Praise for *The*

"*The Heartbreakers* is both equally heartwarming and swoon-worthy… I fell in love with Oliver Perry so fast! This book is feels inducing and every girl's dream—with a side of Heartbreak."

—Anna Todd, *New York Times* bestselling author of the After series

"When I wasn't reading this book, it was all I wanted to be doing. Adorably romantic and fun! I loved it."

—Kasie West, author of *The Distance Between Us*

"Novak creates a titillating tension between her leads… Fans of boy bands will be on this like tattoos on Harry Styles's chest."

—*Kirkus Reviews*

"A fun summer romance that doesn't shy away from the deeper issues of family, illness, and self-discovery."

—*School Library Journal*

Praise for *My Life with the Walter Boys*

2015 YALSA Teens' Top Ten Nominee

"This title will appeal strongly to boy-obsessed readers who will find the romance, particularly the chemistry between Cole and Jackie, to be quite engrossing and the teen voices credible."

—*VOYA*

"A fun, quirky read that will keep a smile playing at the corner of your lips."

—*TheGuardian.com*

"A very addicting book. The writing is strong, and the characters kept me invested and turning the pages."

—*Teenreads.com*

PAPER HEARTS

ALSO BY ALI NOVAK

My Life with the Walter Boys

The Heartbreakers

PAPER HEARTS

—— THE HEARTBREAK CHRONICLES ——

ALI NOVAK

Published by Sourcebooks Fire, an imprint of Sourcebooks, Inc.
P.O. Box 4410, Naperville, Illinois 60567-4410
(630) 961-3900
Fax: (630) 961-2168
www.sourcebooks.com

Library of Congress Cataloging-in-Publication data is on file with the publisher.

Printed and bound in the United States of America.
VP 10 9 8 7 6 5 4 3 2 1

For Jared, the bestest best friend of all the best friends in the history of friendships and, more importantly, the love of my life. Thank you for being with me every step of the way.

CHAPTER 1

Today was my sister's birthday, and I was praying that this year, by some miracle, my mother would forget. She hadn't said anything this morning when I was pouring my cereal—no mention of watching Rose's favorite movies or going to Vine & Dine for dinner like she usually insisted—and I took that as a sign my prayers had been answered.

They hadn't.

Instead, when I got home from volunteering, there was a red velvet cupcake sitting on the table alongside a card Rose would never read. I'm not a religious person, so it made sense that my request to whoever was up above had gone unanswered, but I still grumbled to myself as I dumped my bag on the nearest chair.

I took a deep breath. "MOM!"

It was quiet for a moment, but then I heard a drawer slam in her small bedroom off the kitchen. Two seconds later, the door swung open.

"Hi, honey!" Mom had a towel wrapped around her blond hair, and she was wearing a facial mask and the bathrobe I got her for Christmas two years ago. She hobbled into the room, and that's when I spotted the foam toe separators. My eyebrows went up. Mom only painted her nails for date nights with her boyfriend, Dave.

Okay, maybe this birthday situation isn't as bad as I originally thought.

"How was the diner? Make lots of tips?"

"Mom, I gave up my shift this weekend. I told you that yesterday." Saturdays and Sundays were my best tip days, so she must have been thinking a lot about Rose if she'd tuned out our conversation. Or she was excited for wherever Dave was taking her. Hopefully the latter. "The Children's Cancer Alliance has a huge charity event tonight, remember? I helped with the setup this morning."

"I don't understand why you're wasting time working for free," she said. "You need cash, not good karma." Her bottom lip caught between her teeth in a way that said I was making a monumental mistake. She was always concerned when it came to money. An unknown relative could will her a massive fortune, she could *win the freaking lottery*, and she would still be counting pennies. Of course, after Dad left her with nothing, I couldn't blame her.

"If I want to earn a scholarship, then I need volunteer hours on my college application," I said, my voice tight. There was a rigid feeling in my jaw, and I made a conscious effort to unclench it and not snap at her. We'd gone over this a thousand times before, but she had yet to see how sacrificing a few hours at the diner *now* would benefit me *down the road*.

For the past four years, my heart had been set on attending Stanford. But Mom could hardly keep up with the bills at home, so I knew I'd have to scrape together the money for college on my own. That meant I needed scholarships—lots of them. What better way to beef up my applications than by volunteering for a charity? Mom thought I could pay for my schooling by working at the diner, but no number of shifts would cover the hefty forty-five grand per year that I'd owe, not including housing.

Whenever we argued about tuition costs, Mom would bring up the educational trust funds she and my dad had set up for us before the split. One for Rose, and one for me. She acted like mine would solve all my problems, but there was only enough money to get through a single semester of school, not the eight it would take to graduate. It wasn't that I was ungrateful, but if I was responsible for financing my education, I had to look at the bigger picture. Because I definitely didn't want to spend the rest of my life buried in student debt.

You didn't call her out here to fight about money, I reminded myself. School—more specifically *how* I was going to pay for it—was a frequent argument between us, so it was no surprise that I'd been easily sidetracked.

"But I still think—"

"What's with the cupcake?" I asked, changing the subject.

"Felicity, not this again." Mom crossed her arms and looked at me with narrowed eyes. The green face mask made her attempt at Stern Mom amusing. She'd never been good at disciplining Rose and me growing up, not that I needed a firm hand. I was what she called the perfect kid, all smiles and obedience. Rose was the opposite, a rebellious wild child who could tear through a room like Taz from *Looney Tunes*, leaving behind a wake of toys and juice stains.

When we got older, things didn't change. I followed the house rules, while Teenage Rose would steamroll Mom with one sassy comeback, then sneak out of the house to hook up in the backseat of her boyfriend-of-the-moment's car—on a weeknight, no less.

"Just because you refuse to celebrate doesn't mean that I shouldn't," she said.

"Someone has to be *present* to celebrate their birthday." This particular conversation always had a way of exhausting me, as if each word zapped away my energy. For a moment, I allowed myself to remember the last time I was actually excited for July 23. How the night before I'd painstakingly wrapped Rose's gift—a scrapbook of us I'd spent months making—and placed it alongside my mom's present on the kitchen table, chest swelling with pride. Then there was the cold, nauseous feeling of finding her bed empty the next morning. "Rose is *gone*, Mom. It's been four years."

My mom's face dropped.

She looked so heartbroken that I felt like a mother who needed to console her hurting child, as if the roles between us were reversed. But then I glanced at the cupcake again. It was one of those expensive-looking ones—complete with a mound of swirled frosting and red sprinkles—that could only be ordered at the fancy upscale bakery across the street from where Mom worked. The stupid thing probably cost her more than five dollars, and tomorrow, when nobody had eaten it, the cupcake would be tossed in the trash.

"Felicity," she started, blinking her eyes to blot out oncoming tears.

"Please don't," I said, holding up a hand. I should have known mentioning the damn cupcake was a bad idea. Mom liked to mourn Rose as if she'd died, but I wouldn't grieve for someone who'd abandoned me. "Forget I brought it up, okay?"

The look on Mom's face changed. She stared at me as if *I* had betrayed our family. But I wasn't the one who'd decided she didn't need us anymore. I wasn't the one who ran away and disappeared forever.

"Asha is picking me up at four," I finally said, breaking our stiff silence. "I have to get ready."

I could feel my mom's gaze as I retreated, so I threw my shoulders back and pretended everything was fine. In reality, my eyelids were hot and my chest was heavy, but I waited until my door was closed before collapsing on my bed and allowing myself to cry.

☆ ♭ ♫

Later that evening, after I covered my blotchiness and puffy eyes with a layer of foundation, there was no trace of my breakdown. Getting out of the house helped too. There was something colorful and lively about West Hollywood that helped me forget how much I hated my sister's birthday or, as I referred to it, Desertion Day.

"This is beyond pointless," Asha said. She was leaning against the coat check counter, chin propped in her hand. When she let out a disgruntled sigh, her bangs puffed up like a feather caught in an updraft. "We're wasting our time."

By this point in our friendship, I'd learned to ignore my best friend's constant grumbling. Complaining was something of a hobby for Asha, a way to pass time when she was bored. Still, I cocked my head in question.

How could she *not* be excited?

Even after the fight I had with Mom earlier, I was buzzing with anticipation. Tonight was the biggest fund-raiser of the season—the Children's Cancer Alliance masquerade ball. The most affluent of California would be in attendance, from CEOs to Hollywood stars. There was even a rumor that Beyoncé would be making an appearance, and while I doubted anyone as A-list as she would show up, there would still be a few celebrities in attendance.

For the past month, Asha and I had been working as interns at the CCA. Most of our time was spent calling donors, writing newsletters, and running errands, but today we were in charge of manning the coat check. Our shift was ending soon, and after so many hours spent preparing for this event, I was dying to put on a mask and join the party.

"Nobody is wearing a jacket," Asha continued. "It's disgusting outside."

She had me there. Los Angeles was in the midst of a heat wave, and this morning while I was scarfing down a bowl of Wheaties, the Channel 7 weatherman had reported that the city was experiencing some of the highest recorded temperatures since the nineties. As a result, coat check duty was, as Asha had said, pointless. Not that I minded. The coatroom adjoined the lobby, so if I leaned far enough to the left and craned my neck, I could watch guests arrive off the red carpet. I'd planned to use the downtime to study, but my ACT prep book lay forgotten on the counter in front of me.

"Lighten up, will you?" I said. "This is supposed to be fun."

"*Fun?*" Asha gestured to the empty room around us. "You have a pretty screwed-up concept of the word."

Before I could respond, there was a flutter of movement on the edge of my vision—another guest! I reeled around fast enough to put a kink in my neck, but I only managed to see a flash of tuxedo and blond hair. Judging by the growing commotion, whoever had arrived was important, but there were too many people blocking my line of sight to see who. Just as I was about to turn back to Asha, a tall woman with a pixie cut stepped out from the crowd and made her way in our direction. Even with her mask on, I immediately recognized her as Sandra Hogan, our boss.

"Look," I said, nodding toward her. "Maybe Sandra is cutting us loose early. We could catch the tail end of cocktail hour!" A half grin spread on my lips, but I contained the smile before my excitement grew out of control. There was no guarantee that Sandra would let us attend the ball after our shift.

Using a single finger, Asha twirled her phone in circles on the countertop. "You say that like you plan on staying."

My head jerked up. "Don't you?"

"Definitely not," she said, her nose wrinkling. "As soon as we're done, I'm heading home."

"Aw, come on," I complained, my gaze still focused on our boss. Sandra paused in the lobby to talk to one of the guests, and my shoulders slumped. Maybe we weren't being let off early after all. Still, I said, "You can't leave early. You're my ride."

"Sorry, Felicity." Asha shrugged halfheartedly. "I have a date with my computer. We're going to spend a long, romantic evening on Tumblr."

That was no surprise. Asha had been obsessed with Tumblr ever since her fandom blog about *Immortal Nights*, the hit TV show, went viral. Nowadays, she spent more of her free time creating memes and reblogging GIFs of the actors than interacting with actual people. In fact, that was why she was volunteering for the CCA. Asha's mom had gotten so fed up with her daughter's antisocial behavior that she made her get a summer job. Not wanting to work the local Dairy Dream drive-through or sort shoes at the bowling alley, Asha opted to volunteer with me. And as long as it got her out of the house, Mrs. Van de Berg didn't care what Asha did.

"Seriously?" I asked. "Don't you want to see how the party turns out?"

Asha scoffed. "I have no intention of spending my night with a bunch of stuffy socialites."

"But it's a masquerade ball." Beautiful people, gorgeous dresses, music, and dancing—what wasn't to love?

"And?" Asha said, snatching her phone. She pressed a few buttons and set it back down. Three seconds later, a soft melody started playing. The music wasn't loud—we'd get in trouble if we disturbed the cocktail reception—but there was just enough volume for me to recognize the opening lyrics of "Astrophil," the latest hit from the world-famous boy band the Heartbreakers. If there was one thing that Asha was more obsessed with than *Immortal Nights* or Tumblr, it was them.

After listening to the first few verses, I sighed and answered her question. "*And* the event's going to be glamorous, obviously."

She rolled her eyes. "Yes, and I'm the epitome of glamour."

Okay, maybe my best friend wasn't known for being fashionable. Her normal school attire consisted of yoga pants and T-shirts. And since all the CCA volunteers were required to meet the black-tie dress code, she'd spent three days panicking about what to wear. In the end, she decided on her mother's traditional silk sari, which looked a whole lot better than the getup I'd thrown together.

While I loved wearing dresses, my closet was filled with floral-patterned cotton ensembles that I bought at thrift shops, not ball gowns. I didn't own any formal wear, not even a prom dress. Last semester when I went to the dance, I borrowed my next-door neighbor's in order to save money.

So yesterday morning when I still didn't have an outfit for the fund-raiser, I took the bus to the mall and tore through the sales rack at Macy's. I managed to find a pink, floor-length A-line that didn't clash with my red hair and only had a few ruffles. The price was under a hundred bucks, but I had to dip into the money I'd been saving for college to purchase it. And that meant passing on a new pair of heels and cramming my feet into the pumps I wore for eighth-grade graduation.

"We're already dressed up," I said. "Besides, aren't you the least bit curious to see if anyone exciting comes? What if Gabe Grant shows up?"

That got Asha's attention.

"He won't show," she said, but from the look in her eyes, I knew she was second-guessing her decision to leave. Gabe Grant, Asha's biggest celebrity crush, played the sexy werewolf warrior Luca on

Immortal Nights. She only had about fifty shirtless posters of him taped to her bedroom walls.

"You never know," I singsonged, wiggling my eyebrows suggestively. "How upset would you be if you went home and he ended up coming?" Asha pursed her lips in consideration, so I ambushed her with my best pout. "Please?"

"Okay, okay. You win," she said. "But we're only staying for a little bit. Long enough to survey the ballroom and see who's here. Then we're gone." She turned away. And her avoiding eye contact was the only hint I needed to figure out she wasn't staying because of Gabe.

Asha knew that today was Desertion Day and, more importantly, how much I hated it. That she would stay to keep my mind off Rose made me want to cry, but in a good way, because let's face it: the chance of Gabe Grant coming to the ball was nonexistent. This was something she was doing solely for me. More girls seriously needed BFFs of Asha's standards.

"Yes!" I kissed her on the cheek. "Have I mentioned lately that you're the bestest best friend of all the best friends in the history of friendships?"

"Keep laying it on. You owe me."

"How's it going back here, ladies?" Sandra asked, and I jumped at the sound of her voice. Somehow, in the midst of our conversation, she'd made her way over without me noticing.

"Fabulous." Asha's voice was drenched in sarcasm. "We've checked a grand total of zero coats, but we did point a few people in the direction of the bathroom."

Sandra laughed, pulling up her mask so we could see her properly. "Well, since most of our guests have arrived and nothing has been checked, you're both free to go home."

"Miss Hogan?" I said, and Sandra turned her intimidating gaze on me. "I was wondering if... I mean, you mentioned that we might be allowed to stay?"

"I'm glad you're so eager to help out, Felicity," she said, "but there isn't anything else for you to do."

My smile faltered. "Actually, I meant to stay and enjoy the ball."

Pretty please, I silently begged.

Sandra gave me a hard look as she considered my words. "Yes, I suppose," she finally said, "but you're required to wear a mask, and I can't give away any of CCA's for free. You'll have to purchase one."

"Don't worry. I have that covered." I grabbed my canvas messenger bag from underneath the counter. "I made these last night," I said, pulling out two handmade masks for her to examine. "You know, in case you decided to let us stay."

After the mall yesterday, I'd gone to Craft Corner. By using coupons and shopping out of the bargain bins at the back of the store, I was able to get all the supplies I needed at a relatively low cost. The masks the CCA had ordered for the ball were all different animals—from peacocks and swans to tigers and lions—so I made sure the ones I constructed were as well. For Asha, I'd created a blue jay with an array of white and cobalt feathers that I knew would match her eyes perfectly. My own was a butterfly, made with a dusting of pink glitter and fake jewels.

"I should say no since everyone else is wearing our masks," Sandra said, picking up one of my designs. "But these are simply stunning."

I beamed. "So we can wear them?"

She nodded slowly. "Yes, I suppose so."

"Heck yeah," I said, not believing my luck. "Thank you so much, Miss Hogan. This means the world to me."

Sandra was already walking back toward the lobby, waving a hand over her head without looking back. "Have fun, ladies."

I had every intention to.

CHAPTER 2

The ballroom was glittering. Five massive crystal chandeliers lit the space, their warm glow reflecting in the arched floor-to-ceiling mirrors that ran the length of the room. Music swept down from the mezzanine where an orchestra was playing, and the melody carried beautiful couples across the dance floor.

The amount of wealth packed into the room was staggering. When I first arrived, I saw a woman wearing a necklace that was set with an emerald the size of my fist. No joke. I felt out of place in my department store dress and fake jewels.

"Where the hell are you, Asha?" I muttered to myself as I glanced down at my wrist. But my watch wasn't there. I'd taken it off before the ball, replacing my favorite accessory with a sparkling pink bracelet I'd made to match my mask. Yesterday, I was proud of the jewelry I designed for tonight, but after seeing some of the pieces the guests were wearing, the faux crystals around my wrist didn't seem so special anymore.

Sighing, I turned back to the crowd. Asha had disappeared what felt like ages ago. She'd gone to order sodas from the bar since we couldn't have any of the champagne being passed around by the waitstaff, and I was starting to feel awkward standing by myself.

Besides her, I didn't know anyone here except for the CCA staff members, but they were all too busy entertaining important guests to keep me company.

In Asha's absence, I'd claimed a deserted high-top cocktail table that was set beneath the balcony. My spot was out of the way, perfect for people watching. A sweet-looking elderly couple at the edge of the dance floor were moving slowly to their own tempo, and I easily spotted Ronald Gibbins, the CCA's executive director, who was wearing a ridiculous top hat. I continued to scan the crowd, hoping to catch sight of a celebrity, but it was hard to recognize anyone with all the masks.

That's when I noticed *him*.

Unlike most of the colorful and ornately designed masks guests had donned at the beginning of the night, he'd chosen a simple but sleek black wolf that made his gray eyes pop. Even though he was standing a few yards away, I could see their startling shade as he stared at me without reservation.

He looked younger than most of the attendees. Maybe he was the son of a successful businessman or movie director? It was difficult to gauge how old he was with the upper half of his face covered. Eighteen or nineteen, if I had to guess. Possibly early twenties.

The only thing I knew for sure was that he was beautiful. Not hot like Eddie Marks, the captain of the soccer team who I'd had a crush on since middle school. Eddie knew how all the girls looked at him and used it to his advantage. This boy, whoever he was, didn't do that. I don't know *how* I knew this—maybe it was the way he held himself, tall but not cocky, or the look in his eyes, lonely yet hopeful—but I could tell he wasn't like the Eddies of the world.

We'd never met before, and yet…there was something about him I couldn't put my finger on. Just holding his gaze made me feel like all my insides had been sucked out, and after two more seconds of direct eye contact, I focused my attention on the floor.

Wanting to look busy, I pulled out my phone to see if Asha had texted me. Maybe Gabe Grant *was* here, and she was off flirting in some dark corner of the room with him. But when I checked, there were no new texts from anyone. I clicked on Asha's name and sent a quick message.

Felicity: You kidnapped or something?

I tucked my phone away and glanced up, hoping to see her heading toward me with two sodas in hand and a grin on her face. She wasn't, so I risked peeking at the guy with the piercing eyes. He'd turned back to the people standing around him: a tall man with a streak of silver in his dark hair, but the same gray eyes as the boy; a woman in a green, skintight dress that reminded me of alligator skin; and Judy Perkins, a CCA board member. Wolf Boy was listening to the conversation politely, but never once opened his mouth to comment while I was watching.

After a few more minutes of drumming my fingers on the cocktail table, there was still no sign of Asha. Even the boy, who I'd taken to glancing at occasionally, had vanished, swallowed by the ebb and flow of the crowd. If I didn't go look for Asha now, I would spend the rest of my night standing alone and looking foolish, so I snatched my clutch from the table and stepped out of the shadows.

A massive bar had been assembled on the opposite side of the room—which I knew because I'd helped set it up—and I made my way in its general direction, weaving in and out of clusters of people. I picked up snippets of conversations and laughter as I passed, and submerging myself in the party helped to ease my discomfort.

It took me a couple of minutes to cross the expansive ballroom, and as I caught sight of the glossy wooden counter of the bar, I thought I heard a familiar voice calling my name. Standing on my tiptoes, I scanned the room, hoping to spot the bright blue of Asha's sari. When I didn't, I pursed my lips and spun back around. At that exact moment, someone slammed into my side. I wobbled on my heels, and the half second before I lost my balance seemed to stretch endlessly as my chest fluttered in panic. But before I could tumble over, a strong hand steadied me.

"Thank you—" I started, but then I looked up at my rescuer and froze. Standing before me was the guy in the wolf mask. He was even more gorgeous up close. He said something to me, but I was too stunned to process what.

When I didn't answer, he tilted his head. "Miss?"

I blinked. "Huh?"

"Should I ask the waitstaff for a rag and club soda?" He spoke in a quiet tone, like he didn't want anyone to hear him, but his voice was deep. A smooth, sexy deep.

"Why?"

He pointed to my dress. A brown liquid had spilled down the

front, staining the pink fabric, and that was when I noticed the empty glass in his free hand.

"Shit!" I exclaimed, brushing away a few melting chunks of ice. The brown stain remained. "Shit, shit, shit!"

"I can pay for the dry cleaning if you—"

"No," I snapped, pulling my arm away from him.

I spun around and dove back into the crowd. The closest bathroom was under the mezzanine, and I rushed across the ballroom in half the time it took me before, not caring whether I bumped into people in my mad rush. Barreling into the ladies' room as fast as my heels allowed, I beelined for the sink. After cranking on the faucet, I ripped paper towels from the nearby dispenser.

"Please come out, please come out," I chanted desperately as I dabbed the stain. Some of the dark splotch lifted, but the fabric remained discolored. "Dammit!"

I chucked the useless wet paper in the trash and leaned against the sink, sucking in deep breaths to calm myself. Never in my life had I been so upset about something as silly as a ruined outfit. I wasn't a materialistic person. I couldn't afford to be. My family had never been filthy rich, but as a partner at a law firm, my dad made enough money for us to live comfortably. Not that I remembered that. Dad deserted us before I started first grade.

Mom maintained her lifestyle as an Orange County housewife for as long as possible, but the prenup she signed didn't leave her with much. By the time I was nine, all the money was gone, and she began selling off our things—the speedboat Dad left behind, some of her more expensive jewelry, the foosball table and flat screen from the basement—in order to keep the more important status symbols, like the house and her BMW. But eventually, those things went too.

It was my first year of middle school when my mom finally accepted that our lives had to change. She, Rose, and I were watching *Legally Blonde* (my all-time favorite movie) late one night. Just when Elle was about to get her courtroom victory, the power went out. But it wasn't because of a storm. The electric company had pulled the plug since Mom wasn't paying the bills. I had to give her credit; she put on a brave face. After the shock of the sudden darkness wore off, she dug out enough candles from the garage to light the living room.

For me, the night was a fun adventure. I got to camp out on the floor in a sleeping bag with my family. I didn't realize how bad the situation was until I woke to my mom crying. They were silent sobs, but I could still hear her hitched breathing and occasional hiccup. When I softly called her name and asked what was wrong, she pretended to be asleep. The next day she put the house on the market and started looking for a job.

With a sigh, I returned my attention to the dress. To say I had buyer's remorse was an understatement. I couldn't stop thinking about how much I'd blown on a piece of clothing I'd wear once, especially since I needed every penny for school…so I'd done something kind of awful. When I got dressed for the ball, I'd left on the price tag.

But now I'd never be able to return it. There was a huge wet patch down my torso, and trying to blot out the soda only made a bigger mess. I felt my eyes start to water.

Are you seriously going to cry over a dress? I scolded myself. *Get your shit together, Felicity!*

I yanked up my mask and swatted away the tears in my eyes. I knew saving for college would be difficult. And if I was being honest with myself, the stain was probably for the best. I'd tried to convince myself that returning the dress wouldn't hurt anyone, but I could feel the price tag hanging between my shoulder blades, a constant reminder of my dishonesty.

Shaking out my hair, I squared my shoulders. I was desperate for some fresh air, so I pulled my mask back in place, left the bathroom, and headed toward the set of double doors at the back of the ballroom. One was propped open, and light poured out onto a terrace like a pool of golden water. As soon as I stepped outside, I sucked in a lungful of hot air. Between when I arrived at work and now, the sun had set, but the scorching heat of the day still clung to the night with perseverance.

Taking another deep breath, I walked over to the stone railing, and as I did, the commotion and music of the ball faded into a soft buzz behind me. The terrace overlooked an expansive garden. The only way to describe it was magical, like out of a fairy tale, and I imagined pixies sparkling against the dark backdrop of the night.

Two sweeping staircases led down to a huge circular fountain, and the cobblestone pathway surrounding it disappeared into a maze of tall greenery. Rows of rosebushes were adorned with white lights, and lanterns in soft pastels hung from every nearby tree branch. While I took in the beautiful scene, it occurred to me how much time and effort the decor must have taken, and what a shame it was that I was the only person outside to appreciate it. The CCA had planned for the party to overflow onto the terrace, but with the weather, no one seemed willing to leave the air-conditioning.

I sat on the top step of the closest staircase, propped my chin in my hands, and heaved a long sigh. This was so *not* how I thought my night would go. Did I expect to be swept off my feet like Cinderella? No, but damn, that girl had everything: a beautiful gown free of charge, an evening of laughter and dancing, and a handsome prince to save her from reality. Was it too much to ask for *one* of those things? One stress-free night when I could enjoy myself? When I didn't have to worry about money or work or my future? After the soda-spilling-on-my-dress-and-me-flipping-out incident, stress-free was not the best description of my masquerade experience.

I wove my hands in my hair. It had taken more than an hour to straighten every strand, and after being outside for less than five minutes, I could already feel the waves of my curls taking form. But now, I was beyond caring. The only thing that would make up for my terrible luck was if Asha was having a good time, hopefully with Gabe Grant.

The thought made me smile.

☆ ♭ ♪♫

I don't know how long I was outside, but at some point I wandered down to the fountain. It was even more beautiful upon inspection. The bottom was tiled with colorful glass, giving it the appearance of a waterlogged kaleidoscope. I stepped up onto the smooth concrete base. As I walked the circle, I hummed the Heartbreakers' song Asha had gotten stuck in my head.

"Miss?"

The sound of his voice startled me, and I had to flap my arms to keep from tumbling headfirst into the water. I regained my balance, but my heart was thumping. I pressed a hand to my chest and took a seat before I actually fell in.

I knew it was that boy again without having to look. When I turned to him, I had to crane my neck to see his masked face. *Holy mother*, he was tall! Not like my friend Boomer, but still… I hadn't realized this when we crashed into each other on the dance floor. I'd been too distracted by my soaked dress to make a height comparison. As if sensing this, he took a few steps back so he was no longer looming over me.

"Were you trying to sneak up on me?" I asked, my pulse still thundering in my ears. "Because mission accomplished."

"Sorry," he said, his face neutral. "I wanted to see if you were all right."

"Yeah, I'm fine."

Okay, I wasn't fine. Not bad necessarily, but after my unexpected surge of emotions, I felt disheveled, burned out. Like a battery that had been completely sucked of its juice. My excitement for the ball had already faded, but I wasn't ready to leave yet. Not when I'd be going home to a dark house. There was no way I'd admit this to a total stranger though, even if he was hot in a mysterious way.

He must have known I wasn't being completely sincere, because when I glanced back up, he was studying my face, eyes narrowed in concentration. It felt like an hour passed before he finally spoke.

"Is your dress okay?"

My face got hot. "It'll be fine. Nothing a trip to the dry cleaner can't fix."

"I'm sorry for spilling on you," he said for the second time. "I got that club soda and rag if you need them." He held out the two items as a peace offering.

"You didn't need to do that," I said, barely able to meet his gaze. My face was burning, and I prayed that the lack of light would hide the color of my cheeks. Unlike Mom and Rose, who always had golden California tans, I inherited my grandmother's Irish genes. Not only could my pale, pasty skin sunburn on a cloudy day, but when I was embarrassed, I turned as red as a stop sign.

The boy was still holding out the bottle and cloth, but I was too nervous to reach out and take them. Three long seconds passed. Finally, he strode forward and set them down beside me. Then he stood there, hands stuffed in his pockets, and I couldn't tell if he wanted me to invite him to sit down or give him an excuse to leave. I was too distracted to do either. My thoughts kept returning to the moment of the spill, and with each detailed replay inside my head, my stomach tightened. I had been a total spaz. A bitch even.

"I feel like such an idiot," I confessed, hiding my face in my hands. "I'm sorry for freaking out on you like that. You must think I'm some high-maintenance Barbie."

The boy took my apology as a sign to join me. He sat and pulled something from his pocket: a phone and earbuds. "Your hair isn't blond," he responded. I stared at him, confused by the sudden and strange change of topic, so he clarified: "Like Barbie's."

Oh. He was making a joke. Sheesh, it was impossible to tell with that serious tone and straight-faced demeanor of his. "Right," I said. "Not like yours."

He was towheaded, a blond so light it resembled sunlight reflecting off a fresh bed of snow. And it was styled perfectly, bangs swept up out of his eyes. I almost laughed. He was the Ken to my Barbie. Instead of replying, he reached up and self-consciously touched his hair, checking to make sure every slicked-back strand was in place. When he finished, he fixed his eyes on me again. I waited for him to say something, *anything*, but he seemed content with the silence.

I, however, was not.

"I'm Felicity Lyon, by the way." *Lee-OWN*, like the French city.

I had hoped to keep the conversation going, but for some odd reason, he flinched and looked away.

Okay, weird. Was he too shy to talk to me, or did he not want to tell me his name?

"Never mind," I said. "Pretend I never said anything."

After a few more moments, he draped his headphones around his neck and said, "I'm Aaron." He didn't give a last name, but I could work with that.

"So *Aaron*," I said and tried not to wrinkle my nose. Calling him Aaron felt wrong somehow, but maybe that was because I babysat a little boy named Aaron who enjoyed wearing his Halloween costume year-round and popping out of closets to scare people. "What are you doing here?" As soon as I said this, I realized it sounded like I was asking why he was sitting with me, and I quickly added, "At the ball, I mean."

"My dad was invited," he said without giving a more detailed explanation. I was pretty sure he was frowning, though it was hard to tell because of his mask. I wanted to reach over and pull it off so I could see his face, but I folded my hands neatly in my lap.

God, Felicity. Can you be anymore awkward?

Apparently I could.

"Is that the man with the dark hair you were talking to earlier?" I was trying to get him talking, and Aaron, who seemed to be the silent type, wasn't much help. His lips twitched, and for a split second, I saw what I thought was a flicker of emotion on his face.

"So you did see me."

Oh. My freaking. God.

Embarrassment slammed into my chest like a well-aimed round-house kick. I resisted the urge to run back to the girls' bathroom and hide. My question sounded completely stalkerish and creepy, but then it occurred to me that with his response, Aaron had admitted to noticing me too.

"Well, yeah," I confessed. I pressed my lips together to keep from smiling. "It was kind of hard not to with the way you were staring."

My answer made him look away, like he felt shy about the situation too. As he did, he touched his headphones as if he was making sure they were still there. "When I first saw you standing there," he said, "I thought you were someone else."

Of course, I thought. *Here we go again.* I knew what his answer would be, but I asked, "Really, who?"

"Don't laugh, but I thought you were Violet James. She's the actress in—"

He'd asked me not to, but I couldn't help but laugh. "Yeah, I know who she is."

Violet James, a.k.a. vampire princess Lilliana LaCroix from *Immortal Nights*. The show was her first starring role, and ever since it aired, people insisted we could be twins. I didn't see it. Violet had pale hair and light-brown, almost golden eyes, which was a stark contrast to my red mane and green ones. Yet, whenever I ventured into the touristy areas of LA, people would stop me on the street to ask for an autograph.

It wasn't that I hated being compared to Violet. After all, she was beyond gorgeous, but it always came up when I met someone new. It didn't matter who the person was. I could be meeting the president of the United States or the Little Mermaid, and sooner or later they would point out the resemblance. In fact, I'd heard it so many times that I knew exactly how the conversation would go. Normally I was asked personal questions about Violet (as if looking like someone gave you the power to read their mind), when the next season would start (suddenly I had insider information?), and if I could do that Lilliana quote that everybody seemed to love. (No, I'm not quoting a sex scene!)

But tonight something entirely different happened. Aaron went off script.

"As soon as you glanced my way, I knew you weren't her." He said this like it was amusing.

"Really? How's that?"

"When Violet looks at you, she has a way of making you feel minuscule even if you're six feet tall." Aaron spoke about Violet as if they knew each other, but he was quick to change the subject. "So you never said. What are you doing here tonight?"

"Oh, I volunteer for the CCA."

For the first time since I met him, Aaron smiled. It was one of those slow half grins, and my lips tugged up in response. "Normally my dad has to drag me to these social events, but I have a friend who"—he hesitated, his smile disappearing—"has a close connection to the cause."

…meaning his friend has cancer. Or has a family member with cancer. Either way, it was terrible. My first thought was to offer some type of condolence, but I didn't know anything about his friend's situation, and Aaron clearly wasn't willing to get into the details. The best thing I could do was be friendly and maybe try to wrangle another smile out of him.

"Well, you'll be happy to hear that my particular job is *integral* to the cause," I said, splaying a hand against my chest. "I spent the earlier part of my evening working coat check."

This made him laugh. It wasn't loud or long, but there was enough of a chuckle to make my heart flutter.

"In this heat?" And as if to make a point, he unbuttoned his tuxedo jacket and tugged it off. After folding it neatly and setting it down between us, he reached for his bow tie. "Do you mind if I…?"

"Nope." I grinned and kicked off my heels. "Oh, thank God. These evil things remind me why I'm not fond of formal wear." As fun as it was to get dressed up in a ball gown, the pain in my feet was far from glamorous.

"Aside from your dress," he said, and I couldn't tell if he was teasing me or asking a question.

Dammit, we're back to this topic again?

"I honestly don't care about the stain." I glanced down at the brown spot. Now that it was dry, it was much less noticeable. "It's just…" I didn't know how to explain my plan to return the dress without sounding horrible. Aaron didn't prompt me further. He sat there, staring at me until I figured out what to say. "Okay, I'll tell you why I flipped, but if I do, you're going to think less of me."

Aaron looked me directly in the eye. "I highly doubt that."

"Wanna bet?" I asked, but I didn't wait to hear his answer. "I left the price tag on."

He was quiet for a moment as he considered my words. "That makes you a bad person?"

"Yeah, because I was going to wear it and return it. Look, I've never done something like that before, but all the volunteers had to dress up for the ball and I don't own any formal dresses, and this was the least expensive one I could find, but tuition at Stanford is going to be ridiculous and—"

Before I could finish, he held up a hand to cut off my rambling. "No. I don't think you would have done that."

"How do you know?"

"I'm an excellent judge of character," he said, like it was a fact and not his own opinion.

"How does that work? Wait, don't tell me… Intuition? Spidey senses?"

Aaron shook his head.

"Then what?" I demanded. I needed to know how he under-stood something about me before I did, especially considering we'd just met. Because as soon as Aaron announced that I wouldn't return the dress, I knew he was right. I didn't have the guts to follow through.

"Because," he said matter-of-factly. "I've never seen anyone look as guilty as you do over something they haven't actually done."

He stood and brushed off his pants, and I was positive he was ditch-ing me—*which*, I realized, *is probably a good thing*, because our entire encounter thus far had been mortifying. But then he did something I didn't expect. He sucked in a quick breath and held out his hand.

"Would you like to go for a walk?" he asked, gesturing at the gardens.

He seemed eager and cautious in the same instant, and it put every humiliating second from tonight out of my head. I glanced down at his outstretched fingers, and a slow smile worked its way onto my lips.

Okay, cute guy. Why not?

I put my hand in his and let him lead the way.

CHAPTER 3

The gardens were huge, much larger than I'd originally thought, and it would have been easy to get lost along the mazelike pathways. We wandered beyond the decorative lights and lanterns surrounding the fountain, but the glow of the ballroom perched on the hill behind us helped me keep my bearings.

Aaron hadn't said anything since his invitation. I spent the beginning of our walk trying to come up with conversation starters, but he was moving forward with a purpose, like he was deep in concentration, so I kept my lips pressed together. And the deeper we pushed into the greenery, the less I minded our lack of talk.

At first, his hush made me feel like I had to say something, but the longer we walked, the more I noticed how confident Aaron was in his own silence. It occurred to me that he didn't expect me to say anything, and the steel between my shoulders finally dissolved. Only then was I able to notice the more subtle things going on around me, like the way Aaron and I were walking close enough that our elbows occasionally bumped or how every few seconds he'd cast a sideways glance in my direction.

Before long, the walkway opened up, and Aaron came to a stop where the rosebushes ended. We were standing at the edge of a small square, and in its center was a koi pond. Lily pads dotted the surface of the water, and a tiny moon bridge connected to the path on the other side.

"It's pretty," I said, breaking the quiet between us. There was enough moonlight for me to see flashes of white and orange moving beneath the dark water.

Aaron nodded. "I came here a long time ago with my mother. We fed the fish Doritos."

My eyes widened. "You gave chips to the fish?"

"They'll eat almost anything," he said, shrugging.

"No, I mean why would you willingly throw away something as delicious as a Dorito? Were they Cool Ranch? If they were, I don't know if we can be friends." Chips, whether tortilla or potato, were my all-time favorite snack food. Cool Ranch Doritos were my personal crack. I could devour an entire family-size bag in one sitting. But as long as they had that satisfying crunch, I'd eat any kind.

"They were Sweet Chili," he assured me.

"I suppose that's okay," I told him. "But you have to swear to never again waste a chip."

"Cross my heart," he promised.

We fell quiet again. Deciding to take a page from Aaron's book, I took a seat on the stone bench near the water's edge. Aaron followed suit. Again, he was careful not to sit too close. For the next few minutes, we stared out across the water, enjoying the placidity of nighttime in the garden. Eventually, I turned to face him. He was still clutching his phone, and I watched as he turned it over in his hands.

"Got anything good to listen to?" I asked, gesturing down at it.

Our eyes met again, and Aaron offered me a dazzling smile. I didn't know what kind of reaction I was expecting from him, but that flash of white wasn't it. For the second time, I was momentarily blown away by how beautiful he was, and even though it felt weird to describe a guy that way, *beautiful* was the most accurate word that came to mind.

Aaron didn't notice the effect his smile had on me, because he was already busy scrolling through his music. After a few moments of searching, he found the song he was looking for and shoved one of the buds into his ear. He handed me the other, but we were sitting too far apart, so when I tried to put mine in, I accidentally yanked his out.

"Sorry," I mumbled. For reasons I couldn't explain, sharing headphones and listening to Aaron's music felt intimate.

"Don't worry about it." He fished around for the dangling bud, and once he caught it, he glanced down at the space between us. After a moment of consideration, he scooted toward me and slipped the earpiece back in, and we both focused on the music.

The song was slow—soft in some places and loud in others. It reminded me of a combination of These Beautiful Lies and Sunday's Calling, my two all-time favorite bands. Aaron let me listen to the whole song before pressing Pause.

"Do you like it?" he asked. His lips were slightly parted, and he held his breath as he waited for my answer.

"It was beautiful." There was so much more I wanted to say, like how it was one of those songs that made my heart fly. I didn't know the lyrics or melody, but some part of me welcomed the unfamiliar music like an old friend, as if the artist had used my soul as inspiration when writing it. "What's it called?"

"'Flying Free' by the Silver Souls," he responded, not taking his eyes off mine.

"Never heard of them." But the first thing I was going to do when I got home was download the song.

"They haven't released any music yet."

I paused. *If the Silver Souls don't have an album out, how in the world does he have access to their music?*

"Oh?" I prompted, wanting him to explain, but my curiosity only made Aaron clamp his mouth shut. From the way his shoulders stiffened, I knew my question had made him uncomfortable. *Again, weird.*

I tugged on a strand of my hair and tried to patch up the situation. "So," I said hesitantly. "Mind if we listen to some more?"

He exhaled through his nose and nodded. "Here." He handed me his phone. "You pick."

I took it from him carefully and cradled it in my palm. A few seconds passed as I thought about how unexpected tonight was turning out to be.

Aaron cleared his throat. "Um, Felicity?"

"Yeah?"

He pointed down at the phone. "You have to hit Play for it to work."

"Right." I fumbled with the device for a moment, and then the screen lit up. I quickly jabbed the play button. Another song by the Silver Souls started playing, and Aaron closed his eyes and settled into the bench. I took a second to watch him listen to the music. He was drumming his fingers against his legs, silently mouthing the words. He looked so content I had a hard time tearing my gaze away from him, but I didn't want to be caught staring. Smiling to myself, I copied him and let my eyes flutter shut.

This was by far the best part of my evening, so it was no surprise it didn't last long. We'd only made it through three more songs before I felt something vibrating inside my clutch. When I pulled out my phone, Asha's name flashed on the screen. I yanked out the earbud and answered.

"Hey, girl. What's up?"

"Felicity," she said in an I-mean-business tone. "Where the *hell* are you?"

"I'm sorry, Asha. I didn't mean to ditch you, but I spilled soda on my dress and then I—"

She cut me off before I could explain. "Never mind that. I have to leave, like now."

I glanced at Aaron before moving out of earshot. "Can't we stay a little bit longer?" I whisper-asked. "I met this guy. His name is—"

"No can do," she interrupted again. "Riya called. She finished her shift at the grocery store, but her car won't start. I have to go pick her up."

I groaned. Asha's older sister had a rust bucket of a car. It was a banged-up Ford Festiva their dad drove around in the eighties and smoked lots of pot in. Riya was gifted Michael James—as Asha and I had christened him, since he was clearly a guy and not a Mary Jane—when she turned sixteen.

Because I lived close by, Riya offered to give me rides to school. At the time, I'd been ecstatic. Mom worked in the mornings, so I had to face the social embarrassment of taking the bus. My excitement lasted exactly one day before I reverted back to public transportation, a decision I made for my own safety. When Riya arrived to pick me up, I had to climb through the window into the backseat because the rear doors were bungee-cabled shut.

After that, the only time I rode in her car was when she lent it to Asha. Then I got to sit shotgun where there was a working seat belt. On the few occasions when Riya lent her car to us, Asha and I planned day trips together, like an afternoon at the beach or an outing to Runyon Canyon where we would hike our favorite three-mile trail. Sometimes we only had the car for an hour, so we'd cruise the neighborhood and stop at the Gas Exchange for snacks: Cool Ranch Doritos for me, slushy and Pop Rocks for Asha.

Four years later, it was a feat the car had lasted so long.

"Oh no!" I said with a laugh. "Not the Festiva! We'll have to hold a candlelight vigil to pay our respects."

Asha snorted. "We can thank the Lord for Michael James's passing later. Riya has already called me three times, and I'm running low on minutes for the month."

I sighed and yanked a hand through my hair. "Just go without me. I'll catch the bus."

"You sure? It's getting late."

I was way sure. Although I didn't want to deal with the multiple transfers I'd have to make, I was less inclined to spend the rest of my night listening to Riya moan about her damn car. Complaining ran in the family, and she was more seasoned in the art than Asha.

"Definitely," I told her. "Say one last good-bye to Michael James for me. He's been a semi-faithful companion these past few years."

"Text me when you make it home," Asha said in response. "I want to hear about this guy."

I bit back a smile. So she had heard me mention Aaron. "Sure thing. Talk at you later."

"Peace, Fel." And with a click, she was gone.

I returned to the bench and scooped up my clutch. I had roughly fifteen minutes to find my way back to the ballroom, grab my bag from coat check, and reach the nearest bus stop. If I didn't, I'd have to wait another hour before the next bus came through.

"Is everything okay?" Aaron asked.

"My ride had to leave," I explained. I didn't want to say good-bye like this, but like Cinderella, I had to catch my coach home before it was too late. "If I don't go now, I'm going to miss the bus. I'm super sorry. It was nice meeting you, Aaron."

His face hid it well, but I caught a flash of disappointment in his eyes. "Wait," he said, standing quickly. "I was planning on leaving early anyway. How about I give you a lift?" I blinked, and he must have realized how forward his offer sounded because he added, "Only if you want one, of course."

I *should* have said no. Aaron was a stranger, and for all I knew, he was some dangerous gang leader or mass murderer. But at the same time, I wasn't ready to let go of tonight. Sure, there was the whole soda-on-my-dress incident, but besides that, my time at the ball actually *did* turn out like I wanted. Better even.

I opened and closed my mouth a few times, trying to decide what to say. Aaron was holding his breath, and when a couple of seconds passed without me giving an answer, he deflated. His gaze cut away from mine, and he shoved his hands in his pockets. All it took was seeing that look on his face, and I made up mind.

"All right," I said. "But just to warn you, it's almost a forty-minute drive to my house."

Aaron's smile was filled with relief. "That's okay. I have plenty of music for us to listen to."

☆ ♭ ♪♫

Five minutes later, after taking a wrong turn by the gazebo and losing our way, we emerged from the garden. I immediately came to a halt. Not far from where I'd left my shoes, there was a couple sitting on the edge of the fountain. They were wrapped in each other's arms and much too busy making out to notice us. Aaron followed my gaze, and we exchanged grins before tiptoeing around them, grabbing our things, and scurrying up the stone steps.

"Good thing we got out of there when we did," I said, slipping into my heels again. As much as I wanted to cross the ballroom barefoot, shoes dangling from my fingertips, I knew Sandra would be mad if she caught me disregarding the dress code. "Any later, and we would've caught them in significantly less clothing."

This made Aaron chuckle as he pulled his tuxedo jacket back on, and after adjusting the sleeves, he gestured toward the door that was still cracked to the festivities inside. We fell in step beside each other as we crossed the terrace, and when we reached the back entrance, Aaron moved aside like a gentleman and let me go first.

As I reentered the ballroom, the sudden temperature difference was shocking—from dry and scorching to cool and crisp. I felt like I'd stepped into the walk-in freezer at the diner. I surveyed the room as Aaron stepped in next to me. The shortest route to the lobby was by using the grand staircase, and even though we'd have to navigate the dance floor, I turned in its direction.

"Felicity," Aaron said. He must have had a different route in mind, because when I looked back at him, he shook his head and pointed away from the staircase. I let him take the lead, and we hugged the perimeter of the room, flittering around the edges of the party. Finally, we hit a side entrance, one we could have reached much quicker if we cut through the thick of the crowd, but Aaron seemed intent on avoiding as many people as possible. The door led out into a narrow hall.

"Shouldn't you tell your dad you're leaving?" I asked as we made our way down the long corridor.

"No. He already showed me off tonight." As he said this, something shifted in his eyes. "He won't notice I'm gone." I wanted to ask him what he meant, but Aaron's voice was tight, and I could tell it was a subject he'd rather not discuss.

I stayed silent until we reached the lobby. Someone was locking up the coat check room. "Can you give me a second?" I asked Aaron. "I need to grab my stuff." I dashed across the shiny marble floor. "Hey, wait!"

A custodian glanced at me over his shoulder before returning his attention to the door. There was a ring of gold and silver keys in his hands, and he appeared to be looking for the right one. "Can I help you, miss?" he asked, his tone bored.

"My bag is in there. Mind if I grab it?"

He stopped searching and turned to face me. "I was told I could lock up because none of the guests checked coats this evening."

"I'm a volunteer," I explained. I pulled my CCA employee lanyard out of my clutch to show him. "See? I left my belongings inside when my shift was over."

The man examined the plastic badge like he was a bouncer checking IDs at a nightclub. "All right, go on in. You're lucky you had such good timing."

"Thank you!" I slipped into the dark room and found my way over to the counter where I'd stashed my bag.

After a few seconds of searching blindly, my fingers brushed against the familiar worn material. In junior high, there was a bejeweled designer messenger bag that was all the rage. Every girl in my grade had one instead of a backpack, but Mom couldn't afford it. Instead, she bought me a simple canvas one, and I dressed it up by beading a sun on the front flap in yellow, orange, and red beads. The girls at school asked me where I got it, and I just smiled and told them it was custom made.

I stuffed my clutch inside before lifting the strap over my head. Then I hesitated, wondering if I should take off my mask and put it away too. I didn't need it anymore, but reappearing without it felt weird somehow. Aaron and I had yet to see each other without masks on. I wasn't nervous for him to finally see me, but I felt like once my butterfly was taken off, the night would truly be over, and that made me a little sad.

"Miss, did you find your bag?" the custodian called.

"Yeah, I'm coming."

Before I could overthink it, I pulled off my mask and tucked it on top of my bag where it wouldn't get crushed. Then I hurried out of the room and thanked the man before surveying the lobby for Aaron. He was standing beside the valet counter, headphones in as he waited for me. His head bobbed to the beat of whatever song was playing, and when he saw me coming toward him, he stiffened.

"What's wrong?" I asked when I reached him.

"Nothing," he said, yanking out the earbuds. He stood straighter and nodded at me, but his response was too quick and I didn't believe him.

"No, really. What's up?" Reaching up, I self-consciously brushed a strand of my hair away from my eyes.

"It's just that, well…you took off your mask."

Oh man, that's a bad thing?

My cheeks caught fire. Okay, so maybe my bottom teeth could be a little straighter, and I hated the number of freckles I had, but it wasn't like my face was repulsive or anything. At least, I'd never thought so.

Aaron instantly backtracked, waving his hands in defense. "Crap, I didn't mean it like that. You have a very lovely face…er…I mean, you're really pretty."

"Um, thanks?"

"I'm sorry." He rubbed the back of his neck. "That came out all wrong. What I meant was… Now that you took off yours, I feel obligated to as well."

"And you don't want to?"

"No, it's not that, but…" He trailed off, shaking his head, and took a big breath. "There's something I haven't told you." He paused. "About myself."

"Okay?" I said, my voice rising slightly. Did he not want to give me a ride home anymore? If so, I was totally screwed. I'd probably missed the bus, and there was no way Asha was home from picking up Riya yet, which meant I'd have to call my mom and interrupt her date. She would *not* be happy. "Are you some crazy serial killer?" I joked, voicing my earlier concern. "Aaron the ax murderer?"

"No," he said, "but my name isn't Aaron."

My entire body tensed. "What?"

Why would he lie about his name?

"I'm sorry," he said, slowly untying the ribbon that held his mask in place. "It's just…I didn't want you to think of me any differently." He pulled the wolf away, and somehow I kept my mouth from falling open. I knew his face, but my mind couldn't accept that he was the person looking down at me. "My real name is Alec."

Holy. Freaking. Shit.

"Alec," I repeated. I tried to swallow my shock. "As in Alec *Williams*." Son of Sebastian Williams, CEO of Mongo Records—one of the largest labels in the music industry—and bass player for the Heartbreakers.

He stood there blushing, hands clasped behind his back.

I couldn't wrap my mind around this impossibility, and I thought if I said the truth out loud, then maybe I would actually believe it. Because I hadn't spent my time at the ball with some random cute guy. No, Alec Williams and his bandmates were some of the most famous guys in the whole flipping universe. Even more famous than Gabe Grant and Violet James.

It wasn't like I was crazy obsessed with the Heartbreakers like Asha was. Sure, I liked their music. Heck, I'd even bought one of their albums, but I'd never been to a Heartbreakers concert, and I didn't stalk their lives like a crazy fangirl. But the revelation that I'd unknowingly spent the past hour with an actual *celebrity* was overwhelming. Suddenly, all those embarrassing moments rushed back to me, and I blushed so deeply that my face probably turned the color of my hair.

Alec watched me with a guarded expression as I tried not to freak out. And then I remembered what he'd said only moments ago: he lied because he didn't want me to think of him any differently.

Right now, I was doing just that.

He's just a regular guy, I tried to convince myself. *Pretend he's still Aaron.*

I flexed my fingers and pasted on a smile, but before I could say anything, a woman in a navy ball gown stepped in front of me.

"Alec Williams?" she asked, an uncertain smile on her face. When he nodded, the woman's shoulders relaxed. "I thought I recognized you. My daughter absolutely loves the Heartbreakers. Your music is the only thing she listens to, and she'd be crushed if I had the opportunity to get an autograph and came home empty-handed. Do you mind signing something for me?"

"Of course not." Alec grabbed a pen and a piece of paper off the valet desk. "What's your daughter's name?"

"Zoey."

I watched as Alec scribbled a quick message and his name before handing the paper over to the woman.

"Thank you so much," she said, clutching the signature in her hands. "This will mean the world to her."

Alec nodded again, and the woman said good night. I wondered if it was always like this for him—having to sign autographs, posing for pictures, putting on a smile everywhere he went. As backward as it sounded, living like that must've been lonely, to never have a moment to himself or be just a face in the crowd. I almost felt sorry for him.

When Alec faced me again, his lips were pressed tight, like he expected me to ask for an autograph too. Instead, I smirked.

"Well, I can honestly say I didn't see that coming."

A few seconds passed, and a grin split his face. "Because I'm more the serial-killer type?"

"Yup, totally." We stared at each other with hesitant smiles, and suddenly it was like he was Aaron again, not Alec Williams of certain Heartbreakers fame.

"Mr. Williams?" the valet asked, materializing at Alec's side. "Your car is ready."

Alec took the keys. "Thanks," he said, and my eyes went big when he slipped the man a fifty. He turned to me. "Do you still want me to give you a ride home? There are going to be people out there who will take our picture."

I gulped. Did I want a bunch of flashing cameras in my face? *No*, and I suddenly realized this would be a whole lot easier if I'd kept my mask on. But at the same time, I had a feeling the boy standing next to me was worth a few uncomfortable moments in the limelight.

"Yeah," I said, and my mouth twitched into a smile. "Besides, I probably already missed the bus."

"I guess you're stuck with me." And then he put his hand on the small of my back and guided me out into the night.

☆ ♭ ♪♫

Walking down the red carpet wasn't what I'd imagined. I'd watched the Grammys and the Golden Globes and thought I knew what to expect, but when we stepped outside, there weren't throngs of people screaming Alec's name, reporters and journalists asking for interviews, or a storm of flashing cameras.

Well, duh.

When I thought about it, the lack of commotion made sense. The guests had already arrived, so the red-carpet part of the event was over. I smiled to myself, thinking that our departure would go unnoticed, but Alec knew better.

"Put your head down," he whispered as we neared the sidewalk. There was a group of men lounging against the building smoking, but I was too distracted by the car parked in front of us to pay them any attention.

"Wow," I murmured, shaking my head slowly. I wanted to run

my hands along the sleek lines of the Ferrari, but I kept my arms clamped to my sides. "Is this an F12?"

Alec glanced down at me, eyebrows high. "You know cars?" he asked, but I never got a chance to answer. Someone called out Alec's name, and I turned my attention to the men rushing toward us. A few stragglers were still putting out their cigarettes against the brick wall, but I was instantly blinded by the flashing lights. Paparazzi.

"Alec, who's your friend?" one of them asked. He was a tall, burly man, and when he shoved his camera in my face, I finally took Alec's advice and ducked my head.

Alec didn't flinch at the attention. Ignoring a bombardment of questions, he opened the passenger's side door as the men danced around us snapping pictures. He positioned himself between me and the photographers as best he could, and helped me climb inside.

The car was low to the ground, and I was extra careful not to step on my dress as I moved. It would be just my luck to face plant in the street and end up in next week's edition of *People*. Once I'd settled in and made sure my dress wasn't hanging out, Alec shut the door. He hurried around the front of the car—the men following after him, cameras blazing the entire time—and scrambled into the driver's seat.

The Ferrari roared to life, and before I could tell him how to get to my house, Alec tore away from the curb. Green traffic lights stretched through the next four intersections, and the car shot down the empty street, launching me back against the leather seat.

We were going the wrong way, and I knew I should give him

directions, but I could only focus on how we were flying, because that was what riding in Alec's car felt like. I wished I could roll down the window and holler into the night, but I didn't want to seem like a little kid, so I bottled up my exhilaration and tried to tame the buzz that was surging through my body. There was, however, no way to contain my grin, and it spread across my face, wild and wide.

A few blocks later, Alec slowed the car. He glanced at me before his gaze flickered back to the road.

"You okay?" he asked.

"Considering I'm sitting in a sexy-ass car," I said, "things could be *much* worse."

Maybe later, when I lay in bed reflecting on the night's events, the paparazzi taking my picture would bother me. But right now, all I wanted was for Alec to gun it again so I could feel another rush of adrenaline.

His lips twitched into an almost smile. "Good," he said more to himself than me. Then, as if masked balls, paparazzi, and fast cars were a regular night for him—*which*, I had to remind myself, *they probably were*—he dug his phone out of his pocket and dropped the subject.

The drive was quiet with the exception of my directions and his music. Alec didn't discriminate against any genre, and over the course of the forty-minute trip, we listened to everything from soft rock and heavy metal to pop and rap. An electronic club song was pumping through the speakers, and Alec bobbed his head to the beat as we neared my house.

"Take a right at the stop sign," I directed him. "I live down the street."

He clicked on his blinker, and when we pulled into my subdivision, I cringed. It suddenly occurred to me that I didn't want Alec Williams to see where I lived. Before today, I'd never felt embarrassed about the small one-story, two-bedroom house. Was it a Beverly Hills mansion? No. But it was cute in its own charming way. Rose and I had planted a flower garden along the tiny concrete porch to bring some color to the yard, and a beach-glass wind chime hung next to the front door. More importantly, Mom worked hard to pay the mortgage, and I was proud of her for that.

But as we approached the driveway, I was acutely aware of how tired the house looked. For starters, it needed a paint job. The old beige coat was flaking away from the siding like dry skin, and a few shingles were missing from the roof.

"It's the one with the ladybug." I pointed out our red-and-black mailbox, which came complete with antennae. A flush worked its way down my face and neck. I'd painted the ladybug at a summer camp when I was little and was incredibly proud when Mom proclaimed it "the most adorable mailbox in the postal service kingdom."

Definitely not so adorable anymore.

I peeked at Alec, nervous about what his reaction would be, but his expression remained neutral as he pulled into the drive. He turned off the engine, cutting off his phone midsong, and then his hands dropped from the steering wheel to his lap.

Neither of us moved. A cat emerged from the yard next door and slunk past the front bumper, his fat body illuminated in the headlights. Things were less awkward between us when there was music to listen to. I'd noticed that when we were in the garden too. Now that the music was off, the mood in the car was ripe with uncertainty.

What happens now?

If Alec was still Aaron No-Last-Name, I would probably give him my number. Maybe we'd go out on a few dates before one of us lost interest and stopped texting the other, and then our relationship would become nothing more than a friendship on Facebook. But he wasn't Aaron. Hundreds of girls probably gave Alec their numbers, slipping him a piece of paper with doodle hearts and lipstick marks.

If I did the same—minus the silly decoration, of course—would he think I was only interested in him because of his fame? Was I even interested in him? *Yes*, I answered myself instantly. I'd enjoyed my time with Aaron-Alec. He was quiet and introspective and sweet in a way I never expected Alec Williams of the Heartbreakers to be. When I thought of famous boy band members, I envisioned someone with confidence, charm, and a little too much swagger. That Alec was entirely unexpected made him all the more intriguing.

Pretend he's still Aaron, I told myself for the second time that night.

So I opened my bag and pulled out something to write with. Before I could lose my nerve, I leaned over and grabbed his hand. The tip of the marker shook as I pressed it to his skin. I could have asked for his phone and typed my number in, but there was always the chance he'd refuse. Now he'd have to look at this little piece of me on his drive home. Alec said nothing as I printed on him in blue ink, but his hand was warm against mine. When I finished, I was surprised to find him watching me. His eyes were breathtaking, really, and I decided that gray was my new favorite color.

"Thanks," he mumbled. There was a small smile on his face as he inspected the tattoo I'd given him. I waited for him to move, but he didn't.

"Well," I said, sinking back in my seat. "I should probably head in."

He nodded, still staring down at the digits on his hand. I gathered up my bag, but I wasn't actually ready to leave. I wanted something else to happen—maybe for him to give me his number in return or offer to walk me to the door, but no such luck. His lips stayed clamped shut.

"Okay, thanks for the ride."

Alec's gaze locked onto mine. "You're welcome." There was an electric look in his eyes. His lips parted as if he was going to say more, and I leaned in to hear him better. But then he shook his head ever so slightly, like he'd caught himself doing something he shouldn't, and turned his attention back to his hands. Which was a major letdown. Like reaching the top of a roller coaster and realizing there was no big drop.

It was time to get out of Alec's car.

My fingers gripped the door handle, and then I noticed his black wolf mask sitting on the dashboard. He must have tossed it up there when we got in the car. After a moment of hesitation, I reached over and took it, swapping it with my own.

"To remember tonight," I told him when he gave me a curious look. Not that I would forget tonight, but I wanted something more solid to hold on to than a memory. Sighing, I finally climbed out of the car.

Once I was standing on the driveway, Alec rolled down the window. "Bye, Felicity Lyon," he said, and I blinked.

He remembers my last name? He'd seemed upset when I'd shared it with him, so I was impressed he managed to recall it.

"Bye, Alec Williams," I said as he pulled away. And just like that he was gone, taillights disappearing down the road.

☆ ♭ ♫

I let myself into the house. As I expected, it was silent and dark.

Mom wouldn't get home until late, if she came home at all. It was always like this when Dave wasn't working. My mom's boyfriend was a trucker, and sometimes he'd be gone for weeks, so she spent as much time with him as possible during his days off.

I didn't mind all that much; I liked Dave. Unlike with her past boyfriends, I could tell my mom was happy. He made her laugh, and whenever he came back from a trip, he brought her a little trinket from one of the states he'd driven through. Sometimes there was even something for me.

I flipped on the lights.

My feet felt like they'd been squeezed through a meat grinder, so I kicked off my heels and left them in a pile by the door. A happy sigh escaped my lips as I made my way down the hall toward my room. It had been a long day. Muscles I didn't know I had were achy, and my whole body felt sluggish, but I knew I wouldn't be able to fall asleep. My mind was still turning, trying to compre-hend the events of tonight: *Met cute boy. Cute boy is actually Alec*

Williams. It was hard to believe. Less than five minutes had passed since he dropped me off, but our time together already felt like a lucid dream. I wanted to touch his mask again, just to be sure the experience wasn't something I'd imagined.

At my desk, I pushed a jar of my favorite bugle beads out of the way to make room for my bag. All sorts of jewelry-making supplies were scattered across the surface—crimp pliers, spools of gold and silver wire, clasps, you name it, along with containers and containers filled with beads of every color. I lifted the flap on my bag. Inside was Alec's wolf mask. I pulled it out to examine it more closely.

There was a dusting of black jewels on the brow and a tiny row of silver swirls looping around the eyeholes. It was stunning, and much more intricate than I'd originally thought. Biting back a smile, I set the mask on my bookshelf with the rest of my keepsakes, between the conch shell Asha had brought back from a trip to Florida and the tiny carving of a lion my friend Boomer had made in shop class, back when he thought my last name was pronounced like the animal.

After pulling on my pajamas, I grabbed my phone and flopped into bed. I sent two quick texts to Asha.

Felicity: You'll never guess what happened tonight!!!
Felicity: PS you're going to die of jealousy.

Then I tossed my phone on the nightstand and waited for her response. I couldn't contain my grin. This was the best Desertion Day I'd had in four long years.

CHAPTER 4

The next morning, I woke to the sound of a dog barking. Not fully awake, I nestled further into my pillow without opening my eyes. The barking continued, but I chose to ignore it until there was a knock on the window.

Was someone outside?

No way, I decided. Not when there was a giant thorny bush to crawl through.

Another impatient rap sounded on the pane, and I groaned.

Go away, I thought, but the knocking continued, so I turned over in bed and rubbed the sleep from my eyes. Last night, I hadn't fallen asleep until the early-morning hours. Thoughts of Alec had kept me up and—*Holy mother!*

I shot up in bed as everything came rushing back to me. I, Felicity Ann Lyon, had hung out with an actual member of the world's most famous boy band. I glanced at my bookshelf, and proof that I hadn't dreamed the encounter was sitting right on top of the copy of *Endless Origami: 1,000 Step-by-Step Designs* that Rose had given me.

There was another knock, and it sounded angry enough to shatter the glass. I spotted Asha crouched outside in the bushes. She motioned for me to unlock the latch.

"God, you sleep like the dead. I rang the doorbell for literally ten minutes," she complained, after I dragged myself across the room and pushed open the window. "I'm pretty sure your neighbor thought I was trying to break in."

She passed her dog through the opening for me to take. I'd always been a canine lover, but Lord Pugton was an exception. The wrinkly nine-year-old pug farted so often I was starting to wonder if Asha only fed him refried beans. He peed in my shoe during a sleepover once, and every time he looked at me, I was convinced he was giving me the stink eye. In fact, his bulgy little eyes were focused on me now, sharp and suspicious, as I reached out and took him from Asha.

"I'm watching you," I whispered when I released him on the floor. Lord Pugton made a mad dash toward my bed. He disappeared underneath it, most likely to hunt for another shoe to destroy as part of his reign of terror.

Asha hoisted herself onto the sill and climbed into my room. "Holy amazeballs," she said, wiping her brow as she straightened up. "It's like Canada in here. I'm moving in until this heat wave is over."

I quickly shut the window so none of the heat could seep in. "Battle of the AC still waging?"

"Ugh," she groaned. "It's in full swing. My dad is relentless."

Asha's parents had been fighting about the electrical bill since the start of the heat wave. Her father was a frugal-living penny-pincher who deserved his own show on TLC. He reused everything from coffee grinds to dental floss, and one time when we went to the movies, Mr. Van de Berg dug through the trash for a large popcorn tub so he could get the free refill. His biggest money-saving trick? No air-conditioning. Normally Mrs. Van de Berg put up with her husband's strange antics, but she refused to melt to death in her own house—which, she'd complained, was currently hotter than summertime in Mumbai.

"You know you're welcome to stay, but before you even *think* about sitting on my bed," I said and handed her a towel, "you need a shower. Pronto."

From under my bed, Lord Pugton grunted as if in agreement.

Asha was glistening from her daily run. I never understood how anyone could enjoy running. There were those awful feelings of burning lungs and Jell-O legs, but Asha had fallen in love with cross-country during our freshman year and had been racking up miles ever since. It was two miles from my house to hers. While that was a piece of cake for Asha, I often wondered how Lord Pugton handled the distance. This heat was deadly, and she was absolutely insane for running in it.

"Thanks." She took the towel and wiped the sweat off her face. "I feel like I jumped in a pond. A scummy, disgusting pond. I have so much boob sweat that someone could do laps in my cleavage."

"Asha," I said, "someone could go swimming in your cleavage regardless of the sweat."

Drown in it even. My best friend was curvy in a Marilyn Monroe sort of way, all bust and butt with a waist so small it was like she was born wearing a corset.

I'd always been a little jealous of her for it, starting in the third grade when she pulled aside the collar of her shirt and showed me the pink strap of her first training bra. When I'd gotten home from school that day, I'd begged my mom to let me get one too, but she'd laughed and said, "All in good time." But that time never came. While Asha blew through cup sizes, shedding bras like leaves in autumn, I was stuck with the chest of a little boy. Nowadays, most of the guys on our high school wrestling team had bigger boobs than me.

Asha grinned and shimmied at me before disappearing down the hall. A minute later, the water pipes groaned when she turned on the shower. While I waited for her to return, I changed out of my pajamas—a Harry Potter T-shirt that read *My Patronus Is Pizza* and a pair of baggy flannel pants that had seen better days—and attempted to make my bed. As I was arranging my pillows, Big Blue, my stuffed brachiosaur that I'd had since I was little, fell on the floor. Lord Pugton shot out from the dark space below the bed, snatched Big Blue between his slobbery jaws, and escaped before I could save my favorite stuffed animal.

"Get back here, you little shit!" I dropped to my knees and crouched over so I could peer under the bed. Two reflective eyes stared back at me. Even when I lay down on my stomach and stretched out my arm, Asha's dog was parked an inch beyond my fingertips. "If you don't come out right now," I warned him, "I'm going to kill you. Seriously. I'll make an ugly little hat from your pelt and everything."

"Who are you talking to?"

I straightened up quickly, smacking my head on the bed frame in the process. Asha was standing in the doorway wrapped in a towel, her long, dark hair dripping down her back.

"To that demon you call a dog." I rubbed the lump already forming on the top of my skull. "He stole Big Blue."

She laughed and walked over to my dresser. The bottom drawer was hers, and she rifled through it before pulling out athletic shorts and a fresh T-shirt. "He's doing you a favor then," she said, but after tugging on her clothes, she called Lord Pugton out from his lair and rescued Big Blue from the clutches of evil. Blue's long neck was soggy where it had been chewed, but it was nothing a trip to the laundry room couldn't fix.

"So," Asha said, plopping down on the end of my bed. Her fingers wrestled her thick hair into a braid. "You totally left me hanging last night."

"I did?"

"Um, hello? You can't send me a vague, yet equally intriguing text and never respond. That's cruel."

"You messaged me back? I don't think I got anything." In fact, I remembered staring at my ceiling unable to fall asleep, waiting for Asha to respond. I'd needed to tell someone, to unload the excitement that had built inside my chest, but I never heard the telltale buzz of an incoming text.

Stretching out across my mattress, I reached for my phone on the nightstand. "Crap," I said when the screen refused to light up. "It's dead. I must've forgotten to plug it in. Sorry, Asha."

"It's fine. Just tell me what happened. Otherwise, I'm going to die. My gravestone is going to read, 'The Suspense *Actually* Killed Her.'"

"Okay, okay! So after you went to get us drinks…"

I told her everything. From Alec spilling his soda on me to listening to music in the garden. Everything, that was, except for Alec's real name. I saved that bit for my grand finale.

"He offered you a ride home?" she asked when she thought I was finished filling her in. My best friend was a hopeless romantic, and she heaved a long sigh, just like she did every time we finished watching *The Notebook*. "God, that's the cutest."

"That's not even the best part."

"There's more?" The dreamy look in her eyes cleared, and she sat up straighter. "Don't tell me! Aaron has a twin brother I can date, doesn't he?"

"Nope," I said slowly, enjoying Asha squirming in anticipation. "Better."

"What's better than *two* cute boys?"

I leaned in and paused. Exciting things *always* happened to Asha. She was some kind of magnet for luck, like the time she accidentally dialed a radio station during the middle of a contest and won a weekend getaway to New York City. Or there was the time the van ran out of gas, and who came along to give her a lift to the nearest station? Eddie Marks, soccer captain extraordinaire and man of my dreams. But this experience was all mine, and I was going to savor the moment.

"Come on, spill!" she begged, bouncing up and down on my mattress so that she nearly fell off.

I laughed. "All right, all right!" I said.

And then I told her the truth, Alec's name gushing from my lips in an excited whisper.

Asha's eyebrows furrowed into a V. "Aaron knows Alec Williams? Like from the Heartbreakers?"

"No, no," I said, shaking my head. "Aaron *is* Alec Williams."

☆ � ♪♫

At first, Asha didn't believe me. It took more than five minutes to convince her that Aaron No-Last-Name was a bona fide member of the Heartbreakers, and when she finally acccpted my story as truth, she was upset I didn't get a picture of the two of us. Apparently I needed proof. As if I'd lie about something this monumental.

"I don't understand why you didn't ask for one," she whined.

"Because," I responded, chewing on my fingernail. I was struggling to explain myself. "That would have ruined everything."

"But it was a once-in-a-lifetime opportunity." Asha stared at me as if I'd lost it, and maybe I had…

Then again, she hadn't been there. She hadn't heard the strain in Alec's voice when he admitted who he was, or seen the look on his face after the woman asked for an autograph. I'd wanted to go to the ball for a Cinderella-esque night, a few magical hours where I could put on a mask and pretend to be someone else. And I'd gotten the impression that Alec did too. The masquerade had given him a chance to be a regular guy instead of a teenage heartthrob, and asking for a picture or an autograph would have spoiled that for him.

"It wasn't worth it," I responded and shrugged.

Asha sighed. "But—*Alec Williams.*"

She was still shaking her head in disappointment when my

mom knocked on the door. "Felicity?" she asked, stepping inside my room. Dave must have just dropped her off, because even though she'd already slipped into her bathrobe, there was a Starbucks to-go coffee in her hand. "Oh, morning, Asha. How are you, dear?"

"Hi, Brenda. I'm good. Thoroughly enjoying the comfort of your AC."

"Wonderful," my mom answered, but I could tell she wasn't listening. "Do you mind giving me and Felicity a moment? There're muffins on the kitchen table."

"Ooh, muffins!" Asha was out the door without another word.

I watched as my mom took a spot on the end of my bed. There was a funny look on her face, and I had a feeling she was still upset about our conversation yesterday.

"Felicity, there's something I need to talk to you about," she said, confirming my suspicion.

"I have something super exciting to tell you too," I exclaimed, hoping my enthusiasm would warrant a subject change. I didn't want to revisit Rose or her birthday. That was supposed to be something I only had to deal with once a year.

"Does it have anything to do with this?" Mom pulled a newspaper from behind her back and tossed it between us. Only it wasn't a newspaper. It was one of those daily celebrity tabloids filled with scandals and gossip.

"Holy shit." With a trembling hand, I picked up the tabloid. The front page was a picture of Alec helping me into his car. I quickly flipped to the article inside.

Alec Williams Spotted with Look-Alike of Rumored Girlfriend Violet James

Alec Williams, bass guitarist for the Heartbreakers, was seen leaving the Children's Cancer Alliance charity ball Saturday night with an unidentified woman. What has Hollywood buzzing is not that Williams's date was a mystery, but her resemblance to his rumored girlfriend, *Immortal Nights* actress Violet James. Williams, 18, and James, 20, were first romantically linked after the Heartbreakers filmed a stint on the hit TV show, and then when the two were photographed together at a Malibu restaurant earlier this month. Reps for Williams and James did not respond to a request for a comment.

Everything suddenly made sense: Why Alec noticed me in crowd. Why he brought up Violet. Why it seemed like he knew her. I scanned the rest of the article, which recapped how we left the masquerade together and called me a less-pretty version of Violet.

Ouch. That definitely stung.

"Are you listening to me, Felicity?"

"Huh?" My gaze snapped from the picture to my mom. Her face was pinched.

"Explain this," she said, jabbing her finger at the tabloid.

Explain what exactly? The picture said it all. I twisted my comforter in my hands. "I met Alec Williams last night?"

"So you let a complete stranger drive you home?"

Crap. Her tone was soft, but my stomach dropped. That was my mom's I'm-disappointed-in-you voice, and I hated that voice.

"He's not a stranger. He's Alec Williams," I said as if that explained everything.

"And since you listen to his music, you think you know who he is?" She shook her head. "Felicity, anything could have happened to you. I thought you were smarter than this."

Okay, so was this my best decision ever? No, but it wasn't like I climbed into the back of a sketchy van with the words *Free Candy* painted on the side. I never would have left with Alec if I didn't feel safe.

"Mom, he's a nice guy."

A vein pulsed at her temple, and I knew she'd crossed the line between irritated and angry. "A nice guy wouldn't have paraded you around in front of the paparazzi or flaunted his fancy car," she snapped.

"Hold up." I folded my arms across my chest. "Are you upset because I let him drive me home or because he's rich and famous?"

"Boys like that only want one thing," she said through pursed lips. "I don't want to see you get hurt."

"God, Mom!" I exclaimed, springing up from my bed to move away from her. "It wasn't like that at all."

"Good," she said, matching my tone. "I don't want you getting caught up in the glamour of that kind of lifestyle. You can't be distracted from school or your dreams. Stanford."

All right, now my mom was being weird. What did she think I

was going to do? Drop out of school and become a groupie? How had we gone from discussing a picture in the tabloids to talking about college?

"I'm not Rose, Mom," I said.

I hated that every time we talked about my future, it was as if she thought I was going to make some colossal mistake that would ruin my life. As if I would turn into my sister. And that was a slap in the face. I wasn't the daughter who got a nearly perfect score on my ACT yet didn't graduate from high school because I was too busy partying and wasting my potential. I worked hard for my grades, and I would never, ever abandon my family.

"Honey." The bedsprings squeaked as my mother stood, and two seconds later, her warm arms wrapped around me. "You know I'm incredibly proud of you, right?"

I nodded, and she kissed my forehead.

"You don't have to worry about Alec Williams, Mom," I mumbled into her shoulder. "I doubt I'll ever see him again."

CHAPTER 5

Five days later, when I hadn't received a call or text from Alec, I knew what I'd told my mom was true. I'd never see him again. Which, while disappointing, wasn't the end of the world. Don't get me wrong. I would have enjoyed hanging out more with him, but it wasn't like I had some delusional fantasy that we were soul mates and would live happily ever after.

But the issue was—because there was always some kind of issue, wasn't there?—that Alec Williams had taken over my life. He was everywhere, and no matter how hard I tried, there was nothing I could do to return to my pre-Alec existence. Since the ball, a whole slew of tabloids had printed pictures of us together, which I only knew because Asha made it her goal to track down every single one. According to her, this was a moment I needed to remember forever, and her pile of magazines was quickly taking over my desk.

More annoying were the celebrity news sites that reported fictional stories about who I was and how we met. Their articles always seemed to quote some mysterious "insider" who not only knew me but was willing to spill details of my life. And each story was more ridiculous than the last. Girls from school who'd never spoken to me before were suddenly messaging me on Facebook, wanting to know all about Alec, and every time I turned on the radio, one of the Heartbreakers' songs would come on.

It was all quite exhausting, but the worst of it was the reporters. They came from all the big gossip blogs and entertainment magazines to ask questions about Alec, me, and *Alec and me*. The first one showed up the evening after the ball. I had no clue how she figured out my name or address, but I was quick to turn down an interview. Talking to her would've felt weird. Besides, I didn't get what all the buzz was about anyway. It wasn't like I was dating Alec. We'd been seen together *once*.

"Wouldn't it be easier if you talked to one of them?" Asha asked when I stepped back inside my bedroom. Two minutes earlier, the doorbell had rung, and I'd had to refuse yet another reporter.

"I don't know," I said, not looking at her. She was probably right, but I wasn't interested in sharing something personal with the rest of the world. Our time at the ball was a moment that belonged to me and Alec alone. As soon as I gave an account of what happened, it wouldn't be just ours anymore. Ninety-eight percent of teenage girls would know the story by the end of tomorrow.

I sat back down, returning to the project on my desk. I was in the middle of creating a pattern for what would become a beaded necklace of a bird. Most of the design was done, but I had yet to figure out the challenging part, the wings.

"I think you should do it," Asha said, paging through the edition of *Us Weekly* she'd brought over to add to my collection. "Once you tell your story, they'll go away. Right, Boomer?"

We both glanced at my other best friend, who was sprawled in my beanbag chair with his Game Boy. It was an ancient hand-me-down from his brother, who'd gotten it in the early 2000s. Boomer was addicted to the damn thing. He only had one game, a Pokémon something or other, but he never went anywhere without it. We'd met freshman year when he showed up in beginners' metalworking and took the only available seat in the room—the empty stool next to me.

"Hey, pssst." He had leaned over so I could hear him. Not that he'd needed to; his voice was so loud it was like he came with a built-in megaphone. "Why am I the only guy in this class? Not that there's anything wrong with that. Personally, I rather like this ratio, but it still strikes me as odd."

I'd stared at him for a few seconds before saying, "Probably because this is a jewelry-making class."

"Jewelry?" He frowned and rubbed his chin. "I thought metalworking meant welding. You know, where you melt shit together?"

I laughed. "We might do some soldering."

"Does it require a blowtorch?"

"Nope. No blowtorches necessary."

"Well, that really *blows*." He'd offered me a full-faced grin. "Pun definitely intended."

We spent the rest of the semester goofing off. After that, we decided to take every obscure art class our school offered together, from photography—can you say snooze fest?—to cartooning, where Boomer entertained me by drawing inappropriate cartoons of dicks. When Asha first met him, she said he was childish, but I often wondered if her aversion stemmed from the fact that she *liked* him. With curly, ash-brown hair and chocolate eyes, he had the boy-next-door look that was totally Asha's type. It only took a week of lunch periods for her to warm up to him.

"*Right*, Boomer?" she repeated, her sigh heavy with exaggeration.

"Right, what?" he asked Asha without looking up.

She rolled her eyes. "Don't you agree that Felicity should do an interview?"

He frowned, his thumbs moving at rapid speed. "No, no, no!" he exclaimed, and his shoulders slumped. He tossed the Game Boy to the side. "Goddammit, Chansey is impossible to catch. All the gaming forums say it's Tauros, but I caught that sucker right away. Chansey, on the other hand, has the lowest encounter rate of the game and—"

"Hello? Trying to have a conversation here."

"Oh." Boomer scratched the back of his head. "Sorry, Asha, but I'm totally with Fel on this particular subject."

He pushed himself off the beanbag and stood to his full height. At six foot ten, Boomer was basketball star material, although he lacked the coordination required to play. The only trait that out-shone his freakishly tall stature was the volume at which he did everything—talking, eating, even walking. He was twice as loud as a regular person.

"What? Why?"

Boomer plodded over to my bed and flopped down next to Asha, making my bedsprings squeak in protest. "Because some people value their privacy. Besides, it's not like she has much of a story to tell. The only cool thing that happened was riding in that F12."

I laughed. That was *such* a Boomer thing to say. He had an obsession with cars. His dream was to become a mechanical engineer and work for a NASCAR team, specializing in engine development. If he wasn't playing his Game Boy, he was most likely talking about engines or racing, and during the course of our friendship, I'd inadvertently learned everything I knew about cars from listening to him chatter. Which was how I'd recognized Alec's Ferrari.

"Are you serious? This is about Felicity doing a service for every Heartbreakers fan out there," Asha insisted.

Boomer cocked an eyebrow. "I thought it was about getting rid of the reporters."

But Asha wasn't listening. "She literally lived every fan's dream, and she's not going to share her experience with the rest of the world?"

"Are you calling me selfish?" I asked with a laugh.

"If she is," Boomer said, snagging the package of cookies lying between them on the bed, "I'll be quick to remind her that real selfishness is hogging all the Oreos."

I knew Asha was only joking around, but I still felt the need to defend myself. "Even if I wanted to do an interview, I can't. My mom has been weird about this whole thing."

"Yeah, I suppose. What's up with that?" Asha asked, and all I could do was shrug in response.

"Speaking of moms, I'd better go," Boomer said, snatching the last Oreo out of the sleeve. "I promised mine I'd pick up Kevin from T-ball practice."

"Ugh, lame," Asha said, tossing a pillow at his face. "Fel and I were going to watch the season finale of *Immortal Nights* together."

"I take it you need a ride?" he asked.

"Yeah." She scowled and brushed cookie crumbs from her shirt. "Ever since Riya's car died, I've lost all use of the van. So unfair."

"See you guys tomorrow at Electric Waffle?" I asked as the two stood and headed toward the bedroom door. The Electric Waffle is the diner where I waitressed. We served breakfast only, and every table had a built-in electric griddle so customers could cook their own waffles. While it was a cute idea, the griddles were more of a pain in the ass than anything—impossible to clean out, and people always wanted refunds when they burned their own food.

I worked so often that the diner had become our haunt. During my shifts, Boomer and Asha would make camp in one of the back booths. Usually they did homework or studied, but since it was summer, Boomer wasted his time playing Pokémon while Asha ran her Tumblr account. On my breaks or when there was a lull in customers, I'd go hang out.

Boomer nodded. "Yup. What time does your shift end?"

"I'll be done at six."

"Make sure to call me when *Immortal Nights* is over," Asha said, pointing a finger at me. "We'll have lots to analyze."

"Will do. Bye, guys."

After Boomer and Asha were gone, I focused on finishing the pattern for my necklace. I'd been making jewelry since junior high. One of my mom's first jobs after the divorce was as a sales clerk at a fancy boutique, and I remember being mesmerized by all the sparkly pieces on display. There was no way Mom could afford to buy anything that expensive, so she got a beginners' jewelry kit for me to make my own. Starting out, all I'd been able to do was string a few beads together, but nowadays my work was good enough that people often stopped me on the street to ask where I bought my earrings or bracelet or whatever I was wearing.

I was getting into the groove of working when the doorbell rang again.

"Are you freaking kidding me?" I grumbled, pushing away from my desk. I'd tried to be patient with the reporters, I really had, but their constant badgering was driving me crazy. I stormed down the hall, and a picture of Mom, Rose, and me rattled against the wall.

"If you don't get off my property right now, I'm going to call the police! I'm *not* doing an interview!" I shouted when I threw open the door. "What don't you people understand about that?"

"Felicity?"

I froze.

That voice. I *knew* that voice. It was sexy and deep—a sound I wouldn't easily forget. My hands dropped to my side, and I stared at the person standing on my porch. There was a baseball hat pulled low over his face and a pair of sunglasses hiding the spectacular color of his eyes, but I knew who he was in an instant.

And he was no reporter.

☆ ♭ ♫

"Alec?" I gasped. "What are you doing here?"

He flinched and glanced over his shoulder, as if he expected one of the reporters who'd been stalking me to jump out of the bushes. "Hi," he said slowly, like he wasn't entirely sure why he was here either. "Sorry for showing up without any warning."

"It's okay," I said quickly, but I was glad Mom was at work. What would have happened if she was the one who'd opened the door? Suddenly her voice whispered in my head—*boys like that only want one thing*—and a flush crept across my cheeks.

He glanced down at his watch, but not in an impatient checking-the-time way. More like a surprised wow-when-did-this-get-here way, and he fiddled with the clasp before looking back at me. "Can we talk?"

"Sure." I leaned against the doorframe, trying to look casual. Because teenage celebrities stopped by my house all the time. Obviously.

Alec shifted his weight. "Do you think… I mean, may I come in?"

I hesitated. There was the choice I knew I *should* make…and the one I *wanted* to make. Mom's shift was ending soon, and I didn't want her to come home and catch him here. There was no house rule forbidding me from having boys over while she was gone, though for Rose, it had been an entirely different story. However, I had a strong feeling Mom wouldn't approve of Alec after our earlier conversation. And the last thing I needed was to give her another reason to think I was starting to act like my sister.

But Alec seemed on edge, and when he looked over his shoulder a second time, I couldn't leave him standing on the stoop. "Yeah, okay," I said, and his shoulders visibly relaxed.

I moved out of the way so he could step inside, and he quickly brushed past me with a quiet thanks. I closed the door before turning to face him, and when our gazes met, that was when it hit me—*Alec Williams is in my house!*

After a few seconds of us staring at each other, he had yet to say anything. Wasn't he the one who came to see me?

"So…" I said, as he pulled off his hat and fixed his hair. "I suppose we can talk in my room?"

For a split second, I considered leading Alec to the living room instead. If Mom did come home, it would be better if she found us on the couch than in my bedroom. But I'd been folding laundry in front of the TV before Asha and Boomer came over, and it was still spread out across the carpet. The last thing I wanted was for him to see a collection of my bras or, worse, the pair of pink lace underwear I knew was at the top of the clothing pile.

As we walked down the hall, I twisted my watch around in circles and prayed for my insides to stop quivering. When we passed the bathroom, I caught a quick glimpse of myself in the mirror. My hair was piled on my head in a messy bun, and I had on a Team Luca shirt, complete with an image of shirtless Gabe Grant. Asha had loaned it to me and insisted I wear it for the finale tonight. I was praying Alec wouldn't notice, but once we were in my room, he tried unsuccessfully to hide a smile.

I crossed my arms over Luca/Gabe. "What?"

"*Immortal Nights* fan?"

"Believe it or not, no. My best friend is obsessed enough for both of us."

"Uh-huh," he responded, turning in a circle to inspect my room.

I could tell from his tone that he didn't believe me, which was slightly embarrassing, but then he spotted my closet door, and I learned the true meaning of the word. There, taped next to a picture collage of Asha, Boomer, and me, was a Heartbreakers poster. It was from the band's first album, *Dance till Dawn*, and all four boys looked like babies. Oliver Perry, the lead singer, had long, floppy hair, while Alec looked a least a foot shorter than he was now.

As if he didn't see the poster, Alec glanced away quickly, and I was glad we were pretending it wasn't there. Because really, how awkward was it that I had a picture of him in my bedroom?

He wandered over to my desk, which was on the opposite side of the room from my closet, and examined the bead jars that were lined up in order of the rainbow. The sun streaming in from my window made the colorful pieces shine like the plastic pegs of a Lite-Brite. When he noticed the necklace I was working on, he leaned over for a better look.

"It will be a bird when I'm finished."

He tilted his head. "Why a bird?"

"Homage to my favorite book."

I nodded toward my shelf. On the top row was a collection of my favorite novels: *The Scarlet Letter*, *Fahrenheit 451*, *The Catcher in the Rye*, and so on. The books used to belong to my father. Besides the fact that he was a lawyer, the only thing I remembered about him was that he had a soft spot for American literature. I'd discovered the box of books when we moved out of our old house and hid them underneath the clothes in my suitcase so Mom wouldn't find out. I don't remember why I wanted them. Maybe it was to remind myself that the man actually existed. Whatever the reason, I was glad I'd kept them. If I never learned anything else about my dad, at least I knew we had one passion in common; we both loved reading.

"The one on the far left," I said and pointed. "Can you grab it for me?"

Alec reached up and carefully pulled down my most prized possession. As he did, his shirt rose up, giving me a glimpse of his bare skin. My insides flip-flopped, and I quickly averted my gaze.

"Felicity?"

"Huh?" I was still thinking about that flash of stomach, but then I realized he was offering the book to me. "Oh no," I said, holding up both hands in a you-keep-it way.

"*To Kill a Mockingbird*," Alec said, reading off the title. "I think I was supposed to write a paper on that, but I never ended up reading it."

"You blew off the assignment?" I asked, both amazed and appalled at the same time. I never had the balls to ignore my schoolwork. It made me feel antsy.

He shrugged. "I wasn't much of a school person."

"You don't have to be a school person to enjoy the book," I told him. "If you ever have the time, you should read it. It's a classic."

"So I've heard," he said, inspecting the cover. The main image on the dust jacket was a tree printed against a red-brown background. I always thought it was the most elegant of all the *Mockingbird* covers, even if it was rather simple.

Although it was worn, my copy was probably worth a couple grand. There were only five thousand first edition first printings in existence. If I couldn't save up enough money for college, I'd probably have to sell it, and the thought made my heart hurt.

He opened the book, and his lips parted as he paged through it.

"How many times have you read this?" Every few pages were dog-eared. It drove my mom crazy when I did that. She liked to keep her novels in top condition, as if they'd never been opened, but I was of the opinion that books were made to be loved.

I smiled. "Once or twice." In reality, I'd read the book so often I could recite full passages by memory.

"And you don't mind reading it over?" The upward curve of his eyebrow suggested an unasked question: *Isn't that boring?*

"No," I said, shaking my head. "Have you ever listened to a song on repeat?"

His grin was slow and wide, and I could tell he liked my music comparison. "Yes," he answered. "I suppose I have."

Alec tucked *To Kill a Mockingbird* safely back in its spot on my shelf before resuming his typical, quiet state of being. I watched as he continued to explore my room. When he reached my dresser, he paused. The top was dedicated to my jewelry. I had three fake crystal bowls filled to the brim with rings, a huge clamshell to put my earrings in, and mounds of necklaces and bracelets piled everywhere else.

"Did you make all this?"

"Yup."

He picked up a chunky purple earring, turning it over in his hand. "You're good."

"Thank you." Pride ballooned inside my chest, and it made me feel bold. "Want me to make you something?"

Not waiting for an answer, I sat at my desk and grabbed a spool of brown leather cord. *Where are the scissors?* My hand hovered in air as

I looked around for them, until I finally spotted a pair peeking out from underneath the pile of magazines. After cutting a few pieces, I tied them together at one end and started working. When the back of my neck prickled, I knew Alec was watching over my shoulder.

"What's your favorite color?" I asked without looking up.

"Orange," he answered.

For some reason I was surprised, but I reached for a jar of faceted agate beads in both amber and a rust color. We were quiet for a couple more minutes, and then Alec cleared his throat.

"Is this your family?"

He pointed to the picture frame hanging above my desk. It was a rare photo of all four of us—Mom, Dad, Rose, and me. In fact, it was the only one I had. The picture was taken when we went to Disneyland for my birthday. I didn't remember any of the trip, but five-year-old me looked pretty pleased with herself perched on top of her dad's shoulders.

Shaking my head, I glanced back down at the leather wrap. "It's just me and my mom now."

He paused. "I'm sorry, Felicity."

"It's not a big deal," I said with a shrug. "I honestly don't remember much about my dad. He ran off with an intern when I was six, and they moved to some European country where there's no international child support enforcement. How clichéd is that?"

Wow. Talk about too much information.

The look on Alec's face was impossible to gauge, and when seconds passed without him responding, my ears burned. I searched my head for something to say, some way to fix the bomb I'd dropped in his lap, but I couldn't take back what I'd said. Instead, I concentrated on the to-be bracelet in my hands.

Finally, he cleared his throat. "I can top that," he told me, and my head snapped up at his words. "My parents got divorced three years ago, and my dad is on his third marriage since then. Wife number four is half his age. How's that for a stereotypical shitty dad?"

Whoa. That was so *not* what I expected him to say.

"I'm sorry," I said in a gentle tone. I wanted him to know I meant it, because I knew how it felt to have a screwed-up family. "That must be tough."

He offered me a weak smile, but his entire body had gone stiff. "It's fine."

It clearly wasn't, but I could also tell that he didn't want to discuss it anymore. Which made me remember that Alec still hadn't mentioned why he came over in the first place. I said as much to him.

"Right," he started, but before he could say anything else, the front door opened and closed with a slam.

"Felicity!" Mom called from the hall. "I'm home. I hope you didn't cook dinner. I brought tacos from that Mexican place you like."

I scrambled out of my chair. "Shit!"

"What's wrong?" Alec asked, concerned.

"You can't be here. If my mom sees you, she'll kill me." As I glanced around my room, I realized there was absolutely nowhere for Alec to hide. My closet was too small, and there was only room for Lord Pugton underneath my bed.

"Okay?" he said, still looking confused.

"House rules," I added, even though it was a lie. There wasn't time for a real explanation, and even if there was, I didn't have the heart to tell him the truth. I didn't want him to meet my mom. Because then I'd have to explain her ridiculous assumption and judgment, which would not only be embarrassing, but would probably offend him.

"Oh." He drew his mouth into a straight line. "So…what am I supposed to do exactly?"

My gaze landed on the window. "Quick," I said, shoving it open. "Go out this way."

He seemed taken aback for a brief moment, but strode over to the window with purpose. I glanced over my shoulder at the door and willed it to stay closed until he was out of sight. He slung his leg over the sill and carefully maneuvered himself outside. Once he was crouching in the bushes, he turned to face me.

"Bye, Alec," I said. "Sorry about this."

"Is there a better time for me to come back?" he asked. "Maybe tomorrow when your mother is home?"

"No!"

Alec frowned.

"I won't be home," I explained. "I'm working all day tomorrow." As the words left my mouth, it occurred to me that work was my solution. Mom never went to the diner, so it was the perfect place for us to talk. I grabbed a piece of scrap paper off my desk and scribbled down the Electric Waffle's address.

"Meet me here," I said, shoving the paper into his hands. "We can talk then."

I slammed the window shut.

☆ ♭ ♫

With Alec gone and Mom none the wiser, I went to find her in the kitchen. She greeted me with her usual peck on the cheek and tight hug.

"Honey, do you know whose car is parked in front of the house?" she asked when I pulled away.

My back went stiff. Not knowing what to do, I decided to play dumb. "There's a car parked out front?"

"Yeah, a really nice one."

"Mr. Ramirez's son is a doctor. Maybe it's his and he stopped by for a visit?"

"Maybe." Mom didn't sound convinced, but she dropped the subject, and we sat down to dinner.

Even though the food *was* from my favorite Mexican place, I pushed the beans and rice around my plate without taking many bites. Oblivious, Mom chattered away about her day at the dentist's office where she was a receptionist. Why anyone would want to be the gatekeeper to hell was beyond me, but she liked the stability and regular hours. My mind was too focused on Alec to pay much attention.

I didn't know what to think about him showing up out of nowhere, especially since I was still struggling to come to grips with *who* he was. It felt strange, seeing and talking to him like he was a normal guy and not a world-famous musician.

What did he want from me?

In addition to my confusion was a swelling pang of guilt. It had started as soon as I stepped into the kitchen and saw my mom's smile. I shouldn't have let Alec into the house. Not because Mom's judgment about him was right—I still thought Alec was a good guy—but because she didn't deserve to be disrespected. She worked hard for the two of us and loved me fiercely. I might not agree with her about Alec, but that didn't give me the right to go against her wishes.

"Felicity?"

"Huh?"

"I *said*, Dave gets home on Friday, so I'll be spending the weekend at his place. You okay holding down the fort on your own?"

"Yeah, no problem."

"Good." She dropped her silverware and collapsed back into her chair like she'd finished running a marathon. "That was delicious. Whaddaya say we clean this mess up and watch some reruns of *Gilmore Girls* before that show Asha loves so much comes on?"

CHAPTER 6

The next morning, the heat wave broke with the arrival of a storm. Which was freaky strange. It hardly ever rained in Los Angeles, and when it did, it was usually during the winter months. A thunderstorm in July? It was unheard of.

But the dreary weather complemented my mood.

The Electric Waffle was deserted, and there was nothing for me to do. After wiping down all the counters and tables, refilling the ketchup and syrup bottles, and mopping the floor to keep busy, I'd run out of chores. Miss Daisy, the owner and manager, had sent the rest of the waitstaff home, and without the chatter of the other girls, my only company was my thoughts.

And they were torturous.

I couldn't stop thinking about Alec. Yesterday, I'd been so concerned with getting him out of my room that I'd forgotten to set up a time to meet. Not knowing when he'd arrive made me antsy, so when I wasn't staring at the clock, my gaze was locked on the door. To keep from pacing, I forced myself to sit at one of the counter stools, but that didn't stop me from jiggling my leg or tapping my fingers. It was nearly two o'clock, so there were a few more hours before my shift was over, but I had to acknowledge the possibility that Alec might not come at all. Considering that I practically shoved him out my window, I wouldn't be surprised.

What I needed was a distraction.

Thankfully, Miss Daisy stepped out of her office and told me to take a break. After clocking out and pouring myself a cup of coffee, I took a spot at my favorite booth. It was tucked away in the back of the room but still had a great view of the door.

I had my ACT prep book with me, and I momentarily considered studying, but I was too jittery to concentrate. Instead, I dug to the bottom of my bag and pulled out the first three books my fingers touched: a battered edition of *The Adventures of Huckleberry Finn*, my travel copy of *To Kill a Mockingbird*, and *The Great Gatsby*. Deciding on the last one, I set the first two aside and dove into the 1920s.

As with every book in my collection, I'd read Fitzgerald's masterpiece to the point of memorizing it, but I was still sucked into the story within the first few paragraphs. Just as Nick received his invitation to one of Gatsby's lavish parties, the bell above the door chimed. I looked up, and there was Alec. It was as if he'd came from a photoshoot for a Burberry campaign. He was wearing a stylish gray trench coat with the collar pulled up around his neck, probably to fend off the rain. I always thought popped collars made guys look pompous, but on Alec it was cool.

I stared at him as he pulled off the coat and proceeded to shake away the water droplets that had collected in his way-too-perfect hair. He must have felt me watching because he glanced up and his eyes locked onto mine.

Crap, totally busted!

I shot out of my seat and crossed the room.

When I reached him, I tucked a loose curl behind my ear. "Hey."

Alec looked down at me with his beautiful eyes. "Hey," he said back.

Neither of us spoke.

A magnetic energy of sorts swelled between us. It was charged and electric and impossible to ignore. When I couldn't stand it anymore, I lowered my gaze, and by the time I looked back up, the buzz in the air was gone.

"You came," I said finally. I was still surprised.

He scratched his temple. "You wanted me to, right?"

"Yeah, totally! It's just... I thought that you might... Never mind."

Alec looked at me like I was speaking a foreign language, which reminded me of how I felt when Boomer talked about mechanical engineering. Normally, I nodded my head and offered the occasional *uh-huh* during his rants about heat transfer or energy conversion. Now, I quickly changed the subject.

"Can I get you something to drink? Coffee? Soda? I make a killer blueberry milk shake."

"Blueberry?"

I nodded eagerly. "I promise it's good." In fact, it was my absolute favorite. Mom had a weakness for them, which she'd passed on to me, so whenever blueberries went on sale, we'd fill our shopping basket with as many containers as possible and binge on shakes for a week straight.

"All right. I trust you," he said, serious as ever. Like we were talking about a life-or-death situation and not milk shake flavors. I waited, expecting him to give me his real order, but he stared back at me. When he raised an eyebrow, I realized he already had.

"Ooh, right! Okay, cool."

For reasons unknown, seeing Alec rattled me, even more than when Eddie Marks had sat next to me in geometry last year. I couldn't make sense of what was happening, which left me feeling frazzled. So much so that I was halfway across the room before I realized I'd abandoned Alec by the door.

I spun back around. "Um, you can sit there if you want," I said, pointing to the booth where my books and bag were. "I'll only be a few minutes."

In the kitchen, I pulled everything I needed from the industrial-size fridge—ice cream, milk, blueberries, maple syrup—and set it out by the drink mixer. As I worked on digging a huge scoop of vanilla out of the frozen tub, I wondered what Alec needed to talk to me about. Whatever it was, it must have been important if he was willing to meet me in person twice to discuss it. What if he thought I was the one telling the tabloids all those crazy, made-up stories about how we met? Oh crap, maybe that meant he was mad at me.

But he didn't look mad, I reminded myself. *Stop freaking out.*

Although I could make a blueberry milk shake blindfolded, I measured the exact amount of each ingredient to give myself a few minutes to calm down. When I returned with two bluish-purple drinks in hand, Alec was listening to his music. He yanked out his headphones and dropped them around his neck as I set both glasses on the table.

"Thanks," he said, pulling one of the shakes toward him. The tower of whipped cream on top wobbled.

I slid onto the bench across from him and smoothed out my shirt.

"Pretty good, huh?" I asked when he took his first sip. "I love blueberry-flavored anything, but milk shakes are my absolute favorite. The problem is most places don't make blueberry ones, so when I started working here, I convinced Miss Daisy to add them to the menu. There's this ice cream place down the street from my house that makes them, but theirs were terrible. The ratio was all off—too much vanilla, not enough berry. So I gave them my recipe, and guess what? They totally use it now too!"

Why. Am. I. Rambling?

Alec offered me an amused look when I finally finished. "Your recipe is *killer*," he said, using my earlier description.

Too flustered to drink any of my shake, I swirled the straw back and forth, making a mess out of the whipped cream. "Thanks."

I couldn't tell if he was teasing me or not. Normally, I was good at reading people, but with Alec, it was impossible. I could study him all day long and still not be able to crack his reserved front. The only thing I could make out for sure was the unmistakable intelligence that flickered in his eyes.

And crap. I'd been staring at him for a whole ten seconds.

"So about yesterday," I said with a start. *Might as well swallow my embarrassment and cut to the chase.* "You mentioned there was something you wanted to talk about?"

"Right." He hesitated, and the anticipation nearly drove me mad. "I wanted to say I'm sorry. Both for any trouble the media attention has caused you and for what that one magazine said about you—"

"Not being as pretty as Violet?" I finished, unabashed. I wouldn't take to heart what some poor excuse of a journalist wrote in an attempt to create drama. I had tougher skin than that.

He coughed. "Er, yeah." After a quick pause, he added, "It's not true."

I blushed. "You drove all the way to my house to apologize?"

"Is there something wrong with that?"

"No, but most people would have called." After all, I had given him my number…

It was Alec's turn to blush. "My mother always said it's important to apologize to someone in person."

Ohmygod. A gentleman who isn't embarrassed to talk about his mom?

"Plus," he added, rubbing the back of his neck. "I don't like talking on the phone, and you deserved more than a text."

"Alec, you have nothing to be sorry for." I wanted to reach across the table so he could feel the truth behind my words, but I tucked my hands under my butt so I didn't do anything stupid. "For the record, I didn't believe any of it. What they were saying about me in the magazines, I mean. I don't care about tabloids."

Which was ninety-nine point nine percent true. The only details in the articles that remotely piqued my interest were the bits about Violet being Alec's girlfriend. Part of me wanted to ask him about her, to clarify whether or not she was his girlfriend, but the other part of me didn't want to hear his answer.

Alec didn't bother to hide his relief. "Good."

I sank back into the vinyl cushion of the booth, feeling that same release of tension. Somehow, while making the milk shakes, I'd turned whatever I thought he was going to say into something negative. In reality, he was worried about how the rumors and gossip had affected me. That along with his apology proved to me that Mom was wrong about him. Alec was a genuinely nice guy.

But now that he'd said his piece, I wondered if he would leave. He had no other reason to stay. My heart dropped at the thought. I didn't want him to go.

Say something, Felicity, I thought. *Anything.*

Well, maybe not anything. I'd already humiliated myself enough by going on about blueberry milk shakes. The problem was that a lock of Alec's impeccably gelled hair had come loose, no doubt a result of the rain. It fell right above his eyes, brushing the top of his eyelashes, and made it impossible for me to concentrate.

Or breathe, for that matter.

Just as I was starting to flounder inside my head, he ran a hand through his bangs, smoothing the escaped strand back into place.

He cleared his throat. "You have two copies?"

"Huh?" I was clearly related to Shakespeare or some other great literary genius, because honestly? My talent for words was inspired.

Alec smiled and pointed at *To Kill a Mockingbird*, which I'd tossed next to the napkin dispenser.

"Oh, right! Actually, I have three. The one you saw yesterday is a first edition, so I never take it anywhere. This is my travel copy so I can read it whenever I want, and I think Asha has the third one. She has a bad habit of borrowing things and forgetting to return them."

"Asha?"

"My best friend," I explained. "She was the one who was supposed to give me a ride home from the charity ball."

Alec nodded as if this was interesting information. He took another sip of his milk shake and said, "Can I borrow it?"

"What?"

"Your book. I promise I'll return it."

His question sent a jolt through my body, and I didn't know which I found more exciting: the fact Alec was interested in *To Kill a Mockingbird* or his promise. Probably the latter, because in order for him to keep that promise, we'd have to see each other again.

"You really want to read it?"

"You took the time to listen to my music," he said, as if me cozying up to a mysterious masked stranger at the ball had been *such* a chore. "I want to read your favorite book."

My stomach flipped. I knew he was only being friendly, but still. It was possibly the most romantic thing a guy had ever said to me, that he wanted to read the book because it was *my* favorite.

Alec must have mistaken my astonishment for reluctance, because he played nervously with his headphones. "If you don't feel comfortable loaning—"

"No!" I blurted out, quickly finding my voice. "Not at all." Before he could change his mind, I shoved the paperback across the table.

His eyes searched mine momentarily, looking for any signs of doubt, but then he smiled and picked it up. "I should warn you. I'm a slow reader. You might not get this back for a while."

"That's fine," I told him, "as long as you don't mind my notes. I'm a notorious margin scribbler."

"Margin scribbler?"

"Yeah, like I leave notes in the margins of the book? Mainly thoughts and questions I have while reading."

Alec immediately flipped through the pages to see what I was talking about, and something came loose and fluttered out. We both looked down. Resting on the table was a piece of paper the size of my palm, and it was folded into a delicate heart.

Air whooshed out of my lungs at the sight of the origami folding. I blinked. And blinked again.

"Felicity?" Alec looked from me to the paper heart and back to me again, his eyebrows creased together. "Do you need your book-mark back?"

Unable to respond, I shook my head. All I could think was *Rose, Rose, Rose.*

"Are you sure?" he asked, doubt layering his words.

My throat was thick, but I forced myself to swallow the lump that had risen there. "Yeah, it's fine. I have about a million of those."

"Yes, but it's important to you." His response wasn't a question, but a statement.

Was it that obvious? And, more importantly, what was I supposed to say? While I didn't have any issues talking about my father, Rose was a different story. She was still an open wound—too raw, too personal—even after four years. I ducked my head, needing a minute to collect my thoughts.

"It's not the heart that's important," I said at last, "but the memory behind it." Hopefully, I sounded removed, as if I wasn't on the edge of tears.

But I couldn't fool Alec. "Of someone."

"What?"

"A memory of someone," he clarified. "Someone important to you."

Seriously, how did he see through me so easily? We hardly knew each other. And yet I found myself opening my mouth to explain. "My sister, Rose."

"The other girl in the picture?"

At first his question confused me, but then I remembered yesterday and how he'd asked about my family. "Yes," I said with a nod. "She was obsessed with origami. She'd fold whatever she could get her hands on—napkins, wrappers, receipts—into something beautiful. My favorites were the paper hearts. One year for my birthday she folded… Oh, I don't know, must've been more than a hundred of them, and she hung them from our bedroom ceiling. Her wrist was so sore she had to wear a brace for a week."

I couldn't tell Alec the rest of the story, how after Rose left, I would stare up at those damn paper hearts for hours, praying for my sister to come home. And when she didn't, I'd torn them all down. I'd wanted to throw them out, to burn them even, but a small part of me still *hoped*. So I'd boxed them up and banished them to the back of my closet.

Every now and then, I'd discover a heart covered in dust behind my desk or trapped in the crevice between my headboard and the wall. Finding one was like getting a paper cut, a split second of sharp pain that faded to a dull throb. But seeing one of Rose's paper hearts here? Now? It was a blade in my gut.

"Was?" Alec asked.

I shook my head to clear away the pain and memories. "Sorry?"

"You used the past tense, and yesterday you said it was only you and your mom. Is your sister..." He hesitated, as if he didn't like where he was taking the sentence. "Did she go to live with your dad?"

His question startled me. I turned to the Electric Waffle's big front window as I thought about my answer. The rain had stopped, but judging from the clouds, it was only taking a momentary break.

"No," I said eventually. But the truth was, I couldn't actually answer Alec, because I had no idea where Rose was. For all I knew, maybe she *was* with our dad. It was highly unlikely, considering how angry she was when he left, but there was always a chance. "Actually," I corrected myself. "I'm not sure."

A beat of silence passed. "You...you don't know where your sister is?"

"She ran away four years ago."

I felt the need to provide more of an explanation, but that was the only information I had. And that lack of understanding always ate at me. I'd spent countless hours wondering what made Rose leave so suddenly and without explanation. The only reason that came to mind was a fight she and Mom had had the week before her birthday. It stuck with me because the two of them came home together at two o'clock in the morning, and I'd thought it was strange that Mom was out so late. As soon as they stepped in the door, the screaming started and I'd promptly put on my headphones. Now, thinking back on that night, I wish I'd listened, even if it was only for a minute. Maybe then I'd know why Rose had left.

"So...what happened?" he asked.

My mouth twisted. "We haven't heard from her since." There would be no mistaking the pain in my voice, not with Alec's keen observation skills. I could feel white-hot anger building inside me. "I don't remember much about my dad, but my sister did. From the little my mom has told me, I think the two of them were a lot alike, both headstrong and wild. Mom always said they had more wanderlust flowing in their veins than blood. Rose tried to pretend that him leaving didn't crush her, but months after he moved out, I'd still hear her crying herself to sleep. One night, it was particularly bad, so I crawled into bed with her and asked why our dad would want to hurt us so much."

I paused, reliving the memory: Big Blue clutched against my chest, Rose laughing softly and wiping her eyes, her arms pulling me close so I wouldn't fall off the narrow single mattress. I took a deep breath and released it, letting the air hiss past my lips. "Instead of giving me an answer, she *promised* she'd never do the same thing to me, but..."

"She did," he finished.

"Yes. I want to hate her for it, but I can't."

Alec looked at me for a long moment, as if considering everything I'd told him. Then he said, "I don't blame you."

Whatever reply I'd been expecting, that wasn't it. After all, I'd just admitted to feeling darkly about my sister. "You don't?"

"My sister, Vanessa, and I are super close, so I can imagine how hard it must be for you to be apart from Rose," he explained. "And sometimes the people who mean the most to us, like our family, do things that make it difficult to love them, but we do anyway because that's what love is."

From what he'd said about his father, I had a hunch he was speaking on a personal level. "Is that how you feel about your dad?"

He shifted in the booth before nodding. "Let's just say the relationship I have with him is…complicated."

"But you still love him."

"He's done some pretty shitty things, but yeah. I do."

I wasn't purposely digging for information on his private life, but hearing that Alec didn't have the easiest relationship with his dad helped soothe some of my own self-loathing about what had happened with Rose.

"Speaking of my father…" Alec tugged on the collar of his shirt. "Every year he has this barbecue for all his artists. I hate his parties, but he's making me go, so I was wondering… Would you like to come with me?"

Wait. Did he just… Is he asking me on a date?

Alec kept talking, oblivious to the sudden pounding of my heart. "It's next Friday at noon. The party goes until six, but we don't have to stay the whole time if you don't want. And I can pick you up if you need a ride."

Holy shit. He *was* asking me on a date.

I stared at him, openmouthed and bewildered. When Alec drove me home after the ball, there had been a moment of tense anticipation as we sat in my driveway. It was like in the movies when the guy walks the girl to the door, and she wonders if he will kiss her. Part of me had hoped for the chance to spend more time together, to get to know him. But now that it was actually happening, it didn't seem real. I knew I needed to respond, but words failed me.

"If you already have plans…" he trailed off.

"I don't." Except for work, but Alec didn't need to know that. I could easily trade shifts with one of the other waitresses. "Basically, you need someone to suffer alongside you?" I asked, and satisfaction shot through my chest at my witty, almost flirty response.

His mouth quirked into a crooked grin. "Exactly. It will be terrible. I promise."

"And what does *terrible* include?"

Alec, whose arms were folded in front of him on the table, leaned in on his elbows. "Lots of pain. Lots of torture."

"Well, gosh," I said with a growing smile. "How's a girl supposed to say no to that?"

☆ ♭ ♫

Two hours later, I was clearing my only table of the day—a couple who, judging by their accents, were visiting from Australia—when the door of the Electric Waffle opened with a bang. A pair of heavy boots clomped inside. It was the type of obnoxious commotion that could only be caused by Boomer. Sure enough, he was shaking the rain from his hair when I looked up. Asha stood next to him, struggling to close an umbrella.

"Hey, Felicity!" he yelled in typical Boomer fashion.

"I'm at our regular spot," I called back to him. "I'll be done in a minute."

There was a five-dollar tip pinned under the ketchup bottle, and I shoved it in my apron pocket before grabbing the remaining dirty silverware and heading to the kitchen. After dumping the bus tub in the sink, I gathered our usual refreshments (soda for Boomer, a slushy for Asha, more coffee for me) before making my way over to my friends.

"Two blueberry shakes?" Asha asked as a way of greeting. "Must have been a bad day."

I set the serving tray down and slid into the booth next to Boomer. He'd pulled his Game Boy from his pocket, but Asha shot him a *Seriously?* look, and he heaved a sigh before shoving the gaming device back into his shorts.

"Actually," I said, passing out our drinks, "besides the lack of customers and this god-awful weather, my day was good."

Which was all because of Alec. I tried to keep a straight face as I thought about him, but it was impossible not to smile. A few minutes after he invited me to his father's party, the two Australian tourists had arrived and asked for a table. Regrettably, I'd had to return to work, but he'd waved off my apology as he tugged his coat back on, promising to pick me up on Friday. And this time around, I didn't mind saying good-bye because I knew I'd see him again.

"It was a good day?" Asha ripped open three packets of sugar and dumped them into her cup as if there wasn't already a gallon of high fructose corn syrup in the drink. "Then what's up with the ice cream overdose?"

"I only had one," I said, reaching for a sugar packet. If I didn't snag one now, she would use them all. "The second was Alec's."

"That famous dude with the F12?" Boomer asked. "Did he drive it here?"

"Yes, and no. Well, actually, I don't know," I said.

Boomer frowned and scratched his head, disheveling his already crazy curls.

I quickly clarified, "Yes, it was him, but I have no clue what car he drove."

"Oh, he drove it," Boomer answered even though he was the one who'd asked the question. "You don't own a car like that and *not* drive it places. God, I would have paid to see it."

"Of course you only care about the car," Asha replied with an eye roll, but then she stiffened. "Holy hell. You mean *he* actually sat here?" She looked down at the bench she was seated on, her voice tinged with awe, before glancing at the empty milk shake. "And that was his drink? The straw he drank from?"

I groaned and covered my face with my hands. "Please don't go all creepy fangirl on me."

"I'm sorry, but this is… Wow!" She was shaking her head, her gaze still fixed on the glass, as if this information was too much to handle. "Wait a minute. When did you make plans to meet with him?"

I flinched. Secretly, I was hoping this wouldn't come up, because I knew Asha would be miffed I hadn't told her. "Yesterday after you guys left," I admitted.

And I was right. She was pissed.

"But we were on the phone for over an hour last night! Why

didn't you say anything? I could have come earlier. I could have met him!"

"Which," Boomer said, pointing a finger at her, "is probably why she didn't tell you. Remember the time you met that one guy?"

He didn't need to elaborate. Asha and I both knew exactly who he was referring to. Last year on Boomer's birthday, Asha had spotted Ryan Klan, one of the actors from *Immortal Nights*, while we were eating dinner at Vine & Dine. Not only did she scream Ryan's name to get his attention, but she knocked over a waitress carrying a tray of food in her mad scramble to reach him.

"So I wanted an autograph," Asha said, batting her lashes in an attempt to look doe-eyed. "What's the big deal?"

"You got us kicked out of my favorite restaurant—*on my birthday*," Boomer grumbled, but it was in a good-natured way, and I knew there was no lingering grudge.

"Asha," I interjected, before they continued to bicker. "I wanted to mention it last night, I swear. But our plans weren't concrete, so I wasn't entirely sure he would show up."

"But—"

"Don't you want to hear what happened?" I asked, cutting her off before she could *really* start complaining.

The frown on Asha's face disappeared, and she leaned in, eyes wide and gleaming. "Something happened?"

An uncontrollable grin returned to my face, and I glanced down at the coffee mug nestled between my hands. The steaming warmth was reassuring, and I bit my lip before saying, "I think Alec asked me on a date."

Some of the red slush sloshed over the rim of Asha's cup and onto the table. "*What?*"

"Okay, I don't actually know if it counts as a real date. He didn't use the word *date*…"

For the next ten minutes, Asha grilled me about Alec's invitation, which I assumed was comparable to being interrogated by the FBI. What were the exact words he used? Did he seem nervous or casual? What kind of party was it? Who else would be there? How about the rest of the Heartbreakers?

Eventually we arrived at the scariest question of them all: what would I wear to the party? It made me nervous, because what did one wear to a barbecue/potential date with a celebrity where there would most likely be throngs of other celebrities? I had a feeling there weren't fashion guidelines for this sort of thing.

"How about that purple dress I wore for last year's school picture? The one with the lace sleeves?" I suggested.

Asha pushed her hair out of her face as she considered. "For a barbecue? I don't know, Felicity. I was thinking something more summery. I wish I could come over and help you get ready Friday morning, but I-I already have something going on."

I frowned when she rubbed her nose and looked away from me. She was hiding something, but Boomer, who'd been sitting quietly for the recent part of our conversation, let out an impatient sigh.

"Ladies," he said, "as much as I would *love* to scrutinize every clothing option in Felicity's closet and come up with a *très chick* ensemble, I think my balls are starting to shrivel."

Somehow, in the midst of talking about Alec, I'd completely

forgotten that Boomer was sitting with us. I opened my mouth, but before a single word emerged, Asha roared with laughter.

"It's *très chic*," she said.

Boomer frowned. "What?"

"*Chic*, not *chick*. French for *very stylish*. I can't believe the phrase *très chic ensemble* is part of your vocabulary."

He rolled his eyes. "What you don't know is that I moonlight as a Parisian couture designer," he said. "But seriously, I was trying to get your attention, and obviously it worked. For the love of God, can we please talk about something other than clothes?"

CHAPTER 7

On Friday, my morning started out good. *Really good.* I woke up to a text from an unknown number, and I immediately knew who it was from.

Unknown: Still up for some pain and torture?

Grinning, I added Alec to my contacts and texted him back.

Felicity: What if I say no? ;)
Alec: Too bad. I'll see you at 11:15.

But now, things were not so good. I had exactly one hour before Alec arrived, and I was in panic mode. Yesterday, I'd gone through my closet in search of a *très chic ensemble*, and after trying on half my wardrobe and feeling absolutely ridiculous for doing so, I opted for my favorite blue romper—cute, comfy, and totally me. If it wasn't fashionable enough for a celebrity-studded barbecue, so be it. I'd never been one to dress up special for a guy, not even Eddie Marks, and while I wanted to look good, I wasn't going to start just because of who Alec was.

The issue was, I couldn't find the wedge sandals I'd planned on wearing. They were the cute, beachy kind that weren't totally impossible to walk in and should have been at the front of my closet along with my Keds, flats, and flip-flops. But they were missing—*poof*, gone. Which was strange because they were the only heels I wore on a regular basis. Not that I wore heels regularly. Mom always said a good pair of pumps was a short girl's best friend, but I didn't see the point. My lack of height was obvious, regardless of a few extra inches, so why bother with uncomfortable footwear?

After digging through my closet and finding everything I'd lost since the start of high school (a jewelry design sketchbook, my pink Delta Nu T-shirt, the swimsuit I'd accused Asha of misplacing) with the exception of my wedges, I tore apart my bedroom apart. Still, nothing. And with the combination of butterflies quivering in my stomach and the rushing back and forth as I scoured every nook and cranny, I was starting to sweat. It wasn't a glistening-forehead situation, but full-on bullets and boob sweat. Which made me wonder if I had early-onset menopause.

Crap, is that a real thing?

And then, just as I was considering calling Alec to tell him I'd contracted acute hot-mess arrest or sweaty body syndrome and that I was moving to the South Pole indefinitely for treatment, my mom shouted from the kitchen.

"Felicity! I'm off to work."

I opened my door and called back to her. "Bye, Mom. Have a good day."

"You too, honey. I love you. Remember I'm staying at Dave's this weekend! There are leftovers in the fridge."

The front door slammed, signaling her departure, and that was when it hit me. I knew where my wedges might be. Mom and I had similar-size feet, and sometimes she could squeeze into my shoes. Maybe she borrowed my heels for a date night with Dave and forgot to put them back.

"She better not have stretched them out," I grumbled as I crossed the house in the direction of her bedroom.

After opening the door and turning on the light, I took a moment to wiggle my toes in the plush throw rug that covered the floor as I admired the space around me. I absolutely *loved* my mom's room. It was glamorous in a way that reminded me of old Hollywood, decorated with a crystal chandelier she rescued from our OC house and the lighted vanity mirror where she did her makeup.

I glanced down at my watch: fifty minutes until Alec would get here. Another jolt of nerves made my heart flutter, and I jerked toward the closet. When I opened the door and a stack of boxes toppled out, I heaved a sigh. Though I only owned a few pairs, Mom had a shoe addiction. It took me nearly fifteen minutes to go through all the boxes and the plastic organizer hanging from the door, but my wedges were still MIA. Just as I was about to accept defeat, it occurred to me there could be a few more boxes under the bed.

There weren't.

What I found instead was both confusing and intriguing.

There, pressed against the baseboard, was a lone guitar case.

That was strange. Mom didn't have a musical bone in her body, and my dad never played an instrument—at least not to my knowledge. Which I suppose wasn't saying much, considering I didn't know the guy, but still. If it was his, why had she held on to it for so long? She'd purged all other remnants of him during the move.

I knew it was none of my business, but I knelt down and slid out the case. I don't know what I expected to find—probably an actual guitar and other musical items, like a tuner and picks—but the bundle of letters and postcards tied together with ribbon weren't it.

Maybe they're old love notes from when my parents first started dating.

I untied the ribbon to examine the letters more closely—

And *my* name was scrawled across the front in handwriting that I recognized. Impossible... My gaze shot to the left-hand corner where the sender's address was printed:

Rose Lyon
27 Seawall Street
Galveston, TX 77551

Rose. *Rose.* It was from ROSE!

I stared at the letter in shock. Neither I nor my mom had heard from her in four years. And yet here was proof otherwise, tucked away like it didn't exist. The time stamp was from last year—on my *birthday.* I turned the envelope over and pulled out a single piece of stationery. With trembling hands, I unfolded the page and read:

April 3rd

Dear Felicity,

Today is your birthday. HAPPY 16th! Only two more years until you can legally engage in scandalous bedroom activities and other thrilling adult stuff like voting and applying for credit cards! I must have subconsciously been thinking about you, because you will never guess what happened. YOU were in my dream last night! We were at the park Mom used to take us to when we were little, lounging on a blanket with Elle Woods and Bruiser, drinking margaritas and playing Candy Land. LMAO, isn't that ridiculous? I remember when you were in love with that movie.

Anyway, it was the best dream I've had in ages, all because I got to spend time with you. I wish I could see you, even if it was only for a day or an hour or a minute, so we could do sister things together again, like paint our nails or argue over who gets to use the bathroom first in the morning. I know it's impossible, at least until you graduate, but the thought still makes me happy. God, I probably sound like a rambling idiot. The point is, I miss you.

In other news, Nicoli tried a peanut butter and jelly sandwich for the first time. To say he hated it was an understatement. He thinks American food is *disgusting, which doesn't bother me because it means he does all the cooking! Also, I'm switching characters for my final summer season. I'll be Rapunzel instead of Cinderella, which is way cooler because her costume has this beautiful flowered wig.*

I stared at the paragraph. *Nicoli tried a peanut butter and jelly sandwich for the first time. I'll be Rapunzel. Nicoli and Rapunzel. Sandwiches and flowered wigs.* Rose was talking (well, writing) like she hadn't been missing for the past four years. Like we spoke on a regular basis and I knew what was going on in her life. But who the hell was Nicoli, and what did she mean by switching characters? My whole chest felt tight.

After a minute, I was able to pull myself together and finish the letter.

Again, happy birthday, Fel. I wish I could give you a better gift than these words, but I take comfort in the fact that Mom will spoil you rotten. I heart you more than Starburst and salsa.

xoxo,
Rose

"Heart you more than Cool Ranch and blueberry shakes," I whispered out of habit.

A tear rolled off the tip of my nose before I realized I was crying. Not monster, body-racking sobs, but a silent stream of tears. When another drop fell, hitting the page and making the blue ink bloom beneath it, I wiped my eyes before any more of Rose's words could be ruined. She might not have thought so, but her letter was more than a gift. It was hope. The kind of hope I'd searched for when I'd stared up at her paper hearts, praying she'd come home.

But along with hope, a fire ignited inside me. Why hadn't I seen these letters before now? If Rose missed me, if she wanted to be part of my life the way her letter suggested, then why did she stay away? And why hadn't she contacted me in some other way?

I plucked the bundle of letters out of the guitar case and shuffled through them. Each one was from her, the oldest dating back to a month after she left. There must have been more than fifty pieces of mail. Some were fat envelopes, while others were colorful post-cards, but they were all addressed to me. It didn't take me long to notice every one had been sent from someplace different: Mexico, Jamaica, Brazil, even one from Italy! It was as if Rose was con-stantly on the move, unable to settle down.

Suddenly, I felt as if I'd been awake for weeks. There was some-thing exhaustingly sad about finding these letters, and I felt like the universe was intentionally poking the bruises of my heart. Leaving the bundle and the guitar case of the floor, I went back to my room for my phone and called Asha. My call went to voice mail, so I left her a message.

"Hey, it's me. I know you said you had plans, but you need to get over here. It's an emergency. Bring Boomer."

☆ ♭ ♫

By the time Asha and Boomer arrived at my house, I'd read ten more of Rose's letters. Each one was already open, and they were identical to the first: chatty and full of warmth, but without the answers I was searching for. The more I read, the less everything made sense. Because while I discovered who Nicoli was (Rose's boyfriend from Italy) and why she was rambling on about Rapunzel (she worked as a character on Disney cruises), I was still no closer to understanding the important details, like her reason for leaving or why she wouldn't come home.

"Felicity, you here?" Boomer called from the front hall. "It's me and Asha!"

My voice cracked as I shouted back, "I-I'm in here!"

I glanced at my watch. Only half an hour had passed since my SOS, which was surprising. Boomer lived on the other side of town. There was no way he could pick up Asha and drive to my house in thirty minutes, even if she'd called him right after listening to my voice mail.

With a creak, the door swung open, and light from the hallway spilled into the room.

"How'd you guys get here so fast?" I asked without bothering to look up. It was hard taking my eyes off Rose's letters. Part of me was afraid that if I did, they would disappear like she had.

"I was at Asha's" was all Boomer said.

That was enough to startle me. Asha and Boomer were good friends, but their relationship was the result of their connection to me. It didn't hurt my feelings that I wasn't included in whatever they were doing today, especially considering I had my own plans, but I was confused. The two never hung out alone, and trying to picture it was so…strange. I turned to Asha for further explanation, but she jammed her thumbs into the belt loops of her shorts and looked at the carpet, the walls, anywhere but me.

Before I could ask exactly what was going on, Boomer cocked his head and squinted at me. "Why is your face so blotchy?"

Asha's gaze snapped to me. "Felicity, were you crying? What's wrong?" The sight of my tearstained cheeks must have been alarming. She knew how much I disliked crying. My mom cried enough for both of us, so I figured at least one of us needed to be strong.

The answer to her first question was obvious, so I only bothered with the second. "Look what I found," I said, gesturing to the letters fanned out on the floor around me.

"Let me guess," Boomer said, peering over Asha's shoulder at the mess I'd made. "Your mom is writing an erotic novel and reading the manuscript traumatized—Ow! Son of a…"

"Could you *not* right now?" Asha snapped.

He grumbled a few choice words under his breath, rubbing his stomach where she'd jabbed him with her elbow, but Asha ignored him and crouched down at my side. I didn't say anything as she picked up the nearest letter to examine. Her gaze slid over the first few words, but then cut down to the end to see who had sent it.

"Holy crap!" she gasped. "It's from Rose."

"What? Give it here." Boomer snatched the page from her hands.

"They're all from her," I said. "Apparently she's been writing to me since she left."

Asha frowned. "And you've never seen these before now?"

I shook my head, and the lump in my throat bobbed as I swallowed back my lingering shock.

"Well, where the heck did they come from?" she asked.

"The letters were in there." I pointed at the guitar case. "It was under my mom's bed."

My friends exchanged glances, and Boomer said, "So…she was hiding them from you?"

"No," I fired back, hating that way my voice had risen. "That's *not* possible. If Rose contacted us, my mom would've told me."

There was a long pause. Asha thumbed her ear, and after a few more drawn-out seconds, she asked, "Are you sure?" It was obvious from her tone that she was skeptical, that she thought my mom was behind this.

But Asha was wrong. Wasn't she?

She had to be.

I shook my head again, trying to dislodge the doubt that was creeping into my thoughts. "My mom would *not* hide something like this. You don't understand what it was like for her when Rose left. First her husband, then her daughter. It was as if our whole family was leaving her one by one."

"Okay," Asha said, showing both her palms. "But how did the letters end up here?"

"I don't know. There has to be some sort of explanation."

"Like what? Magical letter-bearing elves?" Boomer said, and Asha elbowed him in the side for a second time.

I tugged my lip in thought. *He has a point.*

There didn't seem to be a plausible answer for how the letters had ended up in my mom's room other than the obvious one, but I refused to believe that she had anything to do with it. That she'd been hiding my sister from me.

"Why don't you ask her?" Asha suggested as I continued to wrestle with the mystery of it all.

Duh, Felicity.

I felt stupid for not thinking of that myself. The only way to know for sure was to confront her about the letters, so I punched in a number I knew by heart and waited. My mom was pretty good about answering her phone, even when she was at work, but today my call went straight to voice mail. There didn't seem to be a proper way to phrase my question in a message, so I sighed and hung up.

"No luck?" Asha asked.

Shaking my head, I said, "It doesn't make sense. Even if my mom *is* lying to me, how could she intercept every letter Rose sent? I'm the one who collects the mail."

"Look at the recipient address though." Boomer pointed at the envelope. "It's a PO box."

He was right. All the envelopes had the same address printed in Rose's loopy script, a box at our local post office. Why would she send letters to a place where I'd never receive them? I was about ready to throw my hands up at the absurdity of the situation, but as I stared down at the mess of paper spread out on the floor, it occurred to me there was another way to get my answers.

"The letters," I said and shuffled through the pile. "Help me find the most recent one."

We spent a minute searching through the mail.

"Here," Asha said, holding up one of the thicker envelopes. "Sent a week ago."

"From where?" I asked. There were so many different return addresses that I couldn't be sure, but I could have sworn I saw one from California. The chance that it was her latest letter was slim to none, but...

"San Francisco," she answered.

"Yes!" After gathering up the rest of the letters and shoving the guitar case back under the bed, I shot to my feet. "This is perfect. Rose might be right here in California. I'm going to go find her."

"Um, okay...but how are you going to get there?" Asha asked as we exited my mom's room and made our way back to mine.

I turned to Boomer. He was the only one of us who had a car, an ancient pickup with a muffler louder than he was.

"Sorry, Fel," he said, his face dropping when he realized what I was thinking. "I wish I could drive you, but I don't think my truck can make that kind of trip. We'd be on the side of the highway calling for a tow in three hours flat."

Damn, I hadn't thought of that. Older than Michael James, Boomer's ride needed constant attention. He was always popping the hood and whispering words of encouragement as he fiddled with the engine when it wouldn't start.

"You could take a bus," Asha suggested.

"I suppose," I said, flipping my light switch. "But how much do you think that will cost?"

"Twenty, maybe thirty bucks?"

More than I could afford, but there was no way around it. I had to find Rose.

"Okay, can you turn on my computer and pull up a schedule? Find out what time the next bus leaves while I pack a bag."

There was a skeptical look on Boomer's face as he leaned against the doorjamb, arms crossed over his chest. "Do you think your mom is going to let you take off like this?"

I pulled a small duffel out from under my bed and brushed a layer of dust off the top. I hadn't used it since the move. "Never in a million years, which is why I'm not going to tell her."

☆ ♭ ♫

"Felicity, this is beyond stupid," Asha said, putting a hand on her hip.

Boomer nodded. "She's right, which says a lot because we never agree on anything."

I sighed as I shoved my toiletry bag into the duffel and zipped it. "We already went over this. It's really sweet you're both worried about me, but I can't let you guys waste so much money."

The bus ticket turned out to be more than thirty dollars—it was double. I cried a little on the inside when I pulled out my emergencies-only credit card to buy one. What made the purchase more painful was that there were buses to San Francisco for as cheap as ten dollars, but apparently Friday trips sold out quickly, and all that was available was a fancy coach. There were cheaper options tomorrow, but I needed to leave today. I had to get back for my shift at the Electric Waffle on Sunday. Or before my mom came home and realized I was gone.

The point was, I couldn't let Asha and Boomer come with me,

even though I wanted them to. Money-wise, they weren't any better off than me. The thought of them dropping sixty dollars on what might be a wild-goose chase made my stomach tighten.

"Helping you is not a waste of money," Asha argued.

And Boomer quickly added, "Besides, I'm not worried about spending a few bucks. I'm worried about *you*." He positioned himself in front of me, a looming mountain, and placed both his hands on my shoulders. "What happens if you get to this address and Rose isn't there anymore? It will be night by the time you arrive. Where will you stay? You're not old enough to rent a hotel room, and you don't know anybody who lives in the city. You shouldn't go alone. You haven't thought this through."

I offered Boomer the most convincing smile I could muster. "I'll be fine. I'm going to San Francisco, not the moon. If Rose isn't there, I'll go back to the station and wait for my bus home. Seriously, you guys are making a bigger deal out of this than necessary. I can take care of myself."

"You know that's not what I meant," he said. "I just don't think you should go alone."

I grabbed his arm in a reassuring way. "I'll have my phone on me the whole time. If something happens, I'll call you right away."

His lips pressed into a small white line, and he let go of me. "A lot of help that will do," he grumbled. "I don't like this."

"Come on," I said, sighing. My voice was soft, apologetic even. While I felt guilty for being the source of their concern, it wasn't enough to change my mind. "If we don't leave soon, I'll be late for the bus."

As gently as possible, I pulled away from Boomer and slung the duffel over my shoulder. Then I grabbed my messenger bag, tucked Rose's letters inside, and strode out of the room before either of my friends could start arguing again. When the door closed with a sharp bang, I knew they were grudgingly following behind me.

After doing a quick lap of the house to make sure all the lights were off and the windows and doors were locked, I was ready to leave. Although his truck couldn't make the six-plus-hour drive up north, Boomer could manage the trip to the bus station. It was only a few miles away.

"Thanks again for all your help, guys," I said, yanking open the front door. "I really appreciate—"

I never finished. Whatever I planned on saying was whisked from my mind at the sight of Alec. He was standing on the porch, hand poised to knock. His lips curved into a timid half smile as he let his arm fall back down to his side.

"Hey, Felicity," he said, and that was all it took to steal the air from my lungs.

I couldn't place it, but there was something different about him. It took me a moment of staring to realize it was his outfit. I'd never seen him dress so casually before, but he still looked sexy in a heart-stopping way. *He could wear a mascot costume*, I thought, *and he'd still make girls swoon*. Today, he was dressed in a pair of plain khaki shorts, Top-Siders, and a blue V-neck shirt. It fit him perfectly, like it was designed specifically with his chest in mind, and the color turned his eyes a seafoam green.

"Oh," I breathed, and the little air still left inside me hissed passed my lips. "Alec, hi." How was it possible that I had forgotten

Alec was picking me up? That we were supposed to be going on a maybe date?

His smile retracted as he took in the surprise that must have been clear on my face. "Is something wrong?" he asked as his gaze darted to the duffel at my side.

I didn't get a chance to reply, because Asha nearly slammed into my back. She made a choking, squawk-like sound and started whacking me on the shoulder.

"Felicity, Felicity, Felicity," she whispered even though Alec was standing close enough to hear. "It's *him*."

The secondhand embarrassment was too real to bear. I squeezed my eyes shut and slowly dragged a hand down my face as I waited for it to subside. After taking a calming breath, I opened my eyes to do introductions.

"Alec, this is my friend Asha." I stepped aside so I wasn't blocking the doorway and glanced at her. She had a hand pressed to her chest, and her entire face had taken on a ruddy complexion. I begged her with my eyes to behave. "Asha, I'm one hundred percent sure you don't need an introduction to know who this is."

"No, nope. Definitely not. Hi, I'm Asha…and you already know that because Felicity just introduced me. Crap. I'm totally rambling now, aren't I?"

Boomer, who was standing behind her with his arms crossed over his chest, snorted. "Was that rhetorical, because I'd be happy to answer for you. Yes, you sound like a dumbass."

Asha momentarily shifted her attention from Alec and whipped around to deliver a well-aimed glare at Boomer.

I quickly jumped in before they bickered. "And this is my other good friend, Boomer," I said. "Boomer, Alec."

Boomer did one of those brusque chin nods as a way of acknowledging Alec before saying to me, "We need to leave soon. I'm going to start the car." Then he blew past us as if the house were on fire, dragging Asha behind him.

"But I didn't get a chance to talk to him," Asha complained as they stepped off the porch.

Alec, who'd been silent this entire time, finally spoke. "You're going somewhere." There was no question in his tone, only disappointment.

"Yeah," I answered, my throat tight. "Something happened with my sister, and to be honest, it completely slipped my mind that you were coming." Saying those words out loud were difficult, but he deserved to hear the truth.

For one who'd been forgotten, Alec took my confession in stride. "You mean Rose? Did you find her?"

His concern was as surprising as it was comforting, and a small smile lifted the corners of my lips. "Not exactly," I answered. "When I was getting ready this morning, I found a collection of letters hidden in my mom's room. They were from Rose. She's been writing to me since she ran away."

"So these letters…" Alec said as a frown crossed his face. "Your mom kept them from you?" He shook his head as if that was the most despicable thing he'd ever heard.

"I'm not sure."

"Is that where you're going then? To talk to her?"

"No, I'm tracking down Rose. At least, I hope to. Her last letter was sent from San Francisco, so I'm taking a bus there today to see if I can find her."

Alec's face remained passive as ever, but he swallowed hard. "I see."

"I'm so sorry, Alec." I wrapped my arms around myself and stared down at my feet. "I was looking forward to going to the party with you, but this is really important—"

"Felicity," he said, holding up a hand to stop me. "It's okay. If she were my sister, I'd do the same thing."

"So…you're not mad?"

"No," he said. "This is something you need to do."

The tension in my shoulders dwindled. I was glad he thought so. The truth was, I wouldn't be able to stop thinking about Rose until I had some answers, but at the same time…there was a heavy feeling inside my chest. Part of me knew that by going after my sister, I would miss out on something that had the potential to be amazing. Something like him.

"Um, Felicity?" Asha said, running up the front walk. She cast a quick glance in Alec's direction before saying, "I hate to interrupt, but we have a problem." She pointed over to Boomer.

The hood of his truck was propped up, and the toolbox he always kept in the back was open on the driveway next to him. He was rummaging through it, presumably trying to find a tool to help stop the smoke billowing out of the engine. Whatever was wrong, it didn't look good.

Shit, shit, shit! This can't be happening.

I stepped off the porch and dashed over to Boomer. "What happened?"

He looked up from his work. There was already grease smudged across his forehead. "This truck is ancient. That's what happened."

"Can you fix it?" I bit my lip and prayed for the answer to be yes.

"Just because I'm good with mechanical stuff doesn't make me a magician, Fel."

"But I can't be late for the bus."

Sighing, Boomer used his shirt to clean the grease off his hands. "And I'm supposed to drive Kevin to T-ball practice tonight. Doesn't look like either of those things is going to happen."

"Wait," Alec said, stepping forward. "You're not going with Felicity?"

The sound of his voice made me turn in surprise. Amid my concern for Boomer's truck, I'd completely forgotten about him. *Again.* What was wrong with me?

"I want to," Boomer replied and crossed his arms, "but she won't let us."

Alec turned his intense gaze back to me. "Why would you go by yourself? That's not safe."

"Thank you," Boomer said, sighing in exasperation. And for the first time, he looked at Alec with what appeared to be acceptance, as if he recognized they were on the same side. "That's another point for Team Common Sense."

"Not you too." I groaned, ignoring Boomer. "We're talking about San Francisco here, not the murder capital of the world. Besides, I can't go anywhere if the truck doesn't start."

Nobody said anything, a silent acknowledgment of the hopelessness of the situation, and Asha pulled me into a side hug. I checked my watch and swallowed hard. There was no way I would make the bus on time, which meant I wasn't going to find my sister.

Alec studied me. I must have looked majorly pathetic because his eyes softened and he cleared his throat. "Of course you're going," he said, stepping forward. "I'll drive you."

I'd completely forgotten he'd driven here until now. I glanced at the car, a Cadillac ATS, parked on the street in front of the house. Obviously it was Alec's. It was new-car shiny and much too expensive to belong to anyone who lived in my neighborhood.

"Really?"

He nodded.

"Thank you so much, Alec. You're seriously a lifesaver." I turned to Asha and said, "Did you write down the address for the station?"

"No, you misunderstood." Alec waved Asha off when she started digging through her purse. "I'm not taking you to the bus. I'll drive you to San Francisco." He straightened his shoulders as he said this, as if he knew I'd argue and was prepared to stand his ground.

"Oh. Um, that's super nice of you, but I already bought a ticket and—"

"You're not going alone," he said, unrelenting. I opened my mouth to respond, but Alec crossed his arms over his chest, and it was impossible not to notice how the sleeves of his shirt crept up over his biceps. "I have a car, and now that you're not going, there's a party I want to avoid."

"But won't your dad be pissed if you miss it?" I asked. I didn't want Mr. Williams to dislike me.

Whoa. Slow down, Felicity.

I was getting way ahead of myself. I'd have to stop turning down Alec's company if I ever wanted to make it to the meet-the-parent stage. Not that I focused on that sort of thing. My mind was on Rose, one hundred percent.

He hesitated for a moment but said, "All the more reason to not attend."

Before I could come up with another excuse, Asha grabbed me by the arm and said to the boys, "Can you give us a moment?" Then she pulled me out of earshot. "Did someone hit you over the head? There's a fine-ass boy offering to take you on a road trip, and you can't say no fast enough. What is wrong with you?"

"I want to go with him," I said, glancing at Alec. He still had his arms crossed. *God, why does stern look so good on him?* "Trust me, I do. But I already paid for my ticket, Asha. I can't waste it."

"Who cares? It's only sixty bucks, Felicity. For once, can you stop thinking about money and have some fun?"

Her words stung. Did Asha really think all I thought about was how much I had in the bank? She made me sound like my mom.

"Fine," I muttered. "I'll let him drive me, but you're wrong. I don't just think about money." I marched back over to the boys and announced, "Alec, I hope you're a good driver, because I get carsick easily." Although I'd already experienced Alec's driving, I couldn't say I remembered much about it. I was too distracted by him and his car to be nauseous.

Alec scoffed and pulled his keys out of his pocket. "I'm a great driver." He spun the key chain around his finger. "We can head out whenever you're ready."

"All right, just let me say bye." I turned toward my friends and found them huddled together a few feet away, speaking in hushed tones. "What's going on?"

Boomer glanced up, and I knew from his expression that the two were up to something. Asha turned around to face me with a fierce gaze and set jaw.

"We've made a decision." There was her I-mean-business voice again.

I raised an eyebrow. "About what?"

"You wouldn't let us come along before because you didn't want us spending money on tickets," she said. "But since Alec is driving, that isn't an issue anymore, is it? We're coming along, whether you like it or not."

"That is," Boomer added quickly, "if Alec lets us." He glanced down at Asha. "It is his car after all."

But Asha didn't back down. As much as she loved Alec and the Heartbreakers, she wasn't going to let his presence weaken her resolve. She looked at him and raised her chin, as if she was daring him to say no. Everything about her posture screamed "She's *our* best friend, not yours."

Alec seemed to understand this, because he nodded in agreement. Whether he was disappointed or not by the company was impossible to tell.

Asha's tough demeanor faded in an instant and was replaced by her normal warm smile. "Good. I'm glad that's all sorted out. Should we get going? This is going to be a long drive." She headed toward the street before anyone could respond, like she was afraid

Alec would change his mind and she needed to hurry us along so he wouldn't have that opportunity. We all stared after her, none of us moving, until Alec shook his head in amusement and followed.

"Hey," I whispered when we reached the car. "Are you sure you're okay with this?"

Alec popped the trunk and held out his hand for my duffel. As I passed it to him, I glanced inside. A guitar case was shoved in the back, and next to it laid a heavy-duty rucksack like the kind used to backpack across Europe. This seemed normal enough, but I frowned at the pair of strange metal objects that looked like sandals with spikes on the bottom. There was also a pickax.

He slammed the trunk closed before I could place either of the two items.

"Absolutely." He held back a smile as if he thought something was funny. "Now will you stop asking me that and just get in the car?"

CHAPTER 8

Asha bolted down the front walk of her house, barely glancing back at Riya, who stood in the doorway with crossed arms and a disapproving frown.

"Hey, Alec," she said when she slid back into the car and slammed the door shut. "I never got to tell you, but I totally adore your guys' music. 'Astrophil' was my favorite song on the new album!"

Alec checked the rearview mirror as he backed out of her driveway. "Thank you," he said with a nod.

A satisfied grin spread on Asha's face as she buckled her seat belt and stuffed an overnight tote between her feet. Alec had offered to swing by her and Boomer's houses before leaving LA so they could pack small bags for the trip.

"Sooo…" Asha said. From the way she was bouncing her knee, I knew she was working up the courage to ask him a question. "Is it true? Are you guys going to be in an episode of *Immortal Nights*?"

"Yeah," he answered. "Three actually."

"WHAT?" she exclaimed, and I flinched at her volume. "*Ohmyfreakinggod!*" She collapsed back into her seat, waving a hand in front of her face.

Boomer glanced up and gave Asha a causal once-over before

diving back into his game. "I think you may have killed her," he said.

"I'm sorry," Alec responded, his brow wrinkling with concern. "Should I not have told her?"

I rolled my eyes. "Give her a minute. She'll be fine. Probably just fandom overload, both *Immortal Nights* and the Heartbreakers together. This is like a dream come true for her."

"She's a bit obsessed, but we love her," Boomer added.

"Oh please," I said to him. "If Alec had driven his F12, you would have jizzed yourself."

Boomer looked me dead in the eyes and said, "Without a doubt."

Alec barked in laughter. "I take it you're into cars?"

"Correction—he lives for cars. Honestly, before I met Boomer, I didn't know the difference between a coupe and a sedan," I explained. "He was so horrified by my lack of knowledge that he had to educate me before we could be friends."

"Well, yeah. I couldn't associate with someone whose dream ride was, and I quote, 'a blue one.' That's just embarrassing." Boomer hesitated, but then asked Alec, "Do you really own an F12?"

At this, Alec rubbed the back of his neck. "It's my dad's car. This is going to sound totally lame, but he insisted we drive it to the ball. He likes…making an entrance."

But Boomer didn't think it sounded lame, and the boys chatted about cars until we reached his house. He was in and out before the song on the radio changed, returning with a backpack slung over his shoulder. Five minutes later, we were on I-5 North. My blood rushed in anticipation. I was on my way to Rose! After four years of thinking I would never talk to her again, I would hopefully get the chance tonight.

I never questioned if Alec knew where he was going, and he didn't ask for directions. He seemed confident enough as he weaved through the traffic, and that was refreshing. Since Boomer was the only one who owned a car, he always drove, but he also had the worst sense of direction. The guy couldn't get from Point A to Point B, even if it was a straight shot between the two, so I was always the designated copilot.

Twenty minutes into the drive, Alec pulled off the highway and I frowned.

Where are we going? I nearly asked, but as soon as the question formed in my head, I realized we were in Los Feliz, a neighborhood known for celebrity residents.

"I hope you don't mind, but I'm going to grab a few things." Alec rolled down his window as he pulled up to a gated underground parking lot. He punched a code into a keypad on the wall, and the gate slid back. "You guys can wait here or come up," he said as he steered his car into an open stall. "Doesn't matter. I won't be long."

"We're definitely coming," Asha said, throwing open her door. There was a feverish look in her eyes, like this was every Christmas she'd ever experienced rolled into one giant holiday.

I unbuckled and got out, although with less enthusiasm. I felt… Was *strange* the right word? This was Alec's apartment. Not his dad's or his mom's. He actually owned his own place. Which was understandable since he was eighteen and had plenty of money, but it made me feel out of my league. He was only a year older than me, but suddenly those three hundred and sixtyish days felt like decades.

Asha hooked her arm through mine as we crossed the garage toward the stairwell. "This is so unreal," she whispered. "Alec Williams just invited us to his apartment."

"You really need to work on your quiet voice," Boomer said from behind us. "Everyone can hear you, including the guy who *invited us to his apartment.*"

I peeked at Alec, who was a few steps ahead of us, keys swinging in his hand. If he'd heard, he made no indication.

Asha snickered. "Of all people, you're one to talk."

Boomer grinned and gave her a playful shove. "That may be true, but that doesn't make you any less creepy."

The elevator ride to Alec's apartment was silent with one exception: Asha was humming to herself. I caught her eye and shot her a look, which was supposed to say, "Can you please *act normal?*" But she just offered me a mischievous smile and carried on. It was only when we reached his floor that I recognized the tune—a Heartbreakers song.

Someone, please. Kill me now.

My face turned impossibly hot, but the embarrassment was quickly replaced with surprise when Alec unlocked the door to his apartment, and we all filed inside.

He flipped on the lights. We were standing in the kitchen, and my first thought was: *This is small.* Small, but nice.

Past the island countertop and bar stools was the living room. A sectional couch and matching chair were centered in front of one of those fake, electric fireplaces. Above the mantel hung a flat-screen TV. The far wall had what looked like a floor-to-ceiling window, but the curtains were drawn, hiding whatever view Alec had of the city. The remaining wall was covered by a huge modular bookshelf. Some of the cubes held books, but judging from our conversation about *To Kill a Mockingbird*, they were for decoration. The other compartments displayed vases and glass bowls and other accent pieces.

I don't know what I was expecting—maybe a penthouse bachelor pad—but this was definitely not it. The space was cozy and warm, and I liked it.

"Well," Alec said. He gestured vaguely in the direction of the living room and then shoved his hands into his pockets. "Make yourselves at home. I'll be right back."

Boomer had no reservation about doing just that. He plopped down on the couch and pulled out his Game Boy. "Alec's not half-bad," he said, glancing at me over the back of the couch.

I shot him a look. "Well, thank God he has your approval."

"I have to pee," Asha announced, starting down the hall in search of the bathroom. I suspected she wanted to see the rest of Alec's apartment and was being nosy, but I said nothing.

Once she was out of sight, I wandered over to the fireplace to inspect the row of picture frames arranged along the mantel. I didn't need an explanation to figure out the first was of Alec and his sister. Vanessa had the same gray eyes and nearly white hair Alec did, and their noses were identical. The siblings were standing at the edge of some desert ridge wearing hiking gear and smiles of accomplishment.

The next frame held two pictures of Alec with his bandmates: Oliver Perry, JJ Morris, and Xander Jones. The first was of them laughing and sitting around a campfire, and in the second they were in what looked like a hotel pool, chicken fighting. Something about the two snapshots was startling. I'd only seen the Heartbreakers in magazine spreads and on posters, so it was strange to see them in such casual settings, like they were regular teenagers and not celebrities.

The fourth photograph was also of the band, but standing in the center of the group was a brunette with a streak of blue in her hair and a nose piercing. My stomach twisted when I saw Alec's arm around her shoulders, but she was holding hands with Oliver, and I remembered Asha telling me he was dating a photographer named Stacy or Sara something or other.

My gaze slid to the last picture of Alec and a beautiful blond woman who could only be his mother. Her head was thrown back in laughter, and Alec, who looked like he was two or three, was propped on her hip. The smile on his face matched his mother's joy, and I smiled to myself. Toddler Alec was adorable.

Out of nowhere, a funny ringing filled the room. At first I thought it was Boomer's game, but he always played with the sound off because it drove Asha crazy. I turned in a circle, trying to find the source of the noise, until I noticed the computer on Alec's desk had lit up. Someone was calling him.

"Hey, Alec?" I shouted down the hall. "Someone's Skyping you!"

"It's probably Vanessa," he yelled back. "Can you answer it? I'll be out in a sec."

"Sure thing!" I rushed over to the computer.

The incoming call was from someone named DoubleJMan. I had a feeling it wasn't Vanessa, but I slid into the chair and answered anyway. It took a few seconds for the call to connect, and when the camera finally blinked into focus, Alec's sister was not on the other end. Instead, there was a guy with dark-brown, almost black, hair. The first thing I noticed was that he was shirtless. And he looked *very good* shirtless, all buff and muscly, with an armband tattoo twisted around his bicep. His face was just as recognizable as Alec's, and I knew who he was in an instant—JJ Morris, drummer for the Heartbreakers.

I was as awestruck as when Alec first revealed his identity, but somehow, despite the uncomfortable flutter of nerves in my stomach, I managed to lift my hand in a hesitant wave and say, "Ah, hi."

"Alec," he said. "You're much prettier than I remember. And ginger. Did you color your hair?"

I inhaled at his greeting. "I'm not Alec," I said, although it was obvious he was giving me a hard time.

This made him smile, and he leaned toward the computer. "Hi, person who clearly isn't Alec. Do you make a habit of answering other people's calls when they're not around?"

"Do you make a habit of calling people naked?" I shot back.

"Half naked," JJ corrected, and he lifted himself from the chair so I could catch a glimpse of the sweats he was wearing. "But if you want me to lose the pants, I would be more than—"

A high-pitched squeal drowned out whatever inappropriate, dirty thing JJ was going to say. I didn't have to turn around to know Asha was back from the bathroom.

"Holy shit, that's JJ!" She pointed at the screen as if it were a one-way video chat and he couldn't see her ogling him. I was tempted to end the call right there and save myself whatever further embarrassment was coming my way, but JJ seemed to find the whole situation amusing.

"Hey, guys!" He motioned to someone offscreen as he tried to contain his laughter. "Get over here. Looks like some crazy fans broke into Alec's apartment again." Three second later, a girl with an aqua streak in her hair moved into view and took the open spot next to JJ. A guy with brown curls and bright-blue eyes appeared behind her, placing his hands on the back of her chair—Oliver Perry. Asha produced another earsplitting noise at the sight of the Heartbreakers' lead singer.

"Oh my God," she exclaimed, repeatedly hitting me on the shoulder. Before I could tell Asha to stop, that she was going to give me a bruise the size of Texas, or explain to JJ that I most certainly had *not* broken into Alec's apartment, the girl spoke.

"She's not a crazy fan," she said. "You're Felicity, aren't you?"

What. The actual. Hell. "Um, yeah."

The girl smiled as if knowing my name wasn't creepy at all. "Hi, I'm Stella."

With narrowed eyes, JJ glanced from Stella to me and back again, trying to figure out what was going on. "Wait, you two know each other?"

"Nope," she responded. Behind her, Oliver was playing with her hair, and she leaned back against him. "We've never met. Hence why I introduced myself, Einstein."

His eyebrows squished together. "Then how do you know her name?" he asked, voicing my own question.

"She's the girl from the masquerade ball, duh."

Alec told Stella about the ball. He told her about me. I was interesting enough to tell someone about! I made myself take a steadying breath.

JJ scratched his head and turned to Oliver. "You know what she's talking about? What ball? I swear, nobody tells me anything anymore."

Oliver flicked the back of JJ's head. "Yeah, because you're a loudmouth," he answered, but I could tell from the look on his face that he also wasn't in the know about the ball. JJ scowled and attempted to swat his friend back, but Oliver dodged out of the way with a smile.

"She's talking about the Children's Cancer Alliance masquerade," Asha blurted out, clearly excited to contribute to the conversation. "It was a charity event, and hi, I'm Asha. I just want to say, I love you guys so much. Your new album is amazing."

A satisfied smirk flashed on Oliver's face. "Thanks, Asha," he replied. She grabbed my arm when he said her name, and I flinched as her nails dug in. "So glad you liked it."

Asha couldn't manage a response. She looked dazed—lips parted, eyes glazed over. It was the same way girls at school looked when Eddie Marks paid them any attention, but this was ten times worse. Oliver had clearly perfected the art of making girls swoon.

A beat passed without anyone speaking, so JJ took advantage of the silence and returned the conversation to me. "So, Felicity, you met Alec at a charity ball?" He sounded casual, but from the way he scooted his chair closer, I could tell he wanted more information.

I nodded. "Um, yeah. He spilled his drink on me."

"Are you serious?" JJ exploded with laughter.

Oliver's lips quirked. "Smooth."

Crap, maybe I shouldn't have told them that.

"It wasn't entirely his fault. I wasn't watching where I was going, and—"

"Hey, I'm here," Alec said, emerging from the hall. "Is it Vanessa?" He glanced down at the screen. "Oh. Hi, guys. What's up?"

A wicked grin slowly built on JJ's face. "You have a secret girlfriend."

"Not a secret," Stella pointed out. "He told me."

"We're not dating," I added quickly. I didn't want Alec to think I'd been telling his friends anything untrue. "We hardly know each other."

"But he invited you over," JJ said. He waved a finger at me like he thought I was trying to fool him. "Alec *never* invites girls over."

"It's not like that," I started to say.

But JJ wasn't listening. He spoke over me to Alec. "No wonder you didn't tell me about her. She's totally bangable."

The flush of humiliation was instantaneous. I peeked at Alec, and to my relief, he was just as red as me.

"*Jeremiah!*" Stella exclaimed. "Why do you always have to be so vulgar?"

"Ugh, how many times do I have to tell you not to call me that? Just because you know my first name doesn't mean you get to use it," JJ complained. "And besides, I wasn't being vulgar. I was paying a compliment."

The two bickered back and forth, and I decided to use their distraction as my opportunity to escape. "I'll let you talk to your friends," I whispered to Alec.

Alec answered with a stiff nod and refused to meet my eyes. His cool behavior made my throat tighten, but I did my best to ignore the sudden change in his attitude. I vacated the computer chair so he could sit down.

"Come on, Asha." I grabbed her wrist and led her out of earshot, wishing we'd stayed in the car.

☆ ♭ ♫

"Hey. You didn't happen to see a Wi-Fi password written down anywhere, did you?" Asha asked. She'd taken a spot next to Boomer on the couch and was scrolling on her phone.

"No, why?" I responded, barely glancing in her direction. My attention was fixed on Alec, who was talking with his friends in hushed whispers. I couldn't hear what was being said, but from the gestures he was making, he wasn't happy.

"I need to update my blog," she said.

That caught my attention.

"But you only post on Thursdays." I narrowed my eyes as I studied her. She was too focused on her phone to reply, so I pushed away from the armrest I was perched on and went to see what was so important. "What are you looking at?"

"Do you like this filter"—there was a pause as she changed the effect—"or this one?"

I frowned, not sure what to make of the picture on her screen. In it was a lone toothbrush inside a toothbrush holder or whatever they were called, and that was it. It wasn't even one of those fun colorful brushes shaped like SpongeBob or a Disney princess to get little kids to brush their teeth.

"What's so cool about a boring old…" I never finished my question. Realization made my stomach roll, and I wanted nothing more than to crawl under the couch and hide there for the rest of eternity. "Please don't tell me that's a picture of what I think it is," I whispered, "because that would be all types of creepy."

"Alec's toothbrush?" Asha smirked. "Totally is. Saw it when I was in the bathroom. I also got a shot of the shampoo he uses. Head & Shoulders for men, in case you were wondering."

No. No, I wasn't.

"Are you joking right now? Because honestly, I can't tell."

Asha's eyes gleamed as she shook her head. "Nope, and I snuck a picture of JJ, Oliver, and Stella when we were Skyping. This next blog post is going to get massive hits. I know my fans expect something *IN*-related, but since the Heartbreakers are going to be on the show, this will be the perfect tie-in."

"No!" My sudden outburst startled Boomer. He glanced up from his game to peer at us, and I quickly lowered my voice to a whisper. "You can't blog any of this, Asha."

For the first time since the start of the conversation, she looked up from her phone. "Why not?"

"Because it's a total invasion of privacy!"

She frowned. "It's a toothbrush, Felicity. Not his diary."

My gaze shot to Alec. Thankfully he was still at the computer. I couldn't imagine his reaction if he found out Asha had snooped through his belongings and taken pictures. *What if he gets so mad he decides not to drive us to San Francisco?* I couldn't let that happen.

"Give me your phone," I demanded.

She snorted. "So you can delete everything? Not going to happen."

Without warning, Boomer leaned over and plucked the cell from her hands. Before she could react, he punched a couple of buttons and tossed it back to her. "There," he said. "Problem solved."

"Boomer!" Asha whined when she saw the pictures were gone. "I totally hate you."

He grinned, obviously not concerned about her newfound feelings, and poked her on the nose. "Just trying to contain the crazy."

"I'm not crazy," she snapped. "Just because I'm passionate about something you're not doesn't mean you can make fun of me."

His face softened. "You're right. That wasn't nice of me, and I'm sorry." He reached out as if to comfort her, but his hand changed direction at the last second, and he picked up his Game Boy instead. "But Felicity is right too, Asha. Posting pictures like that isn't cool. There's nothing wrong with being passionate, but maybe you should take it down a few levels. Otherwise, you're going to freak the dude out, okay?"

Asha blew out her cheeks. "Yeah, okay."

"Sorry for the holdup, but I...er... Is everything all right?"

We turned in unison at the sound of Alec's voice. He stood at the end of the couch, a small suitcase at his side. Instead of answering the question, Boomer coughed and tugged on his collar while Asha stared at the carpet.

I jumped out of my seat. "Yup," I blurted. "Everything's totally fine."

Alec focused on my friends and said nothing. I waited for him to give me a sign that the Skype call hadn't made things weird between us. He didn't.

"Why don't we head out?" Boomer suggested when our silence lapsed into awkwardness. "We've got a lot of road ahead of us."

The trip down to the car was quieter than the journey up to Alec's apartment because this time there was no happy whistling from Asha. There was a tightness to the air. I could feel it as we walked—a strand of energy as taut and sharp as barbed wire, rigidly knit between me and Alec. I wanted to reach out and karate chop it with my hand. All I had to do was open my mouth and say something, but I couldn't think of the right words, and so our footsteps echoed through the deserted garage.

When the Cadillac came into view, Alec unlocked the doors with a click, and I wondered if the entire drive would be this uncomfortable. I didn't know how much longer I could stand it.

Thank God for Asha and her love of the Heartbreakers.

"So, Alec," she said as she pulled her door shut. "I've been dying to ask you…" And then she dove into a series of questions about the band and their music. Alec seemed happy for the distraction, which helped ease my nerves. I settled into my seat as he backed out of his parking spot, and for the next few minutes, I was content with listening to their chatter.

Then I realized we were going in the wrong direction.

"Um, Alec?" I said, sitting up straight. "Not to question your navigational skills or anything, but isn't the highway the other way?"

"I was going to take US 101 through Malibu instead."

"Isn't the I-5 faster?"

"Yeah," he admitted, "but this way is less stressful. More scenic. Not as many big trucks and traffic. Do you mind? I promise I know where I'm going. I used to drive this route all the time."

For the first time since the Skyping disaster, Alec smiled. It was no more than a brief upward curve of the lips, but *God*, how quickly it melted my worry. Suddenly, I didn't care how we got to San Francisco, just as long as we did. Because I was with my two best friends. I was with Alec.

And I was on my way to finding Rose.

CHAPTER 9

We were thirty minutes into our drive, and everyone had settled in for the long haul. Asha and Boomer were in the backseat watching a movie on a tablet he'd borrowed from his dad. Alec and I hadn't spoken much, mainly because he wasn't one to start conversations, and for the time being, I was content with watching out the window. It wasn't until we passed a white mail truck that I thought of Rose's letters.

"Oh!" I sat forward to grab my bag. I'd packed the bundle with the intention of reading the rest on the bus. The stack of letters was in no particular order, so I started with the one on top.

December 26th

Dear Felicity,

Yesterday was my first Xmas without you and Mom. I did all our favorite traditions, like make chocolate snowballs, watch Elf, and listen to "Jingle Bell Rock" on repeat until my ears bled. I decorated my apartment with some garland I found at Dollar Discount, and even put up a miniature tree. But it's not the same. Without anyone to celebrate with, I wasn't in the Christmas spirit. On the upside, my neighbor invited me to a New Year's Eve party, so at least I won't be spending the entire holiday season alone.

I know this shouldn't count as a letter because it's so short, but I don't have the energy to write much else at the moment. Heart you more than Starburst and salsa.

xoxo,
Rose

PS Enclosed is your present. It's not much, but I had fun making it.

With gentle fingers, I withdrew an origami Santa Claus from the envelope. He was shaped like a star, made out of red and white paper, and fit into the palm of my hand. As I stared at him, my eyes watered.

Before she ran away, Rose and Mom got good at fighting. They practiced daily, and more often than not, I had to blast my music to drown out their angry words. It was always the same argument. Mom wanted Rose to go to college, but all my sister wanted was to see the world. She had no interest in school. By the time Rose left, I could recite their exchanges like I was an actress reading from a script. When one of them wasn't home, the house fell quiet, and I cherished those moments of peace.

But not that Christmas.

I'd never forget how empty and cheerless the house felt without Rose—how *lonely* it was. Mom bought me my first pair of wire cutters that year, which I'd begged her for, but I would have traded all the presents in the world to hear them fight again. Because that would have meant that Rose wasn't gone.

Not wanting to squish Santa, I tucked him up on the dashboard where he wouldn't get ruined before turning my attention back to the pile of mail. I wanted answers and figured the best way to understand what had happened four years ago was to start at the beginning. I shuffled through the stack until I found the first letter my sister had sent.

August 15th

Dear Felicity,

If you're reading this, then it means you found my note. I also hope it means you've forgiven me or at least are on your way to doing so. I need you to know that I never wanted to leave, but I had to for my own sanity.

Mom has all these rules and expectations, but I can't be the person she wants me to be. I don't want to waste the next four years of my life getting a pointless degree so I can work a nine-to-five job until I die. I want to have the kind of adventures I

138

can tell my grandkids about when I'm old. I want to see the world. I want to learn by living, and Mom doesn't get that.

If you're worrying about me, please don't. Things are going great. I bought a bus ticket to Phoenix. I have a friend who lives here, and I'm staying with him for the time being. The air is so dry and hot that I feel like I'm living inside a sauna, and the scenery is so different from in California. Everything is a varying shade of brown...that is, with the exception of sunset. That's when the McDowell Mountain Range is painted in the reds and purples of dwindling daylight. It's breathtaking, and I know you would love it!

I found a job working at a local café, but it's not a forever type of career. I'll probably stay long enough to save up money for a flight across the pond, and then I'll backpack across Europe. Or maybe I'll find a job working on a cruise ship and travel the seas! Other than that, there's not much to tell, so I'll write you again as soon as I have something to share. I heart you more than Starburst and salsa.

xoxo,
Rose

Something wasn't right. Clearly, I was missing a piece of the puzzle. What note was Rose talking about? Had she written me a letter before this one? One that wasn't hidden in the guitar case under my mom's bed? Still unable to make sense of my sister's departure, I moved on to the next letter. And the next. And the one after that until I'd read every letter. They were all the same—rambling descriptions of Rose's day-to-day life. I let out a long, exasperated sigh.

Alec cleared his throat and turned down the music. "Are those your sister's letters?"

I rubbed my temples. "Yeah."

"Read something you didn't want to know?"

"That's the thing," I responded. "I want to *know* why Rose left and why she never came home. But there's no explanation. Don't get me wrong. It's wonderful to hear about her life and know she's doing well, but it's so frustrating. It's all meaningless chatter, just... sweet nothings." I shook my head, trying to come up with the right words. "I need more."

"Well," Alec said after a moment of consideration. "It's a good thing we're on our way to San Francisco. We'll get all your answers in person."

"Thank you, Alec. For driving me and for—"

"Don't thank me until we find your sister."

I nodded in agreement. I could live with that.

"Good. Until then..." He paused and dug his phone out of his pocket. "I made a playlist last night. It's short since I didn't expect us to be in the car for so long, but...do you wanna listen?"

"You made a playlist for today?"

"Yeah, with songs and artists I thought you might like."

"Yes, I'd love to hear it."

With a shaky smile, Alec hit Play. It was as if he was both nervous and excited to share this with me, but he had nothing to worry about. That he'd taken the time to find music for me made whatever the result of his efforts perfect in my eyes. An upbeat melody filled the car, and I instantly recognized the song.

A grin split my face. "You listen to Vinyl Theatre?"

Which of course was a silly question. They might be a little-known indie band, but after sampling his music collection, I knew that Alec listened to everything and anything. I wouldn't be surprised if he had a playlist composed of tribal chants.

He nodded. "I take it you've heard of them?" His shoulders dipped slightly, as if I'd spoiled his fun somehow.

"They're tied with Hedley for the coveted spot as my third-favorite band."

My answer made him snort with laughter, and he shook his head as if someone up above was playing a joke on him. "Of course they are."

"What?" I asked. *Was he making fun of me?* My question was answered when the song changed. It was "Crazy for You," one of Hedley's bigger hits.

"And here I thought I was being cool," Alec said.

"This *is* cool," I insisted.

Beyond cool. That Alec was able to pinpoint the artists I enjoyed listening to from the little time we'd spent together was incredible. It also revealed a lot about him. First, that he was more observant than I'd originally thought. And second, that his knowledge of the music world was vast.

"Oh yeah," he said and rolled his eyes. "A playlist with a ton of songs you know by heart."

I waved him off. He was looking at this all wrong. "If I know them by heart, that means they're worth listening to."

Alec paused, considering. "Yeah, I guess you're right," he said, and then he leaned over and turned up the music.

☆ ♭ ♫

We were cruising somewhere along the coast when Alec turned on his blinker and pulled off the highway. A small town rose up to meet us, and in the distance, stripes of sparkling blue flickered between the buildings we passed. I wondered if we were lost, but Alec casually gripped the wheel with one hand, while the other tapped against his leg in time with the music. He looked comfortable, like he knew exactly where he was going, so I let my questions die inside me.

Asha didn't have the same faith. "Is everything okay?" she asked, sitting up straighter to get a better look out the window.

"It's past lunchtime" was Alec's only explanation.

At the mention of food, my stomach rumbled loudly enough for everyone to hear over the music. I placed a hand on my abdomen and looked down in surprise. *Shut up, shut up, shut up!* I commanded. It growled again in rebellion.

"Good thing I pulled off here, huh?"

I could hear the smile in Alec's words, and a burst of laughter spilled from the backseat. "Felicity's stomach definitely thinks so," Asha said.

Ignoring her, I turned back to Alec. "Where exactly is *here*?"

"Pismo Beach," he answered. "A quintessential California coastal town."

He turned onto what must have been the main road, and we passed little cafés and restaurants and palm trees. From the way Alec's eyes lit up as he took in the scenery around us, I could tell that this place wasn't just quintessential, but sentimental.

"You're been here before?" I asked, rolling down the window so I could smell the sea air. A warm breeze whipped through the car, swirling my loose curls around like dancing flames.

"This is where my mom grew up," he explained. "Vanessa and I spent our childhood summers here visiting my gran. There's a restaurant called the Splash Café that has the best clam chowder. Every time we'd walk down to the beach, we'd stop and get a cup. It's a bit touristy, and Vanessa said I only liked going there because it looks cool, but it's still my favorite place to eat in Pismo."

Splash Café lived up to its hype. At least, the facade did—we had yet to taste the food—but it was easy to see why kid Alec loved it so much. The roof and awning were bright blue, and a surfer was mounted to the front of the building, framed by two massive orange and yellow surfboards. A huge beach mural was painted on the side of the building, and judging from the line that stretched out the door, it was a popular spot to eat.

"Crap," Alec said as we parked across the street from the café. "I should've known it would be packed."

I shrugged. The promise of delicious food outweighed my reluctance to wait. "I don't mind. How long do you think it will take?"

"Er…that's not what I'm concerned about."

"Then what?" I asked, but Alec didn't respond. He watched me silently, waiting for me to figure out the answer on my own.

"He doesn't want to be spotted," Asha said as if it were the most obvious thing in the world.

Ohhh!

"Do you want to stay in the car while we go order?" I asked.

"I feel bad ditching you guys," he said, his cheeks turning pink. "But would you mind?"

"Not at all. We completely understand." As soon as I said this, I realized how silly it sounded. As if I had any clue how it felt to be famous. "What do you want?"

"A clam chowder bread bowl," he said, and then, "Are you sure you're okay with this? We could always go through a drive-through somewhere."

"Alec, you're driving us all the way to San Francisco. The least I can do is stand in line for food." I offered him a reassuring smile before grabbing my bag and lifting the canvas strap over my head.

"Okay, but before you go…" Alec reached for his pocket. After a few seconds of clawing at his shorts unsuccessfully, he leaned back and lifted himself off the seat, finally extracting a wallet. He pulled out a crisp fifty and held it out to me.

My fingers itched to accept his offer. But then I remembered Asha's comment about how I was absorbed with thoughts of money, so I waved him off.

"Felicity, take it," he said, but I shook my head and scrambled out of the car before I changed my mind.

Alec turned to Asha with the bill, but she snorted. "Not going to happen."

"Boomer, you coming with, or should I order something for you?" I asked, but he was too engrossed in his game to answer. Asha snapped her fingers in his face.

Startled, he blinked a few times and glanced up. "Huh?"

"Seriously," she said, heaving a sigh. "What's wrong with you?"

"Who, me?" he asked.

"Yes, you. What seventeen-year-old still plays Pokémon?"

He frowned. "I do?"

"*Exactly.*" She reached over and clicked open his seat belt. "Come on."

Boomer looked out the window in confusion as if he'd just realized we'd stopped. "Wait, we're already there?"

"Not even close," Asha said with an eye roll. "We're getting food. Hurry up. Otherwise, Felicity's stomach is going to eat itself."

"Ha. Freaking. Ha," I said.

"Sounds painful." Boomer tossed his Game Boy to the side. After clambering out of the car, he stretched his arms up in the air and yawned. It made him look taller than he already was, and I wondered how he could possibly fit in the backseat. "All right. Let's go feed you, shrimp." He mussed my hair, and I batted his hand away. "Maybe then you'll grow a few inches."

The inside of the café was as colorful as the outside, and the line moved surprisingly quickly. After a ten-minute wait, we were out the door with a steaming bag of food—bread bowls for me and Alec, two fish sandwiches for Boomer, and chicken strips with fries for Asha. As we crossed the street, Alec climbed out of the car. While we were gone, he'd put on sunglasses and, despite the heat, a zip-up with the hood pulled over his head.

"Thanks for getting the food, guys. I appreciate it."

"No problem," I said, switching our meal from one side to another. It was heavier than expected, and without a handle, I had to prop the paper bag against my hip.

"Here, let me." Alec reached over and took it off my hands. "How much do I owe you?"

Boomer, who'd paid for the meal, waved him off. "Nothing, dude. This won't come close to covering gas."

"You don't have to worry about gas," he responded. "I'm the one who offered to drive, remember? I've got it."

Asha crossed her arms. "And we have your soup covered."

The two stared at each other with set jaws, neither wanting to relent, but when Asha leaned in and narrowed her eyes, Alec sighed. "Fine, but I pay for my own meals after this, okay?"

She pretended to consider this for a moment, and then offered him a crisp nod. "Deal."

My stomach growled again, and everyone turned to look at me. A sheepish grin crossed my face. "Can we eat now or...?"

"Yes," Alec said with a laugh. "How about we take our food down to the beach? I know a great place for us to sit."

☆ ♭ ♫

The walk was quick, two minutes at most, and we arrived at a surprisingly large pier. It was nowhere near as big as the Santa Cruz Municipal Wharf, which I'd visited once on a school field trip, but considering the small size of Pismo, it was massive. About halfway down, there was a snack bar/souvenir stall, and at the end, a dotting of fisherman. Their poles jutted into the air like radio antennas, and seagulls hovered on the breeze above them, waiting for an easy meal.

I expected Alec to lead us down the pier, but instead we descended a wooden staircase into the sand below. Scattered along the beach were weather-worn picnic tables, and Alec chose the one farthest from the crowds. We all sat, and I dove into my bread bowl before anyone else had their containers open. The soup was steaming, but I was too impatient to wait for it to cool. I scooped up a huge spoonful, and the scorched-tongue pain was worth it. I'd never tasted a creamier clam chowder in my life, and I quickly shoveled another bite into my mouth.

When I looked up from my food, Alec was watching. "You like?"

Oh no. I'd been eating like a total pig. I swallowed, and the heat of my cheeks was almost as painful as the chowder burning down my throat.

"It's delicious."

He offered me a knowing smile. "I'm glad."

After that, I ate slowly and in silence. The boys talked cars for a while, but Alec was nowhere near as knowledgeable or passionate about them as Boomer was. Alec glanced at me during one of Boomer's particularly detailed discussions about the Porsche 918 Spyder, the world's first plug-in hybrid super car, and I recognized the look on his face. I'd seen it on Asha a million times before, whenever Boomer got excited about a car—eyes crinkled in the corners, lips pushed together to keep from smiling. No doubt, I'd worn the same expression a few times myself. While the subject of his rants was often boring, it was hard not to find Boomer's enthusiasm entertaining.

When everyone finished eating, Asha decided to walk down to the water to dip her feet in. She dragged Boomer along with her, while Alec and I stayed behind.

The sun was scorching. I didn't understand how Alec could stand wearing a hoodie. I could already feel my skin starting to fry.

On the off chance that there was sunscreen buried somewhere in the depths of my bag, I hoisted it onto the table and emptied out the contents. Which were a lot. There were the usual suspects like my wallet, phone, and books, but I also carried a collection of odds and ends with me: double-A batteries for Boomer's Game Boy, a compact first aid kit, enough writing utensils to supply an entire school, a spare charger… Asha called it my Mary Poppins bag, because even though it looked small, I could fit a house worth of stuff inside.

Alec watched me with raised brows as I retrieved a bottle of hand sanitizer and a smushed granola bar. "And what exactly do you need this for?" He held up flat-nose pliers.

"Jewelry making. You use it to bend wire and hold beads and such," I explained. And that's when I remembered. "Oh, I almost forgot! I have something for you."

I unzipped the small pocket inside my bag and retrieved a tiny drawstring pouch. Inside was the leather-wrap bracelet I'd made for Alec, which I finished after my shift the day he came to the Electric

Waffle. This morning when I was getting ready, I'd packed it with the intention of giving it to him at the party.

"Here."

I undid the clasp and held it out to him, but instead of taking my gift, Alec pushed up a sleeve and offered me his arm. Biting back a smile, I leaned over the table and wrapped it around his wrist. My fingers fumbled as I tried to push the wooden toggle through the loop on the end. I could feel Alec's gaze on me as I struggled, which made fastening the bracelet that much harder. But the bead finally popped into place, and I dropped back into my seat.

He held up his hand for a closer look, and the amber beads blazed in the sunlight. "Thanks, Felicity. I love it."

"Yeah?" I couldn't tell if he was being serious or polite.

"Yeah" was his reply. He pushed himself up from the bench like he was ready to leave.

Shit, was the bracelet too much? Did I freak him out?

I was worrying for nothing. Alec took a seat on top of the table and grinned at me over his shoulder. "Come here," he said and patted the empty spot next to him.

His straightforward request threw me off guard, but after a moment's pause, I mirrored his grin, pushed the junk from my bag out of the way, and climbed up onto the table. As I settled beside him, our knees knocked together and a trail of goose bumps shot down my leg. I cast a sidelong glance at Alec, but he was too busy staring out at the ocean to notice. The swells were large, and there was more than one surfer bobbing up and down in the waves.

"Your friends are nice," he said.

I scanned the shoreline until I found Boomer and Asha. They were running through the surf, splashing water at each other like little kids. If they stayed out there much longer, one of them was going to end up soaked.

I smiled. "You mean crazy?"

"Sometimes crazy is good," he said. "And what I meant was that they seem like loyal friends."

"They are," I said. "After Rose left, Asha became my substitute sister. Boomer's family moved to California our freshman year of high school. I think he felt out of place in LA, and I was the first friend he made, so we've been close ever since. They're insane, but amazing. I'm lucky to have them."

Alec was quiet for a moment. "What I've noticed is that when people have real friends in their lives, it's because they've earned them."

I ducked my head, blushing fiercely. "Thank you, Alec. Your friends seem…" I trailed off, unable to come up with a suitable adjective. My goal had been to say something nice, but all I could remember were JJ's pervy comments, how Stella unnerved me, and feeling embarrassed.

"One step past crazy?" he suggested. I clamped my lips together and tried not to smile. That was a perfect description, but I wasn't going to admit that to him. Apparently my opinion of his friends was more transparent than I thought, because Alec chuckled. "They're more like my family than friends, so I suppose it comes with the territory."

We shared a smile, but then Alec's expression unexpectedly

stiffened. A barely there shade of pink spread across his cheeks, and he ducked his head with a sigh.

"Alec?" I asked, confused as to what had gone wrong.

A second of silence passed. He touched his hair, checking to make sure every strand was in place before looking back at me. "I've been meaning to apologize about before," he said. "JJ is one of my closest friends, but that doesn't excuse what he said to you."

"Don't worry about it," I mumbled, not wanting to relive the Skype call.

"He's a great guy, really," Alec went on. "But he's also…"

"Extremely horny?" I offered, as he said, "Immature."

We burst out laughing.

"So," I said, changing the subject while the mood was still light. "How'd you guys all meet?" I could have looked up the answer online or asked Asha, but I wanted to hear it from him.

Before he could answer, we were interrupted. "Excuse me."

Standing a few feet from the picnic table were two girls—a tall blond wearing a swimsuit cover-up and a brunette with Audrey Hepburn sunglasses. When Alec looked in their direction, they both gasped and grabbed each other for support.

"Oh my God," the blond whispered. "I *told* you it was him."

The brunette detached herself from her friend and stepped forward. "Hi, Alec," she said, clutching her phone. "I know you probably get this a lot, but could we possibly get a picture together?"

Alec hesitated, and for a split second I thought he'd refuse, but then he stood and brushed sand off his shorts. "Of course."

When he positioned himself between the two girls, slipping an arm around both their backs, the blond started shaking. "I can't even," she sobbed, waving a hand in front of her face.

To my surprise, Alec's lips twitched into a gentle smile. "Come on now," he teased her. "No crying allowed." Her tears fell in steady streams, but she laughed and nodded her head. "All right, are we ready?" he asked them.

Audrey Hepburn stretched her arm out to take the picture, but struggled with her phone. I hopped off the table before she dropped it in the sand.

"Let me help," I said, holding out my hand.

"Ahh! Thank you." She handed over the phone, but did a double take when she looked at me. Her eyebrows dipped below the top of her sunglasses as she frowned, and I knew she was trying to figure out why I looked familiar. A second later, the connection clicked. "Wow, you look so much like Violet James."

"You think so?" I joked. She nodded, and I smiled in spite of myself. "Okay," I said and took two steps back. "On the count of three."

A photographer I was not, so I took multiple pictures to make sure the girls got one they liked. Afterward, we stood around for a few minutes chatting. Apparently the blond lived on the same street as Alec's grandmother used to, and both girls commented on how much they loved my bag. Then Boomer and Asha reappeared, and Alec told the girls we had to leave. Ten hugs and a chorus of thank-you's later, they finally retreated to the pier.

"Should we head out?" Alec asked. He was surveying the beach, probably on the lookout for more fans. I nodded. If we lingered any longer, it would be well past dark by the time we reached the city.

"Probably a good idea," Asha said. "If Felicity spends any more time in the sun, she's going to look like a lobster." She poked my shoulder, and I felt as if someone had pressed a branding iron to my skin.

I winced and Alec looked at me in concern. "That bad?"

"I'm fine," I grumbled as we trudged back toward the street. "Just another day in the life of Casper, the Pasty Girl."

CHAPTER 10

"You've been driving all afternoon," Boomer said to Alec when we got back to our parking spot. "Want me to take a turn?"

I knew he was itching to drive the car, and from the half smile on Alec's face, he could tell too. Pulling out his keys, he said, "Know where you're going?"

Boomer hesitated. "Won't 101 take us all the way there?"

Alec nodded. "You're not going to drive *and* play that game of yours, are you?"

"I can't tell if you're being serious or giving me a hard time, but in case you need reassurance, I'll keep it in my pocket."

"That was a joke," Alec said with a laugh.

"You need to work on the whole joking part," Boomer responded, his forehead pinched together. "Maybe next time you can smile or something."

"How about this?" Alec dangled these in front of Boomer. "I'll trade you these for the game. I haven't played one of those in years."

Boomer's face lit up like Alec had told him he'd won the lottery. "You so have yourself a deal." He handed over the purple Game Boy. In turn, Alec tossed him his key chain.

Asha leaned over. "Is it just me," she whispered. "Or does Boomer actually think he gets to keep the car?"

We both snorted.

Once we on the road again, I plucked my ACT book out of my bag and tried to study, but it was impossible to concentrate. Alec was sitting across from me playing Boomer's game, and my whole body was conscious of his proximity. Every time my mind wandered to him, I had to reread whatever passage I'd been working on. When twenty minutes had passed and I'd barely made it through a chapter, I tossed the book on the seat between us. Alec glanced up from the Game Boy.

"Sorry," I told him, but he waved me off.

"It's okay. I completed Boomer's Pokédex anyway."

"*What?*" Boomer turned and gaped at Alec. "You caught Chansey? No freaking way. I've been trying to capture that damn thing for three weeks!"

"*Boomer!*" Asha shouted as the car drifted into the next lane. "Eyes on the road!"

Alec just smiled and set the Game Boy aside. Then, he unbuckled his seat belt and slid over to re-buckle next to me. When he pulled out his phone and offered me an earbud, I took it without a second thought.

"I want you to give me your honest opinion about this band," he said as he scrolled through his music library. "They're called Raining Bullets. This is their demo."

When he hit Play, I closed my eyes and concentrated on the song. It was fast and upbeat with loud guitars and a whole lot of rock. They reminded me a bit of the Heartbreakers…only a girl version. Alec didn't say anything when the demo finished, just looked at me expectantly.

"They weren't what I was anticipating," I said, pulling out the headphone so we could talk, "but I liked them a lot."

"Yeah?"

I nodded. "The world needs more awesome rocker chicks."

"My dad's been going back and forth on whether he should sign them. Says they're not radio-friendly, so he's leaning toward no, but I'm working to convince him."

"Are they friends of yours?"

"Actually, we've never met," he said. "But I'm trying to get into the production side of the music business. There's something about finding new talent and working with other musicians that I love."

"Trying?" Alec was part of a successful band, *and* his father owned a record label. How hard could it be to get into the production side of music?

"Let's just say my dad and I don't see eye to eye when it comes to creative decisions."

"So he doesn't trust you."

"It's more that he has a blueprint for running the business and doesn't like to stray from it," Alec said. "But last month I got him to agree to let me produce a record for this new client he's signing."

"Congrats, Alec!"

"Thanks, I'm really excited about it." He gestured for me to put my earbud back in. "Here… How about I play you some more demos?"

As we continued toward San Francisco, making our way closer

to Rose and the answers I so desperately needed, Alec showered me with music. Unlike the playlist he'd shared with me earlier in the day, none of the melodies were familiar, and I didn't know a single lyric, but I couldn't care less. Each time I heard a new song, I felt like I was getting another piece to the puzzle that was Alec Williams.

☆♭♫

Not long after leaving Pismo, we stopped at the Gas Exchange. As promised, Alec refused to let anyone pay for gas. While he fueled the car, Asha and Boomer took charge of stocking up on snacks so we wouldn't have to stop for dinner. They were halfway across the parking lot when Asha spun back around.

"Your usual?" she called. She was still following Boomer, walking backward as she waited for my answer.

"Yeah, and something with caffeine in it." I grabbed a squeegee from the bucket bolted on the side of the pump and said to Alec, "You sure you don't want anything?"

He already had the gas cap off and was selecting a grade. "No, I'm good."

"All right, but don't look at me when you get hungry," I teased. "This girl doesn't share Cool Ranch."

Before he could answer, his phone rang.

"Sorry," he apologized and pulled it from his pocket. He didn't bother looking at the ID. "Hello?" The person on the other end responded, and whoever it was made Alec frown. He listened for a moment before saying, "Something came up." Alec's voice was flat, like whoever he was speaking to had sucked life out of him.

I kept my gaze focused on the windshield, scrubbing a spot that was already clean, and tried my best to look uninterested in his conversation. In reality, I wished he would put the phone on speaker.

"Why? Can't land a deal without me?"

Whoever he was talking to started to yell. Alec flinched away from his phone, and I could make out muffled ranting on the other end. He let it go on for a good minute before finally interrupting.

"King—*King!*" His face went slack, like interrupting had zapped all Alec's energy, and he was too exhausted to fight. "I'm sorry, okay? I promise I'll make it up to you… Well, no. Not right now. I kind of, er, left town."

Was Alec in trouble with this King person because he offered to drive me to San Francisco? The thought made me go stiff. I dumped the squeegee back in the bucket of gray-looking water and stepped out of earshot. Alec's conversation went on for another thirty seconds or so, but I only moved back toward the car after he shoved the phone into his shorts with more force than necessary. I waited for him to say something, but he glared at the cars whizzing by on the road as if I wasn't there.

Mind your own business, Felicity. If he wanted you to know, he'd tell you…

I tried to bite my tongue, but the tension in the air built between us like an invisible wall. I needed to break it down before Alec clammed up. "So…" I said warily. "Who's King? A business partner or something?"

He snorted. "King is my dad."

I gawked. "You call your dad *King?*" Alec mentioned his father was controlling…but making his son refer to him as king? That was just ridiculous.

"It's his name," he explained. "Sebastian King Williams. No clue what my grandmother was thinking when she gave it to him. Actually, she probably knew exactly what she was doing. It fits him perfectly."

"He's mad at you for missing the party, isn't he?"

Alec exhaled through his nose and offered me a curt nod.

My face fell. "I'm sorry. I didn't mean to take you away from your work."

"Don't apologize," he said. "It's not your fault my dad's an ass."

I searched for something to say, but my thoughts and words were muddled with guilt. Alec must have been lost in his own head too, because we both fell quiet. The pump finished fueling as the door to the Gas Exchange swung open.

"Look who scored!" Boomer yelled in his megaphone voice. He held a huge bag of Swedish Fish over his head like he was Lloyd Dobler in *Say Anything*. The smile on his face was all teeth and enthusiasm. Asha followed. In one hand was a cardboard drink carrier with a slushy, a soda, and coffee. In her other hand, she clutched a plastic bag, which presumably held my chips, her Pop Rocks, and whatever other junk food the two had purchased.

"We ready to go?" she asked.

Alec hung the gas nozzle back up and nodded. To Boomer he asked, "You still want to drive?"

I watched my friends, waiting to see if they picked up on the shift in Alec's mood. Neither did.

Boomer gave another toothy grin. "Most definitely. Let's bounce."

☆ ♭ ♫

The rest of the afternoon flew by. Sometime after leaving the station, Alec pointed out the city of Salinas as we passed through. He told me it was the birthplace of John Steinbeck, and that he'd set many of his novels in the area, like *Of Mice and Men* and *East of Eden*. Steinbeck was far from my favorite novelist, but that Alec noticed and remembered my love of American literature was enough to keep me smiling for the rest of the drive.

At some point I must have dozed off, because I woke to the sound of someone gently whispering my name. "Felicity, wake up. We're almost there."

My eyelids fluttered open, and I blinked in confusion. The last I remembered, I was listening to music with Alec, and the sun was still out. Now, dark-blue and purple hues had chased away the daylight. I lifted my head. There was a kink in my neck from sleeping at a weird angle, and my hair was matted to the side of my face. I stretched out my arms and—

Oh God.

I'd fallen asleep on Alec's shoulder.

"Sorry about that," I muttered, quickly straightening up and wiping my mouth. Hopefully I hadn't snored. Or worse, drooled on his shirt.

I felt Alec shrug beside me. "I didn't mind." He was in the middle of wrapping his headphone cords around his phone, and when he finished, he met my gaze with a smile. "Sleep well?"

Warmth bloomed on my cheeks, and I nodded. "Where are we?"

"Just outside the city," Boomer answered. Sure enough, when I glanced out the window, San Francisco loomed ahead of us, glittering against the dark sky. "I have no clue where I'm going," he continued. "Could you give me the exact address? Asha can plug it into the GPS."

"Um…" I hesitated. There was a reason I was always the designated navigator. Asha and Boomer argued like those snippety couples on *The Amazing Race* whenever she was in charge. "Are you sure?" I asked, pulling the most recent of Rose's letters from my bag.

"Oh, just give it here," Asha said, snatching the envelope from me.

Twenty minutes later, we arrived in the Haight-Ashbury district of the city, and after taking a few wrong turns, Boomer finally located the correct street. Even at night, the neighborhood was colorful. The homes were all Victorian-styled townhouses painted in crazy color combinations like lime, teal, and magenta, or lavender, yellow, and cyan. Boomer pulled up in front of a light-pink house accented in different shades of red and turned off the car.

"This is the place," he said.

Everyone was quiet for a moment as we surveyed the house. The tiny patch of grass out front was overgrown, and the potted plant at the top of the steps was well past saving, making it look like nobody had been here for a long time. But the porch light was on.

Please let someone be here. Please let Rose *be here.*

"Are we going to sit in the car all night or what?" Asha asked. She undid her seat belt and threw open the door. "Let's go. I've had to pee for the past hour."

My fingers skimmed the handle on the car door with the intention of following her, but for some reason I couldn't open it, let alone take my eyes off the building before us. The knowledge that Rose had been here at one time or another was overwhelming. Over the past four years, I'd imagined countless places she could have disappeared to—a tiny, one-room apartment in New York or a shack on some Caribbean beach—but they were always intangible and abstract, like scenes out of a dream.

Here was an actual concrete place where she'd eaten and slept and lived.

A hand brushed my shoulder, and even though the touch was soft, my sunburn stung. "Felicity?" Alec asked. "You okay?"

I nodded, still staring out the window.

"You sure? I know this must be nerve-racking. If you're not ready…" He stopped for a second, choosing his words carefully. "I'm sure Asha or Boomer would be more than willing to go knock for you."

"I know," I said, finally waking from my daze. I shook away the lingering fog and offered him a small smile. "Thanks, but I should do this myself."

Alec nodded.

After taking a deep breath, I forced my body to move. I climbed out of the car and marched up the porch steps with Asha, Boomer, and Alec at my heels. Before I lost my confidence, I rang the bell. It was quiet for a long time, and as each silent second passed, my heart slammed against my chest a little harder. Just as I was about to give up, a light in the front hall flipped on. Someone fumbled with the lock, and the door opened.

"Duncan, if you're shit-faced again, I'm not—" The girl stopped midsentence when she realized we weren't Duncan. "Oh, hi." Her curly hair was pulled back into a braid, and her face was red and shiny, as if she'd recently scrubbed it clean. She was wearing glasses, a pair of flannel pajama shorts, a camisole, and a silky kimono bathrobe.

She pulled her robe tighter. "Can I help you?"

I knew this girl, but the problem was, I couldn't remember how. I searched my mind for some kind of connection until I remembered the soccer player Rose was friends with before quitting the team junior year. "Kelsey?" I asked, stepping forward. "Is that you?"

Kelsey adjusted her glasses, eyes squinted at me in concentration, before recognition flickered across her face. "Felicity Lyon? Oh my gosh! I can't believe it. You're so grown up."

Seeing one of my sister's friends fueled my hope. "Thanks, Kelsey. It's good to see you. I was wondering... Is Rose here?"

"Your sister?" She frowned. "No. I haven't seen her since she left."

My heart plunged into my stomach.

I'm too late. She's already gone.

"But she was here, right?" Asha asked, stepping forward. "When did she leave?"

"About a week ago. Why, is something wrong?"

I bit my lip, not sure whether I was going to cry or laugh. I'd missed her by days, a span of time that felt like nothing compared to the four years she'd been gone...but she'd been here. Kelsey had seen her. She was alive. I blinked a few times to clear my eyes and said, "Kelsey, I haven't heard from Rose since she turned eighteen."

"What?" she gasped, pressing a hand to her mouth. "How is that possible? She never mentioned anything like that to me. In fact, she had me mail a letter to you when she left. Here." She pushed open the screen door separating us. "Why don't you come in, and we can talk."

The four of us stepped inside, and she ushered us down the hall into a cozy living room with mismatched furniture. Asha asked to use the bathroom, and after pointing her in the right direction, Kelsey said, "How about I put on a pot of coffee?" as if she knew tonight would be a late one.

Exhausted from our day of travel, I sunk into an oversize couch. Boomer flopped down next to me, dropping an arm around my shoulders and pulling me in for a quick, supportive squeeze, while Alec took a spot on the nearby rocking chair with an afghan dropped over the back.

We waited in silence. Asha was the first to return, and eventually Kelsey came back in with a tray of steaming mugs, milk, and sugar. She set them down on the coffee table and settled into a La-Z-Boy.

Finally, she said, "Tell me everything."

So I did. First, we breezed through introductions—Kelsey raised an eyebrow when I mentioned Alec, but she didn't ask any questions—and then I explained that Rose had disappeared on her birthday, and I'd just found the letters she'd sent me hidden beneath my mother's bed.

"Wow." Kelsey shook her head when I finished. "I knew Rose was going through some stuff in high school, but I didn't realize she'd run away. We lost touch after she quit the soccer team."

"So how'd she end up living with you?" I was desperate to hear how the two had reconnected since my own attempts to track down Rose had been futile. She didn't have a Facebook or Twitter, and even a simple Google search turned up nothing.

"Rose never lived with me," Kelsey clarified. "I can't remember if it was for work or if she was just visiting, but she only stayed in the city for a few days. Running into each other was a total coincidence. I bumped into her on the street, and we spent the rest of the day catching up. I wish I could tell you more, but I don't know anything else."

Something cold and sharp coiled inside my stomach, like a spool of barbed wire. *That's it?* We'd driven all the way here to discover what? That my sister had vacationed in San Francisco? Why had I thought taking this road trip was a good idea? It was the kind of rash, reckless decision that Rose would make. Not me.

Boomer leaned forward, resting both elbows on his knees and folding his hands together. "So you have no clue where she is now?"

"I think she's living in Seattle," Kelsey answered. "I asked for a forwarding address in case her letter was returned. Hold on. Let me go get it." She disappeared to the kitchen again and returned clutching a slip of paper. She handed over an old receipt with crinkled edges and an address written on the back in bright-pink ink.

Everyone was quiet as I stared down at it.

When a full minute passed and I had yet to say anything, Alec spoke up. "We should go."

Startled, I glanced in his direction. "Where? You mean Seattle?"

He nodded.

"Ooh, totally!" Asha said before I could answer. "I love Seattle. My cousin lives there. Last year Riya and I went to visit him, and he took us to the Seattle Center to see this glass exhibit that show-cases some famous artist. I can't remember his name. It's like… Cholula or something."

"The hot sauce?" Boomer asked, and Alec coughed to cover the sound of his snort.

Asha scratched her head, a flush coloring her cheeks. "I knew that didn't sound right."

"Do you mean Dale Chihuly?" Kelsey asked.

"Yes, *him*," she said, snapping her fingers. "There was a garden and a bunch of galleries filled with these colorful glass sculptures. I don't know how to describe them, but it was like being on an alien planet or in a Dr. Seuss book. My cousin took us to some cool places, but that was by far my favorite and—" She stopped midramble, the smile shrinking on her face, and looked at Boomer. "You don't have to babysit Kevin tomorrow, do you?"

"Nope. My dad's taking him fishing. I'm down for Seattle if everyone else is."

"Awesome." Asha clapped her hands together and faced me. "Felicity? What about you? You're super quiet."

"I don't know, Asha…" I didn't want to see the smile fade off her face again, so I lowered my gaze back to the receipt.

When Kelsey had first mentioned Seattle, I'd felt a wisp of hope flicker inside me, but now, as I looked at Rose's handwriting, it was merely a reminder that my sister didn't want to be part of my life anymore. She was obviously running from something. Whether it was her bad relationship with Mom, her heartache over Dad, or a deeper issue I wasn't privy to, it didn't matter. I wasn't important enough to be included in her life. Sure, she wrote me the letters, but the more I thought about them, the more I realized they weren't enough. Why couldn't she spare time for phone calls or holiday visits? Why did she sneak out of my life in the middle of the night?

"What does that mean?" Asha asked, her tone somewhere between anger and alarm. "Fel?"

I pressed my hands to my face and let out a sigh. "It means I don't think it's a good idea."

Nobody said anything, so I peeked out from behind my fingers. Asha was gaping at me as if I'd punched a baby or run over her grandma, and Boomer cocked his head and frowned.

Then there was Alec. Normally he was impossible to read, his thoughts and feelings carefully concealed behind a blank expression. But my response must have thrown him off guard. His eyes were wide, his forehead creased, his lips parted slightly.

He was concerned. For *me*.

As I looked at him, I felt the need to explain myself. "I have to work on Sunday. There's no way we can make it to Seattle and all the way back to LA before then."

"Call in sick," Boomer suggested. He scrubbed a hand through his tight curls like he was still trying to process my abrupt change of heart. "I do it all the time. Say you have the stomach flu or strep throat. It just has to be nasty enough that they don't want you coming in."

"I can't," I said, shaking my head. "Daisy will know I'm lying. I don't want to get fired."

"So you find a new job." He shrugged a single shoulder. "Big deal."

Easy for him to say. Boomer had a bad habit of blowing through jobs like cash. Last month alone, he worked at three different places.

"Yeah," Asha agreed, jumping back into the conversation once she'd recovered from her shock. "Isn't finding Rose more important?"

"Well, yeah. But my mom doesn't know I left. She's going to freak when she finds out I'm gone."

"But you wouldn't be here if she hadn't hid those letters in the first place." Asha poked her tongue into her cheek and sucked in a long breath. I could almost see her editing words in her head, trying to remain civil and composed. "I don't get it, Felicity. You've been dying to know what happened to your sister, and now that you have the chance to figure it out, you're going to walk away?"

"It's not like that." I knew she was frustrated. And I understood that she came from a place of concern, but I also knew that only someone who'd been through what I had—the dread and grief and betrayal—would get how I was feeling.

"Really? It sure seems like it."

I contemplated how to make them understand. "You're right," I told Asha, and her eyes lit up at my words. "I *did* want to know what happened to Rose." Pausing, I watched her shoulders slump as she realized I'd used the past tense. "It just took a road trip and coming away empty-handed to realize that maybe I shouldn't. I've been terrified that something terrible happened to her. That for some reason she *couldn't* come home. But now that I know she's fine, it's obvious she wants nothing to do with me. I don't consider it walking away. It's more like accepting reality."

Asha sighed, a long-suffering, you're-impossible kind of noise. When she didn't fire back with another well-constructed argument, I thought I'd won.

"Is it though?" Alec asked, his quiet voice cutting through the silence.

"Is *what* though?"

"Is it obvious that she wants nothing to do with you?" I was ready with a response, but Alec kept talking. "Maybe her letters seem insignificant weighed against the time you spent in the dark, but I think you'd feel differently if you'd received them when you were supposed to. I don't know what she's written to you, and I won't pretend to understand what you're going through, but I saw the stack of envelopes. There're enough to fill an entire book. Someone who doesn't care wouldn't invest that much time or effort into writing them."

I squeezed my eyes shut. "*Four years*, Alec. I haven't seen her since I was thirteen. How would you feel if Vanessa just left?"

"I'm sure I would be as hurt and upset as you are, but for someone who was hell-bent on getting answers, you're awfully eager to jump to conclusions without them."

There was nothing for me to say to that, no other excuses I could offer. Because he was right, of course. Damn him and his beautiful, see-straight-though-me eyes.

"If it helps," Kelsey said tentatively, "you're all welcome to stay the night." She nodded her head in the direction of the stairs. "There're two spare bedrooms and an office with a pullout couch. Plenty of room for everybody."

"Come on, Felicity," Asha complained. "Say yes. We can crash here tonight and leave in the morning."

My gaze moved to Alec's almost instinctively, and he gave me a small nod of encouragement. He was still willing to help me. We were going to find my sister, and I would get my answers.

"Okay," I said, lifting my hands in surrender. "We can go to Seattle."

Asha didn't need any more conformation from me. She stood from the couch and stretched. "One of you boys help me get our stuff from the trunk. My body needs a bed, pronto."

After the car was unloaded, Kelsey showed us upstairs. Even though I'd taken a nap, my eyelids were heavy as we shuffled up the creaky wooden stairs. Asha and I took the larger guest room, which had a queen-size bed we could share, leaving Alec and Boomer to battle over who got the remaining bed and who was left with the sleeper sofa. Knowing Alec, he'd be too polite to fight Boomer for the better sleeping arrangement.

"Thanks for coming with me today," I whispered to Asha after we'd pulled on our pajamas and climbed into bed. "And, you know, being annoyingly persistent and talking sense into me."

She reached out across the mattress and squeezed my hand. "What are sisters for?"

CHAPTER 11

I woke to the warmth of the rising sun on my face and an empty bed.

Years of sleepovers had taught me that Asha was *not* a light sleeper. Violent was a better description. More often than not, I'd be jolted awake by a wandering elbow or jerking knee. And in the morning, pillows would spot the floor like wounded soldiers on a battlefield, while the sheets were twisted and yanked away from the mattress corners.

But this morning, Asha's side of the bed looked nothing like the war zone I was used to. Her half of the comforter was only slightly rumpled, all her pillows were accounted for, and the sheets were still intact. Maybe she was so exhausted from traveling that there had been no energy left for her usual tossing and turning? Or maybe being in a strange bed kept her from falling asleep?

Whatever the case, she was most likely on a morning run, and I wanted to hop in the shower before she returned. Another thing I'd learned from our hundreds of sleepovers? Asha had a talent for using up all the hot water.

Crouching beside my duffel, I rummaged through my limited wardrobe in search of an outfit. My best option was a casual white sundress that belted at the waist, which hopefully wouldn't look ridiculous with my Keds. I folded the dress over my arm, grabbed my toiletry bag, and stepped into the hall. As I was making my way toward the bathroom, I heard a voice.

"I don't understand why you're so angry about this. I said I was sorry."

It was Alec. He sounded upset. The door to the office was ajar, but I knew this was a private conversation. I picked up my pace with the intention of speeding past his room, but the next words out of his mouth made me pause.

"Violet and I are tight, so I didn't think it was a big deal."

Was he talking about Violet James? I leaned in and cocked an ear to hear better.

"*What?*" he exclaimed, his voice turning sharp. "My own self-interests? Are you serious?" There was a long pause. "But we made a deal. I did everything you asked!" Another pause. "No, don't feed me that bullshit. It's just more lies… Yeah, whatever. Screw you."

The next few seconds passed in silence, and realizing the conversation was over, I jerked upright. *Are you seriously spying on Alec right now?* Embarrassed with myself, I begin to slink away. Because honestly. How mortifying would it be if he caught me snooping outside his door?

"Hey, Vi. It's me," he said suddenly, and I froze again. "I know you left for Paris this morning, but can you call me back when you get this message? We need to talk. Miss you. Bye."

I sucked in a deep breath. *Vi?* I didn't realize the two were on a nickname level of closeness. How *tight* were they?

There was movement inside Alec's room, and before I had time to give anything I'd heard a second thought, he pulled back the door. For a beat we both stood there, staring at each other.

Alec was the kind of person who looked like a magazine spread come to life: perfect hair, perfect clothes, perfect smile. I'd never imagined him as anything less than camera ready, but now he was looking more human than ever before. He was sporting athletic shorts and a white T-shirt worn thin with love. But more startling than seeing Alec Williams in his pajamas was the state of his hair. Like the plastic locks of a Ken doll, his hair was always orderly— bangs swept up and styled, every strand accounted for. Not today. Spikes of platinum shot in every direction as if he'd fought with his pillow in the middle of the night and lost. It made him seem younger, and it was more endearing than I was prepared for.

"Felicity?" He frowned at me. "What are you doing?"

I grimaced as the tingling sensation of embarrassment swept across my face. "Ah, hey. Sorry to intrude. I heard that you were up and I, um…" I was struggling to come up with a good excuse for why I was lurking outside his room. It was too early in the morning for quick thinking, and I hadn't had my daily dose of caffeine.

Oh, coffee!

"There's a Starbucks down the block," I said. "I saw it on our way in last night. I was thinking of picking up coffee for everybody. As a thank-you to Kelsey for everything. Want to come with me?"

"Absolutely."

"Awesome. I'm going to shower before Asha snags it. Give me half an hour?"

"Okay. I'll meet you downstairs."

Twenty minutes later, I was clean and ready to go, but Asha had yet to return. Maybe her run had turned into a sightseeing opportunity? Her phone was charging on the nightstand, so I couldn't text her, not that she'd respond anyway. She never did while running.

Maybe she told Boomer where she went?

That wasn't likely, considering he was a grouch any time before noon, but it wouldn't hurt to check.

The second guest room was still wrapped in darkness when I inched open the door. The curtains were drawn tight to keep the morning out, and when I stuck my head in, light from the hall cut a swatch of golden warmth across the carpet. Even before my eyes adjusted to the gloom, I knew something was off. I pushed into the room, and as I approached the bed, I reeled at the sight before me. A heap of clothes on the floor, tangled arms and bare skin, a coil of charcoal hair spread across Boomer's chest like a drop of ink in water.

I had to process each image individually before my brain could fully grasp what my eyes were seeing. My best friend was *in bed* with my other best friend.

Asha and Boomer.

Boomer and Asha.

A wave of shock rolled through me, leaving me speechless.

The light must have woken Asha, because she lifted her head off Boomer's shoulder and blinked at me. We stared at each other. Thankfully, all the parts of the two of them that I never wanted to see were covered by the comforter, but Asha hitched the blanket up to her chin and elbowed Boomer awake.

"Wha…?" he mumbled, but didn't open his eyes. She tried again, nudging until he sat up. "The hell, Asha? It's too early."

Still speechless, she raised a hand and pointed at me. Boomer's gaze followed the direction of her finger. Emotion flashed across his face like a flip-book—from shocked to panicked to guilty as charged.

A strained silence dragged out between us, but I refused to be the one to break it.

After another tooth-grinding moment, Boomer reached up and rubbed the back of his neck. "Well, fuck."

I opened my mouth, but all that came out were the choked beginnings of laughter as hysteric anger billowed inside my chest. "That's all you have to say?" I sputtered.

Boomer lifted a shoulder, equal parts apologetic and blasé. "What do you expect? It's not like we wanted you to find out this way."

"No." Shaking my head, I held up a hand to stop any further explanation. "I can't deal with this right now."

There was already enough on my plate with Rose and the letters and Stanford. It was impossible to imagine squeezing my friends' love life on there as well. My feet were moving before I realized it. I had to put space between myself and the situation so I could think.

"Wait, Felicity!" Asha cried as I fled the room, but I didn't stop.

☆ ♭ ♫

Alec was already by the front door when I rushed down the stairs five minutes early.

"What's wrong?" he asked, pulling out his headphones.

"Can we just get out of here?" I glanced over my shoulder to see if my friends were following, but the landing at the top of the steps was empty. "I'll tell you on the way."

In contrast to my mood, the weather was perfect—sunny enough to warm my skin, but not so hot that I was constantly plucking at my dress. As we made our way up the sidewalk, I pushed on my favorite sunglasses (a pair of electric-blue cat eyes I'd bought at Dollar Discount and jazzed up by splatter painting the frames), and explained how I'd found Asha in bed with Boomer.

"Wait. You didn't know they were together?" Alec asked, not bothering to keep the surprise from his voice.

I froze on the sidewalk. "Are you saying you did?"

He nodded.

God, I was such an idiot. The biggest of idiots. How was it possible that Alec, who'd known Asha and Boomer for less than two days, had figured out they were together? I was the person who supposedly knew them the best. How had I missed the chemistry between them?

"Why didn't you say anything to me?" I asked.

"I'm sorry, Felicity. I figured you knew."

"Don't be sorry. You're not the one who should be apologizing."

"You're mad at them?"

"Yes!" I said. Then, "No. Ugh, I don't know." I sank my fingers into my still-damp hair.

You're not angry with them, I tried to convince myself. *Don't be a petty, narrow-minded person who can't be happy for her friends.*

But I couldn't stop seeing the image of them tangled together in bed. And then I remembered how strange the two of them had acted when they got to my house yesterday, the vague answer Boomer gave when I asked how they'd arrived so quickly, how Asha wouldn't look me in the eye. They'd been hanging out *as a couple*.

"Hey," Alec said, taking both my wrists in his hands. He gently dislodged my fingers from my hair before I pulled a chunk out in frustration. "Why don't we get some coffee, and then we can figure everything out, yeah?"

I sighed in lieu of responding, but started walking again.

He was quiet for the rest of our stroll, which I appreciated. I knew he was trying to figure out what to say to cheer me up, and his company alone was enough to comfort me. By the time we reached the end of the street, the anger and confusion pumping through my system had run its course, and only then did I realize that one of my hands was still clutched in his.

I stared down at our entwined fingers, suddenly aware that we probably looked like a couple. Which made me wonder exactly what we were to each other. More than friends, obviously. There was no way I could deny the connection I felt with him. But at the same time, we hadn't known each other very long. Then there was the matter of *who* he was, because even if this spark between us blossomed into something more, the longevity of a relationship didn't seem likely. Not with his career. And besides, I had college and my future to consider. Was committing to a relationship even practical at this point in my life?

Am I being ridiculous thinking about all this?

I was lost inside my head, but the bell above the door at Starbucks brought me back to the present. The place was relatively empty for a Saturday morning. The only customers were a couple split-ting a blueberry scone and an elderly man reading a newspaper. A bored-looking employee barely looked up from his phone as we approached the counter.

"You know what you want?" Alec asked as he inspected the glass display case filled with pastries.

I glanced at the menu hanging overhead. "I'll have an iced coffee and a fruit parfait," I said, choosing the first items I saw.

"Anything for the traitors?" he joked.

My lips pursed. I was tempted to say no, but denying some-one their morning coffee was a punishment no one deserved. "Get them each a dark roast."

"Okay." He studied the assortment of baked goods for a moment longer and then moved toward the cash register. The guy behind the counter was still focused on his phone, so Alec cleared his throat. "Um, hi. Can I please have a grande iced coffee, two grande dark roasts, an espresso, one of those parfait things, a chocolate-chip bagel, and a box of assorted muffins? Oh, and cream cheese."

The boy raised an eyebrow as if surprised by the length of Alec's order, but he got to work without a word. When he fin-ished, we found a table on the sidewalk patio and ate our break-fast in the sun.

"So," Alec said, cutting his bagel in half. "Is there something spe-cific that bothers you about Asha and Boomer dating?"

I considered his question, and by the time I'd come up with an answer, I'd inhaled half of my parfait. "It's not them being together that's upsetting. It's that they hid it from me. It feels like…I don't know, betrayal?"

Alec nodded, but said, "They care about you, Felicity. A lot. I doubt they wanted to hurt you."

"I know that." It was the truth—Asha and Boomer would never purposely be mean to me. "I just don't understand why they kept it a secret. It's not like I want them to be unhappy. Did they think I'd get upset?"

"But you *are* upset." He tore open his packet of cream cheese.

"Not because they're together," I said, scooping up a spoonful of blueberries, which I'd saved for last. "I'm upset because they didn't trust me to be happy for them."

"I don't think it was about trust, Fel."

More bitter words were poised on my tongue, but I stopped. Alec had called me by my nickname. Not Felicity, just Fel, and it thawed me.

Sighing, I let my bitterness go. "Then what, Alec?"

"They're probably afraid. Both of hurting you and messing up your friendship."

"So what do I do?"

"Talk to them."

"Well, I knew that," I said. "It's not like I can avoid them forever. We're going to be stuck in the car all day."

"We can always leave them here in San Francisco," he deadpanned. His face was so serious that, if I didn't know better, I would have believed him. "Or tie them up in the trunk. Whichever you prefer."

☆ ♭ ♪♫

Our walk back to Kelsey's was silent, and by the time we reached the red-and-pink house, I felt like a steel pinball had been launched inside my chest. The two lovebirds were sitting on the front steps. Asha had her chin propped up in her hands, and she looked absolutely miserable.

Fingers brushed softly against the back of my hand. "Don't worry," Alec whispered. "It will be fine."

I sure hoped so. Otherwise, this was going to be a long trip. I nodded at him before making my way toward my friends.

Nobody said anything when I arrived at the base of the stairs. Boomer somehow managed to look small as he sat behind Asha. He leaned forward and took her hand in his, and she let out a raspy sigh as their fingers folded together. Her eyes were glassy, and the sight of my best friend on the verge of tears made my throat ache.

What could I possibly say to relieve the tension? This was all so awkward, and I didn't know how to begin the conversation.

Boomer cleared his throat. "We're so sorry, Felicity."

I let out a long sigh. "Yeah, me too."

"Please don't apologize," Asha replied. "It will only make me feel more guilty."

"But I am sorry," I said. "I snapped at you guys without giving you a chance to—"

"No." The word came out firm. "We're the ones who should be apologizing. We shouldn't have kept something this big from you."

"We had every intention of telling you," Boomer added. "It's just… We didn't know…" His voice trailed off, and he pushed his hair back. "There was no good way. We were going to say something yesterday when we got to your house, but then you showed us the letters, and it didn't feel like the right time."

I stared up at the house's decorative red trim as I processed his explanation. "I get it. I mean, I wish you hadn't been so afraid to tell me, because I really am happy for you."

"You weren't this morning," Boomer pointed out.

"Yeah, well—it was a shock."

"For us too. Both our relationship and…um, you catching us."

Our relationship. As in the two of them dating. This would take some getting used to. "So…" I said slowly. "How did it happen?"

Boomer shrugged lazily. "Dunno. It just did."

Asha frowned at his response. "Felicity, don't take this the wrong way, but between studying, working at the diner, and all the volunteer hours…you haven't had much time to hang out. Do you remember the last time we did Monday movie night, all three of us?"

I flinched. "Earlier this month?"

"Not since May."

God. Had it really been that long?

"I'm a shitty friend," I said, hanging my head.

"No, no!" Asha exclaimed. "We understand, Fel. Really, we do. Getting into Stanford is your top priority right now, and while you being busy all the time majorly sucks, Boomer and I started hanging out solo, and…I don't know, things just happened."

"How long?" My voice was thin with apprehension. I wasn't entirely sure I wanted to hear the answer.

It was Asha's turn to flinch. "Since June."

I blinked at the two of them. "You guys have been dating for *two months?*"

"Technically, we didn't start dating until a few weeks ago. Fourteen days to be exact," she said in a rush. "Before that we were casually making out and stuff."

I held up a hand. "Okay, stop." I didn't need to hear about the two of them making out and *stuff*. "Too much information."

We all stared at one another until a sheepish grin tugged at Boomer's lips. He laughed, and then, without any volition on my part, I was laughing too. Like a thawing lake, the tension separating us cracked and dissolved. Asha got up from her spot on the steps and pulled me into a hug.

"Are you sure we're good?" she whispered. "I don't want this to ruin anything between us."

I gave her a tight squeeze before pulling back. "Of course, Asha. I could never stay mad at you dorks forever." She grinned in response, and I quickly added, "But maybe keep the kissing on the DL until I'm used to everything."

Normally Asha dished about whomever she was dating, but I wasn't sure I could handle details about Boomer…

"But I've been dying to talk to you." She lowered her voice so he couldn't hear us. "He does this thing with his tongue that—"

"*La-la-la-la-la!*" I sang, plugging my ears to block out the rest of her sentence. "Scratch that. I don't *ever* need to know about the kissing."

CHAPTER 12

Twenty minutes later, after thanking Kelsey for her hospitality and her help, we were on the road again. According to my phone's GPS, it was going to take us twelve and a half hours to reach the forwarding address Rose had left behind. The boys decided to drive in shifts, and Alec took the first leg. Although the scenery was beautiful, the initial stretch of the trip was uneventful. Asha and Boomer were watching movies again. Meanwhile, I passed the time by poring over my ACT prep book.

Miles stretched on.

The boys traded places. And traded places again.

More miles.

"All right, I got three," Alec announced, drumming his hands on the steering wheel in excitement.

We'd just crossed the California-Oregon border. The faint stink of our McDonald's lunch was hanging in the air, and Boomer snoring in the backseat epitomized the sleepy afternoon mood. I was burned out on studying, so I'd suggested we play a game to entertain ourselves. Right off the bat, Alec nixed the license plate game. Claimed he'd played it one too many times while on tour with the band, so I decided on Two Truths and a Lie.

"You ready?" he asked me.

"Bring it."

"Okay. First, I've climbed Denali. Second, my greatest fear is spiders. And third, my favorite flavor of Hamburger Helper is Cheesy Enchilada."

"What's a Denali?" If I was going to guess which of the three statements was a lie, then I needed all the facts, and I had no clue what he was talking about.

"The tallest mountain peak in North America. Also known as Mount McKinley."

I fell quiet for a minute. Mount McKinley sounded like a difficult mountain to climb—not that I knew anything about mountaineering. But it was a hard-to-believe accomplishment. *Kind of like being part of a world-famous boy band.* But the improbability of Alec's first statement made me all the more willing to accept it as the truth. He probably threw it into the mix thinking I'd never believe him. Plus, there was the equipment in his trunk to consider, not to mention the picture of him and Vanessa at the top of some cliff.

I moved on to the second would-be truth, Alec's alleged arachnophobia. I found it difficult to believe someone so rational could be terrified of a creature a million times smaller than him, but then again, maybe he was trying to trick me with a moment of brutal honesty.

So that left me with one option.

"Number three," I decided. "Nobody likes Hamburger Helper. It's disgusting."

Alec glanced at me, a sheepish grin on his face. "They don't?"

"Ew," I said, my nose wrinkling. "You eat that stuff?"

He shrugged. "I'm not much of a cook."

"Damn! I should've known the mountain climbing was a lie."

"It's not." His smile grew. "I did it back in May. Ever since getting into climbing, I've always wanted to tackle Denali. The entire expedition took twenty-one days."

"Wow. I'm impressed." My voice went high at the end. Hearing about another one of his amazing achievements made me feel inadequate, and I realized I'd done nothing worth noting in my life. Alec seemed to detect the change in my tone, because a funny look crossed his face, so I quickly added, "How does one get into mountain climbing?"

"My family loves hiking. When I was twelve, we went to Mount Rainier National Park to hike the Wonderland Trail. Ever heard of it?"

I shook my head.

"It's this ninety-three-mile hike that encircles Mount Rainier. Takes about two weeks to complete, and you camp alongside the trail at night."

"Two weeks? That's a lot of hiking…"

"Yeah, but it's totally worth it. There's glaciers and canyons, and these amazing waterfalls in the middle of the forest," he explained. "The whole time you're hiking, you're in the shadow of this spectacular mountain. I couldn't stop staring at it and thinking—if it's this beautiful on the trail, how breathtaking is the view at the top? By the time we finished, I'd decided that I was going to make it to the summit so I could see for myself."

"So did you?"

Alec smiled distantly, as if he was reliving the memory. "On my fourteenth birthday. A year later, I climbed Aconcagua, which is the highest mountain in the world outside Asia."

"Wow, I never would've guessed you were so into hiking." He didn't dress like the outdoorsy type...

"Whoa, careful there," he said, feigning offense. "Mountaineering and hiking...two totally different things."

I rolled my eyes. "You know what I meant."

Our conversation lulled long enough for me to wonder if I actually *had* offended him, but then he muttered, "I can't believe you thought I was afraid of spiders."

"It's not totally unreasonable," I said, biting down on my grin. "Lots of people are."

Alec snorted. "I think it's one of those phobias that's exaggerated by the entertainment industry, like in movies and books and such. High-maintenance girl or huge muscleman erupts into chaos at the sight of a daddy longlegs for comedic effect."

I whipped out my phone and did a quick Google search. "Actually, approximately four percent of the world suffers from arachnophobia, so with a population of roughly seven billion that's"—I paused, quickly doing the math in my head—"two hundred eighty million people who are afraid of spiders."

"Okay, Miss Mathlete," he said. "Point proven."

"So what *are* you afraid of?" I asked, unable to contain my curiosity.

Without hesitation, he said, "Clowns."

I was quite convinced I'd misheard. Because there was no way

Alec Williams, slayer of mountains and boy band god, was afraid of *clowns*.

"Really?" I was trying to sort this new bit of information into the mental file of what I knew about Alec, but it didn't fit.

He nodded adamantly. "Ever seen *Killer Klowns from Outer Space*? It's an eighties cult film about aliens disguised as clowns who terrorize a small town." He shuddered as he spoke. "When we were kids, Vanessa made me watch the movie when she babysat. Said if I didn't listen to her, then the alien clowns would come kill me."

The corners of my mouth inched into a grin. That sounded *exactly* like something Rose would do. "How old were you?"

"Like six or seven. I had nightmares for months."

"Aw, poor little Alec."

"All right," he said, as I giggled. "We're done talking about me. It's your turn."

"Okay, let me think."

I wanted to come up with two questionable truths and one convincing lie so I could stump him the way he did me. Because, really? Mountain climbing and Hamburger Helper? Who would have guessed?

"I'm ready," I said a minute later.

"Hit me."

"'Kay. Number one, I won my district spelling bee when I was eleven. Two, when I was a kid, I wanted to be a spy when I grew up. And finally, I can run five miles in under forty-five minutes."

The last statement was my lie, and I crossed my fingers in hopes that Alec would think I was bragging. It wasn't totally beyond the realms of possibility. People always told me I had a runner's body. But as soon as I finished speaking, there was a loud snort from the backseat.

Alec grinned. "I'm assuming Asha just gave you away."

My gaze darted to the rearview. Both my friends had their eyes closed, but there was a curve to Asha's lips, and I knew she'd been listening to our conversation.

"Thanks for that," I grumbled.

"Sorry." She laughed. Clearly she found it amusing that I'd used one of *her* accomplishments as my lie. "But *you* run five miles? Felicity, you can barely make it a block without needing resuscitation."

I scowled and tried to look angry. "That's why it's call Two Truths and a Lie. You know, because you *lie*. Ugh, you suck."

Asha didn't respond. Instead, she pretended to go back to sleep as if she'd never interrupted our game, a smirk still playing on her lips. I grabbed a Swedish Fish from the open bag in the console with the intent of launching it at her cleavage, but Alec distracted me.

"So why a spy?" he asked. "Don't most kids dream about being an astronaut or the president?"

"Because my mom is in love with Tom Cruise. *Risky Business* and *Mission: Impossible* were pretty much Saturday night staples in our house." I popped the candy into my mouth and chewed quickly. "I didn't want to be president because I was afraid of being assassinated."

His forehead furrowed. "But you wanted to be a spy…"

"Yeah, like Ethan Hunt. He's unkillable."

"Are you sure you've seen the movie? His entire team dies within the first ten minutes."

"Well, yeah. That's just to set up the plot. Besides," I added, "I was mainly in it for the cool gadgets."

Alec opened his mouth like he had more to say on the matter, but shook his head, as if realizing there was no point arguing little-kid logic. "Why don't you go again?" he suggested.

Coming up with good statements the first time around was difficult, so thinking of three more would be a challenge, but I wasn't going to let him win. As I deliberated, Alec tapped the steering wheel to the beat of the song playing from the stereo. Suddenly, his phone buzzed in the cup holder. His gaze flicked down to it before refocusing on the road.

"Would you get that for me?"

"Sure." I grabbed his cell. There was one new text.

007: Lord Voldemort called.

"Um, it's from a Double O Seven?" I said, confused by the message. "Apparently Lord Voldemort called."

Alec's lips twitched to a grin. "Can you ask him what for?"

I quickly typed a response:

Alec: What did he want?

"Who's Lord Voldemort?" I asked after hitting Send.

Alec's eyes widened with pretend shock. "Only the most evil dark wizard to ever exist. Has a pet snake and a thing for murdering Muggles. Haven't you read Harry Potter?"

I shot Alec a look. "Not what I meant."

He laughed, a rich, happy sound. "My dad."

Oh. "Gotcha," I said and dropped the subject.

For the next few minutes, I navigated the conversation for him.

> **007:** Wanted to know where you are.
>
> **Alec:** What did you tell him?
>
> **007:** That I wasn't your keeper.
>
> **Alec:** Bet he loved that. Thanks for covering for me.
>
> **007:** So where are you?
>
> **Alec:** On a road trip.

Less than a minute later, the phone buzzed in my hands again, but this time it was an incoming call.

"James Bond is calling," I told Alec. It was such an absurd statement that I had to press my lips together to stifle a laugh. "Should I answer? Maybe he's going to admit that Ethan Hunt is an all-round better spy."

Alec chuckled and held out his hand, so I hit the talk button and pressed the cell into his palm.

"What's up?" Alec answered. He paused for a second before saying, "To Seattle."

This seemed to excite whoever was on the other end, because I could hear their muffled response. I unconsciously leaned on the center console, trying to listen to the other half of the conversation, but my mind caught up to what my body was doing, and I forced myself to sit back in my seat. Pulling my prep book back into my lap, I attempted to give Alec some privacy even though my ears were still perked.

"Safe House? What are you guys doing there?" Another pause. Another nod of the head. "Thanks for the offer, man. I'm not entirely sure what the plan is yet, but I'll keep that in mind… Okay, sounds good. Later."

He ended the call and dropped his cell into the cup holder. I looked at him expectantly, hoping for an explanation. For starters, who was this Double O Seven person, and what in the world did Alec mean by *Safe House*? But I didn't get an answer.

Alec glanced at me, the corners of his eyes crinkling with amusement. He was clearly having more fun keeping me in the dark than alleviating it.

"So," he said, "Come up with two truths and a lie yet?"

☆ ♭ ♫

"Man, you sure study a lot," Alec said, eyeing my flash cards with disdain. They'd come with my ACT prep book, a pack for each section of the test, and I was currently reviewing the science ones since it had always been my worst subject in school.

> An electromagnetic wave with a wavelength longer than that of X-rays, but shorter than that of visible light is in the _____ part of the spectrum.

"I have to," I told him. "Stanford has one of the lowest acceptance rates in the country."

My feet were propped up on the dash, and the sunlight streaming in through the windshield felt like an electric blanket against my skin. I wondered how long it would take before my legs started to burn. My shoulders were tender from yesterday, and even the slightest movement turned the straps of my dress into stinging razor blades.

"So how come you want to go there?"

"It's where my dad went," I said, turning the card over.

> The correct answer is:
> Ultraviolet

Alec tilted his head to the side, like he was trying to make sense of this. "Just to be clear…we're talking about the dad you don't remember because he ran away to Europe, right?"

"Yup." I flipped to the next flash card.

"Okay, explain."

"Well, when my parents first met, my dad was this hotshot lawyer who saved my mom from a lifetime of waitressing. Took her from a one-room apartment in a bad part of town to a nice house in Orange County, where she learned to depend on him. So when he left, he left her worse off than before. Suddenly she had no means of support and two kids to raise," I said. "She has an okay job now, but I remember a time when my mom worked eighty-hour weeks to keep the lights on and put food in the fridge."

"I'm sorry, but…,I still don't understand."

"All my mom wants is for me and Rose to have a better life than she did, but my sister was too busy partying to get passing grades. It killed my mom to see her waste her potential, and I won't make that mistake. After everything Mom has done to provide for us, I owe it to her. And the only way I know how to do that is to become a successful lawyer like my dad. I have to follow in his footsteps: go to the same school, intern at the same firm. That sort of thing. I know it sounds irrational, but it's been my plan ever since Rose left."

The car was quiet except for a the crooning of a country singer and Boomer's monstrous snoring. Alec cast a skeptical look in my direction, as if he thought I was joking. He opened his mouth, and then closed it.

"That's crazy," he said after some time.

I stared out the windshield. "Maybe, but doing this will make my mom happy, and she hasn't had a lot of that in her life."

In the distance, I spotted the red-and-blue flash of police lights. There must have been an accident ahead of us, because traffic was starting to stack up.

"But what about you? Will that make *you* happy?" Alec asked as a black sedan cut in front of us, squeezing its way into the faster-moving lane.

"I won't mind becoming a lawyer, if that's what you mean."

Alec frowned. Whether it was due to our conversation or the current traffic, I couldn't tell. "I don't see it."

"Why?" I teased. "Don't think I could rock a pantsuit?"

"Because you shouldn't make a decision that will affect the rest of your life based on someone else," he said. "You should do your own thing."

"But it is my own thing," I told him. "This is going to sound silly, but I've dreamed of becoming a lawyer ever since I was a little kid and saw *Legally Blonde*."

"You also wanted to be a spy," he pointed out. "Dreams change."

"Not all dreams."

He glanced at me, his gaze sharp and knowing. "Then why don't I believe you?"

I looked at the flash card I was clutching, trying to come up with a way to explain myself.

> The energy an object has when it is stationary is known as its _____.

"Look," I said. "Maybe I'm not as enthusiastic about the plan as I was when I was thirteen, but I've spent the past four years of my life working toward this."

Alec shrugged. "So what? Plans change. You have to learn to adapt."

Was he being serious right now? "Alec, I can't *not* go to Stanford."

"Sure you can," he replied. "Your problem isn't that you *have* to go. It's that you're afraid of not knowing what you'll do if you don't."

"That's not true, and even if it were, I think it's a reasonable concern. Boomer's known he's going to be an engineer all his life, and ever since Asha's blog blew up, she's wanted to be a digital communications major. What would I do? I don't have any interests like that."

"Yeah you do," Alec said. "You're artistic. What about your jewelry?"

"But where's the career in that? I need to be able to support myself when I graduate."

Even though I was no longer focused on studying, I turned over the card.

The correct answer is:
Potential Energy

Alec pursed his lips. "I don't see the point in pursuing a career that doesn't inspire you. If you don't know what that career is yet, so what? Isn't that the point of college—to figure things out? Felicity, you'll never be happy if you're busy chasing someone else's success."

I turned away from Alec.

I knew he meant well, and that he was only trying to help me, but he didn't get it. And he never would. He hadn't grown up in a household that struggled to make ends meet. Even before Alec Williams became a multi-platinum-selling musician, his family had been loaded because of his dad's business. He could afford to chase his dreams. I wasn't so fortunate.

"Maybe you're right," I said at last. "But not everyone can enjoy that luxury."

☆ ♭ ♫

Theoretically, we should've made the drive from San Francisco to Seattle in one day, but a never-ending traffic jam put us way behind schedule. I could tell Alec was struggling to stay awake, and at seven o'clock, he stopped at one of the interstate rest areas so we could discuss our options.

"How much longer do you think?" I asked as Alec found a parking spot.

The lot was empty with the exception of a family and their minivan. The dad was in the process of repacking the rooftop cargo carrier, while the mom tried to wrangle all five kids back into the car. Watching them was stressful.

Alec dropped his hands from the wheel and stretched. "We still have four hours to go."

With a yawn, Boomer leaned up between the front seats. "There's a vending machine over there. If I grab a soda, I can probably handle another shift."

"I have my license, you know," Asha said. "Why don't you let me take over? I can make it the rest of the way." She sounded as enthused at the prospect as I felt about being stuck in the car for another two hundred and fifty miles.

"Maybe we should stop for the night," I suggested.

"Where?" Asha asked, but what she meant was *how*. We'd gotten lucky that Kelsey was nice enough to let us stay at her house, because none of us could afford a hotel. Well, not including Alec. But I didn't expect him to pay for our rooms. He was already doing so much for me. I couldn't ask for anything more.

"Actually," Alec said, perking up in his seat. "I know a place we can stay. Hold on a sec." He plucked his cell out of the cup holder, hit Speed Dial, and climbed out of the car. Whoever he was calling answered right away, because Alec said *hey* before moving out of earshot.

"Who do you think he's talking to?" Asha asked.

I shrugged off her question, although I was curious too. It was strange that Alec needed to make his call in private, especially considering he'd had a heated conversation with King over the phone in my presence. I hadn't learned anything about the mysterious Double O Seven person who'd texted him earlier or what Safe House was.

Why was Alec being so secretive?

The conversation only lasted a minute. "All right," said Alec as he slipped back into the car. "We're good to go."

"And where exactly is that?"

His smile grew crooked. "You'll see."

Fifteen minutes later, we pulled off the highway, and I glanced around in confusion. There wasn't much to see except a one-pump gas station, and nothing but an endless swell of trees. I knew the Heartbreakers were from the Portland area and wondered if he was taking us to stay with one of his bandmates, but we were still an hour outside the city. Alec took a left, away from the only sign of civilization. There was only pavement ahead of us and the blur of nature outside my window. I kept my gaze focused on the tree line. Night had swallowed the sun, and while the scenery was probably green and breathtaking during the day, the gloom of dusk made the landscape look dark and foreboding.

Eventually we came upon a side road that broke through the forest wall. It was so small that if you didn't already know it was there, you never would. Alec slowed the car in time to make the turn. I quickly discovered that the road was not a road at all, but a long driveway that twisted through the foliage and up a hill. As we neared our destination, light from a distant building flickered between the trunks. When we reached the top, the woods came to a sudden stop, opening to reveal a house in the clearing.

Only it wasn't a house. Before us loomed an impressive Tudor-style mansion made of gray brick and dripping in ivy. Every window was lit up, which was a welcoming sight after the suffocating shadows of the pines.

"Whoa." The word slipped out of my mouth. "Where *are* we?"

"Oliver's uncle's place. We call it Safe House. It's where we come when we want to get away from the stress of everything," Alec answered, and I didn't need to ask "Oliver who?" to know he was talking about his bandmate. "Professor Perry is away at a history conference. Poseidon doesn't do well with strangers, so Oliver offered to watch him. Everyone's here."

Huh?

What the in the world was a Poseidon? Clearly he wasn't referring to the Greek god, which made me wonder if Oliver's uncle kept some sort of finicky sea monster in a backyard pond. But, more importantly, what did Alec mean by *everybody*? As in the rest of the band?

I didn't get a chance to ask any clarifying questions, because Asha exploded with chatter. "Oliver's here? We get to meet him? No freaking way!" And then, gesturing at the beautiful home, "This is his uncle's house? What kind of professor makes enough dough for all this?"

Alec laughed. "None that I know of. Oliver bought this place for him about a year back. Not sure why, considering they've never been close, but Professor Perry did take Oliver in after his grandma…" Alec trailed off when he realized he was spilling some-body else's story.

The silence didn't last long, because we'd pulled up alongside a slick, red sports car.

"*Holy hell*," Boomer gasped, pressing his hands and face against the window. "That's a Lotus Evora!" He unbuckled his seat belt and was out the door before Alec turned off the engine.

Asha caught my gaze in the mirror and rolled her eyes. "Here we go…" she muttered, and I allowed myself a small grin. Even though things had changed between the three of us, I took comfort in Boomer's childlike excitement and Asha's obvious exasperation. At least some things were still the same.

We all piled out, and while Boomer fluttered around the vehicle in circles, the rest of us unloaded our luggage from the trunk.

"When it was first released, I thought the facelift on the 400 was a good move. More modern, more aggressive. But wow. This"—Boomer shook his head—"this is so much more beauti-ful in person." His fingers brushed the hood tenderly. "Four hun-dred horsepower. Zero to sixty in four point one seconds. God, the sound of this girl… She's so sexy."

"I don't know which is more upsetting: that you referred to a car as if it's a person, or that you think it's sexy." Asha sounded angry, but I knew she was only teasing. "Can we please go inside? These woods are giving me the serious creeps. It like a scene straight out of *IN*."

Boomer looked like someone would have to drag him away

kicking and screaming before he would leave, and I was convinced he'd sleep outside on the driveway so he could stay next to the car. Thankfully, Alec knew exactly what to say to get Boomer to move. "I'm sure if we head inside, JJ will let you drive it at some point."

Openmouthed, Boomer stared at Alec. "Are you for real?"

Alec shrugged, and that was all it took. Boomer grabbed Asha's hand and dragged her up the front walk so fast you'd think there really were werewolves and vampires lurking in the woods. I hesitated, staring up at the huge house. It was romantic and age-old in a way that suited a historian.

"Felicity? Is everything okay?"

"Um, yeah," I said, pulling the skin at my throat. "It's just… I didn't realize your friends would be here." And by friends I meant JJ. Boys like him were intimidating.

Alec's face softened in understanding. "He'll behave himself. I promise."

"You sure?"

His lips quirked into a half smile. "Positive. And if he doesn't, I'm fairly sure Asha can take him."

CHAPTER 13

Alec rang the doorbell. We stood on the stoop for a solid two minutes, but nobody answered.

"You sure someone's here?" Asha asked, even though the heavy bass of a rock song could be heard pounding from a distant corner of the house.

"Maybe they can't hear us?" I suggested.

Alec frowned. "I doubt that."

He tested the handle to see if it was unlocked, and the door creaked ajar. Alec's forehead wrinkled. He pushed the thick, wooden slab open and inched inside.

"Something wrong?" I asked. I didn't understand why he was he being so cautious. There weren't signs of a break-in or anything else amiss. The last person inside probably forgot to lock up. Big deal.

"Shhhh." He tilted his head as if listening for something.

Biting my lip, I glanced over my shoulder. *What's going on?* I mouthed to my friends. The look on Asha's expression echoed my confusion. She shook her head, and Boomer raised a shoulder in a half shrug.

Not knowing what else to do, I followed Alec into an unlit foyer and set down my duffel. Beyond the tiny room was a magnificent entrance hall decorated with all the elegance and glamour of the 1920s. I felt like we'd stepped back in time. Ancestral portraits of gray-haired men in uniform and women wearing fashion from another era lined the walls, which were covered in an antiqued-silver damask paper. A grand staircase made of mahogany or some other type of warm wood, with carpeted red steps and hand-carved banisters, commanded the center of the hall.

Alec, who didn't seem impressed by our surroundings the way I was, was still looking around with caution. Then a scraping sound cut through the silence as something hard slid across the floor and connected with my foot.

"What the…?" It was a neon water gun. A second Super Soaker was lying next to a laundry basket filled to the brim with water balloons.

At the sight of the plastic toys, Alec's entire demeanor changed. He didn't relax exactly, but the suspicion in his eyes faded, as if he knew exactly what was going on. He scooped up the water guns. He passed the bigger of the two to me and tested his own. A quick blast of water sprayed across the stone floor.

"What am I supposed to do with this?" I asked, staring down at the toy in my hands.

"Use it." His expression was grave. "We're going into battle." He eased down the entrance hall.

Two apprehensive seconds ticked by.

"Double O Seven, target is in sight! Repeat, target spotted!"

The next minute unfolded like a scene out of a movie.

A familiar face jumped out from behind a suit of armor. Unlike the last time I saw JJ Morris, he was fully clothed. He had on a pair of camo pants and a black tank top, with a stripe of war paint under each eye. Clutched in his hands was a plastic water gun similar to ours, only his was bigger. He blasted Alec with a spray.

Alec lunged out of the way and fired back. Without taking his eyes off JJ, he shouted to me, "I got him. You take Oliver!"

Oliver? The only person here is JJ...

But then Oliver charged down the hall in our direction. He wasn't wearing the dorky camouflage his partner in crime was, but a bandana was tied around his head Rambo-style, and his recognizable brown waves curled up around the strip of fabric. Before I fully comprehend what I was doing, I lifted my Super Soaker and aimed it at the lead singer of the Heartbreakers.

Oliver faltered when he saw me, as if he expected Alec to be alone. But he quickly schooled his surprise and charged my way, a war cry tearing from his lips. It was surreal—a celebrity chasing me with a squirt gun—but it was happening too quickly for me to consider. I pumped the handle of the gun until enough pressure built and let it rip once he was in range. Oliver returned the favor, and when a jet of cold water hit me in the face, I shrieked and dodged the stream.

For the next two minutes we dueled across the room, dousing each other in icy showers. Oliver seemed unconcerned about drenching the carpet and walls and furnishings of his uncle's house. I was giddy with the craziness of the current situation, my laughter melding with the chaos. JJ shouted mocking insults at Alec who, silent as ever, seemed to be evading much of the attack, but I was too focused on beating Oliver to pay full attention.

My gun, which was much smaller than his, was the first to run out of water. When I pulled the trigger and nothing came out, a slow smirk spread across Oliver's face. He lowered his weapon to revel in victory.

"Looks like you're out," he said. "Tough luck."

But before he could take aim, another war cry rang out behind me. Boomer and Asha rushed out of the foyer, the laundry basket of balloons swinging between them. Grinning, I tossed the empty toy aside and grabbed three of the water bombs. Oliver's smirk fell. The fight didn't last long after that. With Asha and Boomer as reinforcements, the four of us were able to back JJ and Oliver into a corner and rain balloons down on them until they were soaking.

"Okay, *okay*!" Oliver sputtered, waving his hands in surrender. "Enough already. You guys win." His hair was dripping, plastered to the side of his face, and a huge puddle had gathered on the oriental rug beneath his feet.

There was only one water balloon left, and grinning to himself, Alec plucked it from the basket and lobbed it at his bandmates. It hit JJ square in the chest and exploded. JJ's eyes flickered with irritation, but the paint running down his face rendered his expression comical.

"That didn't go as planned," he said, picking a chunk of broken latex off his shirt. He flicked it in Alec's direction. "We didn't know you were bringing"—he craned his neck to look up at Boomer—"a giant with you."

"Or anyone else for that matter," Oliver grumbled.

"So having an advantage is okay, provided that you're not the ones outnumbered?" Alec asked. He crossed his arms, disgruntled, but the corner of his mouth twitched, and I knew he was curbing a smile. "That's not very fair, is it?"

"All right, Mr. Moral High Ground. We get it. JJ and I got what was coming to us." Oliver yanked off his bandana and shook out his hair, sending a spray of droplets in every direction. "Now," he said, after fixing his bangs, "are you going to introduce us to your friends, or are we going to continue pretending this whole situation isn't slightly awkward?"

"Oh!" Alec turned to face us, two small patches of pink on his cheeks. He gestured at me first. "Oliver, JJ. This is—"

"No introductions needed there," JJ cut in. He showed me a toothy grin. "Felicity from Skype." Alec shot him a warning look, and JJ quickly added, "I was scolded rather severely for being"—he frowned and paused—"what was it Stella called me again?"

"A pervy, womanizing pig."

"Yeah, that's it! My apologies. I swear I didn't mean to offend you."

"His Off button is broken," Oliver added, dropping an arm around JJ's shoulder. "We've learned to ignore him most of the time."

"No worries," I managed to say, although I had yet to make up my mind about JJ and his in-your-face personality.

"Well, I thought you were funny," Asha said, eyelashes fluttering.

I wheeled around and glared. Seriously, what happened to chicks before dicks? Or in this particular case, superhot boy band members. Was that all it took? One attractive celebrity, and suddenly I was chopped liver?

"Hey, I recognize you too. You're Asha, right?" JJ asked. Her eyes lit up when he remembered her name, but that didn't compare to the expression on her face when he pressed his lips to the back of her hand and said, "Pleasure to meet you."

A dark, grumbling noise brewed at the back of Boomer's throat, and JJ cast a curious glance in his direction.

"Who's the tree?" he asked.

"The *tree* happens to be Asha's boyfriend," Boomer growled, crossing his arms over his chest. "My name's Boomer, and for future reference, the tall jokes get old fast."

JJ dropped Asha's hand, but took the news in stride. "But you haven't heard my beanstalk one yet."

Letting out a long sigh, Alec scrubbed his hand down his face.

Oliver kept his features straight for all of two seconds before snickering, and the sound only fueled JJ's grin. "So," he said, when he finally had his laughter under control. "Who's hungry?"

☆ ♭ ♫

Everyone was damp, but Oliver led us through a twisting route of hallways until we reached the back of the house. The heavy rock music grew in volume until we reached its source—a kitchen filled with the scent of freshly baked garlic bread. Oliver's girlfriend, Stella, was setting the table while dancing to the screeching song, and a guy with glasses and messy strawberry-blond hair was chopping lettuce at the island cutting board. Without introduction, I immediately knew he was Xander Jones, the fourth and final member of the Heartbreakers.

"What in the world is this noise?" JJ asked, strolling in and plopping down on one of the bar stools. Alec filed in after him, but Asha, Boomer, and I lingered in the doorway, waiting to be introduced.

"Don't ask me," Xander answered without looking up from his work. "Stella took over the music as soon as you guys left."

"It's Bionic Bones," she said, waving a fork in JJ's direction. "Only my all-time favorite band."

"*Second* all-time favorite band," Oliver corrected. He swept across the room, tugged her against his chest, and planted a kiss on her forehead. "Because you love us more than Freddie K, right?"

She smiled up at him. "The fact you remember who Freddie K is makes me love you that much more."

Looking at the two, it was easy to see how Stella had won the heart of the music industry's most notorious player. They fit together perfectly, all dark clothes and wild hair, prince and princess of punk.

"You two are as bad as this music," JJ said.

Stella looked up, eyes ablaze, but then she spotted Alec. "Alec! You made it!" She dropped the handful of unplaced silverware and threw herself at him. "I've missed you so much."

"It's only been a month," he said, but it was obvious from the smile on his face that he'd missed her too.

I snuck a glance at Oliver, who'd moved over to the oven. He had a wooden spoon in his hand and was checking whatever was simmering in the huge pot on the stovetop. He seemed unconcerned by Alec and his girlfriend's open affection, so I tried my hardest to ignore the rock in my stomach as Alec wrapped his arms around her.

"Yeah, but fall semester starts soon, and then I won't see you guys until Christmas break." I didn't know much about Stella, but at one point during the drive, Alec had mentioned that she was studying photography at the School of Visual Arts in New York City.

"You could always hang a poster of us in your room," JJ suggested, which earned him a withering look from all his friends.

"I'm sure we'll be in New York for some reason or other," Alec assured her.

"So what are you doing in Oregon? Oliver said you were on a road trip or something."

"Yeah, we're going to Seattle."

"We?" She glanced over his shoulder and finally noticed he wasn't alone. A wide smile stretched across her face when she saw me. "Felicity? Oh my gosh, hi! I'm so glad I actually get to meet you."

"Hey." I was thrown by how happy she sounded, like she was as excited to see me as she was Alec. She quickly closed the gap between us, wrapping her arms around me. And holy crap, could the girl give a hug. She squeezed me like we'd known each other forever.

After releasing me, she scolded Alec. "Why didn't you mention you were bringing anyone?"

He shrugged. His gesture was causal, but from the glint in his eye, I could tell he'd wanted this to be a surprise and he enjoyed catching his friends off guard.

I fiddled with my watch, not sure what to say or my place within the conversation. There was a level of comfort among Stella, Alec, and the rest of the band, the kind that made water gun ambushes one hundred percent acceptable and could only be achieved by spending hours of time together. It made me feel like an outsider, despite the warm welcome I'd just received, and I found myself inching toward my own source of comfort: Asha and Boomer. Asha, however, didn't seem intimidated by the tight-knit group. Or the fact that she was standing in a room with her favorite band. She tossed her braid over her shoulder, stepped passed me, and held out her hand to Stella.

"Hi. I'm Asha."

"Stella," Stella said, slipping a hand into Asha's. "You were on the Skype call yesterday, weren't you? Nice necklace, by the way. Love the hearts."

Asha's fingers brushed over the delicate chain at her throat, rattling the cluster of silver heart charms hanging from it. "Yeah, and thanks. Felicity made it for me."

"Wow," Stella said, her eyebrows jutting up. "You made that? You're really talented."

"Thanks." Pride warmed my cheeks. I peeked at Alec, who was smiling and twisting his own piece of my jewelry around his wrist.

A quick pause in the conversation gave Boomer the opportunity to sidle up beside Asha. "Hey, I'm Boomer."

Stella's eyes went wide as she craned her neck. "Hey, nice to meetcha."

"Be careful not to crack any height jokes," JJ said, spinning around on his bar stool. He pointed a finger a Boomer. "That one has a very *short* sense of humor."

I took my bottom lip between my teeth and tried not to laugh. Boomer wasn't the most patient person in the world, and JJ clearly enjoyed pushing anyone and everyone's buttons. I anticipated a scowl or some type of comeback—which, from someone as tall as Boomer, often came off more threatening than it was meant—but instead, he let a breath hiss past the half smile on his lips.

To no one in particular he said, "He's relentless, isn't he?"

The remaining three Heartbreakers chimed in at the same time: "Yeah!"

JJ grinned like he'd won a prize.

Asha opened her mouth again, presumably to barrage the boys with praise and questions, but she was interrupted by a rapid clicking noise. It sounded like a large, clawed monster was charging down the hall in our direction, and I turned in time to see a gray mass gallop into the kitchen from a second entrance. It was a dog, the largest I'd ever seen, and I took a startled step back, accidentally slamming into Alec's chest. He put a steadying hand on my shoulder as the monster-dog hybrid came to a stop in front of us and promptly started barking, the thundering sound reverberating throughout the room.

Oliver turned from the stove. "Poseidon, no barking!" The wooden spoon in his hand was coated with tomato sauce, which splattered on the floor, and in a flash, Poseidon was across the room and cleaning up the drippings.

"Whoa, he's huge," Boomer said. As soon as the words left his mouth, JJ pressed a fist to his lips to contain his amusement.

"Yeah, he's a Great Dane," Oliver said, scratching the dog behind its ears. "Sorry about that. New people intimidate him."

We intimidated him?

After a few more minutes of friendly chatter, dinner was ready.

Oliver had made spaghetti and meatballs—who'd have guessed he could cook?—and Stella added three more place settings to the table for Asha, Boomer, and me. Everyone sat down to eat, and Xander surprised me by dropping into the spot on my left.

"Hey," he said in a tone equally as excited as Stella's had been. "Sorry I didn't get a chance to introduce myself before. I was on salad duty. I'm Xander."

I offered him a warm smile. "Felicity."

Xander Jones instantly put me at ease. He was different from Oliver and JJ in a way I couldn't quite put my finger on. Maybe it was because he seemed more normal—like I could show up for school in August, and he would be sitting in my biology class. His smile teemed with goodwill and friendship, instead of charm and the promise of a wild night.

"So I hear you guys are driving to Seattle?" he said.

On my right, Alec passed me a bowl of steaming noodles.

"We're trying to track down my sister," I answered, scooping a portion onto my plate. When I offered him the serving bowl, he declined with a quick headshake.

Even though he was seated on the opposite side of Alec, JJ must have been listening to our conversation. "How is it possible to *lose* one's sister?" he blurted out.

Both my mouth and thoughts froze at the gall of his question, but before any awkward silence built, Oliver said, "Didn't you lose Jenny in a grocery store once?"

JJ scoffed. "That doesn't count. She ran away from me so I'd get in trouble."

The two proceeded to bicker about the incident, and the discussion quickly developed into an argument about which of JJ's siblings was most annoying. From the way they listed off names, he had a lot.

I glanced at Asha. She was mesmerized by the conversation—an exclusive glimpse into the private lives of the Heartbreakers—and Boomer had to nudge her shoulder a few times before she realized he was holding the bread basket for her. I was grateful the boys' attention was no longer directed at me, because there was no way to answer JJ without the situation getting uncomfortable. I didn't blame him though. He couldn't have known Rose had run away.

"Have you ever been to Seattle?" Xander asked, picking up where we left off while expertly steering away from further tension. "You'll love it. It's one of my favorite cities…"

But I wasn't listening. My mind had shifted to my sister again, and all the pain that came with thinking about her. What if we couldn't find her tomorrow? Or what if we did, and she refused to see me? The possibility was so terrifying my heart felt like it was burning, but not from the searing pain of flames. This was the slow, nerve-tingling ache of frostbite.

A warm hand brushed against the bare skin of my knee, rescuing me from my *what if, what if, what if.*

"Fel?" Alec said softly.

"Yeah?" I asked, and he gestured to my other side with his chin.

I turned. Xander was holding out the salad for me to take. His entire plate was filled with lettuce, so there wasn't much left for me, but I accepted the bowl and emptied the scraps onto my own.

"Thanks," I said, and then without thinking, "Are you on a cleanse or something?" Hopefully he wasn't dieting. The guy was skinny enough as it was.

"No." He laughed. "I'm allergic."

"To what?"

He glanced down at my plate, considering. "Pretty much everything. Well, not the spaghetti sauce, but it'd be weird if I ate that without the noodles and meatballs, dontcha think?"

"Allergic?" I repeated, not because I didn't understand what he meant by it, but because the thought of not being able to eat pasta sounded like a nightmare. Mac and cheese—or any kind of boxed noodle, for that matter—was cheap, which made it a dietary staple in my house.

"Yup. I can't have gluten, nuts, soy, dairy, red meat, or seafood," he said, ticking each item off on his fingers. The cheer in his voice was alarming.

"What *do* you eat?"

"Lots of things. Chicken, eggs, fruit, vegetables. I make a mean smoothie."

For the rest of dinner, Asha bombarded Oliver and JJ with questions with the seriousness of a debate moderator. Unlike Alec, they reveled in the attention, each trying to outdo the other with their answers. On our end of the table, Boomer had roped Xander into a one-sided discussion about cars, while I listened quietly as Stella and Alec discussed someone named Cara.

"How's she doing?" he asked. He'd pushed away his empty plate and was leaning back in his seat, arms folded over his chest.

"Really well," Stella answered. "Just had her annual screening, and she's still in remission."

"I'm so glad to hear that. Does she have any plans now that she's better? Go to college, travel, that sort of thing?"

Stella nodded. "She has a list that's at least twenty miles long."

Their exchange struck a chord with me. I found myself remembering the night I first met Alec, when he admitted he was only at the masquerade because he knew someone *close to the cause*. Whoever Cara was, she had obviously been sick, and I wondered if she was that person.

As if sensing my confusion, Stella said, "Cara, my brother, Drew, and I are triplets. Cara had non-Hodgkin's lymphoma."

"Oh, wow," I exclaimed. "I'm so sorry. That must have been difficult for you."

"It was, but the boys helped me get through it," she said, gesturing at Oliver and the band. "Thankfully she's doing much better now."

"That's good," I said. I didn't know what else I could possibly say.

Thankfully, JJ interrupted, pushing his chair back and standing. "I'm going to put on something dry," he announced. "Maybe we could watch a movie afterward?"

"Good idea," Oliver agreed, throwing his napkin on his plate. "These jeans are seriously starting to chafe."

"Hey, Oliver," Alec said. He glanced over at Asha, Boomer, and me before turning back to his friend. He didn't say anything else, but Oliver caught his drift.

He smiled at us. "I bet you guys want to change too. Let me show you to the guest rooms."

☆ ♭ ♫

After grabbing our bags from the foyer, Oliver led us up the massive front staircase to the second floor. Apparently Alec already knew where he was going, because when we reached the landing, he took a right without waiting for directions, and I wondered how many times he'd been here before.

"See you in a bit," he called to me as Oliver steered the three of us down the opposite hall.

He showed Asha and Boomer to their room first.

Asha peeked at me, as if looking for my approval. It felt weird for them to be sharing, but I flashed my best friend an encouraging thumbs-up. Before they shut the door, we all agreed to meet back in the kitchen in twenty minutes.

Then, it was just me and Oliver.

"About earlier," he said, leading me farther down the hall. "Sorry again for the ambush. If I'd known Alec was bringing you guys, we'd have been more civilized."

It was the first time he'd spoken directly to me, and I took a deep breath as I tried to form a response. There was something about being alone with Oliver that put me on edge, and as I studied him out of the corner of my eye, I realized why. If Alec Williams was day, Oliver Perry was night. His hair—a mop of messy brown waves—was constantly falling into his face, a stark contrast to his bandmate's tidy blond strands. His eyes were sapphire instead of the storm clouds I was so taken with, and unlike Alec, he was outgoing in the way that made boys like him prom king or student body president.

"Well, you didn't have to blast me with the water gun," I teased, remembering his moment of hesitation when he first saw me standing in the entrance hall.

Oliver shrugged, a lazy grin curling on his lips. "I'm an all-or-nothing kind of guy," he said before stopping at a doorway. "Here we are. Hope this works for you."

He held open the door so I could step inside. The space was at least twice the size of my room back home, with a large four-poster bed, a TV sitting area, and an attached bathroom. Looking around, I felt like I was staying at a fancy hotel, not someone's house. What did Oliver's uncle do with so much space?

"Thanks," I said, setting my luggage on the end-of-bed bench. "This is perfect."

I expected Oliver to leave, but he settled against the doorframe. He crossed his arms and looked me over, as if trying to solve a mystery.

"So…you and Alec, huh?" There was that slow grin of his again, the one that made girls weak in the knees. I found it unnerving, and my face went red. Did he know something I didn't?

"We're not together," I told him. It was the second time I'd explained this, but for some reason Alec's friends seemed to think otherwise.

"Maybe not, but there's definitely something going on between you two. It's…intriguing." He rubbed his chin, as if I were a puzzling plot twist in a book he was reading.

"Intriguing?" *Was that a compliment or…?*

"Because you look so much like her," he added.

I ignored the irritation that pulsed in my chest. "You mean Violet James."

He nodded. "You've got a similar face and"—he paused to look me up and down—"well, pretty much everything. Except for her personality, that is. But that's a *huge* improvement in my opinion."

Um, thanks?

"Did they…have a thing?" I felt nosy asking Oliver personal questions about Alec, but he was the one who'd brought it up.

Oliver shrugged. "Alec isn't one to talk about that kinda stuff. They did a scene together in *Immortal Nights*, and they've been friends for awhile, but I don't know anything more than that."

Did a scene together? What did that mean? Like a kissing scene? Something more?

Noticing that I was deep in my own thoughts, Oliver cleared his throat and said, "Anyway, I'll let you settle in." He straightened and pushed away from the jamb. "Think you can find your way back downstairs?"

I nodded.

"Cool. See you in a bit," and then he was gone, closing the door behind him.

For the next few minutes, I stood rooted in the middle of my room, attempting to process everything that had happened during the past two hours.

I tried to regard the situation with a sense of nonchalance, but I'd just had a water fight and eaten dinner with the world's most popular boy band. And now we were all going to watch a movie together. This didn't happen to normal girls. I felt like I'd been written into some cheesy dreams-do-come-true Disney Channel movie—not that my aspiration in life was to share Italian food with the Heartbreakers.

A door slammed down the hall, and the noise jerked me out of my head. Goose bumps rose across my skin as I quickly stripped off my damp dress and discarded it on the floor. The cool air felt euphoric against my sunburned skin. After rummaging through my duffel for a minute, I realized I didn't have anything to wear. The only clean clothes I had were my outfit for tomorrow and a spare camisole. There were also my pajamas—a pair of yoga pants and an oversize Book Nerds Are Sexy T-shirt. I was too embarrassed to wear the tee, so I pulled on the cami. Once I'd finished dressing, I plugged in my phone and freshened up in the bathroom. With nothing left to do, I decided to find my way to the kitchen, even though I still had ten minutes to spare.

Taking a right, I headed back the way I'd come. As I approached the corner, two voices drifted toward me from the hallway.

"...then you should tell her the truth, Alec." It was Stella, her tone high and insistent.

"But it's not like I'm lying to her," came Alec's deep voice. He sounded distressed, and my stomach clenched. I suddenly had the feeling they were talking about me.

"Yeah, well, you're not being honest either. She'll resent you for that."

There was a long pause, and I thought they'd walked away, but then Alec sighed. "What do you expect me to do, Stella? This is my dad we're talking about. He always has to control everything, and I don't want to lose her."

"I already told you what I think you should do," she said. Then, in a softer voice, "I'm sorry, but you know how I feel about your dad. He nearly destroyed my relationship with Oliver."

This conversation was definitely not meant for my ears, and even though I wanted to wait for Alec's response, I felt guilty for listening, so I retreated back to my room before anyone caught me eavesdropping. Collapsing on the bed, I decided to linger for a few minutes to give the two time to finish their talk.

As I stared at the ceiling, I replayed what I'd heard. Neither had mentioned my name specifically, but I couldn't shake the suspicion that I was somehow tangled up in a bigger issue. If that was the case, and Stella thought Alec was being untruthful... I couldn't help but recall the call he'd made this morning.

Does this have something to do with Violet James?

Part of me wanted to be straightforward and ask what was wrong, but I had no desire to admit to listening in. And what if I was completely off base and their conversation had nothing to do with me? Then I'd come off as nosy and presumptuous.

Besides, Alec Williams was not a liar.

Right?

A knock interrupted my internal debate. When I opened the door, Alec was on the other side.

"Hey," he said, stuffing his hands into his front pockets. He was still wearing his khaki shorts, which had dried, but he'd pulled on a fresh shirt and restyled his hair. "You ready? There's something I want to show you."

He smiled, and my heart swelled inside my chest.

With thoughts of Stella and the conversation forgotten, I stepped out into the hall. "Lead the way."

CHAPTER 14

Alec clearly knew his way around Safe House, because he guided me through the mansion without hesitation. I tried to keep track— right, left, down a flight of stairs, left again, through an arched doorway—but the directions began to blur. Eventually we reached a set of stately looking wooden doors with fancy gold handles, and I felt like I was about to enter someplace important, like the Oval Office or the secret meeting hall of the Illuminati.

Lifting his chin, Alec gestured at the room. "After you."

My heart picked up again. I wrapped my fingers around one of the ornate handles and opened the door.

At first, all I could see was black. But then my eyes adjusted to the gloom. We were standing outside a massive library—and an oddly shaped one at that. Rows of towering shelves filled with all sorts of titles stretched in all directions, which made determining the room's exact dimensions difficult. In the center was a collection of armchairs, leather worn dull with use, making it feel like we were visiting a university library instead of someone's private collection. I guess you needed a lot of books as a historian.

I wandered in the direction of the sitting area, my head tipped back as I took in the space.

"Glad you like it," Alec said.

"I didn't say anything."

"You didn't need to," he answered, his voice tinged with amusement. He nodded toward the far end of the room. "Come on. Tour's not over."

As we walked, details emerged from the shadows, the first being an enormous oak desk. It was so solid and heavy looking that I imagined it grew straight out of the polished hardwood floors. There wasn't an inch of work space because the surface was a cluttered mess. The books were the most noticeable, piled haphazardly like Jenga block towers. There were also enough potted plants—from mini ferns to spiky cacti—to form a small tabletop ecosystem. Perched near the front was a shiny nameplate that read *Professor Callum Perry* and was surrounded by an assortment of colored-glass paperweights.

Next to the desk was a floor globe and, behind that, a wall of diamond-paned windows. A standing brass telescope pointed up at the sky, but there was nothing to see outside except for darkness. Not even the moon penetrated the thick cloud coverage. Alec turned on a reading lamp, put both hands on my shoulders, and steered me toward the window seat.

"Wait here," he instructed before disappearing down one of the many aisles.

Taking a spot on the cushion, I noticed a thick book on the seat by the telescope. The binding was battered and worn, so I picked it up and turned to the title page. It wasn't a novel, but an astronomy book. As I waited for Alec, I flipped through the pages, many of which were dog-eared, but one in particular made me pause. It was a section detailing the constellation Hercules, and in the margins next to its picture, someone had scrawled a note:

> You're the song I sing
> You're in every song
> You're in every word I sing
> A constellation of
> And my constellation
> And my star in the dark

I frowned. The poem was somehow familiar, but also not quite right. I stared at the lines until I recognized the words for what they were—song lyrics. And it wasn't just any song. This was part of the chorus to the Heartbreakers most recent hit, "Astrophil."

"Found it!" Alec called, pulling me away from my discovery.

He trotted back into view with a satisfied smile and a paperback clutched in one hand. When he reached the window seat, he sat beside me, his shoulder bumping into mine. In comparison to the first few times we'd sat together, when Alec was careful to put a respectable distance between us, his current ease was so startling that it took me a few seconds to recognize the title.

"Oliver's uncle is more of a nonfiction guy, but I figured he'd have the classics," he said, thumbing through *To Kill a Mockingbird*. "I've been meaning to read it ever since you loaned it to me, but"—he hesitated, lips pressed together to suppress a guilty grin—"last week was a little hectic. Wanna start?"

"You mean like right now?" Weren't we supposed to be watching a movie? Everyone was probably already in the kitchen waiting for us.

"Is that okay?" Alec asked. "Knowing Oliver, he's picked out a James Bond film, and I'm not in the mood."

"Well, you already know I'm more of a *Mission: Impossible* kind of girl," I said. "Although, I'm not one for reading out loud. Maybe we can just read together silently?"

"That's fine," Alec said and turned to the first page.

I looked down and squinted, trying to focus on the opening sentence. It was one of those beautiful first lines, both ominous and deceptive in its simplicity, and if I hadn't already known it by heart, I wouldn't have been able to make out the small font. Alec was sitting inches from me, but I scooted closer until our legs were pressed together.

I felt him look at me.

"Sorry," I muttered, my cheeks prickling with warmth. "I couldn't see."

Alec cleared his throat. "Here." He pressed the book into my hands and moved his arm out of the way, slipping it behind my back and tugging me against him. "That better?"

My body went stiff at the contact. "I... Yeah," I choked out, almost too flustered to speak. A few seconds slipped by, and I relaxed into his side.

Then we read.

Or, in my case, attempted to.

All I could think about was Alec: the way his arm felt wrapped around me, the smell of his cologne, the warmth of his breath on my neck. I willed myself to focus on the book, but it was no use. At my side, Alec's fingers played with the hem of my camisole, and each gentle brush sent a shiver up my back. This went on for a couple of minutes until suddenly his fingers stopped. I tilted my head back to see what was wrong and found him watching me. His sharp eyes searched my own, and I lost myself in their color: stone gray, rain blue, and lightning. I'd never seen a more captivating pair of eyes in my life.

"What do you think?" I spoke each word carefully, so I didn't sound rattled or out of breath, and was relieved when my voice sounded somewhat normal.

His fingers started up again, this time stroking the inside of my wrist, and the simple action made my whole body tremble. "About what?"

"The book."

Alec paused, and I thought he was trying to come up with a polite way to tell me he hated it. "I haven't been able to get much reading done," he admitted.

"Why not?"

"Because of you." He said this plainly and without any reservation, making my heart skip a beat.

I held my breath as he lowered his face toward mine. His eyes fluttered closed, but just before our lips brushed, he pulled back.

"May I?" he asked.

Dear God, yes please! "Mmm-hmm."

I wasn't sure he'd heard my response, but then his head dipped down and—

The feel of his lips was staggering. My hands moved, one reaching up to clutch the fabric at his chest, while the other wrapped around him so my fingers could rake the hair at the nape of his neck.

Way too soon for my liking, Alec broke away. His mouth lifted into a half grin, all lopsided and adorable. "Is this okay?"

It was not okay.

It was better than okay.

Beautiful. Wonderful. Amazing.

There wasn't a word to describe the way his mouth felt on mine. My heart was pounding so hard I was sure he could hear it, and then there was my breathing—shallow and choppy, like I couldn't get enough air into my lungs. I was too jumbled on the inside to answer him, so I nodded my head.

His grin grew. "Good." Then he closed the distance between us again.

This kiss was anything but shy. His lips were hot and demanding, like he'd been waiting for this moment, and when his tongue slipped inside my mouth, I realized I had been waiting too. Alec pushed me back onto the bench so we were lying down, but even with his entire body draped over me, I didn't feel close enough. When his mouth left mine and trailed softly down my neck, I was a goner. My mind hazed over, and all I knew was that I *wanted* him.

And just like that, it was over.

Alec pulled away suddenly, like he realized this was moving too fast for a first kiss, and if we didn't stop soon, we might never.

He sat back, his breathing heavy. "I… Sorry." His voice was raspy, almost regretful, and he lifted a hand, like he was going to run his fingers through his hair, but then stopped and let it fall back to his side.

"I'm not." I pushed myself into a sitting position and patted down my curls. There was absolutely nothing for him to apologize about, except maybe for stopping. Or not kissing me sooner.

This must have eased his guilt because we sat there, timidly grinning at each other, until our smiles faded into reflective silence.

Then Alec said, "So my sister," which was a rather strange conversation starter after a make-out session. "She's getting married at the end of the month, and I thought that maybe—" His phone buzzed, and he jammed a hand into his pocket instead of finishing his sentence. "Hello?" He paused for whoever was on the other end. "Yeah, sorry. We'll be down in five."

"Who was that?" I asked when he hung up.

"Stella. Apparently, everyone is waiting on us."

A deep blush erupted across my cheeks. For the past five minutes, I'd forgotten anyone else existed. As if he was thinking the same thing, Alec grinned and dragged a hand through his bangs. Had I been standing, my knees would have buckled. He was drop-dead sexy, all swollen lips and messy hair.

Outside, the weather had shifted, and the rhythmic patter of the rain against the window helped ease my pulse to a normal rate.

"Well," he said, standing and holding out a hand to help me up. "We should probably go. Otherwise, Stella's going to send a search party."

☆ ♭ ♫

We didn't return to the kitchen.

Instead, Alec led me down another flight of stairs to the basement level, and we entered a large entertainment room. To our left was an air hockey and pool table, and beyond that, an over-the-top flat screen accompanied by movie theater seating. On the other side was a bar with a sparkling granite countertop, glass shelves displaying colorful liquor bottles, and a row of stools. In the corner, a vintage jukebox was blasting "Pour Some Sugar on Me."

A chorus of cheers caught my attention, and I turned toward the small alcove sitting area. Our friends were gathered on two overstuffed couches, and everyone was laughing and pointing at Xander. I watched as he shrugged and took a long chug from the drink in his hand.

"What are they doing?" I asked.

"Playing Most Likely."

"What's that?"

"Watch."

"Your turn!" Stella announced, elbowing Asha in the side. The two were squashed next to each other on the bigger couch, Oliver and Boomer on their respective sides.

Asha displayed a wide grin and pushed a wisp of hair from her eyes that had escaped her braid. "Okay, let me think." Pausing, she looked around until her gaze landed on me. Her grin stretched, and she asked, "Who's most likely to keep someone else's secret?"

On the count of three, everyone turned to me and Alec. Alec's bandmates and Stella were pointing fingers at him, while Boomer and Asha were pointing at me. There was another chorus of laugher. JJ, who was seated closest to us, leaned over the back of the couch and held out his cup to Alec.

"That's four for you, and two for Felicity," he said, grinning at us both.

Stoic as usual, Alec accepted the drink and took four gulps. With a grimace, he wiped his mouth on the back of his hand and passed the glass to me. Before drinking, I made the mistake of sniffing the contents. My nose burned at the smell. It was vodka, which I hated, but everyone was watching me, so I took a deep breath and two small sips.

"Ugh." My mouth puckered, and I shoved the drink back into JJ's hand. "That's awful. Is there anything in there besides alcohol?"

"Does ice count?" he asked, swallowing back his laughter.

I shook my head at him. "That's disgusting."

Across the room, the jukebox flipped records, and another eighties song started playing. The tune was familiar, something my mom would put on when she cleaned the house, but I couldn't think of the title.

"Should we sit down?" Alec asked, loud enough for only me to hear.

His hand found the small of my back, and he guided me over to the last place left to sit, a small loveseat. He plopped down first, and as I shuffled by him toward the other cushion, he took my wrist and tugged me down beside him, nearly in his lap. Boomer's eyes went round while Stella nudged Asha in excitement, but no one was more shocked than me. My cheeks suddenly felt flush, and I wasn't sure if it was an effect of the vodka I'd drunk or Alec's not-so-subtle move.

It was quiet as everybody stared at us, but then Oliver said, "So, you two get lost or something?"

JJ's lips curled in hilarity.

"I was showing Felicity the library," Alec explained.

Among other things...

I could feel Asha's gaze fixed on me, but if I looked at her, my eyes would give away everything that had happened between Alec and me.

Not now, I wanted to tell her. *Not with an audience.*

"You sure, man?" JJ asked. "Your hair's a little messy."

This wasn't true—Alec had smoothed back the stray strands before leaving the library—but he fell for the ruse, his hand flying to his bangs to make sure they were in place, and his friends all roared with laughter.

"You need to be careful with that one," JJ said to Alec, nodding his head at me. "You don't want her to suck your soul out."

"Oh great. A redhead joke," I said, letting out a long sigh. I wasn't as much annoyed with him as surprised it had taken him this long to crack one.

"Don't worry. I have plenty more in the works up here," he said, tapping a finger to his temple. "I've been waiting for the opportune moment. Is it true that you earn a freckle for every soul you steal?"

With an eye roll, I turned to Oliver. "Hey, I found a constellation book on the window seat in the library. There were song lyrics written inside. Is that yours?"

"Oh," he answered, his eye getting big. "Um, yeah. It is. Totally forgot about that."

"A constellation book?" Stella asked, suddenly curious. "What song?"

Reaching an arm over his shoulder, Oliver rubbed the back of his neck. "It's your song," he told her. "I stayed here for a while after we... After everything went down..." His voice trailed off.

I must have brought up something personal or quite possibly painful. I never intended to make him feel uncomfortable. It hadn't even crossed my mind that I could make someone like Oliver Perry feel that way. But I was relieved that everyone's attention was diverted from my prolonged absence with Alec.

Stella smiled at him and snuggled against his side. "I'd love to see it."

"Yeah, sure." He pressed his lips to her forehead. "I'll show you later, okay?"

"As *adorable* as you two are," JJ said, reaching for the vodka bottle set out on the table, "I'd rather not watch any more of this lovefest. Let's move this game along." He looked straight at me. "If you two are going to play, it's time to pick your poison. I make outstanding vodka shots, but the bar is fully stocked as well."

I played with my watch around my wrist and didn't answer. It wasn't like I was a prude. I knew that lots of people my age drank, and I took no issue with them doing so. Sometimes, if Asha dragged me to a party one her cross-country friends was throwing, I'd have a beer. But that didn't happen often.

In the year before she ran away, Rose made a habit of stumbling into our room during the early hours of the morning, wasted from partying. If Mom caught her drunk, it led to screaming matches, so that left thirteen-year-old me to hold back my sister's hair while she puked, change her clothes, and help her into bed. After taking care of her all those times, I didn't find drinking appealing.

Unconsciously, Oliver came to my rescue. "What about the movie?" he asked, frowning in the direction of the TV.

"Nobody wants to watch *Casino Royale*, Oliver," Xander said, throwing one of the couch pillows at him. "Thanks to you, we've seen it a million times."

"Actually, I wouldn't mind," Boomer replied. "There's an Aston Martin DBS in that film."

Oliver beamed. "You like James Bond?"

"He likes *cars*," Asha answered with a snort. And, as if that was reason enough to drink, she held out her cup to JJ, who still had the bottle in hand. He obliged, pouring a shot worth of vodka and sliding it over to her. Without hesitation, Asha threw back the booze in one go.

"That's what I'm talking about," JJ said, rubbing his hands together. "So whose turn is it?"

"I'll go," Alec offered. "Who's most likely to be abducted by aliens?"

"Come on!" Xander grumbled when everyone except me and Asha voted for him. We both pointed at Boomer. "It's like you guys are trying to get me drunk. I'm not putting up with this anymore. It's time for a change of entertainment."

CHAPTER 15

"Why does your team get to be the cops?"

"Because," JJ said. "I'm more manly and overall better looking than you, Xander. Besides, you keep an inhaler in your back pocket."

"I have asthma, not paraplegia," Xander complained. "And what does that have to do with anything?"

Everyone was gathered outside on the back patio of Safe House, and a few feet away from us, JJ and Xander were arguing. The rain had stopped, but the air still had a heavy wetness to it, and every time I took a breath, I felt like my lungs had been hooked up to a humidifier. Not wanting my curls to frizz, I twisted my hair up into a bun.

"Maybe you should decide by seniority," Boomer suggested. He was standing between the two boys, arms crossed over his chest like a referee. All he needed was a whistle.

"In that case, I still win," JJ announced.

Xander threw up his hands. "No way is that fair! You picked first so you could have Oliver on your team. I should at least get to decide whether we're the good guys or the bad guys."

"Is it just me," I whispered, leaning in so only Asha could hear me. "Or do they act like a bunch of little kids?"

I wasn't merely referring to the Heartbreakers' inability to make decisions without squabbling, but their choice of entertainment. Back in the basement, after deciding that Most Likely had run its course, Oliver suggested we play Cops and Robbers.

Outside.

At night.

In the creepy forest that I wasn't entirely convinced was devoid of vampires and other nightmarish creatures.

I'd never heard of the game, and when Oliver detailed the rules, it sounded like a giant game of team tag. Something kids did for fun at recess, not a group of almost adults. Both Oliver and JJ were horrified I'd never played before, claiming I'd missed out on some childhood rite of passage. Maybe it was because I didn't have memories of hanging with the neighbor kids to reminisce over, but the game sounded dreadful to me. There was nothing fun about running. Nothing.

Despite this, tag was preferable to starting another drinking game, so I'd grudgingly agreed.

"Maturity isn't their strong suit," Stella said, answering my question.

Asha and I turned at the sound of her voice. I hadn't realized anyone else was listening, but there she was, standing a few feet away from us, eyes gleaming with amusement.

"I think that's why people like them," Asha said, unabashed that we'd been caught talking about our hosts. "They're real, you know? Just four guys who like to goof off and have fun."

"Yeah," Stella agreed. "It's part of their charm."

"Are you talking about us?" Alec asked, stepping up behind her.

Stella jumped at his sudden appearance and pressed a hand

against her chest. "Jesus! I hate it when you do that." The grin on Alec's face confirmed he knew this, but that he enjoyed scaring the crap out of her more.

"Okay, *okay*!" JJ exclaimed, putting his hands up in defeat. "My team will be the robbers. I make a more ruggedly handsome villain anyway."

"Good, let's start," Stella said. She made a show of covering her eyes and announced, "Robbers have until the count of sixty to get out of here, starting now. One, two, three…"

Oliver and JJ both darted into the night, and that was my cue to leave as well.

"Come on, let's go," Asha said, ushering me down the stone steps.

Glancing back over my shoulder, I stared longingly at the warm light cast around the patio and the four people who stood there. We'd been divided into two teams: JJ, Oliver, Asha, and myself versus Xander, Alec, Boomer, and Stella. I felt bad when JJ picked me second after Oliver, claiming I "looked like a runner," since my athletic skills were dismal at best.

"Keep up, ladies," Oliver called from somewhere ahead of us.

And from behind "…eight, nine, ten…"

I hurried after Asha as she sped across the slick grass, not wanting to lose her. The backyard floodlight only illuminated a small part of the expansive lawn, and the farther we got from the house, the thicker the darkness around us grew. Finally we hit the tree line, and according to Oliver, there was a fence about twenty yards in that served as our boundary for the game. He and JJ were crouched at the base of a huge ash tree, talking game logistics.

"I think it's strategically best if we stick to the trees," JJ was saying. We went over and joined them.

"We should also split up," Oliver said. "Make it harder for them to find us."

Jeez. They were taking themselves way too seriously.

"Are you fast?" JJ asked us.

"Asha is," I said, proudly jabbing a finger in her direction. "Me? Not so much."

"Dang," Oliver said. "Maybe you can find somewhere to hide."

"Yeah, sure," I said, even though the last, *absolute last* thing I wanted to do was wait around by myself in the dark for someone—or something—to find me. I rubbed my hands up and down my arms.

"Are you cold?" JJ asked.

Whoa. Was that actual concern I detected in his voice?

"I'll be fine," I said, ignoring the goose bumps climbing my bare arms. "I'm just not a big fan of running. Or creepy, dark forests."

"Here, take this."

He unzipped his hoodie and yanked it off. When he held it out to me, my brain took a good second to process what was happening. *JJ* was actually being amicable instead of cracking some smart-ass joke.

"Um, thanks," I said and tugged it on. It was way too big for me, and the sleeves hung well past my fingertips, but it was soft on the inside and smelled of citrus from his cologne. "You didn't have to do that."

"Don't worry about it," he said with a shrug.

I half expected him to make a pervy joke about how obvious it was that I was freezing, or maybe something about him not needing an extra layer because he was hot-blooded, but he turned back to Oliver, his attention already refocused on the game at hand.

"So, Felicity," Oliver said. "Are you by any chance good at climbing trees?"

☆ ♭ ♫

"You're kidding, right?" I looked up at the gnarled oak that towered over us. Oliver followed my gaze but didn't seem concerned about the branches twisting in the wind. Which was probably because he wasn't the one who would be risking his life. No, he was offering up mine instead. "You can't actually expect me to climb this thing."

"I was kind of hoping you would," he said. "I'm not big on losing."

This was getting ridiculous. If I'd known Alec's friends would get this competitive over a game of tag, I'd have stayed in the basement drinking vodka and watching James Bond.

"Yeah, well, I'm not big on broken bones."

"Come on," he said. "It's not that high. I'll give you a boost." And there was that Oliver Perry smile again—one part charm, one part magic, and a whole lot of confidence.

But it wasn't going to work. Not on me.

I crossed my arms. "Not going to happen."

Oliver's eyebrows dipped together, and he ran a finger over his lip. "What if I can get JJ to stop with the redhead jokes?"

"Can you guarantee that?"

The grin returned. "Most definitely. You wouldn't believe half the dirt I have on him."

"Fine," I agreed. "But no more comments about Boomer's height. Or making fun of me and Alec." My checks turned pink when I added the last condition, but I knew it was too dark for Oliver to see the color on my face.

"Are you negotiating?"

I started to smile, amused that my rebuff had caught him off guard, but then I looked up at the tree and the feeling quickly faded. I gritted my teeth. "Sure am."

"Okay." His voice was cheerful, like he was glad I'd challenged him and held my ground. "You got yourself a deal."

He took a step closer to the oak, which was either my soon-to-be hiding spot or the place of my last moments on earth, and cupped his hands together, making a cradle for my foot. Since putting him on the spot about the constellation book, I didn't feel as uncomfortable around Oliver as I had when he showed me to the guest room. His moment of self-consciousness revealed he wasn't as imposing as I'd made him out to be, but I was about to put myself in his hands—*literally*—and that made my nerves returned.

"Felicity?" His hands locked together, and he glanced over at me, expectantly.

"Sorry." I sucked in a quick breath and tried to settle my thoughts. I could do this, pretend that the guy boosting me up into a terrifying tree wasn't *the* celebrity of my generation and hide in said terrifying tree all by myself.

All this trouble to win a stupid game.

I stepped into Oliver's hands, putting one of my own on his shoulder for support, and then kicked off the ground, driving myself upward to reach for the lowest branch. He helped lift me, and I managed to wrap my fingers around the rough bark and hoist myself up. It took me a few seconds to arrange myself, but then, panting, I settled against the trunk.

"Hey, guys," I heard Asha's voice call from somewhere in the small clearing. She and JJ had spread out to keep watch. "They're coming. Let's get out of here."

Oliver craned his neck and tried to find me in the dark above. "You good?" he asked.

I sucked in another breath. "I think so."

"Okay, shout if there's a problem," he instructed me. "Otherwise, we'll come back to get you once time's up." Then he was gone, disappearing into the charcoal shadows with the skill of a well-trained spy.

Sitting by myself in the tree wasn't nearly as scary as I'd first thought it would be. I listened to wind play with the leaves and enjoyed the fresh scents of the night. Unlike in LA, the air here smelled clean. Like pine needles and something sweet, and I couldn't get enough of it into my lungs.

At one point, Boomer and Xander ran through the glade together, passing straight under my tree, but I stayed completely still and held my breath, and neither of them spotted me.

More time passed, so much so that I wondered if I'd been forgotten, left to find my own way down from the oak tower. Somewhere in the foliage nearby, a bird screeched, causing my pulse to spike.

The woods grew quiet again, but this time, it didn't feel as inviting as before. I made up my mind to call out for help like Oliver had told me, but then I saw a flash of something white that made me reconsider. I squinted. It was Alec's platinum hair. He was jogging along the edge of the clearing, scanning the open space, and the path he was on would inevitably lead him right to me.

As soon as he was close enough, I called his name. "Alec!"

By giving my position away, I knew my team would lose, but unlike Oliver and JJ, I couldn't care less about winning Cops and Robbers. Oliver would be mad, considering the deal we made, but our agreement was to get me *up* the tree. It said nothing of what I could or couldn't do once I was in it.

Alec stopped short. "Hello?" He turned his head left and right. "Stella, is that you?"

"Up here."

His head snapped back. "*Felicity?*"

"Hi."

"What are you doing in a tree?"

"Ah, hiding?" I offered. Although technically, I wasn't doing a good job of it.

He shook his head once, then, after taking a few steps back, he ran forward, leaped up, and hooked his hands around my branch. He hung there for a moment, waiting for his body to stop swinging back and forth, before heaving himself up and throwing a leg over the solid oak limb.

When he was finally situated across from me, his mouth tugged into a wolflike grin. "Looks like I've found myself a little bird."

I let out a little laugh. "Far from it. I definitely didn't fly up here on my own."

"Meaning…?"

"Oliver had to boost me up. And let me tell you…that was no easy feat, not to mention scary. I have no clue how I'm going to get down."

"What made you decide it was a good idea to climb up here in the dark?" he asked.

"Well, I didn't do a stellar job of selling Oliver on my running abilities, so he thought it best that I hide instead," I told him. "Your friend is insanely competitive."

"And you actually agreed to that?"

"Not exactly. Let's just say we came to an arrangement."

Alec looked at me in suspicion. "What kind of arrangement?"

"Unfortunately, I'm not at liberty to tell," I said with a grin. In all honesty, I didn't want to explain the deal to Alec or, more specifically, the final part of it—that the boys had to stop teasing him about me. By asking that of Oliver, I'd practically admitted something was going on between us. Which, after that kiss, I couldn't deny any longer. But Alec and I had yet to talk about what'd happened, and I didn't want to get ahead of myself. "How about you help me down and we forget I ever climbed up here?"

"I will," he said, "but not until they're done chasing each other around." He pulled his phone from his pocket and checked the time. "There are still ten minutes left in the game. Until then, I like you right where you are."

I raised an eyebrow. "Is that so?"

Nodding, Alec inched himself forward on the branch. "I figure since you're stuck up here…" He trailed off, a smile lighting up his lips as he lifted his shoulder in a partial shrug.

Then he leaned forward and pressed his mouth to mine. The kiss was gentle, his lips like a whisper, and whether that was for safety reasons or because he was trying to control himself, I couldn't tell. One of his hands stayed on the branch for support, but the other slid into my hair.

I wanted to move closer, to drape my arms around his neck, but I kept my back pressed firmly against the tree trunk so I wouldn't fall. It didn't take long before I lost myself in the kiss—his fingers tangled in my curls, the pounding of my heart, a prickle of stubble as his chin brushed mine—and my hands unwittingly moved up and touched his jaw.

As my balance shifted, my stomach wobbled, and I pulled away to steady myself again. "This seems highly dangerous," I said.

"All right, fine." Alec made a point of grumbling, but there was a smirk hidden under his fake exasperation. "I *suppose* I'll help you down."

☆ ♭ ♫

When my feet were firmly planted on the ground, Alec and I decided to lie out in the middle of the clearing. The grass was dewy from the recent rain, and the clouds made it impossible to see the night sky, but I didn't mind. He had an arm wrapped around me, the other folded behind his head, and I was using his shoulder as a pillow. Bugs buzzed in my ear and my yoga pants got damp, but it was nice relaxing together.

"That isn't your sweatshirt, is it?" he asked, tugging on the material.

I shook my head. "I was cold, so JJ loaned his to me." I paused, surprised by the words about to come out of my mouth. "I'll admit, your friends aren't *that* bad."

He laughed, his whole upper body shaking. "They might be obnoxious and immature, but they're all heart and grow on you quickly."

"Yeah," I said. "Stella's super nice too." Since we were already on the subject, I took a deep breath and said, "You and she seem close."

I felt Alec shift. "We are. In some ways, we're very similar, so we've always understood each other."

Whatever similarities he was talking about were lost on me. Stella seemed more like Oliver, outgoing and not afraid to speak her mind, but I suppose I didn't know her well enough to understand.

"You liked her," I guessed.

"When we first met?" He sighed. "Maybe a little. But it was Oliver and her from the start, and it never felt…like this."

I couldn't help it—I inhaled sharply. I wasn't sure why I was so surprised to hear him acknowledge that he felt something between us. Maybe it was because ever since discovering who he was, the idea of us being together—or an us *anything*—was so unimaginable that I did my best to suppress the thought.

"What *is* this?" I asked with bated breath.

At first, he didn't answer, and I willed myself not to fidget. "I'm not sure," he answered honestly. "But I, uh, never finished what I was saying in the library. About Vanessa's wedding."

"Yeah?"

"Would you maybe…be my plus one?"

"Me?" I lifted myself slightly, turning my head to look at him. "I mean, you really want me to go with you?" Going to his sister's wedding was pretty intense first-date material.

"Yeah." He pulled me closer, and I could feel the heat of his body bleeding through JJ's sweatshirt. "I really do."

Before I could shake my surprise and formulate a response, Alec's phone alarm beeped, signaling the end of the game. A few seconds later, several shouts rang through the woods as our friends regrouped. After that, it didn't take long for Oliver, followed closely by everyone else, to find his way back to my tree.

"If nobody found Felicity," he was saying, "then we win." He came to a stop at the base of the oak and tipped his head back. "Felicity, you okay up there?"

"Over here," I called as Alec and I made our way across the clearing.

His face fell when he saw us together. "Damn, he got you?"

I hesitated, not sure how to explain that I'd given myself up, but Alec answered for me. "Well," he said, smirking at the group. "Not *technically* speaking."

Xander frowned. "What's that supposed to mean?"

"I never officially tagged Felicity," he clarified. "Robbers win."

Oliver let out a celebratory victory whoop and pumped his fist in the air.

"But you two were together…" Xander said, his brows still drawn together in confusion.

"Let it go, X-Man," JJ responded, slinging an arm around his friend's shoulder. "The superior team clearly triumphed."

X-Man held up a finger like a lawyer about to argue his case but then sighed and dropped his hand. "Whatever." He shook his head. "I'm not even going to bother."

From behind, Oliver wrapped his arms around Stella. "Does the victor get a kiss?" he mumbled against her neck.

"Only if we're done reliving your childhood memories," she said. "This game is ridiculous, and it's freezing out here."

☆ ♭ ♪♪

There was a wide smile on Xander's face as he slid open the back door and stepped out onto the patio. In his hand was an acoustic guitar. "Found it!"

The rest of us were gathered by the built-in fire pit, warming ourselves after the damp chill of the forest.

"Where was it?" Oliver asked. He was sharing one of the wicker patio chairs with Stella, who was snuggled into his lap.

"In the living room, right where you said." Xander gave the instrument a quick strum and fiddled with one of the tuning pegs. "Any requests?"

Stella pushed her boyfriend's bangs back and smiled. "I wanna hear my song."

Oliver inclined his head. "We can do that."

I inched forward on my seat.

Everyone had been talking around the fire when Alec announced that we needed music. Which, in turn, had prompted Asha to ask if the band could play some of their songs. Now here we were, about to get our own private performance from the Heartbreakers.

A moment of silence passed when all I could hear was the *crackle, pop* of the wood as it burned. I watched Alec in anticipation. He'd retrieved his own guitar from the trunk of the Cadillac, and I was eager to see him in action. JJ started first, magically producing a pair of drumsticks from the waistband of his jeans as if he never went anywhere without them. He had no drum set, but created a simple rhythm against the brick of the patio. Xander and Alec joined in next, strumming a familiar melody. They worked through a few verses before Oliver finally added his voice to the mix.

"'Sometimes the things left unsaid are deadly like bullets and knives,'" he sang. "'Mine cut you deep, girl. We had no chance to survive.'" His voice was gruffer when he sang, but it sounded good with the stripped-down version of the song.

I listened to the performance as intently as I could, but mainly I was focused on Alec.

I loved how he held the guitar as if it were an extension of himself, and the way his fingers maneuvered over the strings. He made it look so easy, as if anyone could sit down and learn how to play in an afternoon. I loved that he closed his eyes and lost himself in the playing, like it was only him and the music. And God, I loved the way his lips moved as he mouthed the lyrics.

"Astrophil" came to an end, and the boys played some of their more upbeat stuff before covering a couple of hits by other artists.

Asha clapped when they finished their final song. "That was awesome, guys."

With a flourish of his drumsticks, JJ bowed. "Our aim is to please. Glad you enjoyed."

It felt like the perfect end to a long day, sitting by the fire and enjoying good music. But something must have been wrong, because Oliver's eyes were narrowed in concentration, as if he were trying to dredge up a long-forgotten memory from the back of his mind.

"Babe, what's up?" Stella asked him.

"Nothing. It's just… I can't remember the last time we played around like this."

"Neither do I," Alec said. "But we should more often."

Everyone nodded in agreement.

"Well, as much fun as this has been, I'm exhausted." Xander yawned and rubbed an eye, nudging his glasses askew. "I think it's time for me to call it a night. It was nice to meet you guys," he said to me, Asha, and Boomer. "I'll see everyone in the morning."

After Xander, people slipped off to bed one by one. When Asha and Boomer vacated the love seat, Alec and I moved over so we could sit next to each other. Before long, only three of us were left.

"Hey, Felicity. I've got a question," Oliver said. "You know that necklace you made for Asha? The one Stella liked?"

I lifted my head off Alec's shoulder. "Yeah. What about it?"

"I've been struggling to come up with a gift idea for our anniversary, but the necklace is perfect. Could you maybe replicate it, but swap out the hearts for stars? I'll pay for the supplies and your time."

"Really?" I asked, sitting up straight. Oliver wanted to give me actual money to make jewelry? This had to be some kind of prank.

"Uh-huh. And maybe earrings to match?" He fiddled with the dog tag around his neck, sliding it back and forth on its chain. "Or would that be cheesy?"

"No, they'd be super cute. And if she doesn't want to be matchy matchy, she can wear them separately. Do you know if she likes dangle, chandelier, or studs?" I was talking a mile a minute, caught up in the thrill of a fresh project. I still had to finish my mockingbird, but that could wait. The promise of a real commission had my whole body buzzing.

"Ah...studs?" Oliver said, and Alec nodded in agreement.

"When do you need them by?" I asked. "And how should I get them to you?" I doubted I'd ever see Oliver after this weekend, so I figured it would be best if we hammered out the logistics of our transaction now.

Oliver shrugged. "Not for a few months, so it's no rush. I'm sure we'll all get together before that, and if not, you can always give them to Alec for me." His response was so casual, like it was a no-brainer that our paths would cross again. Because of Alec. Because he assumed *I would be with Alec*. The thought made my chest feel light.

"Just in case, here." He took my phone. When he handed it back to me, there was a new name in my contact list—007. "Text me if you have any questions."

"Perfect," I said, unable to believe my luck.

"Thanks, Felicity. I really appreciate this," he told me. "You should consider selling your stuff. Clueless boyfriends everywhere would be grateful." Then Oliver stood and stretched both arms over his head. "Anyway, I'm beat. See you both tomorrow."

And just like that, Alec and I were alone.

"Are you excited?" he asked, shifting on the seat to pull me closer.

"Considering I'm getting paid to do something I love, *hell yeah*," I said, no longer able to contain my glee.

"This could be a regular thing, you know. Oliver's right. Lots of people would buy your jewelry." Alec gave a one-shoulder shrug in an attempt to sound offhanded, but I could tell he was alluding to our earlier conversation about college and my future. *See?* he was saying. *More confirmation that I'm right. Forget law school and the pantsuits. Go after your dreams!*

But he was too polite for an *I told you so,* so I mumbled a quick "thanks" and made a point of switching up the conversation. "You were really good tonight," I told him. "How long have you been playing?"

"King started teaching me when I turned eight."

"Your dad plays?"

"Used to. He was amazing, but he's not really into music anymore."

A frown crossed my face. King Williams was the CEO of Mongo Records. How could he *not* be into music? "How come?"

Alec's entire body tensed, and his lips remained clenched for so long that I was afraid my question had offended him. But finally he said, "My dad lost sight of why he started the label in the first place. All he cares about now is making money. Music has nothing to do with it."

"Is that why your relationship with him is complicated?" I asked. "Because of music?" It was hard to imagine that the main source of joy in Alec's life also doubled as the strain between him and his father.

"In part," he said, his voice taking on a sudden edge.

The fire was dying down, and I watched as one of the logs broke apart, collapsing the pile. "And the other part?"

He sighed and raked a hand through his hair, disheveling his always-perfect bangs. "It's not a big deal."

Why don't I believe you? The question must have been visible in my expression because Alec's face softened and he smiled at me.

"Seriously, Felicity. Don't worry about it. The only thing you should concentrate on right now is your sister. Do you know what you're going to say to her?"

It was an obvious subject change, but one with a solid point. Tomorrow I was hopefully—no, *finally*—going to see Rose. The realization made my chest hurt, and I couldn't tell if that pressure was the result of anxiety, elation, or pure terror. Probably a combination of all three.

"I'm not sure." What did one say when they located a long-lost relative? I've missed you? What's up? Where the hell have you been?

None of those seemed eloquent to me.

"Why don't you sleep on it?" He stood before helping me up. "Come on. We should go to bed. You'll have time to think about it in the car tomorrow."

CHAPTER 16

The next morning, my phone buzzed violently on the bedside table, and I jolted awake. I'd forgotten to pull the curtains shut, and although it wasn't California sunny, the natural light filtering in through the window made me blink and rub my eyes. I glanced at my watch. It wasn't even seven.

Ugh. Why is anyone calling this early?

Alec and I had stayed up talking until two, and my body felt drained after such a late night. Still half-asleep, I stretched across the bed toward the nightstand. Right as my fingers brushed against my cell, the buzzing stopped.

Much better.

I burrowed back into the blankets. My alarm wasn't set to go off for another two hours, and I didn't want to waste another minute of my allotted sleep time. But before I could fade back into unconsciousness, the buzzing started again.

"Seriously?" I groaned, throwing off the covers and snatching my cell. What could be so important that someone needed to get ahold of me *right now*? I looked down at the caller ID and my heart sunk into my stomach.

It was my mom.

I'd expected a call from her today, but not this early. She hadn't planned to be home until late. When Asha, Boomer, and Alec convinced me to push on to Seattle, I knew I'd have to tell her I'd left LA. But I'd been hoping to put that off until Monday. My plan had been to say I was sleeping at Asha's tonight, then call her tomorrow after I found Rose. Looked like I'd have to fess up now.

I sucked in a small breath and pressed the talk button. "Mom, hi."

"Hey, baby!" She was unusually upbeat, which I took as a positive sign. Maybe she wouldn't get too upset about my road trip if she was in a good mood. "Your room's empty. Are you at Asha's? I know I wasn't supposed to get back from Dave's until after dinner, but we have some exciting news that I couldn't wait to share."

My shoulders slumped. "So you're at home?"

"Yup. Dave's making breakfast for us. Why don't you have Mr. Van de Berg drive you home, and I'll tell you all about it over bacon and pancakes."

"I'm not at Asha's," I told her.

"Are you working a shift at the diner?" she asked. Then, "Do you want the Italian roast or the French?"

I frowned, unsure why the subject had suddenly changed to coffee, but then I realized she was talking to Dave and not me. I sighed and switched the phone to my other ear. It was time to get this over with, to face the truth whether I was ready to hear it or not. "I found the letters, Mom."

There was a long pause on her end. My pulse picked up, and I pressed my hand to my heart as if it could slow the pounding.

"Honey, what are you talking about?" Mom said at last.

The knot in my chest unraveled a bit, her answer giving me hope that she was as clueless as I had been, that there was no way she could lie about something this big.

"The letters Rose wrote to me?" I was trying to sound calm, but my voice crept up an octave. I could no longer ignore the dread I'd been feeling since the discovery. "They were hidden under your bed."

More silence. Finally, "What were you doing in my bedroom?"

There was no denial in her response. "So you knew?" I whispered. "You knew she was writing to me?"

My mom heaved a sigh. "You don't understand, Felicity. It's more complicated than you think."

I tried to wrap my mind around what she was saying, wondering if I'd misheard her even though I knew I hadn't. "How could you do this?" I exclaimed. My dread was quickly heating to sizzling anger.

"Felicity, baby," she said, and I could picture her leaning against the kitchen counter, dragging her fingers through her bangs.

"Don't!" I snapped. "You pretended you didn't know where Rose was for *four* years. You let me think that she didn't want anything to do with us. With *me*."

"But I didn't always know where she was and—"

"I don't care," I countered, not giving her a chance to explain. "You knew she was okay, that she was alive, and you didn't tell me!"

"You're right," she said. "I kept this from you because I was trying to protect you. I know you're upset right now, but let's not do this over the phone. Come home, and I'll tell you everything."

Too flustered to sit still any longer, I leaped out of bed, hardly blanching when my bare feet hit the cold wooden floor. In fact, I welcomed the cold—it helped cool the flush spreading through my body. If she thought she could gain ground with me by admitting the truth, she was so wrong.

"I'm not coming home, Mom," I said, fuming. "Not until I talk to Rose."

"Felicity." From the tightness in her voice it sounded as if she was on the verge of crying. "Where are you?"

I glanced out the window at the backyard. Now that it was daylight, the long stretch of forest wasn't as foreboding as it had been last night.

"You know that boy you didn't want me to see? The musician who drove me home from the masquerade?" I knew what I was going to say would upset her, but I didn't care. I wanted my mom to hurt, to feel the same anger I was feeling, so I flung my words at her. "I'm with *him*. He's helping me find Rose." Not waiting for a response, I punched the end button and chucked my phone on the bed. Three seconds later, it started buzzing, but I ignored the call.

My whole body trembled.

Ever since Rose ran away, I'd felt protective of my mom because I was all she had left. Everyone else had deserted her. I thought our mother-daughter bond had been strengthened by adversity. It was the two of us taking on the world. That she could deceive me like this seemed inconceivable.

Maybe, deep down, I knew my mom had been lying to me when I found the letters. And maybe I'd overlooked that deception because acknowledging she'd kept me from my sister meant that all the choices I'd made since Rose ran away—choices about school and my future, choices that made me who I was today—were based on a devastating lie. All of a sudden, I felt an overwhelming sense that I'd lost a part of myself, like a bunch of little pieces that defined me were slipping away.

Yesterday morning, after I found Asha and Boomer together, I mistook my feelings of surprise and confusion for betrayal. At the time, I didn't have a real understanding of the emotion.

Now I did.

I couldn't move.

I couldn't think.

I couldn't stop the silent sobs that racked my body.

This was what real betrayal felt like.

Asha's best-friend telepathy must have kicked in, because there was a knock at the door and she poked her head inside. "Hey, Fel. You up?" She glanced at the bed first, and then gasped when she spotted me crying by the window. "Oh hell, what's wrong? Something totally happened, didn't it?" she asked as she stepped inside and closed the door behind her.

Unable to answer, I merely nodded my head.

"What is it?" she demanded. "Did that boy hurt you? Because you know Boomer and I will kick his ass if he did." Her gaze flickered over me, from my face to my feet and back up again, as if she was scanning for signs of bodily harm.

"What are you talking—" I stopped short. By boy, she meant *Alec*. "No, of course not! How could you think something like that about him?"

Asha winced. "I'm sorry. You're right. He's a total sweetheart, isn't he? It's just... The last time I saw you, you were with him, and now you're crying, so I'm freaking out and jumping to conclusions," she blurted out, waving her hands about in a manic fashion. "Besides, I doubt I'd be able to follow through with a promise like that. Not that I wouldn't want to defend you or anything. I don't think I could actually kick someone's ass and—"

The next thing I knew, I was trying to calm down Asha, instead of the other way around. Her rambling had snapped me out of whatever spell I was under. I put both hands on her shoulders, giving her a little shake. "Hey, it's okay," I told her. "You don't have to apologize." There were still tears trickling down my cheeks, and my heart felt like it had a hole in it, but somehow, comforting Asha brought me back to myself.

"Right. I'm going to stop acting like a crazy woman now, and you're going to tell me what happened." Her fingers snaked around my wrist, and she pulled me over to the bed where we sat cross-legged on the comforter. "Okay, so what's this non-Alec problem you're having?"

I squeezed my eyes shut, pressing the heels of my palms against them as I searched for an answer. It wasn't that I didn't know what to say, but that it would hurt even more to admit the truth out loud. "My mom called," I said after a long moment.

"Oh, Fel," Asha replied, her face falling. "She knew about the letters, didn't she?"

The stinging returned to my eyes, and I bit down on my cheek to keep from crying, though it didn't help at all. "Yeah," I managed to get out, and it wasn't until her arms wrapped around me, pulling me into a hug, that I realized my face was wet again.

Without a word, Asha held me until I ran out of tears. My whole body felt spent, like I'd made the trip from LA to Portland on foot and hadn't slept in days.

"Why would she do this to me?" Mom knew how it felt to be abandoned. How could she put me through the same kind of pain?

"You know how moms are," Asha said in attempt to come up with a logical answer, although we both knew there wasn't one. "She probably thought it was best for you."

I swiped at my cheeks with the back of my hand, trying to get rid of the swollen, post-cry feeling. "How is keeping me from Rose best for me? That doesn't make sense."

"I'm not saying it was the right thing to do. Obviously she was wrong, but Rose *did* leave you guys. Maybe your mom thought the letters would only remind you she'd left, and that it would be less painful if she was out of your life instead of on the fringe of it."

Fighting the sigh her words elicited, I turned back to the window and stared out at the clouded sky. Asha meant well, but she didn't understand. Her family was perfect—tight knit, passionate, and most importantly, whole. When it came to her sister, the worst Asha had to worry about was whether or not Riya had stolen her favorite sweater and shrunk it in the wash.

"The most difficult part about these past four years wasn't that Rose left," I said, trying to explain in a way that would resonate with Asha. "It was the uncertainty: Is she okay? Will I ever see her again? Is she even alive? The not knowing kept me up at night. I'd rather have heard the truth, even if it hurt, than to always wonder what happened."

Asha considered this. "Yeah, I guess I'd rather know too," she agreed. "Your mom give you any kind of explanation?"

"No," I said. "She wanted me to come home so we could talk."

"And what did you say?"

"I…ah…kinda hung up on her." I didn't feel bad about this exactly—I was still too upset to feel guilty—but I felt weird admitting what I'd done. We both knew how out of character it was for me to be disrespectful to my mom.

Asha leaned toward me, hair spilling over her shoulder like liquid midnight. "You did not!" she gasped, her eyes widening.

"I know, I know." My mouth curved into a shadow of a grin. "First I leave on a cross-state road trip without telling her, and now this? Perhaps Rose and I are more alike than I thought."

"Oh yeah," Asha said, her gaze flicking heavenward. "You're turning into a regular rebel. Soon you'll be committing grand theft auto and planning diamond heists."

"Well, at least then I'd be able to afford Stanford."

I flopped backward onto my pillow. I knew I sounded bitter. I could taste the acid of my words on my tongue, and I didn't want Asha to think it was directed at her. "Hey," I said, twisting my head so I could catch her eye. "Thank you. For being here and for not saying I told you so."

"I would *never*," she said, biting back amusement, but we both knew that under normal circumstances, like if my heart hadn't been ripped from my chest, she most definitely would. She enjoyed being right. "So…you and Alec," she continued, changing the subject and letting go of the rein on her smile. Her eyebrows wiggled up and down. "*Nothing* happened between you guys? Last I saw, you were looking pretty cozy."

A flush crept up my neck. "Like I said. Nothing happened after everyone went to bed."

Asha raised a single brow. "And before that?"

More warmth flooded my face, and since my own pale complexion had betrayed me, I knew there was no point in lying. "We, um, may have made out once or twice."

I expected her usual over-the-top reaction—a shocked *shut up* to start off, maybe a few *oh my Gods*, and definitely some excited squealing. Instead, her lips parted to speak, but no sound came out for several seconds. "I can't believe you actually kissed *him*," she finally murmured, like he was some kind of mythical being we hadn't spent the past two days with.

"Not this again." I groaned. "I thought you'd gotten all the fangirling out of your system?" I wanted to talk with my best friend about the guy I'd kissed, not a fan of the Heartbreakers who couldn't look past the fact that he was part of the band.

Yesterday, after Alec showed me the library, I kept what happened between us a secret from Asha, convincing myself it was because there were too many people around to have a private conversation. I wasn't ready to deal with Boomer's protectiveness or, heaven forbid, JJ's teasing. Now, as a smile spread over her face, I realized that maybe I'd kept quiet for a different reason.

Ignoring my question, Asha asked, "Do you know how many

girls would give a kidney to trade places with you right now? This is an entirely new level of awesome!" She pressed a hand to her chest as if she were trying to hold back her excitement.

"Yeah, because having an estranged dad, a missing sister, and a traitorous mom is cause for jealousy."

"That's not what I meant," she said with a pointed look. "Regular girls like us don't date celebrities, Felicity. You're living every fangirl's dream."

This wasn't the first time I'd heard how I was lucky, that Heartbreakers devotees around the world would do anything to be in my position. But I couldn't let myself think like that. I didn't want Alec's fame to affect my view of who he was. "First of all, we're not dating," I said, repeating myself for the millionth time. "And second, please don't make a big deal out of whatever this is. I get that to everyone else he's this super-famous musician, but to me... I don't know. He's just Alec."

Asha heaved one of her long, dramatic sighs. "That's possibly the most romantic thing I've ever heard."

I snorted. "You think everything is the most romantic thing you've ever heard."

The smile on her face went stiff before slowly fading, and she collapsed beside me on the second pillow. "Not everything."

Her abrupt mood change left me feeling whiplash, and I pushed myself up so I could see her properly. "What do you mean?"

She pulled a blanket over her face. "Nothing. Never mind."

"Asha, you're literally the worst liar in the world." I yanked the blanket away, and she peeked up at me. "Tell me what's going on."

At first she didn't respond, but then Asha bit her lip and mumbled, "Boomer and I, we kinda… We did it last night."

Whoa. That was the last thing I'd expected to come out of her mouth.

"You mean…you haven't before now?" I asked. When I caught them in bed together at Kelsey's, I'd gotten the impression they'd moved well beyond the kissing stage in their relationship.

She shook her head. "We've done stuff before, but never *it*, and now I'm sorta freaked out. What if this changes things between us? What if Boomer…" She let her fear go unfinished, but I flinched regardless.

"For the sake of my sanity, can we please pretend this isn't Boomer we're talking about?" I compelled myself to think about something ridiculous, like babies riding rainbows or purple elephants wearing top hats, anything other than my two best friends *having sex*. "Let's call him Chad or Ryan."

Asha wrinkled her nose. "I would never sleep with a *Chad*."

That's beside the point, I thought, but I disregarded her response. "I'm guessing things didn't go the way you thought they would?"

"God, no." Her cheeks burned as red as mine had moments before. "It was awkward and uncomfortable and not at all sexy."

"I'm sorry, Asha." I didn't know what else to say. My lack of experience in this particular department made it impossible for me to give her any helpful advice. "Did it hurt?"

She nodded her head. "Yeah, a little. But *Ryan* was really sweet about it. Kept asking if I was okay. It kinda got annoying."

Purple elephant. Purple elephant. Purple elephant.

"Then why are you so worried? That boy is over the moon about you."

Now that I knew they were together, it was impossible not to notice how in love Boomer was with her. I could see it in the way he watched her with parted lips, or how he'd gently brush his hand against her arm. Every Friday, he drove to Bombay Grille to get Asha's favorite Indian cuisine, even though the restaurant was forty minutes away, and one time he sat through an *IN* marathon because he knew how obsessed she was with the show.

Asha tugged on a strand of her hair. "But what if he wakes up and realizes it was a mistake?"

I blanched. "Are you saying you regret it?"

"No," she whispered, and from the tone of her voice, I could tell how much he meant to her. "But what if *he* does?"

"He won't. You're *not* a mistake, Asha. You're the endgame girl." I reached out and clutched her hand, trying to squeeze some confidence into her. "You got that?"

She was unresponsive for a few seconds, but then she squeezed my hand back and nodded.

"Good," I said, throwing my feet over the side of the bed. "Let's go see if we can make some coffee. I think we both need it."

☆ ♭ ♫

The rest of the morning passed in a blur.

Despite our late night, Alec was the first to join Asha and me in the kitchen. His headphones were in, but when he saw us at the table, he turned off whatever he was listening to, draping the cord around his neck like an accessory. Everyone else trickled in over the course of several pots of coffee, until the only person still sleeping was Boomer. It took multiple wake-up attempts, a plate of Oliver's scrambled eggs, and an offer to drive JJ's car to get him out of bed. Once he was finally alive and moving, we said our good-byes to Alec's friends and headed out within the hour.

From Safe House, the drive to Seattle took less than three hours. The closer we got to the city, the straighter I sat in my seat, watching the exit signs and landscape fly by. I tried to relax and listen to Alec's music, but I was too anxious. Each mile we drove was another closer to finding my sister.

By the time we pulled off the highway, nerves were hula-hooping inside my stomach. The sun had come out in the early afternoon, streaking through the clouds to warm the day. When I glanced at Alec for a boost of confidence, I caught a glimpse of the shimmering inlet out the driver's side window. The Space Needle towered ahead of us, its slender legs rising up to support the flying-saucer-esque observation deck. The design was a stark contrast to the remaining skyline, like it was stolen from a futuristic metropolis or a science fiction movie.

Under different circumstances, I'd have been embarrassed to admit I didn't know much about the city besides that it was the birthplace of Starbucks and the setting for one of Asha's favorite rom-coms, *Sleepless in Seattle*. But I wasn't here to sightsee. I was here for Rose.

She had to be here. If she wasn't...

No! I scolded myself. *Don't think that way.*

After weaving our way through traffic, we arrived in Belltown, a neighborhood within walking distance of Pike Place Market. The metered parking lining the road was packed, and I thought we'd have to circle around the block a few times before we found an opening. But like a sign from above telling me we were on the right track, a Prius pulled out of a space directly in front of us. Alec turned on his blinker, claiming the spot. As he parked, I stared up at the building we'd driven so far to find. Like the rest of the street, which was comprised of bars, cafés, and expensive shopping, it was a business, not a residential address as I'd hoped, but I pushed my disappointment down and unbuckled my seat belt.

"Are you sure this is the correct place?" Asha asked from the backseat.

We all glanced to Alec for confirmation.

He reached for the scrap of paper Kelsey had given us to double-check the address. "Yeah, this is it."

I turned back to the window.

The sign above the shop, which was painted a brilliant royal blue, was for Lost Marbles Art. Based on the window display, the gallery specialized in glass. There were colorful vases of various sizes, abstract sculptures that reminded me of sea creatures with spiraling tentacles, and a long row of hand-blown marbles, each one glittering like a gemstone.

"Kind of a ridiculous name, don't you think?" Boomer asked, surveying the gallery with a critical eye.

"It's quirky." *The kind of place Rose would love*, I realized. "Come on, let's go."

Incense was burning strongly inside the gallery—something

spicy, possibly cinnamon or ginger—and the smell hit me as soon as I opened the door. A Guns N' Roses song raged softly from a radio next to the cash register. Not bothering to look around at the wares, I marched over to the boy behind the counter. He was about fourteen or so and completely absorbed in the manga spread out in front of him.

"Welcome to Lost Marbles Art. You'll lose your marbles over our marbles," he greeted without looking up. "My name's Steven. How can I help you?"

"Um, hi. I'm looking for my sister, Rose. I think she might be an employee here or a friend of the owner, and I—"

Steven's eyes didn't leave the glossy pages of his comic. "Sorry," he said, not making an effort to hear me out. "Don't know her."

The quick answer made my throat tight, but I wasn't giving up yet. "Her name is *Rose Lyon*," I started again, as if stressing her name would help. "Maybe she's a frequent customer or possibly—"

"Nope, sorry. No Rose here."

Dread's sharp claws sank into my heart and twisted, but I forced a deep breath into my lungs and tried to stay calm. "Are you sure? This gallery is her forwarding address."

Steven heaved a long sigh, as if answering my questions was an inconvenience. "Hundred percent," he said and turned the page.

The muscles in my face twitched. I wanted to reach over the counter, grab the kid by his collar, and shake him until he spouted answers, but Asha gently grabbed my elbow, her fingers cool on my hot skin, and steered me out of the way. When she turned to Steven, the sympathetic look on her face switched to a menacing scowl.

"Look here, you little shit," she said, jabbing a finger at him. "We drove all the way here from LA looking for her *missing* sister, so the least you can do is look up from your stupid anime and help us."

Lips pursing, he shut the comic with one fluid snap of his wrist. *Shadow Days.* The girl on the front had comically large breasts and a flaming sword held high over her head.

"Sorry 'bout your sister," he replied and casually flicked his bangs out of his eyes. "But like I *already* explained, I don't know a Rose. My parents own the gallery, and the only other employees are my cousins, okay?"

My eyes watered. After everything that had happened since I found the letters, after how far we'd come, I wasn't going to give up now.

"Maybe if you saw her," I suggested, reaching inside my bag. I didn't have a recent photograph of Rose, but I was certain there was an old wallet-size print of her senior picture in the pocket of my bag. For the first few months after she ran away, I'd carried it around and showed it to strangers, asking if they'd seen my sister.

"I know it's in here somewhere…" I dug around blindly until my fingers skimmed a thick square of paper that was worn around the edges after four years of being buried in my bag. "Aha!" I exclaimed, yanking the picture out triumphantly. A few crumbs stuck to the glossy surface, and I brushed them away.

I turned to Steven, and as I did, something caught my attention at the edge of my vision. A line of paper hearts strung on a piece of twine. They framed the back wall of the room, draped in swags like party streamers. I hadn't recognized them right away because they were made out of origami paper, vivid and embellished with flowering patterns, and Rose never used to waste money on the real stuff. Receipts and notebook paper worked fine for her.

My hand trembled as I pointed at the folded hearts. "Who made those?"

Steven twisted on his stool. His cheeks turned pink. "Lizzie did."

Lizzie, as in Rose *Elizabeth* Lyon? I'd never known my sister to go by her middle name, but then again, I hadn't spoken with her in four years. Who knew how much she'd changed?

"Is this her? This Lizzie person?" I asked, holding out the picture for him to examine.

He leaned over the counter. "Her hair is different," he said, "but yeah. That's Lizzie. She's our upstairs tenant."

My heart nearly exploded at his response.

"Why didn't you mention her earlier?" Asha asked before I could sort through my shock.

"Oh, I don't know." His tone was hardened by sarcasm. "Probably because Rose Lyon and Lizzie O'Brien aren't the same name."

Alec cast a worried glance in my direction. "O'Brien?"

"It's my mom's maiden name," I explained. "I've tried to find Rose online before, and now it makes sense why I never could."

"As much as I've enjoyed this impromptu interrogation, I'd really like to get back to my *comic*." Steven speared Asha with a glare. "Lizzie or whatever her name is got back from work an hour ago. If I let you upstairs, would you leave me alone?"

Holy shit.

Rose was here.

Rose was here *right now.*

I gripped the counter for support and took a steadying breath. "Yes," I exclaimed. "Please."

CHAPTER 17

Steven led us through the gallery and out the back of the building into the sun. He stopped in front of another door and flipped through the collection of keys. I clasped and unclasped my hands as he found the one he needed and let us in.

Without another word, he disappeared back inside the shop.

"They really need to work on their customer service here," Boomer muttered, but I was only half listening.

A staircase stretched out in front of me.

The last forty-eight hours had passed in a whirlwind since I found my sister's letters. I'd wanted to track down Rose so badly that I took off without giving myself a chance to consider how reading her words made me feel. And now that I was on the verge of seeing her, I was filled with anger. I was mad at her for leaving, for all the years of not knowing if she was okay. Mad at her for not coming back. It was the kind of long-lasting anger that simmered under the skin, unnoticed for long stretches of time until something like a song, a snippet of conversation, or a paper heart brought it to the surface again.

The only emotion strong enough to cut through my anger was my fear. Rose wrote to me, but she'd also abandoned me. She was going by a different name. What if I knocked on her door and she wanted nothing to do with me?

Calloused fingers knitted with mine, giving my hand a reassuring squeeze. Alec didn't say anything, but his eyes did the asking: *Are you okay?* I couldn't think of a scenario where I'd actually be okay given the situation, but having him at my side, the warmth of his hand in mine… That was exactly what I needed to be brave.

Hitching up a smile, I said, "Okay, let's do this." And then I squared my shoulders and marched up the steps. When I reached the top, I knocked before I had time to panic again. The sound of footsteps followed immediately, along with the chatter of a familiar voice.

"…probably just Steven. He's always thinking of excuses to visit. Oh, not at all! He's totally harmless. It's kinda cute actually."

I heard a click as the deadbolt was unlocked. The door swung open, and—

There, after all this time, stood my sister.

She nearly dropped the phone when she saw me.

Whoever was on the other end said something, because Rose quickly replied, "I gotta go. Call you later." The phone disappeared into her pocket, but neither of us spoke. We took a long moment to study each other, almost as if we could catch up on the years we'd missed by staring. Finally, she pressed a hand to her chest as if she was feeling physical pain. "Felicity?"

"Hey," I responded. *Four years apart, and all you can manage is a hey? Genius, Felicity.*

Rose didn't seem to mind, because she flung her arms out and pulled me into a hug. I tensed at the contact, but as her perfume hit me—vanilla sugar, the same she wore in high school—it was like we'd returned to the night before her birthday all those years ago, before all the pain. We were just two sisters who loved each other, and it was as if no time had passed at all.

"I can't believe it's really you," she said, pulling away after a long squeeze. She placed both hands on my shoulders and gave me a once-over. "God, you look so grown up."

"And you look so…healthy."

I didn't mean to sound surprised. I'd imagined this reunion so many times before. I'd known things would be different between us, that *she'd* be different, because after four years, how could she not? It wasn't like I was the same person she'd left behind. Heck, I was different from the person I was two weeks ago. Meeting Alec, discovering the letters, taking off on an adventure—all of these things had changed me.

But I'd never expected such a transformation from Rose.

The last time I saw her, she looked sickly. She was too thin and her cheeks were hollow, but now she was back to a regular weight, and there was a glow to her face. And instead of having the overbleached, brittle look I'd grown accustomed to, her hair had its natural golden sheen again. Even the dark circles under her eyes, a permanent fixture from her late-night partying, were gone.

"Thank you."

Awkward silence followed, and Asha attempted to fill it. She leaned around Alec and waved. "Hey, Rose. Long time, no see."

"Asha Van de Berg," she replied, her eyes sparkling with recognition. "Why am I not surprised to see you?"

"Felicity's the one person who puts up with my constant complaining, so I decided to keep her around," Asha joked, and she quickly introduced the boys. Surprisingly, she only mentioned Alec's first name, and besides a polite smile and hello, Rose didn't give any indication that she knew who he was.

"So..." my sister said once she was acquainted with everyone. "What are you guys doing here?"

"Do you...not want me here?"

"Of course I do!" Her voice was high with shock and a hint of hurt, like she was insulted I'd suggested otherwise. "Why would you ever think that?"

"How could I not? You left without saying good-bye, and I've spent the past four years wondering if you were alive."

Her skin paled as if I was seeing my sister through a black-and-white lens. "You didn't get my letters?"

I shook my head. "I found them under Mom's bed on Friday. She's been keeping them from me."

Rose didn't respond immediately, but her face was clear enough: eyes thunderous, mouth twisted like she was sucking on a piece of sour candy. "Are you shitting me?" she exclaimed. "That's so typical of Mom." She pulled the door all the way open. "You should come in. We obviously need to talk."

Five minutes later, I was sitting at my sister's kitchen table. Her apartment was tiny, but it was so *Rose* I didn't mind that every time I shifted in my chair, I knocked my head on the low-hanging cabinet behind me. Picture frames containing snapshots of her travels covered the walls, a collection of seashells lined each windowsill, and then there was the origami: intricate flowers with layers of petals, cute woodland creatures like foxes and squirrels, and a fierce-looking dragon that must have taken hours to complete. The paper foldings were scattered everywhere. The coffee table. The living room bookshelves. Even the kitchen countertops. It was as if they sprouted up from any available surface like wildflowers in a forest.

Asha, Boomer, and Alec were out exploring restaurants, so it was just the two of us. The three of them had claimed to be hungry, but I knew they were trying to give us some privacy. A bag of Tostitos and salsa were set out between us, and Rose had enough blueberries in the fridge to make me a shake, but neither of us touched the food.

"So…" Rose said.

"So…" I said back.

There was so much I wanted to say, so many questions I needed to ask, but I couldn't get my brain and mouth to work in unison. Conversations had always been easy between us, but now it felt like forcing small talk with an old acquaintance. It seemed even the natural bond between sisters could break down over time.

Rose was struggling too. She opened her mouth, then snapped it shut. I watched as she tucked her leg up to her chest, propping her chin on her knee. "I don't know where to start."

"How about with why you ran away," I said, fiddling with the spoon in my shake.

"*Ran away?* Is that what Mom told you?"

Surprised by the scowl on her face, I could only manage a nod.

"That's not what happened," Rose said, sitting up straight. "Not even close."

"So tell me what did." Reaching out, I lightly brushed her knuckles with the tips of my fingers. I'd meant to take her hand in mine as a comforting gesture but chickened out at the last second.

Rose deflated in her seat, as if my fleeting touch had punctured her escalating anger. "It's complicated."

I expected her to say more, to start confessing excuses, but she averted her gaze instead.

I blew out a sigh. "I get that. If it wasn't complicated, Mom wouldn't have lied to me, and I wouldn't have had to drive all the way to Seattle to find you."

"I'm still shocked that you never got my letters. I called the post office to make sure they were being picked up, and they were, so I assumed it was you. I never thought that Mom would…" She trailed off, shaking her head. "The night I left, I put a letter on your dresser. It was the first one I wrote to you, and it explained everything. There was a key and instructions inside."

"For the PO box?" I asked.

She nodded. "Mom must've seen it before you woke up. I should have done a better job hiding it, but I was afraid you wouldn't find it."

"But…why? Did something happen between you and Mom?"

"We weren't getting along," she said. "Like, at *all*. Mom had these high expectations for me, and I couldn't live up to them. She wanted me to get into a good school and study something boring like accounting or law, but that just wasn't me, you know?"

"Yeah, I can't picture you doing someone's taxes for the rest of your life." I could see Rose leading safari tours in Africa or running a Jet Ski rental in the Caribbean, but sitting at a desk and crunching numbers from nine to five? Never.

"Exactly," she said. "Besides, it's not like I had the grades to get in anywhere good."

"So then what?"

"Mom kept pushing, so I pushed back. Little stuff at first, like cutting class and sneaking out at night. Then I started partying. Just your typical Friday or Saturday night keggers to blow off steam, but things got bad fast. I would go out every night during the week. I'd skip school during the day and sleep off my hangovers."

This I knew. I'd lived through it. But I could tell there was something more, something she wasn't telling me. "And?"

"The drinking turned to drugs"—she hesitated—"and then I got arrested."

"You got *arrested*?" The question exploded from my lips. "For what?"

"Possession with the intent to sell," she confessed. My expression must have said it all, because Rose was quick to add, "It was only a little weed, and it belonged to my friend Jimmy, not me. He got pulled over on our way home from a party. We'd been smoking, and the cop could smell it, so he searched the car and found bags, a scale, and Jimmy's stash in the trunk. I didn't know it was back there. We both got hauled in, but Jimmy admitted it was his, so I didn't get charged with anything."

"When was this?" I asked. Melted ice cream was running down the side of my milk shake glass, but I pushed the drink aside, untouched.

"The week before I left." Rose let out a humorless laugh. "Mom had to pick me up from the precinct. When we got home, she snapped. Kept going on about how my arrest was the final straw, and how I had to get my act together because she wouldn't be bailing me out of jail anymore. '*Rosalyn, once you turn eighteen,*'" she said, mimicking Stern Mom's voice, "'*I expect you to act like a responsible adult. And if you're adamant about not going to school, then you need to get a job and contribute to household expenses. There will be no freeloading under this roof.*'"

As livid as I was with my mother, her demand wasn't as unreasonable as Rose was making it out to be. "And?" I asked, still waiting for an explanation.

Rose lifted both hands and shook her head. "She wanted me to pay rent *and* follow all her rules. Why would I ever agree to that? If I have to be fiscally responsible for myself, I sure as hell am not going put up with her tyranny."

"So…you ran away," I said, repeating what seemed to be the most logical interpretation of what had happened.

"No, I already told you that," she replied through a taut jaw. "When I refused to sign her ultimatum—seriously, Mom drew up a freaking contract—she kicked me out of the house. Told me to stay out of your life until you'd graduated from high school and got into college."

Mom did what? I pressed my palms flat against the table and tried to remain calm. "What does any of this have to do with me?"

"She was worried about you."

I blinked. "*Why?*"

"Beats me," Rose said, shrugging. "Maybe she was afraid that my mistakes and rebellion would rub off on you. How she ever thought we'd turn out the same is *beyond* me..."

"Because I blindly listen to every lie she tells?" I snapped, unable to keep the venom from my voice. I wasn't mad at Rose as much as I was at myself. I'd trusted my mom so fully and in every aspect of my life. It never occurred to me that she was purposely keeping me in the dark.

"No, because you're driven and dedicated and hardworking... My opposite."

Okay, I'd give her that. We were the inverse of each other: her unruly and me docile. And that major difference made me pause.

If Mom asked something of me, I did what I was told, no questions asked. But Rose didn't have an obedient bone in her body. When Mom told her to do something, whether it was as simple as coming home before curfew or taking out the garbage, she'd made a point of doing the opposite. So why, of all times, did Rose choose to obey her when she wanted to separate us?

Sure, she sent the letters, but that seemed inconsequential considering she'd been cut out of my life. There were no phone calls. No emails. Why didn't she decide to hell with Mom and show up for a surprise visit on the holidays?

"Rose, I'm still confused," I said. "If you cared so little for Mom's rules, why did you stay away?"

She swallowed, gaze fixed on the ground, and I couldn't place her expression. Was she embarrassed about something?

"Felicity, you have to understand. When I left, I had no job, no way to support myself." She bit her lip, and the look on her face finally resonated with me. Rose looked guilty. "I needed the money to get back on my feet."

"What are you talking about?" I asked, eyes narrowing. "What money?"

There was a second or two of silence as she hesitated, but then she said, "The educational trust that Mom and Dad set up for me. I was never going to use it for school, so Mom gave me access on the condition that I keep out of your life."

I stared at her, trying to process the enormity of what she'd said. "Mom *paid* you to stay away?"

"Hey, listen to me," Rose said, stretching across the table for my hand. "Leaving you behind was one of the toughest things I've ever done, okay? But I needed to figure out *me*, and I couldn't do that at home. Not with Mom. Things were too toxic between us."

I pulled my hand away from hers.

No one needed to remind me of how unhealthy my sister and mother's relationship had been. So I understood why Rose had to make a clean break from her—and consequently, me. But that didn't mean the truth didn't hurt like hell.

"Fel?" Rose whispered, and I'd never heard her sound so small before. "Please don't hate me."

I dropped my chin to my chest so she couldn't see my expression. "It's her I hate, not you."

"Don't say that, Felicity."

My head snapped up so fast I smacked it on the cabinet behind me, but I was too surprised by her response to feel any of the pain. "Why not?"

"Because she loves you and—"

"Whoa, hold up." I lifted a hand to stop her. "Are you seriously defending her right now?"

"I'm not saying what she did was right, because it definitely wasn't." Rose said, backtracking. "But take it from someone who spent years loathing her. It's not worth it."

"So you've forgiven her?" I asked, incredulous. "After everything she's done?"

"Not entirely, but I'm trying, because I want to be happy," she said. "Hatred takes up more space in your heart than you realize, and it doesn't leave room for things like love and joy. Trust me."

"You don't understand, Rose. Everything I've done since you left has been for Mom. Everyone who loved her abandoned her, and I felt this responsibility to make up for that." I wrapped my arms around my stomach. "Stupid thirteen-year-old me figured if I study law at Stanford, become a lawyer, and am successful, then maybe she'd be happy again."

"You don't need a fancy diploma or a job at a law firm to do that, Fel. *You* make her happy."

"That's not the point. All the choices I've made over the past four years have been based on a lie!" I exclaimed.

"Are you saying that you wouldn't have studied as hard if you'd known the truth about me leaving, or if I'd never left at all?" Rose asked, shooting me a disbelieving look. "Because if that's the case, maybe Mom made the right decision."

"How can you say that? I've spent all this time focusing on becoming the person I thought would make her happy instead of the person *I* want to be, and now I feel like I don't know who I am."

"You're only seventeen," Rose said with a laugh. "Nobody knows exactly who they are at that age. Shit, I'm twenty-two and I'm still figuring out who I am."

I couldn't think of a response—at least, not one that would help Rose see my perspective. Learning the truth about what'd happened four years ago was exhausting and more emotionally draining than I'd anticipated.

"Look," Rose said when our silence grew too tense to bear. "I've been where you are. When Mom kicked me out, I felt so betrayed. I know you're hurting, but I haven't seen you in so long. I don't want to waste another minute arguing about her."

She was right. Mom had already stolen so much time from us. Why was I letting her take even more?

"Okay," I said, taking a calming breath and trying—at least for the time being—to put Mom out of mind. "Tell me all about Nicoli."

☆ ♭ ♫

"…and here's one of us with his *nonna*," Rose said, pointing to a picture of her, Nicoli, and an older woman.

We'd moved from the kitchen to the living room couch, and Rose was showing me a photo album of the month she'd stayed with Nicoli's family in Naples. So far, I'd learned that her boyfriend was twenty-four, the sous-chef at one of the highest-rated restaurants in Seattle, and that his dream was to open his own bistro.

I ran my finger over the album's plastic page, tracing my sister's grin. Cheeks bunched up high, mouth thrown open in laughter.

I'd never seen her look so happy. "You must've had an amazing time," I said wistfully. I wasn't sad exactly...but knowing Rose had to leave home to find that kind of happiness sent a pang through my heart.

She nodded. "It was the best trip of my life."

"You never said... How did you guys meet?"

"On my first cruise," she answered, eyes sparkling. "There's this tea party where guests can meet the Disney princesses, and he worked it. Obviously not as a princess. He was a waiter, saving for culinary school. Anyway, about halfway through the event, he tripped and dumped an entire pitcher of juice down my dress."

"*That* must've gone over well." I'd never known my sister to be the cool, calm, collected type.

"I was livid," she said, talking with her hands. "But Disney has this rule that we can't break character while in costume, so I had to smile and laugh and pretend the OJ running down my cleavage was no big deal. In reality, all I wanted to do was wring his neck."

I stifled a laugh as I tried to imagine Rose restraining her temper. It was easier to picture her in a Cinderella costume, swearing like a sailor as steam poured from her ears. Little girls crying, teacups shattering as they fell to the floor, while Rose lunged across the table to throttle poor Nicoli.

"I take it he got an earful later?"

"That was the plan," Rose admitted, "but before I got the chance, he cornered me and begged for my forgiveness. Seriously, on his knees *begged*. It was so sweet that I melted. There was nowhere to buy flowers on the ship, but he went to the gift shop and purchased a *Beauty and the Beast* light-up rose. It was cheesy, plastic, and probably cost him a week's salary, but it was so thoughtful."

Rose, *melt*? No wonder Nicoli had lasted so long. Guys normally only made it a month tops with her.

"Then there was the accent," she continued to gush. "God, I was a total sucker for the way he rolled his *R* when he said my name."

"So the rest is history?" I asked.

She smiled. "I think so. We've had our rough patches and obstacles, but things are going really well. We just moved in together, which is a pretty big step, but it feels right. *We* feel right." She shut the photo album and set it on the coffee table before smirking at me. "Now, not that I know *anything* about boy bands, but your friend Alec… Is he who I think he is?"

"Ah, yeah," I muttered, not sure why I felt shy admitting this. "We also met via a spilled drink. I was at a charity event, and he accidentally dumped a soda down the front of my dress."

I spent the next ten minutes recounting the masquerade and everything that happened after, from sharing blueberry milk shakes at the diner to making out in a tree during a game of Cops and Robbers.

When I finished talking, Rose's smile had grown tenfold. "He sounds amazing."

Nodding, I tucked a curl behind my ear. "He is."

"But? You sound…off." She studied me for a beat before cocking her head. "Does his fame bother you?"

I traced the floral pattern of the couch cushion with my finger, considering. "To be honest, we haven't known each other long enough for me to say. I've seen how it affects his life—like everywhere he goes, people want to take pictures with him—but he's generous about that, and it's never gotten to the point of bothering me."

"Then what *is* bothering you? Because something is. I can tell."

Was something bothering me? I stared at my nails as if the answer I sought would suddenly be painted there in my favorite coral polish.

These past few days, I'd been consumed by thoughts of my sister. I was so focused on finding her that I hadn't spent much time thinking about me and Alec. I liked him, I really did…but maybe she was right. After the talk I'd had with Alec last night, I wasn't sure where I stood with him. Were we just friends with benefits? Dating? If ever there was a time to use Facebook's It's Complicated relationship status, it was now.

On top of that, I had yet to get to the bottom of the whole Violet James thing, and I couldn't help thinking back to the conversation I'd overheard between him and Stella. *You're not being honest either,* she'd told him.

And that made me wonder… Was Alec hiding something from me?

The thought made me feel hollow.

The last thing I needed in my life was more lies. First it was Mom with Rose's letters. Then when I found out Asha and Boomer were secretly dating. Now I was second-guessing my feelings.

"Don't laugh, okay?" I said after some time. "At the masquerade, I felt an instant connection with Alec. He's an incredibly reserved person, but he opened up to me. I don't know how to explain it, but it was kind of like hearing a new song on the radio you instantly love. Completely unfamiliar, but it sets your soul on fire. Like it was written just for you, and you want to sing at the top of your lungs even if you don't know the words. That's how it feels with him."

"So what's the problem?"

"I don't think he's been entirely honest with me."

Rose raised a brow. "About what?"

"Well…I'm not sure."

"*Felicity.*" Her tone was light, but so much like Mom's that I flinched. "Didn't you just say you haven't known each other very long? You can't expect him to give up all his secrets right away."

"I get that," I said, smoothing a crease out of my dress. "It's just… There's this other girl. Her name is Violet James."

"The actress?"

I nodded. "There were rumors in the tabloids last month about them dating. All weekend he's been fielding these tense phone calls. I think they have something to do with her."

"*Ah,*" Rose said in knowing voice, which instantly made me feel self-conscious.

"I know I sound irrational," I added, rushing to explain myself. "But I really like him. If he's lying to me…I don't think I can handle it. Not him. Not now."

Ugh. Why was I being so pathetic? Never in my life had I been upset over a guy. Okay, so maybe my heart withered a little when Eddie Marks forgot my name, but he was a stupid crush. I knew Eddie never saw me. I was nobody to him.

Maybe that was why this felt different.

Alec saw me. I *was* somebody to him…but what if that didn't matter? What if the connection I felt with him wasn't enough? What if he saw me and chose her?

Rose moved closer to me, wrapping an arm around my shoulder. "You know there's a simple solution to this problem, right?"

"I do?"

She nodded. "You need to *talk* to him."

"But what if it's all in my head? Maybe there's no huge secret, and I'm jumping to conclusions. I don't want him to think I'm making assumptions about us or to come off as insecure."

"Alec seems like a pretty reasonable guy," Rose replied. "If you let him know how you're feeling, I'm sure he'll understand. And if not, if he *is* lying, then isn't it better you find out now?"

She was right, of course, but her advice didn't make me feel any better. I was saved from responding when my phone buzzed.

Asha: Hey, can you let us in?
Asha: Alec got swarmed by fans at lunch, so we're back early.

"Everything okay?" Rose asked when I pulled away from her and stood.

"It's Asha," I answered. "They're downstairs."

"Hey, Felicity?"

I glanced back at her. "Uh-huh?"

"Talk. To. Him."

☆ ♭ ♫

When I pushed opened the door, Asha and Boomer were the only ones waiting on the stoop.

"Where's Alec?"

Boomer jabbed his thumb to the left. "Should be around the corner. He's taking a call."

Another one?

"All right, I'll wait for him." I stepped aside so they could move past me.

As they climbed the stairs, I leaned against the doorframe and straddled the threshold, one foot firmly planted inside the building, the other outside on the concrete. I didn't want to get locked out, but I also didn't want Alec to think we'd left him. As much as I hated to admit it, Rose was right. I needed to talk to Alec, and this was the perfect opportunity for me to speak with him privately... But where to start?

In theory, it should be easy to come straight out with it and ask about Violet. Alec was an upfront, rational person. We hadn't defined *us* yet, so he'd understand my need for clarity.

But how things worked in theory didn't always match reality. Despite the fact that Alec wasn't the kind of person to judge, there was no good way for me to bring up Violet without coming off as a jealous psycho. What if I ruined everything between us by turning nothing into an issue?

With that being said, I knew I had to say something. The tension in my stomach wouldn't let up until I did.

When five minutes passed and Alec still hadn't returned, I went looking for him. He wasn't around the corner like Boomer said he would be or in front of the gallery. His car was still parked in the same spot, which meant he couldn't have gone far. If he'd retreated into one of the many cafés that lined the street, it would take all night to find him. But knowing Alec, he'd be somewhere quiet if he needed space to clear his head.

I found him sitting on a bench in the park a block away from Rose's apartment. The place was empty except for a mother pushing her daughter on the swings of the playground. Alec's headphones were in, and even though I couldn't see his face, I could tell from the way he was hunched over—elbows on his knees, head hung low, hands clasped together—that he was upset.

I brushed my fingers over his shoulder as I dropped into the spot next to him. "Hey."

Alec tensed at my touch, but when he saw that it was me, his muscles relaxed and he paused his music.

"How'd the talk with your sister go?" he said before I could ask what was wrong.

"Eye-opening." Letting out a harsh breath, I settled back against the bench. "Turns out that Rose never ran away. My mom kicked her out because she got arrested for possession, but the drugs weren't hers. Apparently Mom thought Rose was going to corrupt me or something ridiculous like that, so—get this—she paid my sister to stay away."

"Whoa." He sat up. "That's pretty intense."

"Right?"

A moment of silence slipped by, and then Alec's lips quirked up. "You have to admit, that sounds like the plot line of a daytime soap."

I shot him a look. "So does a mountaineering boy bander who

helps the stranger he met at a masquerade ball track down her long-lost sister."

"Nobody," he said with a snort, "would believe that. But clearly your life has high entertainment value. It's a wonder someone hasn't given you your own TV show."

"Oh yeah," I said, rolling my eyes. "The Kardashians better watch out."

Alec laughed, and the sound made me smile.

"Felicity?" he said suddenly.

"Yeah?"

"I'm glad you found your sister."

A sudden burst of gratitude for the boy sitting next to me coursed through my body—along with hot waves of shame. Alec had only wanted to help me. He'd given up an entire weekend to do so, pissing off his dad in the process, and how did I repay that kindness? By doubting him.

I assumed that because the people closest to me were keeping secrets, he must be too. But just because there was stuff in his life I wasn't privy to didn't mean he was lying. Like Rose said, I couldn't expect him to bare his soul after knowing me for little more than two weeks. Where was the mystery or romance in that?

"*We* found Rose," I said, correcting him. "You told me I couldn't thank you until we did, so now that we have, I want you to know how much it means to me. And I'm not just talking about driving me here. Thank you for not letting me give up in San Francisco and for helping me through the whole Asha-Boomer debacle. I wouldn't have gotten this far without you."

Taking my hand in his, Alec ran his thumb over my knuckles. "It was my pleasure," he said. I knew he meant it—Alec always meant what he said—but the smile on his face quickly faded.

"Hey, you okay?" I asked, bumping my shoulder into his. "Asha texted me about what happened at lunch. Said you got mobbed."

He slumped against the back of the bench and jammed his free hand into the pocket of his shorts. The other stayed locked with mine.

"It's not that," he replied. "I know it might not seem like it, but I really do enjoy meeting fans. Plus, I'm fairly positive Asha was exaggerating. There weren't *that* many people."

"Then what's up?"

Alec forced a smile, but it only made him look more miserable. "My dad."

"He called again?" Even though Alec had told me not to worry, I did exactly that. The frequency of King's calls was increasing at a noticeable rate, which made me think that whatever was going on was serious. "If you need to go back to LA, I totally understand. The three of us can figure out our own way home. I'd hate to think this trip is coming between you and your dad."

"Felicity, I'm not abandoning you in Seattle," he said. "King being a dick is nothing new. I can handle it, okay?"

I frowned, unconvinced, but before I could say anything else, Alec leaned over and brushed his lips on my forehead in a soft, barely there kiss. Then he stood and, like the gentleman he always was, offered me his hand.

"We should head back before they wonder where we've gone,"

he said. I knew he was trying to end the conversation in the nicest way possible, but I couldn't stop my thoughts from circling back to King.

What had he done to hurt his son so much?

CHAPTER 18

We spent the rest of the afternoon hanging out with my sister, and before I knew it, five hours had passed in what felt like a span of minutes. For dinner, I helped Rose make baked macaroni loaded with enough cheese to clog our arteries, and when we finished eating, she forced everyone to play Monopoly.

It ended up being a blast.

"...five, six, seven... Oh, shit," Asha said when she realized where her roll had landed her.

Boomer pumped his fist in celebration. "Thank you for visiting Boomer's Boardwalk luxury hotel and spa. That will be a cool two grand, please."

Asha looked down at her measly pile of ones and fives, sighed, and then pushed everything she had—the pocket change, Baltic Avenue, and St. James Place—over to her boyfriend. "Well, I'm out. Doubt that will cover it."

"I can think of a few ways for you to make up the difference," he suggested with a smirk. "You could start with—"

"*Boomer!*" Asha exclaimed. Red bloomed on her cheeks, and she kicked him underneath the table. "This is a G-rated game. Behave yourself."

"Babe," he grunted as he rubbed his shin. "I'm pretty sure board games don't have ratings."

She pointed at the box. "It says right on the front *ages eight and up*."

"Well, we're not playing with any eight-year-olds," Boomer said, "so you don't have to worry."

Alec turned to him and gestured at his Game Boy, which Boomer had pulled from his pocket and deposited on the table along with his wallet, cell phone, and a crumpled-up receipt from the Gas Exchange. "You sure?" he deadpanned.

Rose nearly choked on a sip of wine, while Asha threw back her head and laughed, embarrassment forgotten. Glancing around at our small group, I was unable to control my smile. I couldn't help but think how perfect this moment was, being here with the people I cared about.

Then Alec's phone rang.

His expression stilled when he saw the caller ID. "Excuse me," he said, pushing his chair back and standing. I tried to catch his eye, to silently ask if everything was okay, but he slipped out of the apartment without a backward glance.

My mouth settled into a hard line. It had to be King calling. No one else could rattle Alec so easily.

Before I realized what I was doing, I pushed away from the table, my gaze focused on the doorway Alec had disappeared through. "Guys, I'll be right back," I said, not bothering to explain myself.

I knew he didn't want me to worry, but I was done letting Alec deal with King on his own. There was no way for me to fix whatever was broken between father and son, but that didn't mean I couldn't just *be there* for Alec. If he wasn't ready to tell me what was going on, I could live with that. It wasn't going to stop me from supporting him. After what he'd done to help me find Rose, it was the least I could do.

As I made my way down the stairs, the sound of Alec's voice drifted into earshot.

"*Please*, Vi," I heard him say, his normally deep voice high with distress. Was he…begging? "I know this isn't what I promised you, but give me a chance. We can work things out."

Wait, what?

I gripped the handrail, not willing to believe what I'd heard. Maybe my subconscious was projecting my nerves into an imaginary conversation.

Yup, that had to be it.

But then he spoke again: "Of course I'm with you on this! After all the time we've spent together, how could you think otherwise?"

A sickening feeling rose inside me as all the doubts and fears I'd tried to suppress crawled out from the pit of my stomach. Alec was fighting for his relationship—with *Violet*. God, I was beyond stupid. Had I really thought he would pick me over someone like her? He was a musician, she an actress. They were perfect for each other.

"No, I'm in Seattle," he said. No mention of why he was here. No mention of me. "As soon as I get back, I'll come see you, okay?"

He went on talking, but I didn't catch any of it. My ears were ringing with words I couldn't get out of my head.

Give me a chance.

We can work things out.

After all the time we've spent together…

One by one, my fingers curled into fists. Maybe their relationship was on the rocks, but nothing, *absolutely nothing*, gave Alec the right to cheat on Violet. I'd witnessed firsthand how my dad's infidelity had crushed my mom, and knowing that I might have caused Violet the same pain made me sick.

Closing my eyes, I tried to take a breath, but my lungs wouldn't cooperate. It felt like my chest was caving in with each strangled gasp I took.

"Felicity?" My eyes flickered open. Alec was standing two feet away, watching me with concern. "Are you okay?"

"No," I snapped. "Not in the slightest."

How could you? I wanted to scream. *How could you kiss me and laugh with me and share bits of your life, when clearly there's someone else who's more important to you?*

He startled at my sharp reply. "Okay…is there something you want to talk about?"

"Sure, Alec. Let's talk." My voice sounded different to my ears—broken, bitter. "How about we start with the fact that I just heard your conversation with Violet."

I had to give it to him. Alec didn't flinch at being caught. "That upset you?" He seemed genuinely confused. "Why?"

"Wow. Considering what I told you about my parents, how my dad cheated on my mom, did you really think I wouldn't be upset?" Shaking my head, I backed away from him.

"Whoa, I don't know what you think you heard, but there's some kind of misunderstanding—"

"No, stop." I held up my hand. Did he think I was stupid? Deaf? "I don't need to hear your excuse."

With a single step forward, Alec filled the space I'd created between us and cupped my face in his hands. Even though I was furious with him, my eyes fluttered shut and I leaned into his touch, allowing myself a moment to memorize the feel of his fingers on my skin.

I knew it would be the last time.

"Did I do something to make you not trust me? Because I don't understand why you're being like this," he said, a tremor of panic in his voice. "After everything we've been through this weekend, you can't give me a chance to explain?"

His words made me yank away. "Explain what? That you've been stringing me along this whole time?" An indefinable emotion swelled inside me. Whether it was rage or anguish I couldn't tell, but I didn't have the restraint to step away and sort it out before I said something I regretted. "What did you expect? That because you helped me find Rose, I owed you? Or is it that I should consider myself lucky, no matter how many people you're seeing, because you're *Alec Williams*?"

It wasn't fair to throw the fame thing in his face, but words were pouring out of my mouth that I'd never say under normal circumstances, like part of my brain had blown a fuse.

Alec's steady composure withered, his expression flipping between hurt and anger. "Is that honestly what you think of me?"

Yes! I wanted to shout, but my sentimental side—the part of me that was still head-over-heels for Alec—made me pause.

"I don't know," I said, hating the way my voice shook. "But I've dealt with too many lies recently, and I'm done with it. I don't have the strength to sort out what is and isn't the truth, especially if the answer is something I don't want to hear."

"So that's it then?" The question came out like ice.

"Yeah," I whispered. "I suppose it is."

"Fine." His face hardened into a mask. Rather than finding the sharp intelligence and kind spirit I normally saw in his eyes, I was met with emptiness. He'd never looked at me that way before, indifferent, like I was nobody to him. "Tell Asha and Boomer good-bye for me."

Then he turned to leave, and I felt my chest split in two.

☆ ♭ ♪♫

"This is *tragic*," Asha said. "Like Rose-not-making-room-for-Jack-on-the-door tragic."

Was she seriously comparing my falling-out with Alec to the *Titanic*?

I ground my teeth together. "Nobody died," I told her as I stared out the rain-streaked window at the forest blurring by. Today's gloomy weather matched my mood perfectly. "Please stop acting like somebody died."

"Your *relationship* died." Asha kept stressing random words as if she hoped one of them would suddenly resonate with me, and I'd realize I was making a huge mistake.

"We were never in a relationship," I reminded her. Why was I always pointing this out to people? What was it about Alec and I *not dating* that people couldn't wrap their heads around?

"Fine. Your romance, love story, whatever you want to call it. You and Alec are over, and that, my friend, is the definition of tragic."

I wished she'd drop it already. Every time she said his name, I felt like someone had reached inside my chest and yanked on my heart. But I had a feeling she wasn't going to let up anytime soon.

Even though I didn't want to go home, we were already on our way back to LA. The only upside was Rose was coming too. She'd called in sick and packed a bag, all so I wouldn't have to face Mom alone. Now that I knew the truth, she figured there was no point in staying away.

Without Alec to drive us, we were forced to find a new way home. Rose didn't have a car, but she was able to borrow the tiny Mitsubishi Mirage Steven's parents owned. The fit was tight—and if I was uncomfortable, I couldn't imagine how Boomer felt—but it was our only choice.

The trip was supposed to take over sixteen hours, so we'd left at the crack of dawn in order to get back before dark. And that meant I had to endure Asha's complaining for another seven. She'd been ranting like this ever since Alec left. When I told everyone what had happened between me and him, I thought she'd be up in arms, ready to fight for me like she had yesterday morning.

Not so much.

Instead, she freaked out and spent the rest of the night lecturing me on all the reasons why Alec was amazing. She was convinced there was no way he could be dating Violet James. *After all*, she argued, *he helped you find Rose and introduced you to his friends. He cares about you, Felicity!* There was a small chance she was right, but Asha hadn't heard Alec and Violet's conversation or felt the desperation in his voice as he begged her.

I had.

It was more than enough to convince me of his feelings for her, and I had no desire to be part of a public love triangle.

"If you called Alec," Asha said, repeating the same phrase like a pull-string doll, "then I'm sure you guys could work things—"

"Hey, can we please drop this?"

"But, Fel, I really think—"

"I don't want to talk about him," I snapped. "Okay?"

Asha's mouth set in a hard line. "Yeah, sure."

She didn't say anything to me for the remainder of the ride, but I didn't mind the silence. With Boomer spellbound by his Game Boy and Rose focused on driving, I had plenty of time to read through my flash cards a second time. Studying helped keep my mind off Alec.

At ten o'clock that night, we arrived at Asha's house. As she and Boomer unloaded, I texted Mom to let her know I was on the way home. It was the only communication I'd had with her since our fight, although it wasn't for her lack of trying. There were five missed calls, two voice messages, and a handful of texts on my phone. The only reason I looked through them was because a small part of me hoped that Alec had tried to contact me.

He hadn't.

Mom was camped out at the kitchen table when we arrived.

"Felicity!" she exclaimed, shooting to her feet as soon as she saw me. "Thank God you're okay. I was getting so worried—" She froze at the sight of Rose.

"Hey, Mom," Rose said. Her tone was tentative, testing the waters.

"*Rosalyn*," Mom gasped, my sister's name falling from her lips like it was something fragile. "You're here."

"Sorry to disappoint."

"You know I didn't mean it like that," said Mom.

Rose didn't bother with a response. She glanced around the kitchen and living room, as if looking to see what had changed in her absence. Not much had, although there was a lack of origami scattered across every surface.

"You look well," Mom continued, trying to fill the silence. "How have you been?"

I cringed at the awkwardness of it all.

"Considering you've been reading my letters, I think you know exactly how I've been," Rose said. "But why don't we play catch-up later? Right now, you need to talk to Felicity."

Hurt, guilt, then anger flickered across Mom's face, but she was quick to square her shoulders and take charge. "Yes," she agreed, her expression turning stern. "You're right. Felicity, why don't you take a seat? Rose, you can wait in your sister's room."

"Uh-huh. There's no way that's happening," Rose replied, all attitude. I flinched, thinking she'd been home less than five minutes, and they were already butting heads. "This is an issue we have to resolve as a family, and I can't wait to hear what explanation you come up with."

Three long seconds passed as Mom stared at Rose.

The tension between the two was so thick I thought it would suffocate us all.

"Fine," Mom said in a tone that made it obvious this was anything but. She offered Rose a spot at the table, but my sister chose to lean back against the counter, arms crossed over her chest. "Felicity, *sit*."

I pulled out a chair and sat. Mom pursed her lips before saying anything, and I fidgeted in my seat.

"I know you're angry with me," she said at last. "But that gives you absolutely no right to leave home, let alone the *state*, without asking for my permission."

"As if you would've let me go," I mumbled. I was still furious with my mom, but it was hard to harness that anger when she was staring at me as if I'd burned down a nursing home or committed an equally unthinkable crime.

"That's not the point. Do you know how worried sick I was? I had no clue where you were, or that you'd even left, until I came home on Sunday. How could I have helped you if something bad happened?"

"I get it, Mom. What I did was reckless, but there was a good reason why I left, and you know that. Punish me all you want, but me taking a road trip without your knowledge is not the issue here." Out of the corner of my eye, I saw Rose nod in approval, so I kept going. "And to be honest, it seems only fair that you were worried about me for a day. In the grand scheme of things, that's nothing compared to the four years you left me to worry about Rose."

"Felicity, what I did was to protect you."

"Yeah, you already said that. But who were you trying to protect me from, Mom?" I asked. "Was Rose so much of a danger that you had to kick her out of the house *and* my life?"

Mom startled. "Kick her out?" She turned to Rose and glared. "I think that's a bit of a stretch. I never forced you to leave."

Rose, who had been silent up to this point, let out a fake laugh. "No, you gave me an ultimatum."

"Which was still a choice. One that *you* made."

"Was it though? How was staying a choice when you knew I'd never agree to live by your rules?" Mom opened her mouth to argue, but Rose cut her off. "Look, I realize you had my best interests at heart, and I fully admit that leaving home helped me grow up. But what you did to me and Felicity, cutting us off from each other? That wasn't right."

"Rose, when you were arrested…" Mom's voice trailed off, and she shook her head. "Being a parent is hard," she started again. "Being a single parent is even harder. There's no one to lean on or solve problems with, no one to reassure you that you're not totally screwing your kids up. When you got arrested, I was more terrified than I've ever been in my entire life. I didn't know what to do, how to help you, and I was all alone. My rules?" She lifted up a hand before letting it fall. "Those were meant to protect you, not push you away."

"But what about me?" I asked. "What does any of this have to do with me?"

"Oh, honey," Mom said softly. "You were always so close to your sister. You collected her origami like it was treasure, and you'd wait up every night to take care of her after she'd been out partying—"

"You knew about that?"

"Of course I knew. I hated that Rose resisted my help and you were the one who had to take care of her. But even at a young age, you knew how to handle her better than I did. What worried me was you being exposed to that lifestyle…the drinking, the drugs. Your sister didn't want to listen to me, and I decided that if she was set on throwing away her future, I couldn't do anything about it. But not you. You are so bright, and I didn't want anything to ruin that for you."

"And by anything, you mean me." Animosity laced Rose's voice, but her chin was trembling. "I get that you wanted to look out for Felicity, but, Mom…I was a troubled teen trying to figure shit out, not some evil drug lord who was tempting my little sister into a life of crime."

Based on past fights, this was when Mom would return the volley. I expected her to lay into Rose, but something completely different happened. She wilted in her chair. "I know. I'm sorry."

Rose looked as shocked as I felt. "*What?*"

"Don't sound so surprised." Mom scrubbed a hand over her face and sighed. "I made a mistake, okay? Sometimes parents do that."

I balked at her words. "You *made a mistake*? Mom, this isn't some little slip-up you can apologize for and expect everything to go back to normal! You chose to cut Rose out of my life and then had the nerve to lie about it."

"I never said I expect things to go back to the way they were."

"You're acting like it!" I could feel my pulse throbbing in my ears, so I made myself take a breath before continuing. "Mom, when I thought Rose ran away, I was so angry with her. I didn't understand how she could throw all of your hard work back in your face, so I promised myself I'd make it up to you. Crazy, right? As if any of this mess is my fault. But thirteen-year-old me didn't know any better, so I've spent the past four years working my butt off so I can go to Stanford and become a lawyer."

Mom frowned. "I thought that was your dream."

"Yeah, but only to make you happy."

"Felicity," Mom said, reaching across the table for my hand. "The only thing that would make me happier than I already am is to see you achieve whatever dream you set your mind to." She smiled, her lips curving up in a way that could only be described as mirthful, and realization crashed over me with the force of an ocean wave. Maybe life had dealt her a difficult hand, but Mom had overcome those difficulties. Now she had a job she loved and a man who would bend over backward for her. She didn't need me to provide her with happiness. She already was happy.

"So...you don't care where I go to school just as long as I do?"

She nodded. "Exactly."

"And what if I don't want to be a lawyer?" I asked. "What if I want to...go into jewelry design?"

This time Mom hesitated. "Well, I'd much prefer you graduate with a degree that will get you a good job, but I know I can't force my idea of success on you. If you want to be a jewelry designer, a poet, a deep-sea diver, I'll support you in whatever your dream may be. I've already made the mistake once of not doing that. I'm not going to do it again."

I tugged my earlobe as I considered my mom's apology. Part of me wanted to wipe my hands clean of her. After all, she'd stolen four years from Rose and me, time that I'd never get back. But the fire I'd felt raging inside me earlier had dwindled to an ember. Because no matter what she did, she was still my mom. What had Alec said? *Sometimes the people who mean the most to us, like our family, do things that make it difficult to love them, but we do anyway because that's what love is.*

Rose broke the silence with a snort. "A deep-sea diver... Really?"

My lips twitched into a small smile. "Yeah, isn't that dangerous?"

Mom laughed and pointed a finger at me. "I hope you know this doesn't mean you're off the hook."

Before I had a chance to respond, Rose gasped. "Holy shit." She was staring at Mom's hand, and when I looked, the ring on her finger sparkled in the light. "Mom, are you engaged?"

CHAPTER 19

My last days of summer dragged on longer than the past two months had combined. I was grounded until further notice, which meant house arrest and no friends whatsoever. The only place I was allowed to go was work, and after my shifts, I had to come home immediately *or else*.

Rose stayed in LA until Wednesday to act as the buffer between Mom and me. It was surreal having her home, like I'd woken up inside a memory from before she disappeared. I knew her time with us wouldn't last forever—she had a job and Nicoli to get back to—and when she returned to Seattle, it was like being wrenched from a perfect dream.

But Rose gave me her word she'd visit soon, and until then, I made do by calling her every night. Yesterday, we'd spent over an hour on the phone, with Rose recounting some of her exciting travel adventures. Like the time she ran with the bulls in Spain or the week she spent sleeping in a hammock on an Amazonian riverboat. I wished I had as thrilling an experience to share with her, but the most interesting thing to happen to me was meeting Alec.

A knock on my bedroom door made me jump.

"Honey, what time do you get off work tonight?" Mom asked.

She was dressed for a night out: red dress, killer heels, Brazilian blowout. Her favorite necklace sparkled at her throat, and as she stood in the doorway surveying my room, she slipped in the matching earrings, one golden hoop at a time.

I was hunched over by my closet, shifting through a pile of dirty clothes. My waitressing apron had to be around here somewhere… I needed to be at the Electric Waffle in thirty minutes, and I couldn't be late. Miss Daisy had let me keep my job even though I missed my shift while in Seattle, but I was on a probationary period.

"I'll be done around eight," I said as I spotted one of the long, black ties poking out from underneath my dresser. I grabbed the garment and straightened up.

"And what are the rules?"

I forced myself not to roll my eyes. "Go to work. Come home. Go nowhere else."

"Good." She nodded in approval. "If you need anything, I'll have my cell. I love you, Felicity."

"Love you too. Have fun."

Tonight was the first time since my grounding that my jailer was leaving me unsupervised for an entire evening. To save money, Mom had decided to skip throwing an engagement party. She still wanted to honor the event, so Dave was taking her to a fancy hotel where they could have their own private celebration. Which meant I had free rein of the house until tomorrow, although Mom would probably call every hour on the hour *and* have one of the neighbors check on me. Because clearly I was going to do something evil like plot world domination.

Basically, things between the two of us were still tense.

I wasn't ready to forgive her for tearing Rose out of my life, and even when that day came, it would take a long time for our relationship to heal. But I was doing my best to be civil. I knew Mom wanted her upcoming nuptials to be a fresh start for all of us, a way to become a family again and move forward. I wasn't going to sabotage that. I just needed time.

When she was gone, my comforter flew back and Asha sat up in bed. "Man! That was way too close. This whole grounded thing is cramping my style."

"Maybe she'll loosen up next week when school starts," I said, although I seriously doubted it. Mom was treating my transgression like a capital offense, one that would only be forgiven when I finished serving my time. Anticipating freedom anytime soon was wishful thinking on my part.

Despite how frustrating and foreign being grounded was, there was an upside: it gave me time to focus on myself. Instead of moping around the house, I'd created an account on Etsy—an online marketplace where people could sell and buy handmade goods—and spent hours designing jewelry. I didn't expect to become the next Tiffany & Company, but who knew? Maybe I'd turn enough of a profit to help pay my tuition. Or at the very least, my books.

Taking Oliver's suggestion to sell my work hadn't occurred to me right away, but after spending my first night home lying awake in bed and stewing over what happened between Alec and me, I knew I needed a better distraction than ACT prep. Jewelry was an easy answer.

"Hopefully. I'm sick of sneaking in through the window." Asha stood and made her way over to my desk. The magazines featuring me and Alec leaving the masquerade were still stacked in a pile, and she paged through the one on top. "So…talk to anyone interesting lately?"

God, she was relentless.

"If you're referring to Alec, then no. We haven't spoken since Seattle, and I intend to keep it that way." Asha opened her mouth to deliver what I knew would be a long-winded speech on how I was *making the biggest mistake ever*, but before she could get a word in, I waved her off. "Don't look at me like that. I've already heard what you have to say. Repeating it for the billionth time won't change my mind."

With a flick of her wrist, she slapped the tabloid shut. "Why are you so freaking stubborn?"

I'm the one being stubborn? I resisted the urge to laugh.

"I just want to move on with my life," I told her, my tone souring. "Why is that so hard to understand?"

"Because you guys belong together." Asha pushed back her bangs, like she was trying to think of the best way to phrase whatever was bothering her. "Felicity, you're so deep in denial that I feel like I'm watching a rom-com. Right now, we're at the part after boy-loses-girl where the female lead refuses to admit how perfect they are for each other. And then there's me, screaming at the TV because she's being so dumb."

"Did you just call me dumb?" I asked.

"Maybe." She grinned, but when I didn't smile back, Asha turned serious again. "I want you to be happy, Fel, but I think you're using what happened between you and your mom as an excuse to cut Alec out of your life."

Rather than responding, I rifled through my bag in search of my name tag. The small plastic badge was in the zippered pocket where I always kept it, but pretending to be busy was easier than answering.

"Please say something," she pleaded. "You're never going to be able to *move on* if you avoid this subject forever."

I wasn't avoiding the subject. I thought about Alec all the time. Not on purpose, of course. Memories of our trip together were painful. But it was difficult to keep my mind from wandering to Alec when my heart still ached for him. Every day I was forced to face my feelings—anger and hurt and longing—because there was no other option. The only thing I was intentionally choosing to avoid was Asha. Couldn't she see that her constant badgering prolonged my healing process? Just when I thought the hole in my chest was starting to close, she'd wrench the wound back open.

"I cut Alec out of my life because he didn't deserve to be a part of it anymore," I said, lifting the strap of my bag over my head. I pulled my curls out of the way and headed toward the hall. "My mom has nothing to do with it."

Asha blocked my path. "Bullshit. You're so terrified of being lied to again that you pushed him away so he'd never have the opportunity to do the same thing."

"But he *did* lie to me." My words had more of a bite than I intended, and when her face fell, I instantly regretted snapping at her. "Look, I'm sorry, but I have to get to work. Can we talk about this later?"

Sighing in defeat, Asha stepped away from the door. "Fine, but it goes without saying that there's only one person in this situation who isn't being honest, and it's not Alec. Stop lying to yourself, Felicity."

☆ ♭ ♫

It was a slow night at the Electric Waffle.

Miss Daisy lent me her laptop during the downtime so I could research different college options. While I still intended to submit an application to Stanford, my plans for the future were shifting, and I had to adapt to those changes. I already knew I was going to apply to UCLA. Tuition there was nothing compared to Stanford, and I could live at home to cut down on the cost. The Fashion Institute of Design & Merchandising was in LA as well, and it offered one of the top metal and jewelry art programs in the country. I was also looking into schools in Seattle, because it would be nice to have Rose in my life again full time.

But the fact of the matter was, I had no clue where I would end up next fall—and I was okay with that. While nerve-racking, the uncertainty of not knowing was thrilling in a way I hadn't anticipated. I felt like the world was spread out in front of me, and all I had to do was pick which direction to go.

I was so absorbed in my work that I didn't notice her until she slid into the booth across from me. As I looked up, she pulled her sunglasses off and shook out her hair.

"Well," said Violet James, smiling as she gave me a once-over. "I suppose we do look alike."

I didn't know what to say. From the smirk on her face, I got the feeling that her sudden appearance was meant to shock me.

"Um, hi." I shut Miss Daisy's laptop and pushed it away, eyeing Violet with a healthy dose of distrust. "Can I help you with something?"

"Actually, yes. I'm here about Alec."

"You can stop right there," I said before she launched into the whole *he's mine* speech. "You don't have to worry about me. I know you two are together, and I won't get in the way of that."

Violet blinked as if I'd sprouted a pair of horns and giggled.

"What's so funny?" I asked.

"We're *not* dating." There was this little grin on her face as if she found the idea amusing.

"I don't understand."

"We're strictly friends," she clarified. "Our moms were college roommates, so we grew up together. Alec is like a little brother to me. He's producing my first album."

Her response made me pause, and I remembered a conversation I'd had with Alec in his car on the way to San Francisco. *Last month, I got him to agree to let me produce a record for this new client he's signing.*

"Wait," I said, my eyes bulging. "*You're* King's new client?"

She lifted her nose as if the idea disgusted her. "Not anymore. That man is a complete dick."

"Okay…" I scratched my head. "Definitely not following."

"It's kind of a long story," she responded, but I had a feeling Violet came here for the sole purpose of telling said story, so I lifted a brow and waited.

"*Immortal Nights* is on its last season, and I needed a break from the whole acting thing," she explained. "I'm interested in launching a music career, so earlier this summer I asked Alec for his help. We spent a weekend putzing around in his dad's studio, and after King listened to the track we laid down, he offered to sign me. At first, I was hesitant because I've heard some not-so-good rumors about King. But he agreed to let Alec produce the album, so I decided to give Mongo a shot. Then, about two weeks ago, King suddenly changed his mind. Told Alec he wasn't responsible enough to work on the project."

My head jerked back. Two weeks ago was when Alec skipped his dad's barbecue. I knew bailing on the party had created tension between the two, but I never considered what Alec had lost because of it.

This was all my fault. I never should have allowed him to drive me to San Francisco.

"Total bull, right?" Violet said as she took in my expression. "If you ask me, King was looking for an excuse to run the show, but not working with Alec was a deal breaker for me. He's actually excited about my music. King just sees me as a giant payday."

"So what happened?"

"Well, I hadn't signed the contract yet and my agent was in contact with a different producer, so I backed out. Which totally sucked, because Alec and I had already done a bunch of brainstorming."

A terrible thought took root at the back of my mind. "Alec begged you to reconsider, didn't he?" I asked.

"Yup. He was in Seattle so we couldn't talk in person, but he convinced me to wait until we could sit down together before making any major decisions."

My stomach twisted. The conversation I'd overheard at Rose's wasn't Alec fighting for his relationship, it was him fighting for what he loved most: music. I swallowed and tried not to be sick.

"I refuse to work with King, and Alec is sick of the way his father treats him, so we came up with a kickass solution. Alec created his own record label." She smiled like a proud mom. "Once all the legal stuff is sorted out, I'll be the first artist he signs."

"He really went against his dad like that?"

She nodded. "Yeah, he's risking a lot for me—his relationship with his father, his career. But that's the kind of a person he is." Violet paused for the briefest of moments and leaned in toward the table. "Listen, Felicity. I don't know what happened between you two, because Alec hasn't been forthcoming. But I do know that he misses you."

For a long time I said nothing.

Asha had been right. Right about Alec not dating Violet. And about me pushing him away so I wouldn't get hurt. About everything, really. The realization of what I'd thrown away knifed through me with sharp, blinding pain.

"I miss him too," I admitted.

Violet's eyes sparkled with excitement, like my response was the best thing she'd ever heard. "So call him. Trust me. He wants to hear from you."

Yeah, right. Thinking about what I'd said to him made me cringe. There would be no coming back from that. Alec probably hated me.

"I know you're only trying to help," I told her, "but I'm not sure that's a good idea. I said some pretty awful stuff, and I just… I don't think things will ever feel the same between us."

"All right," Violet said, holding up both hands. "It's not my business to push." She lifted her purse onto the table and rummaged through it. "Before I go, I have something for you. Alec mentioned returning this, but I don't think he ever planned to."

Her purse was huge, almost as big as my messenger bag, and whatever she was searching for was buried. Frustrated, Violet turned it over and dumped out the contents. A wallet, more tubes of lipstick than I could count, and her phone clattered to the table, along with my travel copy of *To Kill a Mockingbird*.

"Ah, here it is," she said, sliding the book over to me.

But I wasn't listening. Because together with all her stuff, there was a scattering of origami hearts.

"Where did you get those?" I asked, scooping one up. On closer inspection, I realized it was made out of a music sheet.

"Oh, Alec makes them," she said with a dismissive wave. As if they meant nothing. "He watched a YouTube video on it when we were in the studio last week, and he's been obsessed with them ever since. You can keep one if you like. I've got a million of them." Violet repacked her purse before pushing her sunglasses back into place and sliding out of the booth. "Well, I should get going. I have a radio interview tomorrow to prepare for, and I haven't looked at the questions yet. It was nice meeting you, Felicity."

Too stunned to respond, I could only stare down at the heart in my hand. The last time I sat at this booth, Alec had found one of Rose's foldings, and it had been a gut-wrenching experience. But this? The light tingling working its way through my limbs? It was an altogether different feeling. Like finding my sister's letters, the paper heart I was holding sparked a flicker of hope inside me. What if there was a chance Alec would forgive me after all?

A sudden sense of urgency ripped through me. I needed to make things right.

But how?

This wasn't the kind of problem I could fix with a phone call. Alec deserved more than that. He deserved an apology in person. For a second, I considered chasing down Violet to have her arrange a meeting, but then I got a better idea. I scrolled through my contacts and texted the one person who might be able to help me.

> **Felicity:** Hey, this is Felicity Lyon. We met the other weekend? I know me texting you is kind of weird, but I need your help.

There was a huge possibility that he wouldn't respond, especially considering how I'd treated his friend, but I held my breath as I waited for an answer.

A minute later my phone buzzed.

> **007:** Lol. I remember who you are, Felicity. What's up?
> **Felicity:** I screwed things up with Alec. I need to

apologize, but I want to do it in person.

007: I have an idea, but you'll need a nice dress.

I smiled to myself. I knew just the one.

☆ ♡ ♫

Oliver's plan was gutsy.

It required me to sneak out of the house, and considering I was on thin ice with my mom, it was also reckless. But to win Alec back, I was down for anything. I pulled an all-nighter in preparation, finishing both my mockingbird necklace and the jewelry Oliver had ordered for Stella, and at four o'clock sharp the next afternoon, I grabbed my messenger bag and crawled out the window. Mom would discover my absence as soon as dinnertime rolled around, so I'd left a note on my desk in explanation. Whatever punishment she threw my way would be worth it if I could put right the mess I'd made.

I squeezed through the bushes as carefully as I could, and once I broke free of the tangle, I tore across the lawn toward a limo idling at the curb.

Great, that doesn't stick out at all...

I spared a quick glance back at my house. The curtains on the front window were wide open, and I was suddenly nervous that my mom might look out. I should've told Oliver to pick me up around the corner or, better yet, in a vehicle that wasn't so extravagant. Because, honestly. Was a limousine really necessary?

When I reached the car, I yanked on the handle in my hurry to get inside. The door flung open, and I all but tumbled onto the grass. A familiar snicker greeted me.

"Excited to see me, I see."

JJ was sitting in the seat nearest the door. His long legs were stretched out in front of him, preventing me from climbing inside. The smirk on his face made me want to take a deep breath and count to ten, a moment of mental preparation since I would be spending most of the evening with him, but there was no time. Waving my hand in a shooing gesture, I motioned for him to scoot in.

"Hi to you too," he grumbled, but he unbuckled his seat belt and slid over next to Xander, who smiled at me in greeting.

"Sorry," I responded, practically throwing myself into the car. "But I'm grounded. My mom wasn't exactly thrilled about my impromptu road trip to Seattle."

"Is that why you climbed through the window instead of using the front door like a normal person?" I turned to see Oliver, who was sprawled across the middle seat of the limo. He offered me that Oliver Perry smile of his.

"You guys saw that?" All three boys nodded and I winced. "Wonderful."

"We've never harbored a fugitive before," JJ exclaimed. He grinned as if aiding and abetting was an experience he'd been meaning to check off his bucket list.

"Have too," Xander said. "What about that time in Mexico when—"

JJ cut him off. "That doesn't count."

"What was his name again? It was something ridiculous, like Hot Dog or—"

"Dude, we don't talk about Cheeseburger. Ever."

Oliver snorted at his friends before saying to me, "We have to swing by the airport to pick up Stella, and then we'll be on our way. You brought a different outfit, right?"

"Yeah," I said, patting my bag. My dress, heels, and makeup case were packed inside. "But I need somewhere to change."

Unlike myself, the guys were already dressed for the evening. Oliver wore a deep burgundy suit, no tie, with the top few buttons of his black dress shirt left undone. It was the kind of outfit most men couldn't pull off, but looked stylish and cool on the few who could, and he easily fell into the second category. JJ, on the other hand, had opted for a more classic look, a black suit and tie combo, and its slim fit made his already broad shoulders look massive. Of the three, Xander was the only one not wearing a suit. He was sporting dress pants, a white button-down, and navy blue suspenders with a matching bow tie.

"Not a problem. Stella does too," Oliver said. "Once we check into the hotel, you'll have plenty of time to get ready."

"Okay, cool. And speaking of Stella." I retrieved the small, white box I'd wrapped her present in and handed it over. "This is for you."

He pulled off the lid, and his eyes lit up. "Wow. Felicity, these are perfect."

Xander leaned over and peered inside the box. "What's that for?"

"Stella's and my anniversary." Oliver lifted the bracelet out of the tissue paper to inspect it. "She's going to love this," he told me. "Felicity, you rock. How much do I owe you?"

"Don't worry about it," I said, waving off Oliver's attempt to dig his wallet out of his pocket. A few weeks ago I would have been more than happy to let him pay me, but now the money wasn't important. "You're helping me with Alec. Besides, without your suggestion, I never would've started my own jewelry business, so clearly I'm the one who owes you."

Oliver's answering smile was so big, it was as if I'd told him I'd won a Nobel Peace Prize. "That's awesome! How's everything going?"

"Well, I'm not operational yet, but I want to start out small and only sell a couple of designs. Once I get the hang of things, I plan to offer more options and maybe even do custom orders. Fingers crossed people like my stuff."

"You're going to make a killing," he assured me. "And by the way, I still expect a bill. There's no way I'm not paying you."

Before I could decline a second time, Oliver knocked on the glass separating us from the driver. Then we were on the move, disappearing down the street before my mom realized I was gone.

☆ ♭ ♫

"Pretty sure that bathtub is larger than my bed," I said when Stella flipped on the light. Oliver had rented a suite for the evening, and everything about the room was over the top, bathroom included. "There should be a sign: No lifeguard on duty. Bathe at your own risk."

Stella laughed. "Believe it or not, I've seen larger."

"For real?" Why anyone needed such a huge bathtub was beyond me. Unless, of course, they were hosting a swim meet or playing the world's largest game of Marco Polo.

She nodded and claimed a spot next to the sink, unzipping her toiletry bag before dumping its contents out on the marble countertop. A package of face towelettes, a toothbrush, and a tube of Colgate fell out, along with travel-size bottles of shampoo and conditioner.

"Do you need to shower?" I asked. After a six-hour flight from New York, I was willing to bet she felt grimy.

"You don't mind, do you? I'm going to rinse off, and then we can do our makeup together."

Twenty minutes later, we both had changed into our dresses and were standing in front of the mirror, me with a stick of eyeliner and Stella with a mascara wand. I was trying to make my wings even, but my fingers were shaking, and the left side looked more like a heart-monitor line than the crisp edge I was going for. Some strange screamo band called the Sensible Grenade was blaring from Stella's phone, but when I heaved a sigh and tossed the liner onto the counter, she hit Pause. "You okay?"

"I'm nervous," I admitted.

What if Alec won't accept my apology? Or maybe he's already moved on? My thoughts were spiraling, each new scenario I imagined worse than the last. *Oh God, what if he refuses to talk to me at all?*

"Don't be." Stella set down her mascara and smiled at me in the mirror. "You two will work things out."

I drew my bottom lip in between my teeth. "You sure? I was pretty horrible to him."

She touched my shoulder. "I promise."

"But..." I hesitated, not sure I wanted an answer to the question I was about to ask. If Alec had confided in anyone about how things ended between us, my guess was that he'd chosen Stella. "He told you what happened, right?"

Her smile faded. "Yeah."

"And…you don't hate me?"

"Well, it's not like I'm happy with the way you treated him," she said, placing a hand on her hip. My throat tightened, but then she sighed. "That being said, I know Alec isn't an open book. Sometimes misunderstandings happen, and people say stuff they don't mean. What matters is that you're sorry, because he needs you, Felicity. You're good for him."

My cheeks warmed at the compliment, but I frowned. "How can you be so sure? You hardly know me."

"Because I know Alec, and I've never seen him smile the way he did that night around the bonfire," she explained. "What's more, he's been completely miserable since Seattle."

I wanted to argue with her, but a knock at the door interrupted us. Oliver was standing at the edge of the bathroom, and he quickly settled into a comfortable position against the doorframe. As he looked at Stella, the corners of his mouth turned up into a dimpled smile. It was so different from the slick, arrogant grin he wore for the media that I almost didn't recognize him.

"You look beautiful," he told his girlfriend. Then, remembering they weren't alone, he glanced at me. "You too, Felicity. Nice dress."

I glanced down at my masquerade gown, smoothing out the fabric that was now stain free. "Thanks," I said. It was the only dress I owned fancy enough for the occasion, and wearing it felt poetic, considering this might be the last time I ever saw Alec.

"So, you girls ready?"

"Give us two minutes," Stella answered. "I'm just going to help Felicity fix her makeup, and then we'll be right out."

"Two minutes it is," he said and backed out of the room.

When he was gone, Stella picked up my eyeliner and gently tugged me toward her. "Close your eyes," she instructed. Two seconds later, I felt the gentle brush of her hand on my cheek and the tip of the charcoal pencil against my lid. "I know you're scared to talk to Alec, but it's going to be all right. He's hurting right now, and believe it or not, that's a good thing. If he wasn't, it would mean he didn't care about you. People don't agonize over someone who hasn't touched their heart."

She had a point, and it helped ease the churning of my stomach. "Thanks, Stella."

"No problem. Okay, you can open up." She took a step back and inspected her handiwork. "There! Alec won't know what hit him."

I glanced at the mirror. Somehow Stella had managed fix the squiggly line above my eye.

All right, I thought, sucking in a deep breath. *You can do this, Felicity.*

It was time to crash Vanessa Williams's wedding.

CHAPTER 20

"I'll be back in two hours tops," Oliver told me as JJ, Xander, and Stella filed out of the suite.

I raised my hand in parting. "Have fun."

As much as I wanted to make things right with Alec, I wasn't going to ruin Vanessa's big day by upsetting her little brother. I'd decided it would be best to wait until the ceremony and dinner ended before confronting him. The nuptials were taking place in the hotel's grand ballroom, and once the party was in full swing, Oliver would pull Alec away from the reception and bring him upstairs.

Which meant that strictly speaking, I was only crashing the wedding in the broadest sense of the term.

"If you get hungry, order room service," Oliver told me. "I'll try to save you a piece of cake, but with JJ at the table, I can't make any promises."

"Don't worry about me," I replied. "Never been much of a frosting fan anyway."

JJ gasped. "*Told* you she has no soul."

Oliver rolled his eyes as he stepped into the hall. "See you in a bit," he called, and then I was alone.

Not quite sure what to do with myself, I turned in a circle and surveyed my surroundings. There was a piano tucked into the far corner, a wall of shelves filled with books, a glass rock fireplace, and a handful of other luxuries I never expected to find in a hotel room. Any other day I would have been impressed with the grandeur of it all, but it was hard to appreciate when I could feel my heart fluttering around my chest like a caged bird. Without anyone to keep me company, my mind immediately found Alec. I had this terrible image in my head of him storming away as soon as he saw me, and I kept playing it over and over like some kind of sick movie.

When my palms started to sweat, I knew I needed a distraction. Some way to kill time so I didn't have a heart attack before he arrived. I grabbed my travel copy of *To Kill a Mockingbird*, the one Violet had returned to me yesterday, and took a seat on the couch. I was too worked up to focus on reading, but there was comfort in holding my favorite novel.

As I flipped through the first chapter, I noticed something different about the usually familiar pages. Beneath my margin scribbles someone had left comments in near-perfect penmanship.

I drew in a sharp breath.

It was Alec's handwriting. I was sure of it.

Not only had he read the book, but he'd responded to each of my thoughts. There were answers to the questions I'd posed, along with his own ideas and analyses. He even jotted down part of a song after the passage where Atticus tells Scout about Tom's shooting. The lyrics were unfamiliar to me, but they fit the story so perfectly it was as if Harper Lee had written them herself:

With these wings we fly
Toward the clouds, sun, and sky
Until the dark of night arrives
And shatters us forever

From cover to cover, Alec had filled my book with fragments of himself. I was so absorbed in reading them that I didn't realize Oliver had returned until I heard him speaking.

"This will be real quick, I promise."

"Can't it wait until tomorrow? I should be with my family right now."

My head shot up at the sound of Alec's voice.

"I know, I know. But this is important," Oliver told him. "Just bear with me."

I tossed the paperback onto the cushion beside me and jolted to my feet. A second later, the boys stepped into the room, and my chest hitched at the sight of Alec. The tux he wore sent me back to the night we first met, back to before I'd ruined us. His brows were knit together in a frown, as if he was trying to figure out why he'd been dragged away from the party. As I watched, he patted his hair, checking to make sure every blond lock was in its designated place.

Heart throbbing at the back of my throat, I waited for him to spot me. Finally, he glanced up, and when our gazes locked, he came to an abrupt stop.

"*Welp*, I've done my part," Oliver said, rubbing the back of his neck. "I'm going to leave you two alone now." He shot me a thumbs-up before inching backward in the direction of the exit.

The moment we were alone, I wanted to rush into Alec's arms. Instead, I planted my feet and lifted a hand in greeting. "Hi."

For a long time, a *painfully* long time, he said nothing. I stared at him, my breath bottling inside my chest as I waited for a response. If he didn't say something soon, I was going to run out of oxygen.

"Felicity." His tone was guarded, careful. "What are you doing here?"

The question stung, but I ignored the pain and answered. "I wanted to see you."

"Why?" he asked, his steel eyes narrowing.

I felt myself wince, like his words were a slap across the face. To have him look at me like that—like I was poisonous—was excruciating. *Things could be worse*, I tried to convince myself. *At least he's talking to you.*

"Because," I said. "A super smart guy once told me that his mother said it's always important to apologize in person."

Alec crossed his arms and waited. Okay, so he wasn't going to make this easy for me. I guess I deserved that.

Taking a quick breath, I started over. "Violet came to see me yesterday."

That got a reaction out of him. "What? Why would she do that?"

"To set the story straight," I replied and began inching my way across the room. "She said King went back on his promise to let you produce her record, and that you begged her to reconsider when she contemplated signing with another label."

I stopped a yard away from him and gave myself a moment to work up enough courage for what was coming next. *You've got this,*

Felicity. All you have to do is open your mouth and say you're sorry for being the biggest ass in the world.

"I know this isn't the best time, but I need to apologize for what I said in Seattle." I glanced at the carpet, tucked a loose curl behind my ear, and then looked back up at him. "Alec, I'm so sorry. You were nothing but kind to me, and I automatically assumed the worst. I-I didn't trust you, even though you never gave me a reason not to."

"Why?" he asked again. It was quickly becoming his catchphrase of the evening.

"Why am I apologizing?"

"No." He swallowed hard. "Why didn't you trust me?" His voice broke at the end of the question. Clearly, he'd been torturing himself over the answer.

I was at a loss for words. The honest truth was that I didn't have a good response to give him.

"Um, well…I may have overheard your conversation with Stella when we were at Oliver's uncle's place. I thought you were talking about me. That combined with your phone calls to Violet, and I just sort of figured…" My explanation was so terrible I couldn't even finish it.

But then something amazing happened. Alec took an actual step in my direction. Now we were only two feet apart. Close enough to reach out and touch him, but still too far in all the important ways for me to actually do so. "Felicity, I would've told you anything you wanted to know. Why didn't you ask me?"

He made it sound so easy, which felt a little unfair, especially coming from someone as reserved as him. Alec and I had clicked from the start, but that didn't mean we'd settled into the ease of a long-term relationship, one where we were completely comfortable with each other. Nobody could let their guard down that quickly.

"I guess I was afraid," I told him.

"Of what?"

With a shrug, I focused my gaze on the swirling pattern of the carpet. "I don't know. Lots of stuff, I suppose. I didn't want you to think I was crazy or ruin things between us by making assumptions."

"But you *did* make assumptions." His voice was gentle, which made me feel worse. Why was he so calm and composed? Couldn't he just yell at me? The pain in his eyes would be so much easier to deal with if he was angry.

"Everyone was lying to me, Alec," I said, forcing my gaze to meet his again. "My mother was keeping this monumental, life-changing secret, and my two best friends were purposely hiding their relationship from me. I know it's no excuse, but I felt like nobody was being honest anymore."

It happened so fast that I couldn't be sure, but I thought I saw Alec's lips twitch. "I've always been honest with you."

Not when we first met, a petty part of me wanted to say. *You said your name was Aaron!* But that wasn't fair. We hadn't know each other then.

I hung my head. "Yeah, I know."

There was a long pause during which I chewed on my lip and tried to think of something else to say, some way to make things right, but I came up with zilch. And maybe that was because there was nothing left to be said. Maybe I didn't deserve his forgiveness.

"Well, I've said my part," I told him, swallowing the lump in my throat. "I-I understand if you can't forgive me. God knows I don't deserve it, but I wanted you to know how sorry I am. Give me a minute to grab my things, and then I'll leave."

Turning away from Alec, I pressed a hand to my lips. *Don't cry, don't cry, don't cry.* I wasn't going to let him see my tears, so after giving myself a second for the heat behind my eyelids to subside, I moved toward the couch to collect my book and bag.

Then Alec spoke.

"The mockingbird is beautiful."

I was so caught off guard by the sudden change of topic that at first I didn't know if he'd actually said something or I'd imagined his voice. On top of that, I wasn't entirely sure what he was talking about—the book or my necklace?—but I turned to face him.

Alec closed the gap that was separating us. My pulse exploded when he reached up and fingered the beads at my throat, his knuckle gently sweeping across my collarbone. "I know I've said this before, but you're really talented."

"I… Thank you," I whispered, holding as still as possible.

Is this really happening?

"I took your advice about the whole do-what-inspires-you thing," I rambled, a desperate attempt to keep Alec here in this moment. "Told my mom that I was ditching law school for jewelry design. Turns out you were right: I had this step-by-step plan for my life, and even though I would've been miserable, the thought of throwing it all away was too terrifying."

His face remained as blank as it had been for most of our

conversation, but I didn't miss the spark that flashed in his eyes. "And?"

"Well, I don't have everything figured out yet, if that's what you're asking, but I'm in the process of researching what schools would be a good fit for me." I allowed myself a small grin. "Who knew not knowing every detail of my future could be so liberating?"

"What did your mom say?"

"She was surprisingly supportive."

He smiled for the first time since I'd ambushed him, but there was something off about it. He wasn't looking at me, but through me. "You're lucky," he said, and I immediately knew he was thinking about his dad.

My shoulders slumped as my momentary spurt of happiness faded. "I'm sorry about what happened with King."

He shook his head. "Don't be. It's for the best. If he hadn't reneged, I never would've had the motivation to do my own thing. I was being a hypocrite, preaching to you about taking a risk when I was too afraid to take one myself."

"I think the situation is more complicated than you being afraid to go out on a limb," I said. "But I'm glad you figured things out. I want you to be happy, Alec."

"I want the same for you," he replied. After a moment's pause, he tugged me into his arms, and somehow, it was like I'd never left. We stood like that forever, holding each other as the walls between us crumbled away.

"Felicity?" he said, after some time.

"Yeah?"

Alec dropped his forehead onto mine, but didn't answer. He didn't have to. I knew exactly what he was thinking. I could feel it in the way he looked at me.

I missed you.

I missed you too.

☆ ♭ ♪♫

"Holy purple."

Alec smiled as he guided me into the ballroom. "It's my sister's favorite color."

"Really?" I teased, glancing around at the party. "My guess would've been yellow."

Vanessa's wedding planner had turned the expansive room into a magical garden of varying shades of violet. Overflowing bouquets of lilac filled the centerpieces; mauve drapery surrounded each crystal chandelier like petals of a flower, dipping down from the ceiling in half-circle loops before uniting with the rafters; plush periwinkle sofas were arranged in groups around the hall so guests could relax and chat if they grew tired from dancing, and the up lighting cast the walls in a lavender glow.

Everything about the decor was extravagant. As horrible a person as King Williams was, he didn't spare any expense on his daughter's big day.

Stella must have been watching for us, because we'd only made it ten feet inside before she materialized at my side.

"Hey, you two!" Her greeting was overly cheerful.

"Everything's fine, Stella," Alec said, even though she hadn't asked a question. He lifted up our hands, which were locked together. "See? We've made up. No need to worry."

"Okay, first," she replied, holding up a finger, "I never said I was worried. I had the utmost faith you guys would work things out, and Felicity can attest to that. Second, I didn't come over here to check up on you guys."

Alec and I exchanged looks, and then he made a face at Stella as if to say, *bullshit*.

"What? I'm serious." Stella propped a hand on her hip. "I'm here to keep Felicity company while you guys preform."

"Already?" Alec asked, craning his neck around.

I followed his gaze to a stage where a live band was playing, and to the side of the platform stood the remaining three Heartbreakers— Xander was tuning his guitar while JJ repeatedly poked Oliver with his drumsticks.

Turning back to Stella, Alec said, "Isn't it too early?"

She shook her head. "Vanessa's been asking."

"But—"

"No buts." She gave him a gentle shove in the direction of the stage. "You're the one who promised your sister a show, remember? It's only a few songs. We'll be right here when you're done."

"I'm not going anywhere," I told Alec when he looked to me for confirmation. "I promise."

"All right," he said with a nod. "See you in a bit."

I watched as Alec skirted around the party to join his friends. As soon as he had the strap of his bass over his head, the Heartbreakers took the stage. I expected Oliver to greet the crowd, but he hung back and let Alec step up to the microphone.

"Hello?" He tapped the mic. "Can I have everyone's attention please?"

A hush swept through the ballroom, and I couldn't stop myself from smiling when Alec brushed a hand over his bangs.

"Um, hi," he said once it was quiet. "I didn't make a toast during dinner, so here we go. For those of you who don't know me, my name is Alec and I'm the very proud little brother of the beautiful bride. I want to start off by congratulating the newlyweds and thanking you all for making the trip here today. Many of you flew in from different parts of the world. I believe that's a testament to how amazing the couple standing before me is, that we all want to be here to celebrate this special day with Vanessa and Chris. On behalf of the entire Williams clan, I would like to welcome my new brother in-law into our family and…"

Stella leaned over and whispered in my ear. "I don't think I've ever heard him say so much in one go before. Color me impressed."

"I'm not," I answered, my eyes still locked on Alec. He must have shared a funny memory or cracked a joke, because the crowd laughed. "One of the first things he told me about himself is how close he is with Vanessa. He would do anything for his sister, even give a speech." Alec and I had that in common, and it was one of the main reasons why we understood each other so well.

Stella tipped her head. "Makes sense. I can relate to that on a personal level—Ooh, look! Oliver's up."

Back onstage, Alec had passed the microphone to Oliver, who

adjusted the stand before charming the audience with his trade-mark smile.

"Good evening, party people! I hope everybody is having a fantastic time so far tonight. As per the bride's request, we are going to play a few songs. So without further ado, we're the Heartbreakers and we hope you all enjoy the show!"

JJ counted the band in, smashing his drumsticks together over his head, and they kicked things off with a cover of "Marry You" by Bruno Mars. As they played, Stella and I sang along. Five songs later, Alec whispered something in Oliver's ear, set down his instrument, and hopped offstage. He cut through the mass of wedding guest as if he was on a mission, and I quickly lost sight of him.

"All right, ladies and gents. We're going to slow it down in here for the next few minutes," Oliver announced. "This next song is dedicated to the little lady dressed in pink at the back of the room. Hi, Felicity! Sorry about this. Alec promised you'd turn bright red, so he alone should be held responsible for any embarrassment I might be causing at the moment."

Laughter filled the room, and not only did my face burst into flames, my entire body flushed.

"Aw," Stella gushed, and I gave her a small shove to shut her up.

"I'm going to kill him," I muttered.

"How about you dance with me instead?" Alec asked, stepping back into view. He didn't give me a chance to turn him down. Taking my hand, he led me onto the dance floor and tugged me against his chest. My embarrassment dissolved as he placed a hand at my waist and held me close.

"This is going to sound totally lame," I said, "but I've never danced with anyone before. Sorry in advance if I crush your feet."

"You've never *danced* before?" Alec's mouth gaped. "How is that even possible?"

Well. This was more humiliating than I anticipated.

"No, I mean with a *guy*. I don't go to school formals. Between homework and actual work, my weekends are booked solid."

I didn't add that I'd never been asked to one before. No point in embarrassing myself further. Asha always had an endless supply of guys wanting to be her date, but I was never that lucky. Usually Boomer and I hung out at the diner—me waitressing and him playing Game Boy—while she went to Homecoming or Spring Fling. But this past year, Asha wouldn't let us miss out on Junior Prom since, according to her, it was the kind of memory that would last a lifetime. So Boomer and I went together, strictly as friends. The thought of slow dancing with him was strange, so we'd spent most of the night by the punch bowl, laughing at people's bad dance moves and the couples who needed to get a room.

My response made Alec happy, I could tell. He offered me a smug grin and spun us in a circle. "So I'm your first then, huh?"

With the best brows-arched, are-you-shitting-me look I could muster, I said, "Better watch out. You're on the verge of sounding like JJ."

Alec laughed so hard we had to stop dancing right in the middle of the floor. The other wedding guests glanced at us in curiosity as they drifted by, but I hardly noticed. The sound of his happiness was dazzling.

"You know," he said, grasping my hand and tugging me back against him once his laughter was under control. "I wanted to dance with you the night we met. It was when I saw you walking around the garden fountain. You were humming 'Astrophil,' your hair was starting to curl in the heat, and even though there was an extravagant masquerade taking place a few yards away, you were completely lost in your own world. It was the most beautiful thing I'd ever seen."

My breath caught in my throat. "So why didn't you?"

He shrugged—or made what passed as a shrug since his arms were wrapped around me. "We didn't even know each other."

"And yet," I said, as the song slowly faded. "I would've danced with you all night."

A grin returned to his face. "Good, because that's exactly what I plan on doing."

EPILOGUE

We were finishing off a pile of Nicoli's homemade French toast when Rose's phone vibrated against the table. She wiped her mouth with a napkin before glancing at the text. As she read it, her eyes went round.

"No way!" The chair she'd been sitting on jerked backward as she shot to her feet. "I can't believe it!"

Asha froze, a fork poised halfway to her mouth. The last bite of sausage she'd speared fell off and hit the pool of syrup on her plate. "What's wrong?"

"Nothing. This is perfect!" Rose turned to me. "When I found out you were coming for a visit, I arranged a surprise for you." She was speaking at full tilt, like she couldn't get her words out fast enough. "I didn't know if my idea would work timing-wise, but something came up and now we're in business!"

I smiled despite my confusion. Man, was it good to be with my sister again.

My grounding had lasted through the end of September, six full weeks where I was cut off from Asha, Boomer, and Alec. It was easier to handle not spending time with my friends because I saw them at school, and since things with Asha were tense, we didn't talk much anyway.

With Alec it was different. Between his work schedule and my imprisonment, we'd only been able to hang out twice following his sister's wedding—both times when he'd stopped by the Electric Waffle during one of my shifts. Being apart from one another was maddening, especially considering we were still in the heart racing, stomach fluttering stage of our relationship. Nevertheless, we made the most of a bad situation by texting every day.

But more than anyone, I missed Rose. We had so much time to make up for, and I hated that she lived so far away. The miles between us made me feel like I'd found her only to lose her again, so when my punishment finally came to an end, the first thing I did with my renewed freedom was go for a visit. Without a second thought, I purchased the cheapest flight I could find from LA to Seattle. I flew out to Washington on a Friday after school, this time with my mom's permission.

The only small hitch was Mom didn't feel comfortable letting me travel alone, so I'd bribed Asha into coming with me. She'd needed a victim to rewatch all four seasons of *Immortal Nights* with her before the fifth and final season aired, and that was a price well worth paying. The marathon turned out to be a blessing in disguise. During the eighty plus hours of Lilliana LaCroix and her supernatural gang, I was able to mend the rift I'd caused in our friendship, no groveling required. Asha was so eager to hear about my rekindled romance with Alec that she forgave me on the spot.

All things considered, I felt like my life was back on track after being derailed by the turbulent end to my summer.

"What kind of surprise?" I asked, pulling my robe tighter.

Undeterred by the October weather, Rose had the kitchen window propped open, allowing a crisp, morning breeze to drift through the room.

Her mouth curled into a sly grin. "Go get dressed and then you'll see."

I nodded, then brought my dirty dishes over to the sink before heading to the guest room Asha and I were sharing. Rose was in scheme mode, I could tell. Whatever she was up to, it had better not interfere with today's touring itinerary. I had our entire weekend planned out down to the minute, and today was no exception.

There were so many places I wanted to go in Seattle, like the Chihuly glass exhibit that Asha had mentioned. I'd read up on the city since my last stay, and in addition to the main tourist attractions like Pike Place Market and the Space Needle, visiting the Fremont Troll and the Museum of Pop Culture were at the top of my to-do list.

When I returned to the kitchen ten minutes later, Asha was already gone. She'd made plans to hang out with her cousin but would return later tonight in time for our flight home.

Sitting at the table in her place was my *boyfriend*.

I stopped midstride and did a double take. "Alec? What are you doing here?"

Based on his outfit, it looked as if he'd just returned from a wilderness expedition. He was wearing a red and black lumberjack flannel, and there was a windbreaker draped over the empty chair at his side. A gray beanie was pulled over his head, and strapped to his feet was a pair of heavy-duty hiking boots. Most surprising of all, however, was the stubble on his face. He was normally clean-shaven, but Alec appeared to have lost his razor. That, or he really had been traversing the wild these past few days.

I'd never envisioned him as an outdoorsy type, not even when I learned of his love for hiking and mountaineering. But now, seeing Alec dressed like someone out of a North Face catalogue, I was able to appreciate this other side to him, a side he didn't often share with the rest of the world.

"Wow," he said, standing to greet me. "That wasn't the warm welcome I was hoping for. What gives? Not happy to see me?"

Alec's teasing cured my shock, and I threw myself at him in response, wrapping my arms around his shoulders as he lifted me off the ground. "Of course I am," I laughed. "It's just that I don't understand."

"He's your surprise, dork," Rose responded. She was leaning against the countertop, observing us as she sipped at her morning caffeine. Her lips curved up over the top of her coffee mug. "I figured you guys haven't seen much of each other lately, so I extended an invitation to him."

"I didn't know if I'd make it, so we decided not to tell you," Alec added. "The band was supposed to have a major meeting about our upcoming tour tonight, but our manager Courtney came down with the flu. I caught the first flight out as soon as I heard it was postponed."

"That's awesome!" I exclaimed, and when Alec raised his brows, I quickly backtracked. "Well, not the part about your manager getting sick. I hope she feels better soon. What I meant was, I'm super excited to see you."

Alec grinned and brushed back one of my escaped curls. "I know," he said, planting a kiss on my forehead. His face felt like sandpaper. "I'm excited to see you too."

Twenty minutes later, we were cruising down the highway in the Jeep Wrangler Alec had rented at the airport. It was just the two of us, since Rose claimed she had errands to run. But we all knew she was only making an excuse, giving Alec and me an opportunity to spend time together.

I couldn't be more grateful.

Although this was supposed to be a sisters' weekend, there was no telling when I'd get another moment alone with him—and that was because of my mom. She was still wary of Alec, which wasn't a surprise considering his association with the biggest rebellion of my life. The two had yet to meet, but when that finally happened, I knew Mom would see the same, caring person I did. Not an aloof rich kid or just a guy in a band. Alec Williams was so much more than that. He was someone who wasn't afraid to chase his dreams. Someone who inspired the people around him. And he was the boy who held my heart, because the music rooted in my soul, an inherent tune that made me who I was played in his as well.

"Can you pretty please tell me where we're going?" I asked for the fourth time, batting my lashes for good measure.

Alec's eyes cut from the road to me. "Nope." As usual, he was enjoying keeping me in the dark. The smirk on his face was evidence enough.

"How about a hint?"

He freed a hand from the steering wheel in order to lace his fingers with mine. The leather strap of the bracelet I'd made him brushed against my wrist. "Not going to happen," he said. "But if you pay attention, I'm sure you'll figure it out."

Biting down on a smile, I focused my gaze out the windshield. I had a hunch where we were heading. In the distance, a snowcapped mountain pierced the clear blue sky—Mount Rainier. I decided to concede to the mystery of our destination, so I settled into my seat and basked in the stunning scenery that surrounded us. If there was one lesson I'd learned this summer, it was that the best things in life are often the ones we never plan for: a surprise birthday party, a chance meeting with the future love of your life, a spur-of-the-moment road trip.

So even if today turned out to be a total disaster, I knew everything would be fine.

Sometimes all you needed was an adventure.

ALEC'S PLAYLIST FOR FELICITY:

"Love Won't Sleep" by Lostboycrow

"Tear in My Heart" by twenty one pilots

"Meteorites" by LIGHTS

"Paris (Ooh La La)" by Grace Potter and The Nocturnals

"Crazy for You" by Hedley

"What I Like about You" by The Romantics

"Tell Her You Love Her" by Echosmith

"Raise Hell" by Dorothy

"Lightning in a Bottle" by The Summer Set

"Gold" by Vinyl Theatre

"Secret Valentine" by We the Kings

"Living Louder" by The Cab

"Amen" by Halestorm

"Mindset" by Every Avenue

"Geronimo" by Sheppard

"I Must Be Dreaming" by The Maine

"Hit Me with Your Best Shot" by Pat Benatar

"On Top of the World" by Imagine Dragons

"Little Bird" by Ed Sheeran

"Hallelujah" by Paramore

ALEC'S FAVORITES:

"Gorgeous" by X Ambassadors

"Bottoms Up" by Brantley Gilbert

"The Otherside" by Red Sun Rising

"Runaway (U & I)" by Galantis

"Hotel California" by Eagles

"Find Your Love" by Drake

"Paralyzer" by Finger Eleven

"Must Be Doin' Somethin' Right" by Billy Currington

"Feel So Close" (radio edit) by Calvin Harris

"Numb / Encore" by Linkin Park and Jay Z

"Say My Name" (featuring Zyra) by ODESZA

"Simple Man" (rock version) by Shinedown

"Beautiful Lasers (2 Ways)" (featuring MDMA) by Lupe
   Fiasco

"Superheroes" by The Script

"Mr. Brightside" by The Killers

"Powerful" (featuring Ellie Goulding and Tarrus Riley) by
   Major Lazer

"Wicked Games" by The Weeknd

"Dear Agony" by Breaking Benjamin

"My Kinda Party" by Jason Aldean

"Soundtrack 2 My Life" by Kid Cudi

INSPIRATION FOR WRITING *PAPER HEARTS:*

"Hold It Against Me" by Sam Tsui

"Enchanted" by Taylor Swift

"Renegades" by X Ambassadors

"Life Is a Highway" by Rascal Flatts

"Send Me on My Way" by Rusted Root

"Bones" by Alex G

"Young Volcanoes" by Fall Out Boy

"Better than Words" by One Direction

"You and Me" by Lifehouse

"Kiss Me" by Ed Sheeran

"I Was Made for Loving You" (featuring Ed Sheeran) by
   Tori Kelly

"It's Time" by Imagine Dragons

"You" by The Pretty Reckless

"Don't Say Goodbye" by Jamestown Story

"A Drop in the Ocean" by Ron Pope

"Tear Down the Stars" by The Years Gone By

"Beside You" by Marianas Trench

"Army of Angels" by The Script

"Shut Up and Dance" by WALK THE MOON

"Her Love Is My Religion" by The Cab

ACKNOWLEDGMENTS

Hands down, writing *Paper Hearts* has been the most difficult project of my life. There were more late nights, cups of coffee, and breakdowns during its creation than there have been in my entire career. But along with the countless challenges this book presented, there was an amazing team of people who saw me through every draft.

First, I want to thank Annette Pollert-Morgan, for her never-ending patience during this novel's lengthy birth. An epic poem could be written about her heroic editorial deeds. Thankfully, a poet I am not. Further thanks to all the talented people at Sourcebooks Fire: Elizabeth Boyer, Alex Yeadon, Diane Dannenfeldt, Stefani Sloma, and many, many more.

To my Wattpad readers, who loved Alec and Felicity before I wrote this story. Thank you for the thousands upon thousands of hilarious, laugh-out-loud comments, the sweet messages that encourage me to keep writing, the names you give my asterisks, and believe it or not, even the "UPDATE!"'s. *Every. Single. One.* I'm also eternally grateful to all the extraordinary people on the Wattpad team, who shower me with unconditional support. I will never be able to say this enough—thank you for making my dreams come true.

Thank you to my kick-ass agent, Alex Slater, for his tireless work on my behalf, and Grandma Fletcher and Aunt Jennifer Fletcher, for catching my many mistakes.

Much love to my family: Mom, Flynn, Jackie, and the rest of you crazy bunch!

And finally, thank you to Jared Kalnins. You kept me sane while I pursued something as crazy as writing a novel, and in my book, that makes you a rock star. I heart you more than Cool Ranch and blueberry shakes, and Starburst and salsa.

DON'T MISS
THE HEARTBREAKERS

OLIVER IS THE LEAD SINGER OF THE WORLD'S HOTTEST BAND.
STELLA HAS NO IDEA.

CHAPTER 1

Cara was clutching the latest edition of *People* as if it were the Holy Bible.

"If I didn't have you to bring me magazines," she said, "I'd go stir crazy locked up in this place."

"I had to fight off some soccer mom for the last copy," I told her. And I was serious. Fresh reading material was a hot commodity among inpatients and their families at the hospital.

Cara didn't hear me. She was already tearing through the magazine, eager to consume her daily dose of celebrity gossip. Beside her, Drew was camped out in the room's only armchair, staring down at his phone. From the scowl on his face, I knew he was either reading about last night's baseball game or discovering that the spotty Wi-Fi was being particularly fussy.

Unlike a typical day at the hospital, today I actually had something to keep me occupied during visiting hours. After pulling a chair up to Cara's bed, I started scrolling through the pictures I had taken with my new Canon. My parents had bought me the camera as an early birthday gift, and I had tested it out at the Minneapolis Sculpture Garden this morning.

"God, could he be any more perfect?"

I looked over, and Cara had the magazine open to an interview with one of the guys from the Heartbreakers, her favorite band. The headline read "Bad Boy Still Breaking Hearts." Underneath it was an abstract with a quote: "I'm not looking for a girlfriend. Being single is too much fun." When I glanced back up, there was a look on Cara's face—eyes avid, mouth partially open—that made me wonder if she was about to lick the page. I waited a moment to see if she would, but all she did was heave a sigh, the kind that implied she wanted me to give her a reason to gush over her favorite celebrity.

"Owen something?" I asked to be polite, but my attention was already focused back on my camera.

"Oliver Perry," she said, correcting my mistake. I didn't need to look at Cara to know she was rolling her eyes at me even though I had made my dislike of the band clear on multiple occasions, like every time she blasted their music through the house. I didn't care enough about the Heartbreakers to learn their names; they were just another boy band whose popularity would sputter out as fast as it had shot up. "I swear you're like a forty-year-old stuck in a teenager's body or something."

"Why?" I asked. "Because I don't know the name of some boy band member?"

She crossed her arms and glared. Apparently I had crossed the line. "They're not a boy band. They're punk."

There were two reasons I didn't like the Heartbreakers. First and foremost, I thought their music sucked, which should be explanation enough, but I had another reason: the Heartbreakers tried so hard to be something they weren't, parading around as rockers when really, they were just a boy band. Sure, they played instruments, but no amount of vintage band tees and ripped jeans could mask the watered-down lyrics and catchy beats of songs that were undoubtedly pop. The fact that their fans had to constantly remind the world that the Heartbreakers were a "real" band only proved otherwise.

I pressed my lips together to keep myself from laughing. "Just because they site the Misfits and the Ramones as their inspiration doesn't make them punk."

Cara tilted her head to the side, eyebrows scrunched together. "The who?"

"See?" I reached over and grabbed the magazine. "You don't know what real punk is. And this," I said, gesturing down at the page, "is not it."

"Just because I don't listen to all your underground weird stuff doesn't make you more musically cultured than me," she responded.

"Cara," I said, pinching the bridge of my nose. "That's not what I meant at all."

"Whatever, Stella." Cara slid the magazine back into her lap. She looked away from me, shoulders slumping. "Honestly, I don't care if you don't like them. I'm just in a bad mood because I wanted to go to their concert."

The Heartbreakers had performed in Minneapolis this past month, and even though Cara had desperately wanted to go, she had decided not to purchase any tickets. It had been a tough decision, especially since she had been saving up for months, but in my opinion, it was the right one. Because, when it came down to it, it didn't matter how much she wanted to go. Her body was giving her all the signs that she couldn't—nausea, vomiting, and fatigue just to name a few—and she knew it. One important lesson that Cara's cancer taught us was that there's a time to be hopeful and a time to be realistic.

Two weeks had passed since Cara started her first round of chemotherapy. The treatment worked in cycles—three weeks where countless drugs were pumped into her body, followed by a rest period before the whole process started over again. Then, after the regular chemotherapy killed off all the bad stuff in her body, Cara would be zapped with a single round of high-dose chemo just to make sure the bad stuff stayed dead.

I was never really good at science, but Cara's trips to the hospital taught me a lot. Ordinarily, chemo doses are restricted to small amounts due to the threatening side effects. A higher dose might kill the cancer, but it also destroys bone marrow, which I've learned is kind of essential to life. But sometimes, regular chemo isn't enough.

That's how it was for Cara. After two recurrences, her doctors thought it was time for a more serious treatment, so once she received the high-dose chemo she would need to have an autologous stem cell transplant. An autologous transplant was where Cara's own stem cells were removed from her bone marrow prior to her treatment. The cells were frozen and kept safe during her chemo, and they would be given back by a blood infusion. Without it, she wouldn't be able to recover.

A small sigh escaped me, and I was careful with my words. "I'm sure there'll be more concerts in the future," I said and offered her a weak smile. "I'll even go to one with you if you want."

At this, Cara giggled. "Drew's more likely to join a cheerleading squad." At the sound of his name, our brother looked up and raised an eyebrow at Cara before returning to his phone.

"It was just a suggestion," I added, but I was glad she found it amusing.

"You, at a Heartbreakers concert?" she said, more to herself than to me. "Yeah, right."

At this, we both went silent. A thick kind of quiet settled around us; I could feel its weight bearing down on my chest, and I knew we were both thinking of stuff that was unhappy. Long days at the hospital tended to do that, and after a while, bad thoughts came more easily than the good ones.

A knock on the door pulled me back into my surroundings, and Jillian, Cara's favorite nurse, stepped inside. When I saw her, I glanced up at the clock and was surprised to see how fast the day had disappeared.

"Stella, Drew," she said, greeting the both of us. "How are you both?"

"Same as usual," Drew said as he stood up and stretched. "You?"

"I'm doing well, thanks. Just here to check up on Cara." To her she said, "You need anything, dear?" but Cara shook her head.

"Are you kicking us out?" I asked. Visiting hours would be over soon and that meant it was time for Cara's nightly meds, which included penicillin and a long list of other stuff I couldn't pronounce.

"No," Jillian said. "You still have time, but I figured you'd want to run down to the cafeteria before it closes."

The thought of food made my stomach rumble. I'd gone straight to the hospital from the sculpture garden, so I hadn't eaten anything since breakfast. "That's probably a good idea." I wrapped my camera strap around my neck and stood up. "See you tomorrow, punk."

I wanted to lean over and give her a kiss, but I couldn't.

Cara had non-Hodgkin's lymphoma. It was a type of cancer that originates in lymphocytes—white blood cells—which are part of the body's immune system. Normally, people with non-Hodgkin's were treated as outpatients. They would come to the hospital on a daily basis to receive treatment before going home, and during her first two bouts of cancer, Cara was an outpatient too. Every day my mom would drive her to the hospital and her drugs were administered through an IV. It normally took about an hour, and sometimes Drew and I would tag along and do homework in the waiting room.

But Cara recently had complications with her appendix and it had to be removed. Since her white blood cell count was so low, her doctors were concerned she was at risk of infection, and she had to stay at the hospital for a few weeks. When we visited, we were required to wear masks over our mouths, and we couldn't touch Cara because there was a chance we could get her sick.

I knew being away from home was hard for her, and it was frustrating that I couldn't even comfort her with a hug.

"You know where to find me," she said and rolled her eyes.

"Get some rest for me, okay?" Drew said in parting. Then he turned to me. "Ready? I'm hungry."

"Yup," I responded. "Me too." We said one last quick good-bye, and then we were out the door, heading in the direction of the cafeteria.

"Think they'll have those caramel pudding cups today?" Drew asked as we made our way down the familiar hospital halls.

"Man, I love those things," I said, "but I doubt it. Haven't seen any in a while."

"Lame."

"Yeah," I said, thinking about our day. "Pretty lame is right."

☆ ♭ ♫

Every day, Drew and I would mention one positive thing that had happened during the time we spent with Cara. The thing about hospitals is that they're breeding grounds for fear. If you don't constantly remind yourself about the good, the bad will seep in and take over. Because when one of your family members gets cancer, you all get cancer. It might not be the same kind, but it will still eat at you until there's nothing left inside.

The tradition started when Cara was diagnosed the first time, back when we were freshmen in high school. It hadn't really hit me that my sister was sick, that I could actually lose her, until she had a diagnostic treatment and stayed in the hospital while her doctors identified the location, extent, and stage of her cancer. Our mom brought Drew and me in to see her, and all around us were children in various stages of decline, some further along than others.

That was the first time I felt the fear. It buried its nails in my chest, lifted me clear off the ground, and said, "See those kids?

Those kids are actually dying." And that made me wonder—if my sister was here, did that make her one of those kids too?

"What's your positive?" I asked Drew when we reached his old Honda Civic on the far side of the hospital parking lot. He was fiddling with his keys, and even though I knew my door was still locked, I yanked on the handle.

"The caramel pudding cup," he said. The locks popped up with a click when he found the right key. "That shit was delicious."

"A pudding cup?" I repeated as we both climbed into the car. "That's your positive?"

"It's that or the fact that the Wi-Fi was in an obliging mood today."

I was battling with my seat belt, trying to untangle it and pull it forward, but Drew was being so odd that I let it fly back into place. "Are you being serious?" I asked as I stared at him. "Because I honestly can't tell right now."

"What does that mean?" he said. "Pudding cups are serious business."

I blinked slowly and deliberately. Up until today, our positives had always been meaningful, something to keep us going. If pudding became the only redeeming part of our day, then we were in trouble.

Drew started laughing, and I smacked him on the shoulder. "Not funny," I grumbled.

"I was only teasing, Stella. Lighten up."

"Sorry," I said, reaching for my seat belt a second time. "I only narrowly avoided making Cara cry today."

"You know why she's upset, right?" Drew asked me then. "She thinks she's never going to go to one of their concerts."

"Why does she have to be all negative like that?"

I didn't expect Cara to be sunshine and roses all the time. In fact, she deserved the right to be angry with God or the universe or whoever had dealt her the shittiest hand of all. But I hated when she spoke in definites—*I'm never getting out of here, I'm never going to college, I'm never going to see the Heartbreakers perform*—like her death was already a done deal. It made me feel like I had no control over my life, like it really was all left up to fate.

"No, not like that," Drew said. "Apparently there's a rumor going around that the Heartbreakers are breaking up. Some kind of rift between the members."

"Oh! Well, no surprise there," I said, but I silently hoped that the rumors weren't true. Shocker considering I wasn't much of a fan, but I wanted to prove Cara and her definites wrong. She would see the Heartbreakers perform because she was going to get better.

Placing his hand on my headrest, Drew craned his neck to see if there was anyone behind us before whipping out of the parking spot at full speed. Visiting hours were officially over, and some of the hospital staff had already left for the night, so the lot was relatively empty. When we reached the exit, Drew swung the car into the left-turn lane and flicked on his blinker. We both just sat there for a second, neither of us talking, as we waited for a gap in traffic.

I remembered that Drew had yet to answer my question, and I was the first to break the silence. "So what is it then?" I asked.

"What's what?"

"Your positive."

"Oh, right," he said, his head twisting back and forth as he checked to make sure there were no more oncoming cars. There weren't, so he slammed his foot on the pedal and shot out onto the road. "I came up with an idea for Cara's birthday present."

"Really?" I asked. I turned my full attention to Drew. "What is it? Tell me."

Not only was next Friday the Fourth of July, but it was also Cara's eighteenth birthday. It was mine and Drew's as well; we were triplets. Every year, we had a competition to see who could get each other the best present, and Cara normally out-gifted us. This year, Drew and I decided to team up and beat her, but so far, we had yet to come up with anything worthy of winning.

"Okay, you know how you've been going on and on about that photographer's art gallery?" Drew asked, glancing at me. "The one that's opening in Chicago?"

"You mean Bianca Bridge?" I edged forward in my seat. I had no clue what Cara's birthday gift had to do with my all-time favorite photographer, but wherever Drew was going with this, I had a feeling it would be good.

Bianca was my inspiration and everything I wanted to be in life. As one of the most famous photojournalists of the modern world, she was known for eye-opening street photography that featured people from all walks of life. I had painted a quote from her on my bedroom wall, and all my best pictures were tacked up around it: "The world moves fast, changing everything around us with each new day. Photography is a gift that can keep us in a moment forever, blissfully eternal."

Whenever someone asked me why I enjoyed photography so

much, I would recite Bianca's quote as if it were my own personal mantra. I was enthralled with the idea that, with one click of a button, I could somehow beat time.

"Yeah, her," Drew said as he sped up to make a yellow light. "It just so happens that her gallery is only a few blocks away."

"A few blocks away from what?" Drew was purposely dragging out his explanation to build suspense, which was nothing short of annoying. "Come on!" I was bouncing up and down in my seat. "Tell me!"

"No patience whatsoever." He shook his head, but there was a glimpse of a smile on his face. "It's a few blocks from a radio station where the Heartbreakers will be doing an autograph signing this weekend."

"Are you for real?"

Drew lifted his chin, and a smirk flashed across his face. "Well, Cara was really disappointed about not being able to go to the concert, and that got me thinking. There has to be something else Heartbreakers-related that would make her happy. So I googled a list of their public events. We could drive down and get one of their CDs signed or something."

"And?"

"And visit your art thing."

"Yes!" I exclaimed and pumped my fist in the air. "Cara won't stand a chance of beating us this year."

"I know," he said and brushed off his shoulder. "No need to thank me."

I rolled my eyes but smiled inwardly. Something inside my chest was shifting.

When Cara's cancer came back again, I knew it was different than the first two times. The knot in my gut told me that if this treatment didn't work, Cara would never get better. It was a heavy feeling to carry around, almost as if a hundred weights had been tied to my heart.

Even now, I knew there was nothing I could do that would make Cara's cancer disappear. But for the first time since the recurrence, I felt like those weights were slowly being cut loose. It was silly, because what would an autographed CD do? But if it could lift Cara's spirits, then maybe she stood a chance.

"Do you think Mom and Dad will let us go?" I wondered, chewing on the inside of my cheek. If they didn't, my surge of hope would dissolve and bring me lower than before.

Drew shrugged. "We'll be together," he said, "so I don't see why not."

"Okay, good," I said, nodding at his answer. "Are we really doing this? Road trip to Chicago?"

"Yeah," Drew said. "Road trip to Chicago."

CHAPTER 2

I pressed my forehead against the passenger's side window and let my eyes drift over the buildings slipping past me. Drew and I had been driving all night, and thankfully we arrived in Chicago well before the morning rush hour. It was still dark, but a faint purple light on the horizon hinted at the coming sun. Even though it was too early to check in, we were making our way through downtown to find our hotel. Drew wanted a place to park the car and leave our luggage.

I stayed awake during the drive to keep my brother company, and now I was too tired to focus much on anything. If I didn't get caffeine soon, I would never make it through the day. Just as my eyelids began to flutter closed, a green sign caught my attention. I shot straight up in my seat.

"Drew, stop! It's a Starbucks!"

He jumped, accidentally jerking the wheel to the left, and the car swerved a foot into the next lane. There wasn't much traffic to crowd the five o'clock streets, but I could see the alarm on his face.

"Jesus, Stella, you could have gotten us killed," he said and let out a shaky breath when he successfully pulled our car back into the right lane. "That scared the crap out of me."

"Sorry," I said as he found a parking spot on the side of the street. "Coffee's on me. What do you want?"

"Just a regular cup of joe. None of that creamer crap."

I wrinkled my nose. "That's disgusting," I told him as I unbuckled my seat belt.

"That's how you're supposed to drink it," he told me as he settled back into his seat to wait.

Grinning to myself, I climbed out of the car and headed toward the shop. When I stepped inside, a bell rang above me and the smell of freshly brewed coffee greeted me. There was one employee behind the counter, a middle-aged woman with frizzy hair, and she was taking the order of the only other customer in the shop.

As I waited for my turn, I studied the boy in front of me. He was tall and lean and must have been around my age, but I couldn't get a good look at his face. Light-brown, wavy hair poked out from underneath a beanie, and he was wearing a fitted white T-shirt, designer jeans, and a pair of gray Vans: simple but stylish. I couldn't help but look him up and down a second time. Normally I was into guys with big muscles and facial hair, but something about this boy was interesting. His whole look screamed artsy, and I liked it.

"That will be two ninety-five." I watched as the boy retrieved a wallet from his pocket, pulled out a five, and handed it over. After giving back his change, the woman said, "I'll be right back. Gotta grab the soy milk out of the other fridge."

"That's chill," he answered and tucked his money away.

The barista disappeared through an employees-only door, leaving me alone with the boy. As he waited for her to return, he beat his hands against the counter, re-creating the rhythm to a song. I cleared my throat to let him know he wasn't alone, and he turned, finally noticing I was standing behind him.

He offered me a smile. It was one of those full-face smiles accompanied by an adorable set of dimples, and all I could do was stare like an idiot. Something about him struck me, almost as if I knew him from somewhere, which was ridiculous since we had never met. I touched my camera out of habit, and his smile faltered. Neither of us moved for a moment, but then the boy forced another grin onto his face and waited, like he expected me to say something.

Unable to stand his gaze any longer, I glanced up at the huge chalkboard menu hanging above us. Even though I already knew what I was ordering, I deliberately studied each item. They really should have another employee working. He was still watching me, and I tried my best to ignore him.

"So," he said, finally ending the silence. "That's a nice camera. I take it you're into photography?"

I jumped at the sound of his voice. The boy was leaning back against the counter, his arms crossed casually over his chest. "Um, thanks," I responded. "It's an early birthday gift. And yeah, I'm into it."

"What kind?"

"Portraits are my favorite," I told him, as I fiddled with my lens cap, popping it off and on. "But I'll take a picture of just about anything."

"Why portraits?"

"Have you ever heard of Bianca Bridge?" I could feel a smile growing on my face, and I didn't wait for the boy to answer. "She's, like, the best photographer ever, and she does these amazing shots of people from all over the world. I'm actually in Chicago to visit her photo gallery."

"Hmm," he said, tilting his head to the side. "Never heard of her." Pushing away from the counter, he took a step toward me. The dog tag around his neck caught a beam of light from above, and it shimmered back and forth. "Mind if I have a look?" he asked and pointed at my camera.

My fingers tightened around it, and I hesitated. "Umm," I responded, not knowing what to say. The Starbucks employee trotted back into the room clutching a carton of soy milk, and when I glanced back at the boy, he lifted an eyebrow at me as if to say, "Well?" Slowly, I nodded my head. In any other instance I would have said no, but something about him was confident and charming. Plus, I wanted to see that smile again. I lifted the strap from around my neck, and he moved in to take the camera. As he did, his arm brushed against mine, making my skin prickle.

"Like this?" he asked and snapped a close-up of me. I found it hard not to grin. He was holding the camera all wrong and clearly had no idea what he was doing.

"No," I said, reaching over to help. "You probably have to adjust the focus. Here, I'll show you." I put my hand on top of his and demonstrated how to move the lens. The boy looked up at me for a moment, my hand still over his. This close to him, I could see the thick lashes that surrounded his dark-blue eyes, and my stomach flipped in circles.

He moved the camera up to his face. "Smile," he said, but I

looked away and let my hair cascade in front of my face. "What? The photographer doesn't like having her picture taken?" he asked as he snapped another one.

"Not really," I answered and took back my camera. Dropping the strap back around my neck, I held it in my hands and let out a huge breath. "I much prefer looking through the lens," I told him. I focused it on his face for a moment before swinging around to my right and capturing the barista at work. I held the camera up so he could look at the image on the screen. "It's best when they don't know you're looking at them. That way you get the real stuff. Real is when it's the most beautiful."

"What if they know you're looking?" He was closer now, and even though he had spoken in a barely there voice, I heard every word.

Taking a deep breath, I counted to three in my head to work up some courage. Then I stepped back and focused the lens on him. He leaned in with an unwavering gaze, but with the camera between us, he was less intimidating. I only saw a subject. My finger hit the button three times before I pulled away to study the portraits. They were easily the best pictures I'd taken in a long time.

Finally, I answered him. "Those can be beautiful too."

His lips quirked up in a smile, but before he could respond, the barista finished his order. "All right, one caffè latte with soy," the woman said, handing the boy his drink. "Sugar's around the corner if you need it."

"Thank you," he told the woman, but he never glanced in her direction. He kept his eyes on me as he reached over and grabbed his drink. Finally, after three long seconds, he turned and made his way over to the sweeteners and stir sticks.

"Sorry about the wait," the woman continued. "What can I get for you?" I gazed at her with parted lips. I had completely forgotten why I was even standing in Starbucks. "Hon?" she prompted me.

"Right," I said, tucking a loose strand of hair behind my ear. "Um, can I have a grande of your regular brew and a tall hazelnut macchiato?"

"Anything else for you today?"

"No thank you."

She pressed a few buttons on the register. "Okay, that will be eight ninety-eight."

I pulled my wallet out of my purse and searched for a ten. "I know I have some cash in here somewhere..." I muttered to myself. I didn't want to have to run back out to the car—that would be totally embarrassing—but all I could find was my plastic, and I was only allowed to use that in emergencies.

"I got it." The boy slapped a twenty down on the counter and winked. My fingers fumbled as I looked between him and the money, and my credit card slipped out of my hand.

"Crap." I rushed to pick it up, but he was already there, bending down and plucking it off the floor. He turned it over in his hand as he straightened back up, his eyes glancing down at my name.

"Here you go," he said, holding it out for me to take.

"Um, thanks."

"It was nice to meet you, Stella Samuel." A half grin yanked on the corner of his mouth as he said my name. "Have fun at the gallery today." Then he turned and exited the coffee shop. I stood in place and watched the door swing closed behind him.

"Here you go, darling. One grande coffee and a tall hazelnut macchiato." The barista pushed the drinks across the counter to me. "Your friend left his change behind. Do you want it?"

"Keep it," I told her, not bothering to look back. I grabbed the cups and rushed out the door to ask the boy his name, but when I reached the sidewalk, there was nobody in sight.

"What took you so long?" Drew complained when I finally slid back into my seat.

"Oh, you know. Soy milk, camera," I rattled off. My mind was on that boy.

Drew choked on a sip of coffee. "You spilled soy milk on your new camera?"

"Huh?" I focused my attention back on him and then realized what he was asking. "Oh, no. Never mind, it was nothing."

My brother watched me for a moment before shaking his head. "Drink that caffeine up. I think you need it."

☆ ♭ ♪♪

"That was awesome!" I exclaimed as Drew and I stepped out of Bianca's gallery.

Unlike this morning, I felt energy streaming through my body, enough for me to skip the five blocks to the radio station where the signing was taking place.

"Maybe not the word I would use," Drew responded.

"Oh, come on," I said, bumping my shoulder into his. "Don't you feel inspired?"

"Not overly," he replied. "We just spent all morning looking at a bunch of pictures on a wall."

This conversation was familiar. I'd had similar experiences with every member of my family in the past, when I'd shown them new Bianca pieces that I was obsessing over. Nobody ever appreciated the photos, and I'd learn to shrug off their lack of interest. Mom liked to blame her sister, my aunt Dawn, for what she referred to as my "artistic arrogance," which was when I got all snobby about a certain photograph and tried explain the vision behind it.

My aunt Dawn was one of those posh, East Coast ladies who drank martinis like water and only bought art if the price tag had enough zeros. One time, when I was twelve, she took me to an art auction in New York. We spent three hours meandering through rows of artwork, and Dawn taught me which paintings were quality and which were not, a skill no twelve-year-old should be caught without. Of course, her definition of quality was vastly different than mine. Dawn's choice of favorites hinged on who the artist was, not the subject, while I preferred the black-and-white photographs tucked away in the back of the gallery. There were different people in each image, which made me wonder who they were and what they were thinking.

"But they were pictures that mean something," I said, turning to look at Drew. I knew he wouldn't understand, but that didn't stop me from hoping he would. I wasn't snobby about art the way Dawn was or the way my mom thought I was; I was just passionate about photography. And my mom could only blame that on one thing—my not-so-typical high-school experience.

When Cara first got sick, our mom made an effort to try to keep my and Drew's lives as normal as possible. But Cara's treatment was long and grueling, so she started homeschooling. The three of us didn't like being apart, not when things were so serious, so Drew and I begged our mom to let us be homeschooled too. That way, we could be with Cara and still receive an education. She finally agreed, and we never went back.

Until freshman year, I'd loved being a triplet. It set us apart and made the other kids our age think we were cool. It was like we were exotic animals at the zoo that everyone wanted to see, and we always got asked questions like whether we could read each other's thoughts or feel when one another got hurt. We always responded by putting on a show. Drew would pinch himself, and Cara and I would grab our sides and grimace as if we had felt his fingers too.

It wasn't until high school that I realized people only knew me as one of the Samuel triplets. During English class on my first day, the girl sitting next to me asked, "Are you Cara or the other girl?" as if I could only be defined by the fact that I was one of three. That was when I decided I needed to stand out from my siblings, to declare who I was and all that independent stuff. The problem was that I didn't really know how to go about doing it.

I thought about the girl from my English class. She had one of those scary nose rings that made her look like a bull, and her dreadlocks were dyed purple. I was willing to bet that nobody forgot who she was—not when she looked like that. But I wasn't as daring as her.

Although my ears were already pierced, getting a nose ring scared me. On top of that, I was nervous the maintenance required to keep all of my chestnut hair a solid blue—my favorite color—would be too much work. In the end, I settled for a single streak of aqua in my bangs and a small, sparkly stud in my left nostril to start my metamorphosis from Stella the triplet to Stella the individual.

High school was going to be my chance to break away and discover who I was, and during those first few months of freshman year, I started to. Drew, who was built like our dad, tall and thick, easily made the football team. Cara had always been the most outgoing of the three of us, so it made sense when she joined the cheerleading squad and yearbook committee. But even though we normally did everything together, I decided not to try out for the squad.

Instead, I signed up for as many clubs as I had time for—from student council, which I hated, to academic decathlon, which I also hated. Art club became my fast favorite. Not only did I love the quirky cast of kids, but there was something about imagining and shaping and creating that I found intriguing.

I packed my schedule so tightly that, during those two months, it was as if I didn't have siblings anymore because I saw so little of them.

But when Cara got sick, all of our individual growth folded in on itself, and we just became the triplets again. Sometimes I would catch a glimpse of who we could've been from those few high-school fragments that stayed with us. Cara never went anywhere without at least three different lip gloss options, and Drew always tried to make a competition out of things, whether it was beating me in a game of Scrabble or seeing who could get a better test score.

That's why I held on to photography so tightly. It was my only takeaway from a time that was supposed to be mine but never really was. One of my art friends introduced me to it, and even though I wasn't a natural, I enjoyed it enough to make an effort to improve. So while every other teenager was blundering their way through high school, experimenting and making mistakes, I was at home staying how I always had been, whatever that was—but at least I had one thing that was all my own.

Before I could dive into the details of why Bianca's work was so meaningful, I spotted a great shot farther up the sidewalk. "Oooh, look!" I said and rushed ahead to snap a picture.

"Stella," Drew said when he caught up to me. "That's a fire hydrant. We have those back in Minnesota."

"Yeah, but look at the way the sunlight is hitting it," I said and adjusted my lens.

Drew scoffed. "Please don't tell me there's some symbolic meaning in the contrast between the light and the shadows or some artsy bull like that."

"No," I said and crouched down to get a closer picture. "I just think it's pretty."

"But it's a fire hydrant," Drew repeated, and crease lines—something my mom always warned us would become permanent if we frowned too much—formed on his forehead.

Knowing there had to be at least one good picture out of the ten I took, I straightened up and poked Drew in the side. "Sure, but it's a very *symbolic* fire hydrant."

At this, Drew opened his mouth to argue, but then decided against it and shook his head. "Come on, expert photographer," he said. "We're going to be late for the signing." He turned and continued up the sidewalk, expecting me to follow.

"All right, all right," I said, laughing before jogging to catch up with him. "I'm coming."

☆ ♭ ♫

It only took us ten minutes to walk to the radio station, but Drew was right. We were late.

"I don't get it," I said as we took a spot at the end of a long line. "The signing isn't supposed to start for another hour."

Crossing his arms, Drew shot me a look. "Really, Stella? You're surprised that a ton of people are waiting to see a world-famous band?"

"Okay, maybe not," I admitted. "We probably should have gotten here earlier, but I didn't want to leave the gallery."

"I know," Drew said, his tone lighter. "Hopefully this won't take too long."

"Hopefully," I responded, but as I gauged the line in front of us, I had serious doubts.

Ninety-nine percent of the crowd was female—a few moms with little girls, but mainly teenagers dressed up in floral sun-dresses or cute tops. They made kissy faces as they posed with friends for Instagram pictures and squealed over each other's Heartbreaker merchandise.

Eyeing the girls around me, I felt like an impostor in my plain T-shirt and Converses. I patted my hair and regretted not brushing through it this morning. Instead, I had pulled it back in a sharp pony-tail that showed off my bright-aqua strand. A few girls glanced at us in curiosity, and I couldn't tell if they were looking at me because I stood out like a sore thumb or if they were checking out Drew. While being distinct from my siblings was important to me, I didn't like feeling out of place. I skimmed the crowd to make sure nobody was looking before yanking out my hair band and tugging my fingers through my bangs. Nobody else had a stud in their nose or multiple ear piercings like me, but I wasn't going to take those out too.

Finally the mob of estrogen rushed forward as the doors to the station were opened. I briefly bowed my head in thanks, but my relief didn't last long. Once inside, I saw the long, roped-off line that twisted through the huge lobby. We were at the end of it.

"Are you kidding me?" I exclaimed.

Drew started to say something, but he was cut off as an uproar rippled through the crowd. Clasping my hands over my ears, I tried to block out the sudden screams of hundreds of fans.

"Ladies and gentlemen!" a man announced with a megaphone. "Please put your hands together for the Heartbreakers!"

Even standing on my tiptoes, I couldn't see the group of boys that had caused the commotion. Too many girls were jumping up and down in front of me for me to get a good view.

Another round of screaming made the room shake when a song started blasting through the building's sound system. Drew pulled his iPod out of his back pocket and put his headphones on. I groaned out loud, knowing that if I checked my backpack, mine wouldn't be there. I had left my iPod in the car, and Drew chuckled when he saw the panicked look on my face.

"Rock, paper, scissors for it?" I asked with my best puppy-dog face.

"Can't hear you, Stella," he said with a smirk. "My music's too loud."

He turned the volume up and started to head bob to whatever he was listening to. I closed my eyes in frustration. The rest of today was going to suck.

✩ ♭ ♫

My head was pounding. Between two hours' worth of cheesy lyrics, screaming, and a stuffy room, my brain felt like it was exploding inside my skull.

Cara and I were scary similar in so many ways. We both could quote every line from every episode of *Friends* like we had written and produced the show ourselves. We hated peanut butter because of the way it made your tongue stick to the roof of your mouth, and neither of us had ever had a boyfriend.

But if there was one startling difference between us, it was our choice in music. As Drew and I stood in line waiting for an auto-graph, I couldn't for the life of me understand how Cara enjoyed the Heartbreakers. From the look on Drew's face, he couldn't either. His iPod had died about an hour ago, so now we were both suffering.

"She's totally adopted," I muttered, which made Drew snicker.

"You're identical."

"Irrelevant," I said and shook my head. "I mean, honestly? Where did she go so wrong?"

"I think it was that girl at the hospital Cara's friends with."

"The one with leukemia?"

"Yeah, her. She made mixed CDs for all the pediatric patients."

"We should sue."

Drew laughed and rubbed his temples. "Seriously, though. I think this prolonged exposure to musical garbage is wearing on me. You'd think they'd move the line along a little faster."

"Seriously," I agreed.

The Heartbreakers' new CD was playing on a loop, but every time the song changed, another round of screams ensued. By now I could sing along with every song if I wanted.

A girl in front of me turned around. "Oh my God! This is their best song!" she exclaimed, as if we hadn't heard it a million times already today. "I love the Heartbreakers!"

I restrained myself from rolling my eyes. Every song must be their best song. Closing my eyes, I inhaled a deep breath. "How close are we?" I asked Drew for the tenth time. I still couldn't see the front of the line, but we had to be close. If we weren't...well, I didn't know how much longer I could stand this torture. Drew, who was a good foot and a half taller than Cara and me, craned his neck over the crowd and looked in the direction I assumed the band was sitting.

He smiled down at me. "Looks like it will only be ten minutes."

"Oh, thank God!" Reaching into my backpack, I pulled out a few of my sister's belongings—a Heartbreakers CD, a poster, and a tour shirt. If she didn't go crazy over this present...

As the minutes passed, we moved slowly up the line. The closer we got, the more often I could catch a small glimpse of the band through the crowd. Cameras flashed as people took pictures. Soon we were only a few people away from the front of the line. A group of girls huddled around the table moved away, and—

I could finally see the Heartbreakers. I scanned the table and my heart stopped.

There were four boys. On the far right sat a broad boy in a muscle shirt and with close-cropped dark hair. On his upper left bicep was an armband tattoo with black spirals that twisted together. Next to him was a tall, lanky guy with messy strawberry-blond hair and thick glasses. The third boy was blond as well, but his hair was styled to a T and drenched with gel to keep every strand in place. A pair of headphones hung around his neck, and he kept fiddling with the earbuds.

The final boy was the one that made my eyes pop. He had a familiar mop of wavy hair and a killer smile: the boy from Starbucks. I felt my face go red as I stared at him. He was talking with a fan as he signed a poster, and then he reached across the table to give her a hug. When she walked away, I could see the tears streaming down her face. My mind was on hyperdrive. I had been flirting with one of the boys from my sister's favorite boy band? Someone famous?

The line moved forward, and I realized I would have to talk to him again. What would he do when he saw me? Would he remember? *Of course he would*, I told myself. We'd flirted for a good five minutes, and he paid for my drink! But then again, he'd probably flirted with a million girls. My palms were sweaty, and I quickly wiped them on the back of my shirt.

I didn't want him to remember me, I realized. I'd told him that I was in Chicago to see an art gallery, not to meet the Heartbreakers. When he saw me standing in front of him asking for an autograph, he would probably laugh and think I was just another crazy fan.

"They look like little kids," Drew said, startling me from my thoughts. I tore my eyes from the boy.

"What?" I responded, my heart thumping.

"The band." Drew looked at me funny. "You okay, Stella? You're kinda pale."

"What?" I said, forcing a laugh. "I'm totally fine. And yeah, you're right—little boys." My brother was still staring at me like he knew something wasn't quite right, so I continued the joke. "I mean look at the scrawny guy on the left. Can't be older than twelve."

Drew looked up at the boy I'd met this morning and cracked a smile. "I don't know, looks thirteen to me."

The girl from before turned back around again, but this time she had a sneer on her face. "Oliver is eighteen. Stop making fun of him. It's not nice."

Oliver, I thought, churning the name over in my mind. Suddenly I knew why he had seemed so familiar. He was the guy from the magazine article Cara had been reading, the one that called him a heartbreaker.

"You're kidding, right?" Drew responded, his mouth hanging slack.

She put a hand on her hip. "Does it look like I'm kidding?" When my brother didn't answer, she continued. "The Heartbreakers are the most talented band ever, and Oliver is amazing. Keep your stupid thoughts to yourself."

After a few moments of staring with his mouth open, Drew finally recovered and surprised me by apologizing to the girl. "Well, Mrs. Perry," he started, looking down at her shirt. It read: Future Mrs. Oliver Perry. "I profusely apologize for insulting you. It won't happen again."

"Don't apologize to me," she snapped and pointed at Oliver. "Apologize to him."

"Next!" one of the bodyguards called. The girl spun around, and her sneer transformed into a smile that must have bordered on painful. I blinked in surprise. During the argument, I hadn't noticed how close we had gotten to the front of the line. My empty stomach flipped over.

"Drew, I think you were right," I told him, shoving my sister's stuff into his arms. "I feel sick. I need to go to the bathroom."

"No way, Stella." My brother reached out and grabbed my shirt as I tried to run away. "You're not getting out of this one. You can puke on the band for all I care, but I refuse to go up there by myself."

I felt my arms start to shake, dread setting in. There was no way I could face Oliver. "But, Drew…" I whined.

He looked at me with hard eyes. "We are doing this for Cara."

I bit my lip. Drew was right. My sister was a billion times more important than my pride. Sighing, I hung my head. The bratty girl and her group of friends moved away from the table, and I held my breath. Hopefully the lack of oxygen would calm my nerves.

Suddenly the band stood up and headed off the stage. "Wait, where are they going?" Drew demanded.

"Sorry," a husky security guard answered. "The boys are done for today. They have to rest for their concert tomorrow."

Forgetting my embarrassment, I snapped at the man. "We've been waiting in line for hours."

"Yes, and so has everyone behind you," he pointed out. "The boys can't get to everyone. There are just too many fans. Better luck next time."

"But I'm not here for me. This is for my sister's birthday present. She—" But it didn't matter what I had to say. The Heartbreakers were already gone.

CHAPTER 3

I was spread out on my bed in the hotel, staring up at the ceiling. It was sweltering in our room, and the heat was tiresome in a way that made it impossible to move. If I did, I could feel sweat drops trickling down my neck, and every time I took a breath, my skin stuck to the fabric of my shirt. I let my head roll to the side to look at my brother, who was on his own bed.

"Could it get any hotter?" I asked.

After a silent walk back to our hotel, Drew and I had been glad to finally check in and crash for the night. Our luck, however, was still in a downward spiral, and we ended up receiving a room with a broken air-conditioning unit. Lying on the bed, I couldn't help but think that this trip hadn't been worth it. It had been fun to see Bianca's gallery, but at the moment, all I could think about was how frustrating the rest of the day had been. More than anything, I had wanted to see Cara's eyes light up when we presented her with an autograph from the Heartbreakers, and now that wouldn't happen.

My brother glanced up from the book in his hands. "Please don't jinx it," he said before returning to reading.

"We should find somewhere with air-conditioning. Wanna grab dinner?"

This time, Drew didn't bother to look up from the page. "Maybe in a little bit," he said. "I want to finish this chapter."

For the past month, Drew had been consumed with completing his summer reading list. When summer was over, he was leaving to attend school in Minneapolis. Freshman registration wasn't for another two weeks, but Drew wanted to major in English and had already picked a literature course he hoped to take. He was so excited about starting college that he'd decided to read the course material before the semester even began.

I turned away from my brother when my throat grew thick. Freshman year, before Cara was diagnosed, I'd set my heart on NYU. I'd decided that New York would the perfect place for me to discover who I was, independent of my siblings. At the start of senior year when Cara went into remission and I received my acceptance letter, things finally started to feel real. I was going to college.

By the time summer rolled around, I wasn't so excited anymore. New York was calling out to me and I wanted to answer, but at the same time, the thought of leaving was terrifying. My mom told me the flutters I felt were normal. Leaving home for the first time was a big step, and it was good to be nervous. But what I felt inside my stomach didn't feel like butterflies. It was more like killer bees.

Before I could make sense of anything, the cancer came back.

And just like that, the bees were gone. I knew I couldn't leave while Cara was undergoing treatment, so I decided to defer for a semester. It was different for Drew. Minneapolis was only an hour and a half drive from Rochester, so he could come home on the weekends to visit Cara whenever he wanted. I would be states away, completely and utterly alone. I wasn't bitter about having to put off school, but part of me wished I'd followed Drew's example and applied to a university close to home.

A drop of sweat started to trickle down my forehead. "That's it," I said and sat up.

I needed to stop feeling sorry for myself. Yes, it was disappointing that I wasn't going off to school like my brother, and yeah, I hadn't been able to get the perfect birthday present for my sister, but there was no way I could deal with this discomfort any longer. Pulling my hair onto the top of my head in a bird's-nest fashion, I decided to do something about our room.

"I'm going down to the front desk to complain. Don't have a heatstroke while I'm gone."

"You're going down like that?" Drew questioned me.

I glanced in the mirror. Okay, so I looked like hell with my sweaty bangs plastered to the side of my face, but I was way past caring. "Yes, I am, so shut up. It's not like I'm going to run into anyone important."

"Just saying," Drew said. His gaze dove back down to his book, and I watched for a moment as his eyes tore across the page. Suddenly he gasped at something unexpected. "No way," he whispered to himself.

Rolling my eyes, I left my brother to his reading and headed out of the room.

☆ ♭ ♪♫

"What do you mean, there are no more rooms left?" I complained to the concierge. He'd already informed me that the hotel maintenance man had left for the night, so no one could fix the AC.

"Sorry, miss, but everything is booked up." The man's eyes shifted around the lobby as he answered my question, almost as if he was expecting something bad to happen. I followed his gaze and noticed quite a few girls waiting around.

I placed both my hands flat on the counter. "Well, is there a manager I can talk to? I didn't pay to melt to death."

But the man wasn't listening. His face went pale and he stared past me. "Oh crap…"

"Oh my God!" someone squealed. "They're really here!"

The muscles in my shoulders went rigid, and I grabbed the edge of the counter with a grip tight enough to turn the tips of my fingers white. I'd heard a sufficient number of screaming girls for one day, and I sucked in a deep breath before turning around. Just as I was about to tell off whatever idiot had screamed, all of the girls lingering around the lobby rushed to the front doors.

"It's the Heartbreakers!"

Four boys stepped into the lobby, bodyguards swarming around them on both sides. Outside, police were manning the door so a stampede wouldn't rush into the hotel. I caught a glimpse of familiar wavy hair and my stomach dropped.

"You have got to be shitting me."

This wasn't seriously happening, was it? I mean, how was it even possible to run into the same celebrity so many times in one day? These kinds of things happened in movies, not real life.

"Ladies, ladies," the concerned concierge called out. "Please give our guests some room." His request went unnoticed.

"Xander, I love you!"

"Alec, marry me!"

"JJ, over here!"

"Oh my God, Oliver!"

The band paused to greet a few of their fans, and as I looked on, I decided that this would go down as one of my craziest days ever. Cara was never going to believe me when I told her. I continued to watch the Heartbreakers until Oliver glanced at the counter where I was standing. I quickly spun around before he spotted me.

I knew it was irrational, but I almost felt as if he'd lied to me by not telling me who he was. Or maybe I just felt stupid for not knowing. Either way, it would be awkward to talk to him again.

After a minute of negotiation with the desk clerk, I managed to get our room for free, but it wasn't much of a comfort. Just thinking about spending a whole night feeling hot and sticky made me want to yank my hair out. But there was nothing else I could do, so I headed for the elevator.

"Stupid boy band," I grumbled as I stepped inside and hit the button for the fifth floor. It was childish, but it helped to have someone to be angry with.

"Hold the door!" Glancing up, I spotted a bodyguard pointing at me. The Heartbreakers were being led across the lobby, their guards trying to hold back the growing group of girls. I jabbed the "door close" button multiple times, hoping I could escape, but no such luck. The group slipped into the elevator, the doors almost shutting on the last guy.

"Thanks so much," the boy with glasses said. "That would have been a nightmare."

"I didn't know appreciating your fans was such a chore." The words tumbled out of my mouth before my mind even registered what I had said.

Oliver's head popped up at the sound of my voice. He stared at me for a moment before breaking out into a huge grin. "Stella!"

He remembers me! My heart leaped, but for some reason I couldn't bring myself to respond, and I watched as the smile slipped off his face.

Nobody seemed to hear Oliver's comment, and the boy with glasses readjusted his frames as he tried to get a better look at me. "Say what?" he asked.

"What do you mean, not appreciating our fans?" The boy with the big muscles crossed his arms in an intimidating sort of way, and the tattoo around his bicep stretched. "We had an autograph signing today."

"Yeah, I know that," I snapped. "I waited for three hours only to get right to the front of the line and watch you all leave."

"Oh, an unhappy fan?" he asked. His expression did a one-eighty as a grin spread across his face.

"We can definitely fix that," Glasses Boy added. He pulled a Sharpie out of his pocket. "Do you have a camera?"

I let out an unattractive snort. "You think I'm a fan?" Pausing, I shot him a glare. "Not a chance in the world."

The boys glanced at each other, not sure how to respond. "I

think she might be crazy," Muscles whispered to the boy with the perfect hair, who still had a pair of headphones draped around his neck. He had yet to speak, and he only gave his friend a quick nod of agreement.

"The only thing that's crazy is that people actually listen to your music." I could feel my pulse fluttering with each word I spoke. "I was at the signing today—which was torture, considering I was forced to listen to the same CD until my ears bled—for one reason only: to get my sister an autograph. And if she weren't my sister, I'd probably disown her for listening to crap."

The band stared at me, mouths gaping.

"Anything else?" Glasses asked.

"Yeah," I added with one final burst of irritation. "You guys suck."

The elevator stopped and the door slid open.

"I think I kind of like this girl. She's got sass," Muscles said with a smirk. "Can we keep her?"

"Screw off," I told him, and then, without looking at Oliver, I shoved past the Heartbreakers onto the fifth floor.

ABOUT THE AUTHOR

Ali Novak is a Wisconsin native and a graduate of the University of Wisconsin-Madison's creative writing program. She started writing her debut novel *My Life with the Walter Boys* when she was only fifteen. Since then, her work has received more than one hundred million hits online. When she isn't writing, Ali enjoys Netflix marathons, traveling with her husband Jared, and reading any type of fantasy novel she can get her hands on. You can follow her on Wattpad, Facebook, Twitter, and Instagram @fallzswimmer.